A Different War

A Different War

CRAIG THOMAS

G.K. Hall & Co. Chivers Press
Thorndike, Maine USA Bath, England

This Large Print edition is published by G.K. Hall & Co., USA
and by Chivers Press, England.

Published in 1997 in the U.S. by arrangement with
Little, Brown & Company UK.

Published in 1998 in the U.K. by arrangement with
Little, Brown and Company.

U.S.	Hardcover	0-7838-8281-5	(Mystery Collection Edition)
U.K.	Hardcover	0-7540-1067-8	(Windsor Large Print)
U.K.	Softcover	0-7540-2043-6	(Paragon Large Print)

Grateful acknowledgment is made to the following for
permission to reprint previously published material:

Six lines (page 67) from *Poem of the Melon Garden* in *Wang Wei: Poems* translated by GW Robinson (Penguin Classics, 1973). Copyright © GW Robinson, 1973. Reprinted by permission of Penguin Books Ltd.

Three lines from *Canto* LJJ in *The Cantos of Ezra Pound* by Ezre Pound. Reprinted by permission of Faber and Faber Ltd.

Three lines from *Changing of the Guard* by Bob Dylan: every effort has been made to trace the copyright holders and to clear reprint permissions. If notified, the publishers will be pleased to rectify any omission in future editions.

The text of this Large Print edition is unabridged.
Other aspects of the book may vary from the original edition.

Set in 16 pt. Plantin by Juanita Macdonald.

Printed in the United States on permanent paper.

British Library Cataloguing in Publication Data available

Library of Congress Cataloging in Publication Data

Thomas, Craig.
A different war / Craig Thomas.
p. cm.
ISBN 0-7838-8281-5 (lg. print : hc : alk. paper)
1. Large type books. I. Title.
[PR6070.H56D54 1997]
823′.914—dc21
97-28009

Laisser-faire, in short, should be the general practice: every departure from it, unless required by some great good, is a certain evil . . .

. . . as a general rule, the business of life is better performed when those who have an immediate interest in it are left to their own course, uncontrolled either by the mandate of the law or by the meddling of any public functionary.

J S Mill, *Principles of Political Economy,* V, 9

PRELUDE

1st April, 199–

And I have told you how things were under
Duke Leopold in Siena
And of the true base of credit, that is,
the abundance of nature
with the whole folk behind it.

Ezra Pound, *Canto* LII

All Fools' Day. The markets had been telling him that — laughing at him, in effect — ever since they had opened that morning. The share prices, the snippets of information, the rumours, the heavy selling, the nervousness of the banks . . . Like the chuckling of people at a joke at his expense.

Twenty million dollars had been wiped off the asset value of Winterborne Holdings in a matter of hours. Wall Street, open an hour earlier, had caught the infection and the stock of the US subsidiaries was sliding downwards in price. It could be fifty million dollars by the day's end. All Fools' Day.

In enraged frustration, David Winterborne stood up and walked to one of the full-length windows of the first-floor drawing room which overlooked Eaton Square. The London traffic filtered politely through the square, sunlight was dappled in the gardens. There were a few well-dressed pedestrians enjoying the spring sunshine. The scene appeared painted, formal, like a landscape he had commissioned to celebrate ownership. Yet, as if in the moment of an earth tremor, the whole vista of wealth, exclusivity, decorousness was rendered shimmeringly unreal by the shocks of a threatened financial disaster.

Fraser, who remained seated on the sofa behind him, was just another of those bringing the *bad* news, a functionary reporting that the Oracle hadn't found in his favour. One long-fingered hand smoothed his orientally straight black hair — but he realised that even Fraser, a mere employee, would see that the gesture was entirely pretence. He turned to face the room, catching sight of his slim figure in a mirror above the Adam fireplace. His Jermyn Street shirt was crumpled, his tie askew. His Eurasian features appeared unhabitually thunderous, stubbornly defiant.

He had spent millions of his own trying to block the hole in the dyke. To little or no effect . . .

'I may have to base decisions — important ones — on your assessment, Fraser. Are you *certain?*'

Fraser shrugged, a moneylender's gesture.

'I — look, sir, this is *good* inside information. Possibly the best. MoD Procurement and the Treasury are digging in for a very bloody campaign.' Fraser's Scots accent came and went, like the sophistication of his vocabulary, in the manner of a weak, intermittent radio signal. 'The Treasury is twisting the DTI's arm up behind its back *not* to support the European helicopter, but to side with them over the American machine.' His mouth distorted in a congenital contempt.

'It's *cheaper* than ours — *yours.*'

'It's not mine —' Winterborne began angrily. But it was, wasn't it? That was the whole problem. Winterborne Holdings in the UK had become far too close — symbiotic, they said — to Aero UK, senior manufacturing partner in the European consortium building the helicopter the British army was supposed to buy. 'You must be mistaken — your sources are misguided. The government just couldn't do it . . .' Fraser's expression remained dourly cynical. Winterborne turned away.

The government — the damned *Tory* government who had seen almost a quarter of a million of his money to help their last election campaign — would do it, if it suited. 'It would be the finish of a great many companies. The unemployment would be embarrassing . . . It would — *could* — be the end of Aero UK.' He was speaking to the painted, formal scene beyond the window. He felt he was staring at the family estates, watching for the small army of bailiff's men who would soon be coming up the drive to dispossess him. Then, to Fraser: 'You're *sure?*' He cupped his narrow chin with one hand, adding: 'Is it no longer a simple matter of more money — ?'

'We can't buy influence at that level. It's in the hands of the grown-ups, not the greedy kids. Aero UK's board and you could wrap yourselves in the flag, talk about job losses . . . It might work.'

'But you don't believe it. When do they decide between Eurocopter and the American rival?'

'Some time in the next two months — before

the end of May.'

David Winterborne turned to face Fraser.

'They *will* do it?'

Fraser nodded.

'That's the betting. That the Treasury will force MoD to buy American because of the relative costs.'

'So, Winterborne Holdings has a huge stake in Aero UK, in a dozen wholly owned subcontracting companies, in various other offshoots . . . While *already* Aero UK has a new airliner no one in the world wants to buy! *And* a Eurodefender fighter project that's almost four years behind schedule in the development phase alone. Now Aero UK will lose the helicopter project, too — worth at least two hundred and fifty million sterling! Have I left anything out?'

Fraser suppressed a grin and shook his head.

'No, sir. Nothing.'

In the gardens, small dogs were barking around young children and nannies. It was all so bloodily — mockingly — *normal,* a flattering image of the world he had bought for himself.

Which was now threatened. Cash-starved because of Aero UK, and even more because of his involvement in the urban regeneration project in the Midlands, his largest investment outside the US. His borrowing was at a record high, his profit at a ten-year low. He had lost twenty million because of a couple of hostile newspaper articles over the weekend and a follow-up in *The Times.* Just because of that damned unsellable airliner alone — ! When all the other skeletons tumbled from the cupboards, Winterborne Holdings would be finished.

'It has to be stopped — the rot,' he announced.

'Sorry — sir?'

He turned to Fraser. His decision, which had leapt out of the dark at the back of his mind, shocked and thrilled like a sudden, unanticipated sexual encounter.

'I'm propping up the share prices and it's costing me a very great deal. That must cease.'

'Yes, sir.' Fraser appeared unsettled, as if he were about to be accused of not supplying a solution to the situation. He was like a hamster trying to get further into its straw. Perhaps he sensed what was coming . . .

'I need *someone*. Someone *you* would know, your kind of person.'

'To do what, sir?'

'Help me to sell airliners — since Aero UK have singularly failed to do just that. I need someone who can help me deal with that mess.'

He moved towards the sofa, plucking that morning's *Times* from the arm of a chair and dropping it into Fraser's lap. The business section was folded open at one of its inside pages. The fateful follow-up to the weekend articles on Skyliner and Aero UK that had cost him so much. There were two photographs, side by side. One displayed the bulk of the Skyliner that no one wanted to buy, looking like the profile of a winged dolphin. The other was of an American airliner — the new Vance 494 longhaul. It, like the US helicopter soon also to become his bane, was *cheap*. Much cheaper than Skyliner to buy, lease, operate. Those carriers not waiting for the new

Boeing were poised to buy it, once its early commercial flights were successful.

Potential Skyliner purchasers would soon be queueing to buy the Vance aircraft.

Fraser looked up at him ruminatively, doubtful of the reality of his inference. Then his expression became carefully, patiently neutral.

'Find someone — someone who can do something . . . about *that.*' *Vance 494 — the airliner of the future,* the caption beneath the photograph read. Beneath that of the Skyliner were the words, *Euro-boast — any future at all?*

'I — think I understand, sir. I'll bring you some names, a scenario — tomorrow?'

'Tonight.'

'Sir.'

He heard the doors of the drawing room close behind Fraser. There seemed a finality to the sound, as if he had closed the doors on some other kind of space. Scruples? he mocked himself. But he sensed that some sort of Rubicon had been crossed, just by intimating this design to Fraser. Very well, he had made no final decision, he could always rethink, withdraw . . .

And yet he was almost certain he would not change his mind, retreat from the place where he suddenly found himself. He reached out and pressed the bell on his desk. Coffee, which he had not offered Fraser, appealed. He glanced at his watch —

— realised he had forgotten that he had promised to accompany Marian to Covent Garden that evening, for the revival of Dowell's production of *Sleeping Beauty* — with the magnificent Maria

Björnson sets. He would have to go. His absence would be remarked — create further problems. Damn . . .

And yet . . . He savoured his decision. Problem-solving through other channels. Business by means of —

David Winterborne smiled, feeling himself looking back towards a rock ledge he had traversed; a high fence he had hurdled with ease.

PART ONE

Machines and Shadows

Fortune calls.
I stepped forth from the shadows, to the marketplace,
Merchants and thieves, hungry for power, my last deal gone down.

Bob Dylan, 'Changing of the Guard'

CHAPTER ONE

Business Arrangements

'Look, Major —' The FBI agent employed his former rank without respect, as if it was a shrivelled fruit bitter on his tongue. 'It's in your own interest to cooperate with the Bureau . . .'

There were two of them in the small apartment's main room. Fall sunlight exposed the age of the carpet, the weary furniture. If he craned his neck, he would catch a glimpse of the Washington Monument in the distance, narrow and sharp as a missile against the faded blue of the sky.

'I know nothing about Alan Vance or his business deals,' he replied for perhaps the fourth or fifth time. Midmorning traffic three floors below the window protested like animals caught in quicksand with the squeal of horns and brakes.

'For Christ's sake, Major, you were married to his daughter until a couple of years ago!' It was spoken by the senior of the two, his back to the room, his face in half-profile irritated, squinting into the light as if it challenged him. 'What d'you mean, you know nothing? You were *family,* Major!'

They were short-tempered with frustration, with a kind of righteousness. It was entirely probable that his former father-in-law was as crooked as they came, and their investigation overdue. Vance in trouble with the federal authorities amused him — however much he resisted being drawn back, even at such a tangent, into the morass that his brief marriage had become. The FBI men threatened to reawaken painful memories. He squinted towards the window.

'I wasn't family, McIntyre — never family.'

The younger of the two, seated opposite him in a narrow armchair that seemed designed more for interrogation than comfort, appeared embarrassed. McIntyre remained at the window, his features set in a grimace that expressed a determination to disbelieve. Then he turned to him.

'For Christ's sake, you don't owe the guy a free beer, Major! Why cover for him now?' He came closer, wafting ahead of him the scent of a masculine aftershave and tobacco. And moral outrage. He stood before the sofa, hands clenched at his sides. 'We're going to get Vance, Major — for bribery, tax evasion, corruptly obtaining government funding — the works. I don't see how you can refuse to help us with your record.'

'*My* record?' he mocked, sensing himself smaller, more compact than the man who bulked over him, the soft hair above his collar haloed by the sunlight.

'Desert Storm, Major — you were there. Instructor on Stealth Fighters, you even flew missions. Your other work for the Company, your air force record . . .' His effort suggested there had to be some button he could push that would activate the human being he confronted.

'Trying to wrap me in Old Glory won't do it,' he remarked, angering McIntyre. The younger man's bland, pale features extinguished the beginnings of a smile.

McIntyre turned on his heel.

'What the hell is it with you, Gant?' he snapped. 'Your file says you're an asshole. I *believe* the file!'

'Your privilege, McIntyre. I told you, I know nothing about Vance's aircraft company. I flew his company jet, I married his daughter. I left his company, I left his daughter.' With a deliberateness that was designed to anger, he glanced at his watch. 'I'm late for work, McIntyre — you through with me?'

'Not by a long way, Gant — not by a long way,' McIntyre threatened.

'What happened to *Major?* It kind of dropped out of sight —'

'Why are you siding with a guy who screwed up your job and your marriage, Gant? Tell me what you *owe* him.'

'Nothing you'd understand, McIntyre.' He realised he was leaning forward tensely in the chair, in some vague, reminiscent form imitating the posture of someone refusing to answer an interrogator. His Vietnamese interrogators, KGB questioners . . . it was of no significance which memory was evoked. It was important only that he was once more confronting the world as something pitted against him, antagonistic and dangerous. 'I don't owe him anything — I just don't *know* anything.'

McIntyre was leaning forward as he stood, large hands clasping his thighs like a footballer paused for a set play.

'The Senate Committee is going to call him to give evidence. *We* already got a great deal of data against Vance. Don't be a hick from Iowa all your life, Gant. Wise up. Help us . . . It ought to be your *duty* as a Federal employee, for Christ's sake — !' His exasperation was entire, consuming. That helped. 'This guy', McIntyre continued, his arm wildly addressing the younger man while he continued to stare with a baffled rage at Gant, 'let me tell you about this guy, Chris. This *hero* dropped out of high school — this *hero* demonstrated against the war in Vietnam, in Iowa, for Christ's sake, then he went there himself! He was arrested at the age of fourteen for one of those Peace March things — all that Kennedy crap.' Gant made a noise that was almost a growl, and McIntyre battened on the small betrayal of emotion, grinning. 'Maybe the guy didn't know — living out in the boondocks — that Jack and Bobby were both *dead.*' Chris, whose surname he had forgotten, looked at him as if watching a father or uncle being humiliated.

'Jack and Bobby,' McIntyre continued, 'neither of them could keep their pissers in their pants, not even on Inauguration Day. Jack and

Bobby . . .' He sighed theatrically. 'Your *hero* here is just a fucking liberal, like them. And a pain in the ass ever since.' Gant remained immobile, passive in his chair. 'That Camelot bullshit — eh, Gant? Haven't you wised up yet?'

Eventually, into a silence that seemed hot and tense, Gant said: 'What for? To look at the world through your eyes, McIntyre? I'd rather be dead.'

'Jack and Bobby and Camelot screwed up your life, Gant. Go get yourself another one.'

'So you can put it all on file?'

He stared at Chris. The young man wore the suit of a junkbond dealer and just happened to be a federal agent. He seemed already without hope and possessed of nothing but a shallow ambition; and perhaps a fragile, incompetent decency. One day, he'd wake up to find he'd become McIntyre. Gant sighed audibly, and shook his head. Then he said:

'You've got all of me on the computer file, McIntyre. Why don't you just add a statement I never made? For the sake of neatness?'

'Vance is a damn' crook, Gant — !'

'Whoever got arrested in the land of the free just for that?' He stood up, surprising them. 'I'm late, McIntyre. Go bother some of those assholes with fifty assault rifles and ten thousand rounds of ammo who think they're defending life, liberty, the American way and Mom's apple pie — I don't need this. I can't help you —'

McIntyre snorted.

'Can't help — or won't help?'

Chris hovered by the window like a repo man

who had discovered his belongings valueless and the condition of the apartment embarrassing. Perhaps, as McIntyre had claimed, Chris thought of him as some kind of legend who could only disappoint in the flesh. Suddenly, he was angry with them both. They had brought his recent past back into the room and it had spilt on the carpet like paint, staining it. He had walked out on Alan Vance and Barbara. Left that part of his life behind. The sense of failure, even of shame, that he had felt at the breakdown of his marriage had been reawakened. He'd spent two years trying to bury it.

'You're in trouble, Gant —'

'I hear you.'

'It's a long time since you were a hero — untouchable.'

'Sure. I hear you playing the music, McIntyre — I just can't dance.'

'You will, Gant, you will. Two left feet and all. For the Senate Committee. I promise.' He glowered at Chris. 'Let's get out of here — I need some fresh air.'

'It's in short supply in this town, McIntyre — and I'm more used to an oxygen mask than you.' For the first time, he smiled. 'Don't believe his version of anything, Chris,' he added to the startled younger man. 'Especially life. McIntyre doesn't know anything about *real* life —'

'Says you —'

McIntyre confronted him for a moment, then his expression became dismissive. Gant turned away, knowing he had made another enemy. But then, people like McIntyre only ever wanted to screw you. Petty power never did have much sense of humour.

'See you, McIntyre,' he offered ironically.

'Soon.'

The door of the room closed behind them, then the front door slammed. At once, Gant wanted to get out of his apartment, as if it might make some move to restrain him, begin the interrogation of memory again. He'd tried to forget the failed marriage and Alan Vance, and make the quarrel a personal one between himself and McIntyre. He could deal with that.

He put on the jacket and tie to which he had long become accustomed, picked up his briefcase, locked the door behind him and headed for the office. Had he lived, Jack Kennedy would be almost eighty now, and people would remember him with the cold clarity of the familiar, the ordinary; the half-failed rather than half-completed. Like McIntyre remembered *him.* Mitchell Gant closed his mind on the thought.

Tim Burton had spent the previous evening and night at Alan Vance's desert home outside Phoenix, in the shadow of the Superstition Mountains. It was a place as unlike his London home or the surroundings of his Cotswold mansion as he could ever have imagined — white walls heated only by the splashes of Indian rugs and woven blankets, by Mexican artifacts and reddish-ochre tiles, and hard-edged modern furniture. It was only one of Vance's homes — and not a home at all in the sense that Cardleigh Manor or Holland Park were *his* homes.

There had been mane-tossing, half-wild horses near his bedroom window in the first heat of the morning, and the unexpected strips of grass gleamed after the ministrations of arching sprays of water.

He had nevertheless felt comfortable, embraced by the stark ranch-style house beneath the high desert air and sharp grey mountains where miners had died following golden illusions. Now, squinting at the gleaming aircraft at the end of the desert runway, as specklike as a stranded gull in the morning heat haze, the high air tickled his agoraphobia, however mildly, and he resented the mood of exposure because it tainted what was to be savoured — the tide of his expectations. He was eager, he realised — as eager as he had been at the very beginning of Artemis, his company, when the only aircraft they had had were two old, hired Boeings with which to take on British Airways and the Americans.

As eager, he realised, as he had been at the very beginning of everything, when the figures on the balance sheets had proclaimed that he had made his first million. *This* — well, that really, that at the end of the runway, still unmoving — was another beginning. The first of his order of six of Vance's aircraft waited to begin its pre-delivery flight — waited to begin his revenge.

The flight crew were to rehearse the press flight while they tested the systems. When they returned, reporters and cameramen would be loaded aboard and flown on a sightseeing, publicity-serving junket, awash with champagne and knee-deep with caviar and canapés, over the

Grand Canyon and back to Phoenix. *Maximum* exposure, locally, nationally, internationally, for Artemis Airlines and Vance Aircraft. *Sounds good to me,* he thought, suppressing a satisfied, anticipatory smile.

Cameras fussed around them. Vance, inexpressive behind sunglasses, had summoned the media as if by magic — they had come to see the man being investigated by the Senate and the man who had always been the maverick of the US planemakers, the dazzling, flawed boy whose firm jaw was now padded with the jowls of success and power. Beside Vance, his daughter Barbara, Executive V-P in charge of Corporate Affairs at Vance Aircraft, was darkly power-suited against the mood and heat of the morning.

Burton tensed as he saw the plane straighten, and the cameras turned towards it as to a new bird seen in an unexpected place. The tension was palpable. The low hangars and factory buildings were crouched around them beneath the desert sky, which diminished the aircraft, and made it more fragile as it began to accelerate. The Vance 494 airliner was no more than a distorted, shimmering image as it rushed towards them through the heat. Burton felt Vance's hand on his arm, but with a questioning touch. Momentary loss of nerve? Success was as important to Vance as to himself . . . His daughter's features seemed varnished with a glossy anxiety. Other company people were in suits and overalls, or dresses that attempted competition with the hard sunlight. In his own concentrated anxiety, he had forgotten how many people there were, arranged as for an

American funeral or graduation ceremony on white chairs in neat rows in front of the hangar from which the airliner had been rolled out an hour earlier. Local politicians and dignitaries, businessmen, faces that habitually adorned the Arizona social and charitable functions and glossy magazines. The delivery of the first of Burton's six ordered planes was important to Arizona, to the whole south-west sunbelt.

The employees and executives had moved into what might have been a protective fence around himself and Vance.

A plume of dust billowed out behind the accelerating plane and its noise was beginning to cannon back at them from the mountains. It was a projectile being fired down the runway. Burton felt his mouth dry and his hands grip at themselves, holding certainty in a fierce grip or suffocating doubt. Then the gleaming metal bullet *sailed* . . . moving effortlessly into its natural element above the desert and the roiling dust. A great silver insect against the mountains, then against the sky like a star. There was clapping, but the reflected, magnified engine noise drowned it.

As the noise diminished, he heard Vance's chuckle of celebration and relief. Barbara held the big man's arm. His jaw was firmer, younger again, and his blue eyes glinted challengingly as he removed his sunglasses. The cameras whirled around them once more like seductive dancers, and Vance was answering the reporters' questions about bribes and misappropriated funds. His manner was confidently dismissive. Burton moved to his other side and shook his hand for the photographers. Above them, high above, the plane circled slowly, a distant, winking speck. Burton's mood was elated, but fierce as a weapon. After all the dirty tricks, the attempts of the big national carriers to keep him out of Heathrow, JFK, O'Hare, Europe's international airports — after the vast bank loans, the rescheduling of debts as regularly as bowel movements — this was a real beginning.

It had been exhilarating, climbing the mountain against their hostile weather. Then his own country's national carrier, privatised but anticipating monopoly, had attempted to steal passengers, spread black propaganda, question his liquidity, the safety of the huge loans. They'd settled out of court, eventually, but their actions had declared that now it was a dirty war. One he had taken on with a ruthless alacrity that had surprised him.

Now, with the 494 in service within six months, regularly flying the Atlantic, he would undercut all competition.

He pumped Vance's hand, perhaps his sudden exhilaration surprising the American. Then Vance slapped his shoulder — they slapped each other's shoulders in their released, gratified nervousness; brothers under the suits. Vance had begun in overalls, as he had in bright, even lurid sweaters and with much longer hair. Now, neither of them could be stopped.

'Let's get a drink!' Vance bawled, his arms embracing the cameras, the guests, his small desert kingdom. 'Or drunk! Come on, Tim-boy — it's our day!'

His enthusiasm was tumultuous, enveloping. He dragged Burton to his side like a lover, his arm on his shoulder, and steered him towards the hospitality marquee, its gaudy, flounced sides flapping in the desert breeze.

Vance had begun designing and building executive jets, rich toys for richer boys. Then he'd copied the Boeing philosophy, stretching and fattening the fuselage until he had the skeleton of the 494. A long-haul workhorse on to which he had bolted the two big Pratt & Whitney engines he had helped design, some fancy avionics he'd bought in and his own design for the fuel management system — and the airliner possessed a better load-to-range ratio than any of its rivals. It was the most effective and cheapest transatlantic carrier in existence. Burton knew that as certainly as did Vance . . .

. . . but the people wouldn't buy it. Not yet. They were waiting patiently in their lightweight suits and silk ties in their boardrooms for him to be their guinea pig. The big carriers would flock to Vance and stand in admiration with the desert dust blowing over their polished shoes and squinting against the sun — *once* his airline, Artemis, had shown how good and cheap the 494 was. Until then, they would stick with their Airbuses and their Boeings. So, Vance needed him like an addict — just as he needed Vance. He smiled reassuringly as they approached the marquee. He could hear the canvas cracking in the breeze like old wood. *Fuck the rules, don't tell me about them* . . . It could have been a pledge between them. Bankers patted Vance on the back as his smile preceded them into the marquee's illusory cool. Local politicians seemed lit by his confident flame.

The 494's two big engines had faded into the distance beyond Phoenix. *Thanks, Alan,* he thought. *Oh, thank you, Alan . . .* He had been given the means to shaft the European and British carriers who had tried, for a decade, to ensure his failure.

Barbara Gant — or did she call herself Barbara Vance Gant now? No, he remembered, she had remarried and there was a child . . . She, too, was smiling, glad-handing. He was given a glass of chilled champagne and raised it to her. She returned the salute with a quiet triumph.

'Of course — a wonderful aircraft,' he offered in reply to someone in a light-grey suit with the distinguished grey coiffure of an American banker — or mafioso. 'Local employment?' He remembered. The state senator. 'Employment will be *no* problem —' he grinned. 'Give me six months on the New York route and they'll be flocking here, Senator. I guarantee!' His confidence embarrassed him, his habitual reserve reminding him of its right to his smiles, his manner. '*I* won't let the plane down,' he could not avoid adding with a laugh. 'Next spring, at the latest, they'll be falling over themselves to buy Alan's baby!'

He moved further into the undergrowth of the crowded marquee, among species he had forced himself to be able to confront and confound. Vance was without that English apologetic tic in the forebrain which moderated self-congratulation. His arms waved above his head in broad, unquestioning gestures. The money-men, the politicians, the executives, the advisers — all of them were people from whom he had masked himself behind his money and his most trusted deputies, even behind his dazzling wife. His long hair, his sweaters, his apparent naivety; all had been defences against intrusion, bolsters of an assurance he found it difficult to maintain. He sipped more champagne.

Bright chatter, then, or amusing asides. He sensed his path through this forest of money, influence and dependence in the role they forced upon him — St George, riding to Vance's rescue. The *sound* Englishman. It must be the pepper-and-salt in his hair that gave him the appearance of maturity over Vance, since the American was ten years older than himself. His hands, too, began to wave, like those of Vance; smaller, politer imitations. The marquee became hot with bodies and success. The mingling of expensive perfumes and aftershaves was heady. He clipped his glass to the plate on which a helping of salmon and salad had arrived, unrequested. He pecked at the food, his excitement unable to digest. Nodding as he listened to a Phoenix matron inviting him to her *salon.*

'A great shame,' he murmured, 'but I'll be back in London before Thursday . . . Of course, on my next visit. Delighted!'

The matron floated away, having tamed if not captured him. He smiled after her. Charlotte was definitely required on his next visit, if he was to trawl the Phoenix social world . . . He must ring her and the boys, tell them the plane had flown and he would be home a day early. What time was it in London? He glanced at his watch surreptitiously. Seven hours' difference, was it . . . ? It was — time for tea or G-and-T in Holland Park. He grinned a private pleasure and glanced towards the entrance of the marquee. The desert seemed to smoke with heat rather than dust —

— Vance? Alan Vance was outside, and a man in shirtsleeves was gesticulating in what might have been anger . . . No, the anger — the baffled fury — was all Vance's. Smiling, nodding, sidling, Burton moved towards the gap of desert between the canvas and flounces. Voices caught at him like gentle hands, but he managed to evade them. Vance's features were thunderous with knowledge and rage.

'What is it — Alan? What is it?'

Vance turned to him, his eyes like those of something dangerous, cornered and wounded, but far from finished. Something that wanted to hurt, damage.

'What is it?' he repeated inadequately.

'The — *my* plane . . . it's gone down. Crashed. The crew's not answering. It's gone down, Tim. My plane crashed —'

The image of Her Majesty stepping from the fuselage of the Skyliner into a hot, tropical light and a breeze that ruffled cotton dresses and unsecured hats became that of the newsreader, then the symbolic portcullis of the House of Commons as the channel returned to its coverage of a Commons Select Committee. At once, Giles Pyott sat forward in his armchair, to Aubrey's renewed amusement. He sighed with gentle mockery and Pyott, swilling the clinking ice in his glass of gin and tonic, acknowledged the noise with an inclination of his head.

The Chairman of the European Affairs Select Committee was an MP known to both himself and Giles Pyott. He had been an unsuccessful Foreign Office junior minister and later had spent an equally fruitless sojourn at MoD. In the former post he had buckled before Aubrey, in the latter had been implacably opposed by Giles. But he was rabidly pro-European, of the party of government, and his present eminence was thus fully accounted. Seated next to him was Giles' daughter, his *shining girl* as only Aubrey, Clive Winterborne and Giles himself were ever allowed to call her. In riposte, they were still to her, even in their collective dotage, the three musketeers. As the sound of her voice was faded up — her first words making her father chuckle with indulgent approval, as if he were witnessing some kind of successful training exercise for a violent assault by special forces — Marian was haranguing the man giving evidence to the Committee; the CEO of Aerospace UK, Sir Bryan Coulthard. He appeared sullenly resentful, despite the media coaching he must have had over the years and especially just prior to this appearance on the box.

Money, Aubrey thought — it was always money. A tropical storm of it, running down the drains of the European Union, disappearing into the sands of corruption, grandiose dreams, bureaucracy. In his retirement, he had found a lofty, indulgent aloofness. Giles, because his daughter was angry at waste, incompetence, corruption — and Europe — was angry in his turn. He sipped with a quiet, satisfied savagery at his drink as the industrial knight inadequately fended off the redoubtable Marian.

Aubrey recollected the bloated, gleaming fuselage of the Skyliner from which the monarch was disembarking on the news film. British Airways had two of them, employed for junkets, tourist trips, celebrating Lottery winners and the like. The costs of production had escalated — become mountainous — and the airlines jibbed at buying what was yet another pompous, Louis Quatorze-like dream of European glory by France and the UK with the full complicity of the European Commission in Brussels. Indeed, it was a dream more like those of Brussels than his own country — for Aerospace UK it had been born of desperation at the end of the Cold War . . . and it was too damned expensive for anyone to buy, this *future of airline travel,* as it was usually touted. Even Her Majesty's endorsement on her State Visits would hardly recommend it to realistic, hardheaded airline chairmen around the world.

'Your shining girl's fishing,' he murmured, glancing into his malt whisky and catching a scent of the beef Mrs Grey was preparing for his dinner with Giles. 'She's bluffing.'

'Ah, Kenneth — but Coulthard doesn't know that,' Pyott replied in triumph. No one was as clever as his girl, no one quicker on their feet than his only daughter.

Outside, home-going traffic was muted and the sunlight lay strongly on Regent's Park. Aubrey stirred comfortably in his armchair, enjoying the restrained interrogation.

'Why won't they buy his dream, Giles — that Skyliner thing? Cost alone?'

'Probably. Ludicrous situation,' Pyott barked. 'As far as I can understand it —'

'This is *Marian's* view, is it, to which I'm to be treated?'

Giles Pyott snorted with laughter.

'A hit — I do confess as much . . . yet, it is. It's the old sad story — overcapacity in the industry and falling revenues. They want *cheap*, as she puts it, not *flashy*.'

'But they won't buy American planes either.'

'They'll have to start replacing their fleets soon — and it's either American or it's this costly bugger. Brothel with wings, Marian calls it.' Aubrey laughed. 'But Coulthard and the Frogs are sweating over Marian's acquaintance, Tim Burton, and his choice of plane. That *is* cheap — relatively . . . HMG and the French have poured so much money into *developing* the damned Skyliner they won't bale out the airlines with subsidies to *buy* it!'

'Then we have another Concorde on our hands.'

'With this difference — BA was the national carrier back then and government could make them buy Concorde. Now they're in the private sector, they think they've done enough by taking two on appro and flying the champagne and gold-medallion set on junkets.' Pyott tossed his head, still thickly crowned with grey hair. His aquiline profile appeared bleak in expression. Full-face,

Giles found it harder to frown effectively. The retired soldier gestured at the screen, absorbed in his daughter's casual, intent duel with Coulthard.

Aubrey had heard as much in the whispering gallery of the Club, and elsewhere where he still encountered men of present or resigned power. The Skyliner was a luxury, ocean-going liner of the air, a grandiloquent gesture appropriate to a more extravagant age. It was opulently appointed, it attempted to carry too many passengers, its engines were inefficient by comparison with the newest generation of propulsion units, its sumptuousness ruined its payload-to-range-to-price equation. It was an overdraft, negative equity, a spendthrift gesture quite out of tenor with the straitened times.

If one airline bought it, then others might. But the Germans had never joined the project, using the money they had saved on Eurodefender to help efface the cost of rebuilding the industrial horror of the former East Germany. Bonn would never allow Lufthansa to acquire a fleet of Skyliners for the US and Far East routes. Air France *couldn't* afford it and the Elysée wouldn't afford it on behalf of the national carrier. The Belgians couldn't even dream of it, like the Dutch, and the British privatised national airline was not prepared to make more than a gesture.

If young Tim Burton succeeded, the Skyliner was sunk without trace . . . which was what infuriated Marian so much, the billions of ecus the project had cost. Aubrey shook his head.

'You can assure this Committee, Sir Bryan,' Marian was saying, 'that when the Skyliners under construction are completed, you will have found buyers for them? Or is the short-time working announced at one of your subcontractors in my constituency the shape of things to come?' Marian's smile remained dazzlingly innocent as her words worked like acid on the crumbling brickwork of Coulthard's self-confidence.

Marian was wearing her blonde hair drawn back from her face, accentuating her wide blue eyes and the high, prominent cheekbones. The mouth was firm in the generosity of her smile, her neck long. Even seated, she appeared to possess her father's stature, as well as his determination and confidence. To Giles, she was as beautiful as her mother had been. Most men, indeed, found her attractive, desirable — then, eventually, too dauntingly intelligent for their entire comfort. She had, however, discovered two or three men sufficiently up to scratch to partner her in affairs.

Pyott grunted with pleasure at Marian's remarks. Aubrey's mood was complacent. He was an aged senator returned to the Forum from his farm, to find himself little more than amused at antics he had once taken with the deadliest seriousness. He sipped at his whisky, enjoying Giles' pleasure at his daughter, and the scent of the promised meal. A cork popped in the kitchen, sliding seductively from a bottle of very good claret.

'There will be buyers — there is a great deal of interest, my dear lady,' Coulthard replied, his eyes narrowed into creases of fat, his demeanour so ruffled that he had publicly patronised his inquisitor — to Marian's intense satisfaction. 'I didn't know our sales and marketing division interested honourable members quite so closely,' he added, his anger incapable of restraint except in sarcasm.

'Our interest, Marian . . .' the chairman began, leaning to her so that his words became a mutter in which was distinguished a tone of ingratiating reprimand.

'You're right, of course, Chairman,' Marian murmured. 'This Committee is simply interested — are we not? — in seeing some return on the EC subsidies that were made into research and development, here and in France. Hence our interest in the sales prospects —' She paused, as if stung by an insect or a revelation. The camera cut to Coulthard, who appeared ever more uncomfortable — before his eyes became hooded and inexpressive. It was no more than a moment, but something had been revealed. Aubrey's ancient, rusty curiosity was aroused.

'What happened there, Giles? She scored a hit without realising it — how?' At once it had become a diversionary game, of course; nothing of real or immediate interest to him. Real interest was confined to dinner and Giles' amicable, comfortable company.

'I saw that, too, Kenneth. Research subsidies, grants — whatever the Black Hole of Brussels calls them these days . . . we all know they got a bucketful of ecus at Aerospace UK, just like Stendhal-Balzac, to get the project off the ground. Funny . . .' He studied the screen, but the camera had passed to an interjecting left-wing MP who had taken up Marian's cry concerning jobs. There had, apparently, been redundancies at a subcontractor in his constituency. Why the lay-offs, he asked in broadest Lancashire, if there was the immediate prospect of sales?

Coulthard had recovered his habitual condescension, his corporate arrogance. Whatever Marian had caught on the wing was gone. A glimpse of her features showed that she, too, had dismissed the moment . . . as Aubrey did. For, as Giles said, they all knew how much the European Commission, in one of its fits of anti-Americanism and *Le grand Europe* moods, had poured into the initial research programme for the Skyliner. That was all above board, allowable. Coulthard had looked, for a moment, like a man caught with his hand in the till.

Mrs Grey appeared in the doorway and mouthed *ten minutes* to Aubrey, who nodded and turned to Giles.

'Another drink, my dear Giles?'

'Why not? That beef smells wonderful, Mrs Grey.' Aubrey's housekeeper retired to her kitchen suitably recompensed. General Sir Giles was an always welcome guest of Sir Kenneth.

Aubrey shuffled across the green carpet towards the drinks tray on the Victorian credenza near the bay window. The early summer evening gleamed on the grass of the park and from a hundred windows. Traffic murmured like flies. He poured himself another whisky, clinked ice for Giles' gin, and dismissed the nag of curiosity. Remembering with amusement a time when he would, in Marian's place, have worried at Coulthard like a dog at a bone — *a terrier at a rat*, as one of his field agents had always preferred to phrase it. But, in his case, the interrogation would have been of someone unshaven and without sleep and who posed a threat. That had been a kind of war, and this was not. It was merely business . . .

'There you are, my dear,' he announced brightly, handing Pyott his tumbler. 'Cheers — to us, and to our very own St Joan!' He gestured his glass towards the television. Giles Pyott raised his own almost with reverence towards Marian's image.

He was still awake when the telephone rang in the bedroom of the apartment. The illuminated dial of the bedside alarm showed him it was two in the morning. The whole apartment was quiet, empty, the traffic outside seeming to pass it furtively, with a sense of uncertainty. When he heard her voice, he wondered for an instant whether some anticipation of her call had been what had kept him awake.

'Mitchell — it's . . . Barbara.'

He had known she would call — either her or her father. The TV news had been awash with images of the crashed 494, scorched fuselage lying like an old artillery shell in the sand of the Arizona desert, surrounded by the immobile vehicles of the rescue team, the fire department, the accident investigation. Speculation, the fall of Vance stock on the Dow, rumours of jumpy nerves among the bigger creditors, the half-dozen banks Vance had charmed money from . . . it had been like watching a garment unravelling, its designer label mocked by its shoddiness.

'Sure, Barbara,' he muttered, sitting up in bed and switching on the table lamp beside him. The room did not seem to warm in its glow; the place expressed his mood, even the memories that he at once entertained. The shabby, bitter last year of their marriage, the months of the divorce. 'What — how are you?' he asked, changing the question, drawing back from why she must have called.

There was an exasperated exhalation, a sound he had thought not to hear again, then she said abruptly: 'Daddy needs your help, Mitchell. He's in trouble —'

He snapped back: 'I watch the news on TV. You can't miss him, Barbara.'

'Oh, for Christ's sake — !'

'The good Lord isn't why you're calling, Barbara. How is — what's his name? Tom — and the baby?' Again the exasperation, even hatred, in her breathing. He felt cheap — and satisfied.

'*Will* you help him?'

'What went wrong?' He *was* curious, he admitted. There had been nothing but speculation on TV and in the newspapers, and by men whose credentials he either suspected or dismissed. *Pilot error* . . . how they *loved* that old dog. The oldest, most inclusive slur and easiest escape route for guys who shaved safety and quality for profit, extended maintenance schedules, ignored routine checks.

'We — he doesn't know . . .' She sounded doubtful, angry.

'He hasn't told you what he suspects? What

about the flight recorder?'

'Nothing to account for — the crew died, Mitchell.' He wondered, disliking himself at once for the suspicion, whether the lack of information was just another persuasive tactic.

'It was on the news.'

'The banks are crawling all over him, Mitchell. He could be *ruined* by this — !' The element of hysteria in her voice was uncalculated, genuine. He knew the tone only too well.

'Did he ask you to call me?'

After a silence: 'No . . .'

'No. He wouldn't. What could I possibly know he didn't know already — the guy who flew his personal jet and disappointed his daughter?'

'Please — not now . . .' She sounded wounded, exhausted. Then hard-edged as a flint. 'Will you help, Mitchell? Just a simple yes or no, then we can end this —'

'How badly is he hurt?'

'You've seen the Dow? The banks are panicking. Burton, the man who's agreed to buy the first six planes — he's suffering, too.' Then her filial outrage overmastered all other feelings. 'He doesn't deserve to fail, Mitchell. Even *you'd* have to admit that! They're all waiting for him to fall — he's on his own and he's on the edge. For God's sake help him!'

He felt as if he was listening to the sound of a collapsing building. Her noises were dry sobs, grasps at air and calm. Where her husband was he could not guess — or from where she was calling. He owed Barbara precisely nothing — except her continued apprehension of the truth that he was responsible for the failure of their marriage. She was entitled to that prop to her confidence, that investment in her new marriage. He owed Vance even less. Headlights slid across the curtains like a searchlight seeking him, then they were gone.

He went on listening to the silence from the other end of the line. Was she waiting for his reply, or did she think she had already heard it in his silence? Perhaps she was clinging to the phone like a lifebelt. What in hell could he do, anyway — even if he was a better accident investigator than most, probably than the guys picking the plane to pieces in Vance's hangar outside Phoenix? It had been a pre-delivery, routine flight. Nothing had seemed wrong, everything was registering normal or satisfactory, the status of every working part . . . Then the pilot had reported sudden engine failure, declared an emergency — and felt the plane carrying him drop out of the sky, determined to kill him and everyone on board. It was the *pilot* who hadn't deserved it.

'Barbara,' he said eventually, his voice level.

'Yes?' Unreasonable hope mingled with self-protective contempt.

'A guy reminded me, two days ago, I was a federal employee. If I come to you — if I *find* anything — then the FAA will have to know. I won't cover up for Alan — or you. That's the risk. If the plane's guilty, I'll have to say so — whatever it does to the stock and however much it frightens the banks.' He paused, then murmured: 'That's the deal.'

She was silent for no more than a moment, then she asked abruptly: 'Can you be here tomorrow?'

'Maybe. See you —' But the connection had already been broken, as suddenly as if they were lovers and her husband had walked unexpectedly into the room from which she was making the call. He looked at his receiver, then replaced it.

He had expected the call, he decided. It had been that anticipation that had kept him awake. He lit a cigarette and blew smoke at the ceiling. He rested against the headboard, arms folded across his chest. Had he *wanted* her to call? Maybe . . . probably. He sensed, from the TV news and the scuttlebutt at the FAA offices, that it was the plane that was at fault, not the pilot. Alan Vance's dream, become a reality, was faulty — it *didn't work*. And he would prove it. And, because he was a senior accident investigator, he would be able to tell the whole of America — on TV. *Good Morning America* . . . He grinned sourly. Barbara hadn't thought it through, hadn't realised how much he still hated Vance and resented his treatment at the man's hands as the marriage accelerated down its slippery slope to its day in court. Vance had lied about him, blackened him — made out he was the jerk of all time and violent, too. He'd told the newspapers, anyone who'd listen and repeat the slurs.

He continued smoking. Now Vance needed him. Better than that, Vance didn't even know he was coming, didn't know that his beloved only daughter had *invited* him . . . Yes, he had waited, *really* waited for her call . . .

When she returned to the Holland Park house from the board meeting of one of the unfashionable charities she helped shepherd, Charlotte Burton found her husband in the first-floor drawing room, the younger boy, Jamie, on his lap. Both of them had, apparently, been lulled to sleep by the book that lay fallen on the Chinese carpet. She paused in the doorway, studying him as he struggled awake. The youth that sleep, however exhausted, had given his features, vanished. Jamie stirred and, looking at her, Tim hugged the child.

'Hi,' he said. 'Er — we must have fallen asleep . . .' He grinned apologetically.

She crossed the room and stood behind the sofa, her hands resting on his shoulders. At once, his cheek rubbed against her fingers, intent as the gesture of a small, dependent animal. Jamie had probably been tired out by the grim, dedicated intensity Tim always brought to play with his children when he was deeply worried. It was almost as if he were enjoying them for a final time. His lovemaking at such times was, by contrast, apologetic, tender and guilty, as if he had betrayed her.

'Rough day?' He nodded against her fingers. 'Are you in this evening?' His head shook.

'Sorry, Charley.' He stretched his head back and stared up at her. 'You're so beautiful,' he announced, and she quailed inwardly. He was ragged, becoming unravelled. It was even obvious in the way he carefully handed Jamie to the carpet, as if he was dealing with something Ming and fragile, bought with a loan he could not repay.

'That bad?' she steeled herself to say, adding: 'Has Greta made your tea, Jamie?'

Jamie, pushing tracks of a toy lorry into the thick pile of the carpet, nodded. He was still Daddy's boy, herself and the au pair just females for the moment.

'Yuck. I left it — salad. That's all she eats. Yuck!'

'Where's Tony?'

'Cricket nets,' Jamie replied. There were three years between them, but they still attended the same prep school. Next year, Tony would begin at Winchester, Tim's old school. 'Cricket — yuck.'

Burton, stroking her hands with his own as they rested on his shoulders, chuckled.

'Disgraceful slur on the beautiful game.'

'Footballers and golfers are richer than cricketers,' Jamie observed, idly turning the pages of the book from which Burton had been reading. *Lord of the Rings* — of course. It was Tim's idea of literature as well as what children should imbibe with their mother's milk — or their au pair's salads.

'Richer than me, too, before very long,' Burton murmured, and he flinched as her grip involuntarily tightened on his shoulders. 'Sorry,' he added, patting her fingers.

'Who are you wooing this evening?' she asked, staring over his head, across the room to the marble-topped sideboard, the two Louis Seize chairs, one on either side, and at their figures reflected in the French mirror with the trumpeting angel surmounting it. She always — and perhaps to her slight, shameful disappointment — appeared the more mature of the two, the more purposeful, self-confident. Quite often, especially in mirrors and when unaware, Tim was still the schoolboy who had desperately sought, even bought, his friendships; who had always played amanuensis, second fiddle to boys better at sport, or more intellectually equipped. *Life's eternal straight man,* as he said of himself. 'Anyone very important?' She shrugged his shoulders, as if plumping them like cushions.

'Sir Herbert of Bank A, Lord Sisfield of Bank B, Mr Martin of Bank C, Herr Adler of Bank D . . . The biggest creditors' biggest guns. Crikey — !' he added self-mockingly. Charlotte was forced to answer his ingenuous, open smile. They studied one another in the tall mirror. Burton sighed.

'Ten more minutes of this and I'll be able to carry it off,' he murmured, then continued: 'They're giving Alan Vance an even harder time, I gather. Really *squeezing* —'

Angrily, she snapped: 'Never mind Alan Vance! If his aeroplane hadn't fallen out of a clear blue sky *you* wouldn't be in the midden!'

'I took the lead, Charley — I really did. *I'll take the brunt of it,* I said to him. He wanted a creeping barrage, like a Great War general — some small American carriers, maybe a Far East airline, a few of the holiday charter firms . . .'

She gripped his shoulders fiercely.

'I know all that, Tim — I know!' she said

through clenched teeth. 'But it was the plane that failed, not you. Now —' She was quickly sitting beside him. Jamie had wandered off towards the kitchen and Greta or the housekeeper. '*Now,*' she repeated, 'how bad are things? Really.'

'Cash flow is down. The big carriers are trying to undercut me — cut my throat, more likely. They can stand the loss. Maybe I can't. I'm not sure yet. The team's doing some projections for me . . .' He tried to lean against her but she remained sitting bolt upright, hands folded on the lap of her narrow cream dress. He smiled at the effort of restraint she indulged in order to appear frowningly assertive, inquisitorial. He raised his hands in mock surrender. 'Alright, alright. Seriously, a few months more of it — all the summer traffic across the Pond — and my losses could be enormous. Which means the debts will not be serviced properly — interest payments and the like — and I won't have a cheaper plane to put into service to recover the losses. Unless, my darling girl, I can charm the pinstripe trousers off the men in suits tonight and every other night they demand to have dinner with me —' In spite of her resolve, she smiled for a moment. He grinned back. 'Unless I can, I won't be able to buy new aircraft, I won't be able to fly the Atlantic cheaply. I won't' — his features at once became angry, filled with a hateful disappointment — 'be able to open the Australian route. The big carriers — all the bastards who've been trying to screw me for ten years . . . they'll have won. I'll go the way of Freddie Laker, Charley. I really will!'

She put her arms around him and pulled his head on to her breast.

'Nice,' he murmured.

Not nice, she thought. Not the prospect of financial ruin. She would live in a hut with him, on crusts and love, if necessary — though she wouldn't choose it. She remembered the grotty flats, the dingy Victorian terraced house in north London they couldn't afford to do up or alter . . . She did *not* want to return to them. For there was, naturally, little in her name, not even the house here or in the Cotswolds. Tim — daft bugger — had always used *his* money as collateral. One of those perfectly awful magazine features only two months earlier had named him in the top two hundred wealthiest people in Britain . . . which, *then,* was the measure of the value of Artemis and his other interests. *Outside* the business, he was not independently wealthy. There was no crock of gold in Switzerland or anywhere else. If the business failed, so did he — and *she* wasn't wealthy either. Tim hadn't cared enough about money, only about achieving, about *winning* — which he never measured in millions.

'He'd better make that aircraft work, then, hadn't he,' she murmured into his thick, greying hair, 'your friend Alan Vance? So he can get you out of the mire — and me and the children with you. Oh, you silly bugger, Tim, why didn't you give me a million or two against a rainy day!'

He laughed, quite genuinely.

'I didn't think I needed to,' he confessed. 'And you never asked!'

'When do you have to start flying the Vance aircraft? *Latest?*'

'I should have had it for this summer. The banks have been happy to wait because the two we've got stoogeing around Scandinavia are performing well and bringing in passengers. There's one small airline with two 494s in New Mexico. They're turning in good figures, too. But — I don't think they'll wait, not *now.* You've seen the papers, the TV — Christ, you'd think the bloody plane was held together with string and sticky tape and flown by means of a rubber band!'

'What *is* wrong with it, then?'

He threw up his hands, then sat up on the sofa. He looked at her with such an exaggerated seriousness that she felt he was mocking her. Then he said:

'Vance doesn't know. He doesn't bloody know, Charley. And if he can't find out, we really are in the shite — we really, really are! Up to our necks and beyond.' He stood up and began pacing the room. Their confidentiality and intimacy were at an end. His mind was already marshalling argument, proposal, charm, fabrication in anticipation of the evening meeting. 'But it must be bloody serious to make an aircraft fall out of the sky without the slightest warning! So serious it might be impossible to remedy. Oh — *shit!*' He tugged his hands through his hair. 'Oh, shit, shit, *shit!*' He turned to her as if to a stranger, his eyes gleaming. 'I can't see any way out, Charley — I think we've bloody had it. Artemis is going out like a dim bulb, and I can't do anything to save it!'

She towelled her blonde hair in a rough, pummelling motion, as if it had somehow offended her, watching her actions in the mirror above the carved wooden fireplace, positioned to make her sitting room seem larger. Her cheeks were still pinked from the shower. Her eyes, blue and without make-up, stared knowingly back at her, examining the first crow's-feet of her late thirties. Laughter lines, she pretended, just like those on either side of her mouth. However, she smiled at her reflection and knew she wasn't doing too badly for her age. She continued to watch herself, almost with that strangest of childhood sensations, seeing the person in the mirror, reflected back, as oneself. *Was she really that person?* She possessed her mother's high forehead and cheekbones, her full mouth. And Giles' piercing blue gaze, finished off by her grandmother's blonde hair, worn shoulder-length. It wasn't a bad amalgam, she admitted indulgently.

Then, aware of her vanity and the recollection of men's admiration bubbling just below the surface of her thoughts, she moved to the window of the sitting room and studied the fall of the evening sun across the Chelsea Physic Garden which lay behind the mansion block of flats. Hers was on the top floor.

Sipping at her gin and tonic, she grazed the rows of neat, white-painted shelves which housed her books and her collection of records and CDs. Then she scowled suddenly as she recalled herself to the day's last duty and flicked the answerphone to replay the messages she had missed while at the Commons that afternoon. The Prime Minister, to the embarrassment of the greater part of his own side of the House, had stumbled like a three-legged dog through PM's Questions, challenged on Europe, Ulster and sleaze with equal — and equally impotent — ferocity.

She listened half-heartedly to the voice of her constituency agent detailing the business of her Saturday-morning surgery, then with much more pleasure to her father's voice reminding her of their lunch date the following day. Then two calls from lobbyists — one of them a fellow MP — which made her long to switch on some music . . . and, finally, a call from Brussels, from Michael Lloyd. She smiled with anticipation. Michael was a senior researcher and aide to the EC Commissioner for Transport, a Frenchman — but then he spoke four languages fluently — and had once been one of her more dazzling undergraduates during her time as a junior Fellow at Oxford. And he was her conduit into the Byzantine politics, gossip and machinations of the European Commission.

'Hi, Marian,' she heard.

'Hi, Michael — what news?'

He sounded slightly breathless, but it was often his amusement to make much of little, act the role of a conspirator or double agent. Probably, he would have been recruited by dear Kenneth during the Cold War. Now he was her man in Brussels, an alliance that had sprung as much from mutual amusement at the EC and its bureaucratic labyrinths as from any other motive.

'. . . whether it's significant, I can't say, Marian

— but I know my Commissioner has a very big meeting arranged for tomorrow . . . with, among others, the CEOs of Aero UK and Balzac-Stendhal, and your friend David Winterborne. It's not taking place at the Commission, but one of the big hotels. I'll try to find out more — might be interesting, you never know . . . It was arranged at the last minute, and my Commissioner looks a little put out, to say the least. Like someone who's had his breakfast stolen from under his nose.' The young man laughed. Marian pictured his long fair hair, easy charm, stereotypical good looks. Her mother would have characterised him as perfect for modelling knitting patterns. He had employed all that considerable and effective charm for the purpose of seducing his tutor in modern history — she had been able to resist it, she remembered, smiling at herself in mockery as she continued to watch the streaming sunlight working like fingers among the planted rows of the Physic Garden. *Just* resist. Michael had forgiven her, with as easy a charm as he had employed in his seduction, and become instead her friend and ideological acolyte. 'I still can't put my finger on *anything* that suggests the slightest impropriety regarding funding — I think, my darling woman, you're barking up the wrong tree there. Even in this hall of mirrors it would be very difficult to hide wholehearted subversion of EU funds and subsidies . . . Sorry about that. I'll ring off now — talk to you soon.'

She finished her drink as the tape rewound in the answerphone. Working day at an end. Idly, she flicked the remote control for the hi-fi, and the music began. At once, the intense, swelling drama, the celebration of human joy, the rhythmic intoxication of Beethoven. Her lips moved, her fingers tapped around her tumbler, in time to the music.

She was disappointed — but, then, the idea had always seemed too brilliant; too unlikely therefore to have any foundation in reality. She had asked Michael whether there was *any* evidence of continuing, secret and illegal funding from the Commission to the planemakers, the partners in England and France engaged in building the monumentally expensive Skyliner. She knew that the Commissioner for Transport was engaged as deeply as a major shareholder in lobbying the national airlines to buy the plane — but she had wondered whether there was more than influence, more than lobbying and arm-wrenching and seduction involved . . . whether, in fact, money had changed hands. *Taxpayers'* money going into the pockets of private industry without the knowledge of the Council of Ministers and the House of Commons.

Kenneth Aubrey had somehow encouraged her suspicions . . . but it wasn't, after all, like one of his Cold War bedevilments. There was no truth in the suspicion. Aero UK was bleeding from the wound of the Skyliner's costs, its banks were nervous — even the sale of its car division to the Germans hadn't made its books much healthier. However, by her father's best guess, they should be in pole position to acquire the contract for the army's new attack helicopter, which they'd developed in cooperation with the Germans and Italians. It would certainly be less controversial to buy third-British than wholly American. Anyway, apparently Aero UK was not being kept afloat by secret subsidy.

Too much to hope for, she acknowledged, smiling at her disappointment; it was as if she had lost the matches that would have lit a fierce blaze under the pro-Europeans in her own party and the government. It would have been so *nice* to have been right about large-scale corruption . . .

Gradually, she let herself move into the music, into the hypnotic, intensifying dance of the symphony's allegretto, moving like a dancer around the lounge of the flat in her cream silk robe, her fair hair drying unregarded. Then, as the music reached a further height of intoxication and purpose, she caught sight of her flushed, angular features in the mirror behind the French clock. Her hair was making every effort to become a fright-wig, her cheekbones were livid, her full mouth opening in realisation.

Michael had sounded frightened . . . no, nervous rather, like someone trapped in a small, fragile car, hearing the unavoidable approach of a juggernaut. She switched off the music and hurried to the answerphone, accelerating the tape through the mundane in a rush of incomprehensible, birdlike calls, until she heard his voice.

'. . . taking place at the Commission, but one of the big hotels . . . It would be very difficult to hide . . . I'll ring off now — talk to you soon.'

He *was* frightened — like someone who had woken to a strange noise in the night and remained awake, hardly breathing, waiting to hear it again. The layers of pleasant assurance were penetrated by a sudden doubt, as if the implications of what he had said had only just struck him, so that the farewell faltered in his throat. Michael had had some insight regarding that meeting in Brussels which had unnerved him.

She replayed his words twice more. It was, she thought, almost as if he were not alone in the room . . .

CHAPTER TWO

The Needle and the Damage Done

The telephone brought Marian quickly awake. The radio alarm showed some minutes after six-thirty, and she groaned with irritation. Light was promisingly bright beyond the heavy, closed curtains.

'Marian Pyott.' She cleared her throat.

'Marian — it's Bob here.' The breathless voice of the young, ambitious MP with whom she shared an office in the Commons. Formerly in advertising, currently in self-advertisement in the hope of a junior ministerial post.

'What is it, Bob?' She made no attempt to disguise her irritation.

'I thought you'd like to know' — he was strangely, childishly disappointed at her apparent indifference — 'the papers are full of an MoD leak about the new helicopter contract. The army's going to award it to the Yanks. The Mamba, or whatever the machine's called.'

'What?' she breathed, feeling winded, and

weirdly guilty, as if she had committed some obscure betrayal. 'It's still at the level of a rumour, this leak?'

'Looks pretty deliberate to me — you know. "Don't let me catch you leaking this to the press, but here's the editor of *The Times*' number, just in case you've forgotten it." '

'Oh, *shit!* Aerospace UK will — God, this could absolutely finish the company. The banks will be circling like sharks. Where's the leak?'

'*FT* and the *Telegraph* — but it's already on the radio and TV.'

'Then it's the minister who's leaking. And the PM's caved in to the Treasury and the Chancellor on the grounds of cost. He said he wouldn't . . .' She had had a private meeting with the PM — briefed by her father and his group of lobbyists in favour of the Eurocopter — only the previous week. And had been assured, really *assured,* that it would be a decision based solely on quality, not cost.

Into her silence, Bob offered:

'I just thought you'd like to know — well, not *like,* but . . .'

'Yes. Yes, thanks, Bob.'

She put down the telephone loudly, with abstracted clumsiness. *Dear God* — there were thousands of jobs suddenly at risk, hundreds of them in her own constituency. And in all the component and avionic companies who were involved in the helicopter project in the UK, France and Germany. David Winterborne would take a battering, too. David was up to his ears — so many of his companies were committed to the project

. . . why did she feel guilty?

She remembered. She had pummelled Bryan Coulthard over Skyliner in the Select Committee. Now, it seemed she had been kicking someone who was already down. Bloody silly feeling — but real, nevertheless.

She scrabbled for her cigarettes and lit one. Heaved herself out of bed and drew back the curtains. Morning sun gleamed like paint on the Physic Garden. She tapped her fingernail against her teeth as she stood at the window.

Her father had been lobbying hard, together with a group of senior, mostly retired military figures and dozens of MPs like herself who had companies in their constituencies whose future depended on the army buying the British helicopter . . . Two hundred and fifty million sterling was a conservative estimate of the size of the business. But the Treasury had persuaded MoD that the Mamba, an old airframe with shiny new bolt-on goodies, was good enough. And *cheap*. And the Chancellor had persuaded the PM, obviously.

What a *bloody* mess! She puffed furiously at her cigarette. She'd fought for the helicopter just as she'd fought against Skyliner and its hideous costs. Now, however, there was *no* good news for Aero UK. Skyliner was unsaleable and the helicopter was grounded. Who'd buy it if the British army wouldn't, for crying out loud?

She flung herself away from the window and out of the bedroom. The newspapers lay on the doormat like IOUs come home to roost. She snatched up the *Telegraph* and scanned the front page. Yes, there it was . . .

The report estimated the worldwide, total business to be derived from the helicopter — *if* it had been chosen by the army — at more than a billion pounds. Later in the piece, sombre rumblings with regard to the future of Aero UK and the even more dire future of the whole British aerospace industry. Angrily, she threw the newspaper along the hall. Its separated pages fluttered like wounded grey birds.

Giles would be apoplectic — as she was. The government was getting the decision — unpopular as it was bound to be — out of the way now just in case the PM called an autumn election. People would have forgotten by October. It was outrageous . . . hundreds of her constituents faced redundancy. Oh, *bugger — !*

The hangar was the garishly lit stomach of a great marine mammal, ribbed and sparred to support its own size. The scorched wreckage of the aircraft lay on the stomach's floor like a half-digested meal. Gant felt the surge of sadness that was now a part of his professional self — for the people who had died as an aircraft changed into this mockery of a machine partially reassembled. The machines which he had always loved and to which he had always felt closest killed people occasionally — sometimes in their hundreds.

Vance was waiting for him, surrounded by his own people and the investigators from the southwest NTSB office. He detached himself from the group with evident reluctance, moving uncertainly towards Gant, who put down his sports bag on the stained concrete floor, aware of the desert dawn behind him, beyond the open hangar doors. Barbara — thankfully — was not there.

Vance held out his hand. But his habitual, enveloping charm, his energy, failed to ignite like a cold, sullen engine. He was weary and defeated, baffled for so long and so completely that even the anger at his own impotence had drained away. His blue eyes, bleared with lack of sleep, revealed nothing more than a worn cunning; all the challenging confidence was gone. Yes, he resented Gant's presence, his need for him.

'Mitchell.' One big hand gripped at Gant as at a lifebelt, the other was on his shoulder at once. Vance loomed over him, his stature pressing Gant back towards his hated beginnings and his childhood. Barbara had happened because he had wanted to be an adult, not the perpetually half-formed thing his flying skills had made of him, and which Vance had exploited. His hold over him had never been Barbara, but the fact that he created beautiful flying machines. As such, he had always been the gifted adult, Gant the dazzled child.

'Alan.' He returned the man's grip.

'Good flight?'

'OK.'

There was an aftershock through his hand of the anger Vance must have felt when Barbara had told him she had called. Then that, too, was gone. He was forced by circumstance to invest Gant with magical, visionary powers.

'What — you need to rest up?'

Gant shook his head.

'No.'

Vance's relief was audible.

'What do you want to look at? Most of the airplane is here, the flight recorders have been computer-analysed . . . instrument check is completed, the engines have been . . .' And he wound down like a child's toy made to talk by a battery which was now spent. Offering that inventory had exhausted not only him but his options, his optimism. The accident investigators had no answer, there were no clues in the flight recorder, the wreckage, the engines. 'I — don't know what else . . .' he faltered, then dried again like a terrified actor.

Gant disliked the empathy he felt for the man. Vance was a chained and beaten dog, that was all, and still capable of savagery.

'Let me look at the fuselage . . . just look. On my own.'

Vance nodded.

'Sure — but go easy, OK? These people — just handle them right. My people, the team — ?'

'Sure. I learned the trick,' he added. 'I can work with people just like a grown-up.'

As if affording proof, he brusquely greeted others. People he already knew from Vance Aircraft, others whose names or voices he knew from the Accident Inquiry Office in Tucson. They were suspicious of him — either because they knew him, or because they knew *of* him — the former fly-guy hero . . . or because he was Washington and his being there was an implicit criticism. He was free of them in moments, leaving vague reassurances, instructions, and walking towards the wreckage. Their murmuring behind him was a chorus of Vance's own need of him. He'd talk to them later —

— walking towards the wreckage as urgently as if there was some faint hope that someone was still alive within the cracked, skeletal fuselage. He passed trestle tables and long benches on which smaller pieces of wreckage lay, and gutted instruments, scattered bolts and fixings; all of it like tumours already excised from a diseased body. There were computer terminals and their leads like those of a life-support system. The flight recorders lay opened and empty, their tapes already futilely analysed. He would come to all of that later.

He stopped close to the cracked tailplane, its markings — those of Artemis Airways — scorched like a house wall after an explosion. He clambered into the rear section of the fuselage.

The central aisle, down which duty-free perfumes and drink would have been trolleyed and meals delivered, was broken like a road dug up for new conduits. Wiring dangled, together with oxygen masks and torn fabric. Everything smelt of smoke, scorching, extinguisher foam. The overhead lights of the hangar glared through a gap in the fuselage like sunlight between buildings. The fuselage had snapped in three on impact with the desert. The wings had broken off. Seat after seat as he moved lay torn away, crushed, drunkenly tilted. He shied from them as if a passenger had died in each one.

He glanced through one of the gaps in the fuselage at a huge engine. Pratt & Whitney people were among the crowd that had gathered again around Vance like uncertain children. That engine hadn't restarted — though the pilot's last words, the TV had said over and again, claimed that the instruments were telling him that nothing was wrong.

He jumped across the gap of concrete to the flight deck, aligned like a broken neck with the rest of the fuselage. Fiercer scorching here. The overhead switch panels had dropped to hand like surprised jaws. The control columns were distorted like trees sprouting in a gale, the throttle levers were bent. The instrument displays of all three crew positions were disrupted by damage and removal, so that eye sockets and blank panels looked back at him. There was blackness on the crew seats, of dried blood perhaps. Some plastic had melted on the flight deck in what seemed to have been an intense but very brief fire. He stored the impression against comparison with other cockpit fires. How much fuel had there been? There should have been more damage. This fire would only have helped kill Pat Hollis and his co-pilot and flight engineer, if they had even been alive after the impact. He wondered who they had been — Lowell, maybe, Hollis' shadow and idolater . . . and the flight engineer had probably been Paluzzi. Which meant that three women had been widowed, nine — no, ten — children orphaned. He shuddered, remembering cockpit fires in other places, other times. *This* crew hadn't had the option to eject as he had done twice in his life with the airplane on fire. They'd had to sit in their seats and *burn* . . .

. . . like the Vietnamese girl who now, so many

years later, hardly ever intruded on his dreams.

Almost every instrument from the pilot's centre panel, which had housed the engine instruments, was missing. What remained was labelled or tagged. Name tapes, neatly computer-typed, fluttered from the overhead panels, from the flight engineer's panel. Each one, he knew from their colour, offered a negative — no explanation of the cause of the crash. He turned his head and stared through the flight deck's shattered side window. Through the cobweb pattern reminiscent of bullet damage, he glowered at the engine that was beached some yards from the broken fragments and spars of the port wing. Its position, in a kind of ominous isolation, suggested guilt. Fuel, fuel computer, booster pumps, fuel flow monitoring, the tanks, the lines, the compressors . . . *Check, check, check, check,* the team would tell him, again and again. The Tucson NTSB Inquiry Office had as good a reputation as any other.

He heard a noise behind him and half-turned — at once surprised and unsurprised to see Vance heaving his bulk into the cramped, crushed tin can of the flight deck. His breathing was that of an old, asthmatic man — as if the accident had aged him, cleaned the dye from his hair and given him instead dark stains beneath the blue eyes.

'Well — you cosied up enough to your wreckage?' Vance was impatient. No one interrupted a senior investigator in his or her meditative first exploration of a crash site, or of a reconstructed wreck, or of a *single piece* of wreckage. They left you alone until you wanted to talk . . . but Vance was hurting and Vance was an egoist and a bully and Gant had once been his son-in-law. He assumed he still had rights of demand, of appropriation. 'Any feelings?'

'Cold. Melancholy.'

'You know what I —' Vance choked the words off.

'Sure. I *know,*' Gant snarled. 'You're hurting in your billfold, Alan, and you need an answer quick! Don't crowd me, Alan — don't push . . .' His own words faded. It was obscene, the continuation of their guerrilla war in that confined, damaged space where people they had both known — and respected — had burned to death. 'Just take it easy,' he forced out.

'OK — sure. I apologise. What can I tell you? Is there any — ?'

'The engine. Before I talk to the Pratt & Whitney guy who is going to fire off in defence of his baby.'

'The engine was perfect. So far. Your people are almost through with it — with both engines.'

'Which one stopped first?'

'Port — that one.'

'Seconds later, the starboard engine suffered flame-out. Right?'

Vance nodded in a sullen, aggrieved way. 'Right.'

'Hollis didn't make a mistake and cut the other engine?' Vance shook his head. From the pocket of his jacket he produced a small tape recorder.

'You want to hear it? It's on here — the fragments that were left of the cockpit voice recorder after the cabin fire.' He proffered the machine but Gant shook his head.

'Later,' he murmured, as if he had been offered the portfolio of an atrocity. Vance must have been carrying his copy around, listening to it constantly, tormenting himself with it . . . or maybe just hoping that Hollis or Lowell or whoever else was on the flight deck had screwed up and he, like everyone else hustling for a buck in the airplane business, could cry *pilot error.* 'Later,' he repeated.

Something . . . ?

'How much of the cockpit record tape survived?'

'Not much. The fire was pretty intense in here . . .' *First to arrive at the scene of an accident* was how pilots tried to laugh the prospect of a crash into unimportance.

Intense . . . ? *Fire — ?*

His mind wandered back down the twisted, scorched passenger compartment, between the leaning or lurching seats and the dangling wires and masks . . . not much fire, not *that* much. Not as badly damaged as here —

— glanced to one side, through the starred window, to where the broken wing lay like smashed planking beside the huge engine. Other crashes, other scenes, had a lot of fire damage, but the images on the TV news of the 494 taken from a helicopter . . . dulled metal, untarnished flaps . . . didn't show much fire damage — not *enough* fire damage?

He concentrated on the flight deck.

'What else was there?' he asked. 'Before flame-out in both engines?'

'What — ? It's hard to tell. Hollis was a tight-ass. You knew him. He was above keeping in radio contact with the ground on a routine flight. He reported the failure of both engines — but nothing before that . . .'

There was something, though.

'What else, Alan?' His voice was icily calm.

'Instability. There's some exchange about the ship becoming unstable —' Vance threw up his hands, as if he had been made to admit to minor fraud. 'Look, Gant —'

'Suddenly, I'm Gant — what happened to Mitchell?' His eyes held no amusement. 'What *happened?*'

'OK, so there was some instability — difficulty handling the plane, and controlling the trim —'

Not enough *fire damage.* His stare hardened, as if he were dredging Vance's recollection by means of hypnotism, willing the answer.

'It's impossible to say how bad, for how long . . . The computer realisation of the pilot's instruments shows it must have been pretty violent. I don't know what caused it.'

'Fuel?'

'Uh?'

'Fuel flow, fuel management?'

Vance shook his head vehemently. 'All the readings for the fuel flow, the booster pumps, the lines, the management system, the fuel computer — they're *all* normal. Nothing was happening to the fuel to make the ship unstable. And the weather didn't do it, either. Look — we're agreed, all of us, that the instability problem isn't linked to the flame-out in both engines!'

'OK. For now.' He had no insight. Hollis may, or may not, have exacerbated the instability by over-correction, by distraction. He'd have to study the computer realisation and judge for himself, as a pilot. He owed that and a great deal more to Hollis, who had listened to him too often, as they had gotten drunk together, on the subjects of Vance and Vance's daughter — and the bitter taste of his life after the airforce and the combat and the heroics with the MiG-31 and the operation they had code-named Winter Hawk. It wasn't going to be *pilot error* except as the coldest of cold facts. He owed Hollis' patience with his own self-pity that much at least.

'Did you find *anything* wrong with the engines?'

'Not with either one. They just didn't restart. There was cactus and sagebrush ground to dust in each one, so they were rotating. But there was nothing burnt — so, no flame. Neither engine relit. They tried —'

'Flight engineer's panel?'

'Everything was reading normal — and on the central panel. You can hear Lowell —' It was Lowell, then, who had died in the seat on which Gant's hand rested as he remained squatting on his haunches. Bright-eyed and hero-worshipping. He had been cruel to Lowell — often — because the boy had loaded him with his old identity and asked him to relive it, day after day. What had initially flattered had rubbed like salt on raw flesh after a while. 'He and Hollis repeat all the read-outs after the port engine failed, and Paluzzi confirms every call. That's the most unspoilt part of the cockpit tape . . . There was *nothing wrong*,' he ground out finally, his big hands clenching again and again, as if tearing at something or strangling it.

'There was. They died.'

'I know that — !'

'The airplane killed them, Alan. Either the air-frame you designed or the fuel management system you boasted about or the Pratt & Whitney engines *you* helped modify . . .' His eyes were glacial and he sensed Vance's anger and confidence quelled, momentarily. 'One way or another, Alan, *you* let Hollis down.'

'*He* could have made a mistake! He could have unstabilised the ship —'

'The instability isn't linked to the flame-out. Your words. You tested other engines — on the ground?'

'Of course.' The anger was snuffed out like a flickering candle. Gant and Vance faced each other like crouching animals within the crushed metal box of the flight deck. The desert breeze shouldered its way from the hangar doors into the confined, hot space. Vance shrugged his much bigger frame. 'We ran all the checks. Look, I know that engine, the fuel flow monitors, the computer . . .' He spread his large hands. The fingers were stained with oil. Leaning back against the seat in which Hollis had burned, he said: 'Sol Zeissman over at Albuquerque Airways has grounded the two planes he's leasing from me. He'll be asking for a refund before the week-end — ! They're libelling my ship in the newspapers, on TV, every day and night! Scare stories.

No one is going to buy unless I can *prove* she's safe.' The appeal became more evident as he burst out: 'You were around the early stages of development, Mitchell — you know she's a good ship!'

Gant was forced to concede a brief nod. Then he looked away from Vance, from the ageing process of his bewilderment and profound, impotent frustration, through the starred windows of the flight deck. Like a storyboard for some projected movie, huge blow-up photographs of a desert landscape and the stranded 494 formed a semicircle at one end of the hangar. They were the wall against which Vance's energy and remaining youth had spent itself. It would be a horror movie, about the destruction of dreams. The computers, the group of men, the pieces of the plane were the accoutrements of a funeral scene.

'No bird ingestion, no fuel line blockage, no fuel computer failure . . .' he murmured to himself, as if reciting charms that would ward off what he sensed in Vance — what the man *really* wanted from him. Vance shook his head at each item and instrument. 'Fuel starvation . . . ?' Even with the economy forced on the adapted Pratt & Whitney engines to meet Vance's specifications, the calculations for the pre-delivery flight wouldn't have been wrong. 'Were the fuel calculations wrong?' he asked mechanically.

'No.'

Gant felt suddenly hot, despite the sensation of the breeze on his face and bare forearms. He knew — now — why Barbara had called, and he knew it had to have been at Vance's instruction. Vance didn't want his current expertise. He wanted the hero to make a comeback, the *flyer.*

'You're out of your skull, Alan.'

'What — ?' Gant turned to look at Vance and saw the admission plainly in Vance's face. 'I —'

'You got Barbara to call me, knowing I'd just love to come down here and make some cheap shots at your expense. Fool around with the team from Tucson, then ground the 494 for a while. You took that chance, just to —'

Vance clenched his fists.

'I need you to fly that plane —'

'Other people said much the same, a long time ago. The priorities seemed bigger, back then.'

'All that out there — it could take weeks, even months. You know that. I don't have *days* — and neither does Tim Burton, who has ordered six — *six.* He's run into his own brick wall. You *have* to help.'

'I don't.'

'Christ, Gant — !'

Vance stared at him in challenge, even hatred. He was trying to goad him into acting like a crazy man. Pretending there was no way out for Gant without losing face, running scared. He'd known he would come. Now he thought he could force him to fly another 494, duplicate the flight plan Hollis had been flying, prove that the accident was a freak, a once-only. It would make the TV news on NBC, CBS, ABC, CNN. National coverage of the *hero* giving Vance Aircraft his backing. Giving the airlines and the public a guarantee of safety . . . Gant, formerly of the USAF and well connected with the CIA, now of the National Transportation Safety Board — what more could Vance ask or the public receive? It would be like a basketball player like Michael Jordan endorsing sports gear — a surefire winner.

'You'll pay me millions for the endorsement, right?' he murmured.

'What — ?'

He was expected to underwrite the plane's safety.

'It won't work out. If another airplane goes down, you'll never get out from under. And I'll be *dead* —'

'You can't refuse.'

'Until we know what went wrong, it could happen again.'

'We're not going to find out, down here.'

'Not quickly, maybe, but we will find out.'

'They'll foreclose on me like I was a share-cropper. But maybe that's what you want.' Gant shook his head, resting on his haunches, his eyes fixed on the empty eye sockets in the pilot's instrument display. The twisted control column was like a broken catapult. 'All right,' Vance announced heavily, his breathing ragged and loud. 'I'm *begging* you. Isn't that what you want? Save my company. Save the airplane.' Gant looked up at him. Alan's eyes remained flinty but his voice was uncertain and aged, that of a very old man waking in a strange and dark place. Yet he *knew* Gant's answer before he replied. His features claimed, with utter certainty, that Gant would seize the opportunity to recapture something of his past, that he would risk his life to help a man who despised him, just for the sake of discovering a former self staring back at him from his shaving mirror. Vance knew that he would do *anything* just for one more fix, because his whole existence was continuous cold turkey and withdrawal symptoms.

The anonymity of his days stretched before him in an unending succession; and Vance, like the devil, now offered him his own version of the kingdoms of the earth — his former identity, his sense of himself as the best, as unique.

Eventually, he said: 'I can't ask the Tucson team to fly with me — I can't risk that.'

'I — er, I can fly as engineer. You need a co-pilot?'

Gant shook his head.

'*You*'ll fly?'

'See? You don't have any choice.'

Gant rubbed his cheeks.

'Is the simulator available?'

'All set up.'

'You're an asshole, Alan — a real, made-in-America asshole.'

'Sure. Just save my plane, uh? *And* my ass.'

At first — for perhaps as much as an hour — he was unaware and then uncertain that he was himself under surveillance. Now he was sure of it. Sitting under the sodden, garish umbrella over his table outside the café, Michael Lloyd had gradually felt his confidence subside into a fidgety, bemused, unnerved sense of himself.

He thought there were two of them, one in a parked car whose wipers flicked occasionally to give the driver a clear glimpse of him, and a second man inside the café, at a steamy window seat, a face half-hidden in fog. There might be others, near him or around the Grand' Place, moving or still among the hurrying flocks of umbrellas and raincoats. The patience and immobility of the two he was aware of — their very lack of distinct or direct threat — was more intimidating than action would have been. The summer storm splashed from the umbrella over the table as well as from the awning on to the cobbles.

He could leave now, of course — go back to his office in the Commission — casually, indifferently, as if he had never noticed the two men. After all, he couldn't barge into whichever conference suite they were using in the Hotel Amigo for their meeting. He'd seen them all arrive, including his own Commissioner, Etienne Rogier, whom he'd followed through the Brussels rush hour. Bryan Coulthard and David Winterborne from Aero UK, their equivalents from the French planemaker, Balzac-Stendhal, various functionaries, the Commissioner for Urban Development — he was something of a surprise but it probably meant nothing except more lobbying — and assorted minions, hurrying under black umbrellas, the skirts of their trenchcoats or crinoline-full raincoats flapping and flying around their legs.

There had been no secrecy about their arrival . . . so why was *he* being watched? He tried to laugh off his mounting nerves as childish pique at the unfairness of it. It had been stupid to come — he'd thought it witty at the time, something to amuse Marian Pyott — and to photograph them going into the hotel. That must have been how he had drawn their attention to himself.

The rain drummed on the sodden canvas over his head. A wet raincoat brushed his cheek as someone blundered past into the interior of the café, a look of surprise on his face as he saw Lloyd sitting outside in a rainstorm. He tried not to look at the parked car, or towards the windows of the café. *Caught in the crossfire,* he tried to joke. He thought the man in the car was using a mobile phone. He felt frightened, *lost in a dark wood.* Dante. Why Dante now, for God's sake? The wipers flicked again. Yes, he was using a phone. Summoning others?

And what had he seen, anyway? There was no hidden message, no secret pattern to be discerned. What had been worth attracting the attention of these people, whoever they were? They were not Commission security people, he was certain. All he'd discovered was that EU Commissioners and a Euro MP for an English constituency were meeting prominent businessmen. Great! They did it every day — feathering their nests, aligning their post-Commission futures on the boards of major companies, creating their grand designs, dreaming their unrealisable dreams . . . Snouts in the trough or heads in the air, it was all so usual and *expected.*

His suspicions of the previous day, his sense of his Commissioner's nervous attempts at secrecy and deflection, now seemed ridiculous.

The man in the car, still on the phone, worried him to an unexpected and unnatural extent . . .

'. . . about to piss himself, poor little sod.' There was a hard, barking laugh in Jessop's ear more like a dismissive cough than amusement. 'What's he up to, anyway?'

He flicked the wipers again and glimpsed Lloyd's slumped, tense figure through the rain. Fraser, talking to him now, was warm and dry in the hotel, unlike that poor pillock who thought he was playing detective or something . . . What was he taking pictures for? For *whom?* It hadn't done him much good, he was practically crapping himself with worry now, ever since Fraser had told him and Cobb to show themselves and their interest. Declaring their surveillance had frightened this bloke but not driven him off. So, what was he doing, and who was he doing it for? The papers? Fraser wouldn't like that.

'What does the great white chief say?' Jessop asked.

'He's thinking.'

'He's always doing that.'

'Unlike you, Jessop.' Fraser was a deeply unpleasant person. But he paid handsomely. At least, his boss did. Mind you, the stupidity of holding a *very secret meeting* in one of the best hotels in Brussels . . . not clever. But it was typical of Brussels bureaucrats — if they were going to be seduced, they wanted the roses and the candlelit dinner and the best wine before they got into bed with you. They couldn't pass up a free lunch in the plushest surroundings for the life of them.

'Do you want us just to sit here, then?'

'If he moves, you move. Otherwise, sit tight. When he does go, find out who he is and who he represents. And don't bother me again until he does move.'

Jessop put down the phone. He'd always disliked Fraser. Most people in the service had done. He was dangerous to be around because he didn't look after you. In the private sector, Fraser was, if possible, even more dismissive and contemptuous of his subordinates. On the other hand, there was a certain new and definite ruthlessness attached to work in the private sector, after the restraints of the intelligence service. You didn't have prissy old farts like Aubrey running the show, forever worrying about the moral dimension and the *weight* of one death or more. A facility in the arrangement of untraceable, unsuspicious *accidents* was much more recognised and rewarded — even if the game plan remained as mysterious and remote as ever. Fraser bullshitted with the best, but he didn't know much, either.

Jessop lit a cigarette and idly flicked the wipers once more. There he still was, poor little bugger. Moving closer every minute to being turned off, he was . . .

They'll follow me the moment I get up to go, Lloyd realised with a numbing fear. He seemed to look down on his hunched, immobile form from a height, seeing the ridiculous loneliness and isolation of his figure under the drenched table umbrella, the rain still lashing down, the parked car, the openness and betraying space of the Grand'

Place at the end of the street. *They'll follow me back to the office, back home, they'll know who I am* . . . Rain had soaked his raincoat collar, that of his jacket, his shirt. He shivered, the coldness coming from inside him. *Oh you idiot, you bloody idiot — !*

Why had he thought it so clever to ring Marian Pyott, why had he denied, when she'd called him only hours ago, that there was anything wrong, that this meeting had nothing to do with her suspicions . . . when he had already begun to suspect that she might be right, after all? *Her* suspicions had put him here, she had seduced his curiosity and left him between the man in the car and the man in the café — and at the mercy of whoever was on the other end of the phone. Oh, *shit —*

It didn't happen. Not here, not like this, not *that* kind of thing . . .

The flick of the wipers. The man had finished on the phone, he was smoking a cigarette. Before rain slid down the windscreen again, he saw a white hand wave. Instinctively, he turned his head. Beside the clouded face in the café window was another waving white hand.

Both of them were waving at *him —*

Fraser caught the mood of the meeting as clearly as he would have sensed a threat to himself. His impressions were like listening to a bug that had developed an intermittent fault, but the quiet, suppressed desperation of the people in the conference room was evident. Their features and hunched furtiveness were unmistakable.

The door closed again. *Find out,* he had been ordered, *who he is — then find out his interest in this meeting.* Fraser stood in the corridor that smelt of new carpet and recently tinted walls. Ten yards or so away, a maid fussed at her trolley of cleaning fluids, fresh towels and linen.

His mobile phone trilled in the pocket of his raincoat.

'Fraser.'

'He's on the move.' It was Jessop. 'You want us to follow him, right?'

'I want an ID, quick. Photograph, address, background.'

'Is he important?'

'You tell me — by lunchtime.'

He snapped shut the mobile phone and leaned back against the wall. The unexpected surveillance worried him because it *was* unexpected — and from an amateur. Jessop was certain of that. But not newspaper or TV. Yet there had been photographs . . . Fraser rubbed his smooth, blunt chin. Whoever he was, he was a rogue, unanticipated element of the situation. He stared at the closed doors as if watching the meeting taking place behind them. Aero UK's CEO, screaming rape by MoD because the helicopter contract was going to the Yanks — *and* the shiny new airliner they were building with the Frogs, who were in there, wasn't selling . . . to *anyone.* The Euro Commissioners, both of them, squealing because of the pressure they were under to armlock the national carriers and the various aviation authorities into buying and flying and approving routes and slots for the Skyliner . . . Everyone hanging on for the new Boeing 777 or — he smiled — the Vance 494, which had just so *conveniently* fallen out of the sky.

Aero UK might be going to the wall, which meant his employer would lose millions, and limp away wounded from the collapse. Blackmail, bribery, cut-rate special offers . . . none of it was working in favour of the Skyliner. The man was *angry* . . . and his anger could turn against Fraser and his minions.

He rubbed his face. Took out the mobile phone and dialled Jessop.

'Where are you?'

'Rue de la Loi, near the Commission —'

'Is that where he's heading?'

'You'll have to wait for an answer — I'm not a mind-reader.'

'I'll wait.'

The line sounded like a tunnel through which a wind blew coldly, then, after perhaps a minute in which Fraser waited as patiently as a machine:

'He's dropping down into one of the underground car parks — must be a fully paid-up —'

'Is Cobb with you?'

'Yes.'

'Then find out *who* he is now.'

'How?'

'Use your imagination!'

He switched off the phone, the skin of his cheeks and jaw tight with angry suspicion. The European Commission building . . . He worked there, in some capacity or other, because he had a car park pass, accreditation. He glowered at the conference suite's closed doors. There were two Commissioners behind them, engaged in confidential talk with prominent businessmen . . . which was not criminal. But it interested the man who'd photographed them. He'd wanted to know who, why . . . *Why?* Why keep people he worked for, or worked alongside, under surveillance? Was he working for the Euros in the meeting? Against them or against the business interests in the room? Working for the Frogs, who were never to be trusted in anything?

He waited, itchy to move, act — but one place was as good as another to wait. The maid had drifted out of sight now and the corridor was empty, airlessly warm, desiccated.

'Well?' he demanded when the mobile eventually offered him its peremptory chirping. 'Who is he?'

'His name's Lloyd — Michael Lloyd. A researcher for one of the Commissioners. It's cost Cobb his mobile. Claimed Lloyd had left it in the café and he tried to catch him before he drove off . . . followed him public-spiritedly to return it. Good deed in a naughty —'

'*Which* Commissioner?'

'Transport.'

Who was behind those closed doors at that moment . . . He had been keeping his *boss* under surveillance.

'He'll be put on his guard getting a phone delivered that isn't his,' Fraser observed. 'Never mind. OK, find out everything about this Michael Lloyd. Who there is around him, behind him, in the shadows. He's interested in what's happening here — why should he be?'

'Will we — ?'

'Take measures to prevent his further interest? I should think so, Jessop. I really don't see why not.'

'Just a minute, Daddy — I want a word with that weasel over there. Sit tight for a moment —'

The Commons Terrace was, as yet, unlittered with MPs. There were a few early arrivals scattered at the darkwood tables that reminded Marian of nothing so much as garden furniture from a DIY chain store. There had been no morning business in the House, and there'd be nothing more than written answers to questions on the helicopter contract. Neither the PM nor the Minister would appear — if they were wise. But the junior procurement minister from Defence was seated at one of the tables, a gin and tonic sparkling in the sunlight clutched in his long-fingered hand, some constituent or contact opposite him, dazzled by the locale, the occasion.

'Hello, Jimmy,' she announced portentously, standing close to him so that he was less likely to stand. The junior minister was languidly, gracefully tall, as all former Guards officers seemed to be, and her protest would be more effective if he remained seated. No, she did not recognise the other man. He was not a Member.

'Marian — not here, I think,' the junior minister warned.

'Perhaps I should let my rebuke *leak* out, then?' she snapped.

On the slats of the table lay a jumble of the

day's papers, their headlines uniformly gloomy. She had already read every newspaper as if cramming for an examination. Jimmy's guest appeared slightly wary, intensely curious, as if a spectator at some arcane bloodsport. The junior minister uncoiled from his chair, stood up and steered her firmly away from the table.

'Minimum embarrassment factor, Marian,' he murmured.

'Jimmy — what the hell's going on? You've been issuing the smoothest assurances for weeks —'

Sunlight splintered from glass towers across the river. The flanks of the Commons were serenely biscuit-coloured. Small craft on the Thames were like scraps of coloured paper.

'It's no more than a leak at this stage, Marian —'

'A creeping barrage, Jimmy! *Why,* for heaven's sake?'

She confronted him, hands on her hips, the breeze rustling her full cotton skirt around her. The minister smiled condescendingly.

'It's a very good helicopter, the Mamba,' he soothed. 'My minister —'

'Has been bought off, Jimmy. It's a bloody disaster for Aero UK, for the subcontractors. It shouldn't have been allowed to happen!'

'Ah, my dear girl, if only we could always do what was most obviously the *right* thing.'

'Your height allows you to patronise me, Jimmy — your age and brains don't.'

The junior minister flushed, then said: 'The generals wanted the Mamba. It makes sense — to *experts.*'

'I'll be sure to tell my constituents as much, Jimmy. I'm sure it will be a great comfort at the Job Centre.'

'By God, she's beautiful when she's angry,' he mocked.

A senior Labour backbencher passed, winking at her. She pretended not to notice.

'Angry I am, Jimmy.'

'Marian — the battle's lost.'

'A warning?'

'Just friendly advice — from a fervent admirer.' He grinned, his early-greying hair distressed by the breeze. He brushed it smooth. 'But you'll no doubt receive the usual encomiums in the press for your stalwart defence of the British aerospace industry . . .' He was warned by the clouding of her features, and added: 'Is that Sir Giles with you? Lunching at the House? I must have a word with him. Excuse me, Marian. Go easy on us poor mortals in government from the moral ramparts of the back benches, won't you?'

He waved a languid hand and returned to his guest. Marian felt her anger tight in her chest. She had hardly begun to discharge it before the conversation was terminated. Reluctantly, she returned to her father, who was engaged with a knight of the shires and senior member of the 1922 Committee. They parted as Marian approached.

'I never cease to be amazed how that man ever rose above the rank of second lieutenant,' Giles murmured. 'And you, my girl, look as if you've just suffered a nasty bout of indigestion. No joy?'

She shook her head.

'No hope, Daddy. It's been decided — everything's cut and dried. No amount of complaining is going to get us anywhere!'

'Sit down.' A Commons waiter had brought their drinks. 'I'm desperately sorry for Aero UK, for the Italians and the Germans . . . and your constituents. The problem is — there was always very little on paper between the two helicopters, ours and the Americans. In military terms, there isn't a good case to be made in objecting to —'

Her mobile phone trilled and she plunged her hand into her bag to locate it. A lipstick and a handkerchief emerged with it. The tiny folded triangle of cotton flew away on the breeze and Giles followed it, crouching like a hunter.

'Marian?' It was her researcher-secretary, Rose. 'Someone called Egan just rang. Wonders whether he could snatch a moment with you this afternoon, around three?'

'Egan?'

'Sam Egan. Something to do with the Millennium Project work in the constituency. Egan Construction — mean anything?'

'Yes, I know him. Did he say what he wanted?'

'No. Made it *sound* important.'

Marian glanced at her watch.

'Tell him three-thirty. Meet him in Central Lobby, will you, Rose? Thanks —'

Giles had recovered the handkerchief.

'Anything important?'

'Nothing that will interrupt lunch.'

'Good.'

'Contractor on the fabled Millennium Urban Regeneration thing. Probably wants me to lobby for a bigger EU grant. Nothing unusual.' She smiled. 'It won't put people out of work, at least!' Giles was studying her intently — as he did habitually, like a doctor for the first signs of disease. 'Daddy,' she warned.

'Sorry. Drink up — I'm feeling more than a little peckish!'

He had mislaid the number of her mobile phone . . . mobile phone. He stared again at the phone that had been brought up to his office by one of the commissionaires. Someone had handed it in — one of the men watching him — after he had left it on a café table. It had terrified him. It was the Black Spot, he had tried — and failed — to joke. Evidently, it had been the excuse to discover his name, his function at the Commission. They knew he worked for the Transport Commissioner, Rogier, and that he had been spying on his own superior. That knowledge would be like a taunt, or the first step in a seduction which would madden and arouse. They would *have* to know his motive now.

Her home number answered his call, her voice on the answering machine. *This is Marian Pyott, I can't take your call at the moment but if* . . . He waited for the extended, pinging tone, then said breathlessly:

'Sorry, Marian — but they're on to me. Some people circling like sharks around that meeting, I don't know who. I'm back at the office now — they've taken the trouble to find out who I am . . .' There seemed nothing he could add, however much he disliked the bleak promise of the facts. 'I — I'll call you again if I learn anything more . . . 'Bye.' He put down the receiver quickly.

He sat back from his desk, pushed his chair on its castors to the window. The rain had stopped and the Boulevard Charlemagne gleamed like a mirror. The Schuman station hunched at the end of the boulevard, shiny as a great snail shell. He sat near the window like a mockery of surveillance. How could he pick them out from this high vantage, how possibly?

He was no longer so afraid of them, now that they were again invisible, unidentifiable figures on the crowded streets or on the *place* in front of the Commission building — the curving ugliness of which Marian Pyott had once described as *the revenge of concrete on good taste.* They were lost to him in the space down there, and he had been able to become calmer, even after the jolt of the phone being delivered to him, masquerading as his own.

Yet he knew no more clearly how to deal with the situation than he had done, stranded beneath the sodden umbrella at the café table. Knowledge . . . but he had none. There was nothing lying carelessly on his Commissioner's desk, no cryptic indication in his appointments book, nothing that would suggest the *need* for the men who had had him under surveillance to provide a protective screen around the meeting. Their presence suggested secrecy, an added importance to what he had thought mere bribery, influence-seeking venality.

The men who had taunted him with white,

waving hands had altered the construction, even the meaning, of the small drama he had created; they had acquired it, and made its plot cloudier but larger, its action more febrile and mysterious, its figures more sinister. It was as if he had set out to create a mocking little satire upon bureaucracy and they had insisted it become a drama of danger, threat. But he could not, simply could not, comprehend something that would unite the Commission and *danger* . . . It was a bad joke. He *knew* all those people at that meeting, for heaven's sake — !

He picked up the telephone and dialled the number of his flat — before remembering that Marie-Claire was already on her way to Rotterdam to report to Royal Dutch Shell on the lack of success of her lobbying at the Commission. Brent Spar still floated on the company's horizon like a ship flying the skull-and-crossbones, endangering image and sales alike. The Commission was sympathetic only in strict privacy, and was the colour of chlorophyll in all its public pronouncements. Lack of success was slowly driving his delectable partner up the proverbial wall.

He put down the receiver, then once more picked it up. The Commissioner's secretary answered.

'Michael,' he said. 'M'selle Fouquet — sorry about this, but the Commissioner asked me to research some background for' — he hesitated momentarily, before reminding himself that they were already only too well aware of his unauthorised interest — 'Aero UK, the British planemaker, and — and Mr David Winterborne's companies.'

He lightened his voice. 'I think the Commissioner thinks they're lobbying too hard, m'selle. Do you have any idea how urgent it is?'

'A moment, M'sieur Lloyd.' His charm was like thinly spread margarine when applied to Mlle Fouquet. He heard her riffling pages.

'M'sieur Rogier is to be the guest of — yes, David Winterborne at the family home this weekend. He did not tell you this? I presume he requires your work on his desk before he leaves on Friday. At midday.'

As he replaced the receiver, he could not but laugh, even though the noise merely became the exhalation of nerves after a moment of amusement.

Rogier was meeting Winterborne again, in a few days' time. In England. And he hadn't asked for a background briefing from his senior researcher, something the Frenchman was habitually punctilious about. They joked among the Commission's junior ranks that Rogier required a detailed briefing before he used the toilet or took his next meal. Secrecy again . . .

. . . David Winterborne. Was he the reason for the security screen? Why? As Chairman and CEO of Winterborne Holdings, a Singapore-based conglomerate, he was a major shareholder in Aero UK, in some of the subcontractors working on Skyliner — and on the helicopter — and a prompt and determined lobbyist for EC funds on each and every possible occasion. And he was a friend of Marian's — they'd practically grown up together. He was just another businessman.

Once more, he picked up the telephone. Her

answerphone offered its assistance.

'Marian? Is there — ?' No, that's not the question. Try again, Lloyd. 'Rogier is staying with David Winterborne this weekend. Mean anything? Doesn't to me . . .' He hesitated, then added: 'There's no reason for *security,* unless there's a hidden agenda and this isn't the usual bribery and corruption. Marian — is David Winterborne a likely candidate? Your *friend* Winterborne, that is? Call me —'

He put down the receiver, nerved by a sense of activity and insight. He was intrigued; curiosity masked fear, for the moment, and offered him a return of confidence. Marian's question returned to his mind, together with the sensation that when he had left that message for her the previous day, he had almost believed the supposition that lay behind it. Perhaps *this . . . ?* The actors in the scene at the hotel were, indeed, the necessary cast for such a play. He scribbled their names on his legal pad. Rogier — *Transport,* he underlined. Laxton — *Urban Development,* a former Cabinet middleweight now punching above his talents in Brussels. The Euro MP Campbell, Winterborne, Coulthard, Bressier from Balzac-Stendhal, his deputy . . . which meant Skyliner had to be the subject under discussion . . . *Urban Development,* funds for rundown regions, for grandiose renewal projects — those in Italy and Spain notoriously corrupt, acting like desert sand on EC funds. Marian had asked — speculated — whether funds could be diverted, moved by disguise to the Skyliner project . . . The cast for the proposed play stared back at him in his large, untidy handwriting. It would require secrecy . . . surveillance —

He glanced out of the window. The streets were drying. Fugitive sunlight glanced from thinning cloud, making blinding squares of windows and car windscreens. The pace of pedestrians seemed slower, less urgent. The scene had recaptured its innocence. It was — *if* it was — corruption; just worse than usual and more secret. It was within his province, familiar to him . . . The sense of threat receded, the men who had been watching him were stripped of their stature in his fears. The names on the pad were *familiar,* after all, they remained fragments of the ordinary, the expected — politicians, businessmen, functionaries. The men who provided their security screen were images of their guilt and paranoia, nothing more.

He breathed deeply, regularly for some moments, in imitation of a half-remembered Buddhist exercise of meditation, the name of which he could not recall. That had been a passing college thing . . . He did feel more calm, he realised, more in control, even when he glanced at the names on the pad and delved into the shadows at the back of his mind where Marian's suspicions had become his own. Then he grinned.

He would send the undeveloped film he had taken, and the handwritten sheet from the legal pad, and post them to Marian. She could ring him, for a change — *she* could make the next move.

'Well?'

Jessop shut the door of the Peugeot behind him and grinned at Fraser, whose morose, demanding expression did not alter.

'Easy.'

The old house, eighteenth century for the most part and floridly bourgeois in its external decoration, was fifteen minutes' drive from the Commission. Trees in full leaf lined either side of the quiet street. Children in bright clothes played on front lawns, sprinklers making screaming games and rainbows in the afternoon sunlight.

'Well?'

'There's a woman living there, with him.' Jessop loosened the buttoned overalls. A reported smell of gas — never failed. 'She's away overnight, so the inevitable nosy concierge told me. He's usually back around six.'

'Find anything?'

'No, funnily enough. Looks like he's just begun this new job of his, watching *us* and ours. No tapes, no film, nothing in writing. Last-number redial on the phone was interesting, so was the answerphone. British MP — Marian Pyott. Asking him questions —' He held up his tape recorder. 'Played it back, got it on here. She's quite nosy —'

Fraser stared through the windscreen at the passage of an estate car, then a 4WD. Collecting-the-kids-from-school time was almost over, gin-and-tonic time almost here.

Fraser nodded, Jessop switched on the tape. Two messages from Marian Pyott — one to warn him to be careful, but to try to get good photographs of anyone he thought might be attending the meeting . . . timed earlier that morning . . . second message just telling him she would be out that evening and to leave anything he had on the answerphone. The woman's voice contained a residue of anger, frustration. Her interest did not seem urgent or precise, but it wasn't merely casual, either.

'Well?'

'Pat on the head, Jessop,' Fraser offered sarcastically. 'I'll buy you an ice-cream for being such a good boy.'

'What do we do?'

'I don't think there's much to worry about. Not yet.'

'Oh, I found some coke — a social amount, nothing heavy.'

'Tut, these fashionable young men and their thrill-seeking,' Fraser mocked. 'Doesn't it disappoint you that their lives are so empty of meaning that they pursue such courses?'

'What course are we going to pursue?'

'I shall consult our employer, Jessop, like the dutiful subordinate I am. I shall recommend that the obstruction be cleared — while it's still a stone rather than a rock in the road. I wonder why *she,* of the six-hundred-odd self-seeking bastards in the House of Commons, is interested in us . . . ?'

'How?' Jessop asked with the intent and innocent malice of a child.

'You mentioned cocaine, Jessop. These trendy people, they don't stop at sniffing cocaine, you know. No, indeed. Very soon, it's the needle and the hard stuff — stuff you have to know *just* how to handle, if you're not to do yourself a great deal of damage.'

Jessop sat back in the passenger seat, his eyes

closed, a beatific smile on his face.

'I suppose this drug habit of his is nothing new?' he murmured, seduced by the detail.

'I'm sure the Brussels police will find *plenty* of corroborative evidence in the young man's apartment,' Fraser replied with a smile, his expression that of a gourmet consulting a titillating menu.

CHAPTER THREE

On-Site Analysis

The desert already shimmered in the heat of the early morning, and the mountains surrounding Vance Aircraft moved in and out of focus, gained and lost weight and massiveness, like an army of giant shadows repositioning for some final assault. Gant squinted even behind the filtering of his sunglasses. Heat struck through the soles of his boots and the stifling warmth of the hangar seemed cool the moment he left its shade. Vance, beside him, had begun to sweat freely. The airliner glared in the sun. Dust devils whirled like conjuror's handkerchiefs in the chokingly hot breeze.

Around the 494, the ground crew fussed and then stilled as they saw the two men approach. The plane was adorned with the livery of Artemis Airways, red and blinding white; the image of the virgin-goddess as huntress on the high tailplane, hair flying with two sleek hounds at her heels. The heavy tug had towed it from the hangar to the edge of the taxiway, and the walkround inspection had been done by the ground engineer. Both Gant and Vance could make straight for the flight deck. Pausing while Vance spoke to his ground engineer, Gant looked back at the buildings of Vance Aircraft. The faces that would be at countless windows were obscured by the sun dazzling back from tinted glass, but there were small knots of workers at the open doors of the two main assembly hangars, others straddling a line of shadow and light at the entrance to the service hangar. The Superstition Mountains already seemed to seep into the drained blue sky, as if their mass and colour were being leached away. His mouth felt dry.

Vance was listening and nodding, then reluctantly took the engineer's outstretched hand. Barbara must have been dissuaded from accompanying them out to the 494.

'OK,' Vance muttered throatily, and followed Gant up the passenger steps into the main embarkation door situated just aft of the flight deck.

Shadow, coolness. The air-conditioning was already operating from the APU. There was the shadow of a technician at the door to the flight deck. He merely nodded at Gant and then swiftly glanced aside, as if he had seen warning or disease on his features. Vance closed the main door behind him and locked it.

Slowly, aware of the brightness of metal, the cleanness of plastic, the clarity of glass, Gant settled into the pilot's chair. Nothing was burned in there, no one had died there . . . The flight deck smelt new, as aseptic as the flight simulator in the boxlike confines of which he had spent most of the previous day. The flight engineer's chair behind him creaked as Vance lowered himself into it. Vance would have to act as co-pilot on take-off, and double as flight engineer during the rest of the flight. He heard the man's stertorous breathing. Gant touched the control column and released it almost at once as it became instantly slippery with sweat from his palms.

After the simulator had come the analysis of the cockpit voice recorder and the computer-realised record of Hollis' last flight. The instability of the aircraft had been progressive, frightening. Just prior to flame-out of both engines and the inability to restart them, the oscillation had been as violent as if they had been flying through a hurricane. The plane had lurched and swayed, dipped and threatened to roll like a ship in great waves. He had known that it would have had to have been that bad for Hollis not to have gotten it under control . . . which was why he had committed himself to the simulator, prepared himself for the flight, before he had looked at the images of the aircraft on the VDU, behind the superimposed instruments which looked like searching gunsights and the 494 like a fighter plane trying to evade a pursuer.

The voice recording was fragmentary — Vance had admitted that in the burned-out fuselage — and provided no clues. Hollis, Lowell and Paluzzi *didn't know what was happening to them,* it was as simple as that. And neither did the flight recorder. There was *nothing to account for* what had happened, either the instability or the engine failure . . .

. . . and now he was going to repeat the precise pattern of the flight Hollis and his crew had made — and wait until it happened to him, until the 494's twin sister killed him, too. Because it couldn't be a freak — there was no weather, no pilot error, no mechanical, hydraulic, electrical or manual failure to account for what had happened . . . *no* system had failed.

It was, he realised, as if that ground-to-air missile was on the Phantom's tail again, over 'Nam, and even though the instruments told him it was closing, he couldn't outmanoeuvre or outrun it. It would hit his craft and the plane would catch fire . . . He found himself gripping the control column and hearing Vance ask:

'Pre-flight checks?'

'What?'

'You ready?'

He did not even half-turn to Vance, merely muttered:

'Sure.' Then, with a greater emphasis that even to himself sounded like defensive anger, he repeated: 'Sure.'

The technician had already switched the three INS sets to align and inserted the plane's exact present position. The INS gyros had spun up and he could begin the instrument checks; all their displayed failure flags had retracted. He felt a bead of cold sweat slip down his cheek, over his jaw, into the collar of his denim shirt. He began his scan check at the top right of the overhead display panel, his eyes moving up and down through each piece of equipment, then down across the autopilot and the autothrottle and zigzag across the centre panel; finally, the centre console. Vance — he turned now, knowing the man would be absorbed in his own work — was making a similar scan check of his instrument panels . . . fire warning, engine instrument displays, the fuel system, fuel contents, fuel computer, booster pumps. Somewhere there . . . ? The instruments had shown that all of the systems had been functioning. The engines hadn't relit but there was no reason they shouldn't have.

He knew the passengerless weight of the plane plus the two of them and the fuel, and set the markers on the airspeed indicator for the take-off speeds at V1, V2 and VR. Hollis' engines hadn't failed at take-off . . . He put the thought aside and stopped himself staring through the glare shield at the vanishing length of runway and the desert. He tuned the VOR. Clamped on his headset, which at once made him aware of how much he was sweating. There was dampness, chill against his ears, then heat. The seat and the rudder pedals had already been adjusted to suit his height and frame.

'Engine start check?' he heard Vance ask.

'Engine start check.'

Circuit breakers . . . INS . . . oxygen . . . radios, altimeters . . . boost pumps . . . start pressure . . . start engines . . . Gant swallowed.

'Let's go,' he heard Vance breathe in his ear. The man's hand was heavy on his shoulder then it was gone again. Its weight had seemed filled with a gambler's desperation. 'Starting number two,' he heard Vance announce over the intercom to the ground engineer. The ignition switch was selected to ground start to turn the engine.

Gant heard the ground engineer's voice.

'N-One.' The fan was beginning to turn.

'N-Two rotation and engine oil pressure rising,' Vance murmured. Then: 'Twenty-two per cent.'

Gant moved the start lever to idle and started the stopwatch. Twenty seconds to completion of start-up. Fuel was now being pumped into the engine and the igniters were firing.

'Fuel flow normal,' Vance called. Gant's instruments confirmed. The exhaust gas temperature began rising steadily. The engine had lit.

'Fifty per cent.'

The engine was now self-sustaining and Vance would have released the ignition switch.

'Starting number one . . .' The process was quicker, it seemed, as if the engine start was being hurried in order that he would be placed in control of the airplane . . . 'Fifty per cent.'

He swallowed. His mouth was dry.

'Ground?'

'All cleared away —' There was the slightest hesitation, then: 'Good luck, sir.'

Gant checked the start levers were at idle, the stabiliser trim, power hydraulics. Over the VHF, he contacted the huddled buildings and the toylike, glass-topped control tower at the far end of the runway.

'Request taxi.'

'Clear to taxi.'

Gant released the brakes and moved the thrust

levers with his right hand, his left on the control column to steer the 494. There was no more than a momentary sense of the bulk of the airliner being drawn behind the tiny flight deck. He could hear the engine whine as the two huge Pratt & Whitneys spooled up. Vance began reading the take-off checks. Flaps at ten per cent, speed brakes checked, flight controls — *check,* trim set — *check,* annunciator panels — *check,* pressurisation — *check* . . .

'Travelling down the taxiway . . . *threshold.*'

He turned the airplane like some lumbering marine mammal stranded on a desert beach on to the end of the runway. Then the plane was still, massive. The desert air made the runway melt, re-form, melt again. It was hallucinatory, unnerving. The mountains seemed starker now, crowding around the dwarfed, distant buildings and the tiny, isolated plane. The sky was almost colourless, utterly cloudless.

'Boost pumps on, fuel system set, hydraulics, brakes . . . ignition switches to flight start . . .' In case the engines flamed out on take-off, he could restart them . . . Hollis hadn't been able to relight the engines . . . forget that. 'Body gearing switched to off . . . instruments, flaps set, trim set . . .'

He waited. Behind him, Vance waited on him. He was aware of the man's presence like a weight pressing at his back; felt the man's almost lunatic desperation, the madness of his enraged frustration — and his fear.

The voice from the control tower startled him. '494 — cleared for take-off,' it repeated.

'Let's *go* . . .' he heard Vance mutter, his voice as small as that of someone mumbling prayers.

Gant placed his hand on the throttles, tensing his right foot on the rudder. The 494 began to strain against the brakes. Vance took up his flight engineer's position between and just behind the two pilots' seats in order to monitor power. He was leaning forward, precisely adjusting the engine pressure ratios of each of the thrust levers. Gant had to rely on him to scan the instruments as any co-pilot would have done.

'OK, Alan — here we go,' he murmured, his throat tight and the sweat in rivulets on either side of his taut neck. He moved the throttle levers to vertical, then forward to just below the required power setting. The centre line of the runway stretched ahead, quivering in the desert heat or his imagination. The grey, dusty runway itself continued to melt, re-form, melt again in the haze. 'Here we go,' he repeated quietly through clenched teeth.

He released the brakes and the plane leapt forward as if released from a chain. There was no sense of its size behind him as it skimmed the runway, reaching eighty knots. Gant felt the rudder become effective. The airspeed indicator needles flicked upwards. A bird flashed across and beneath the nose of the 494. The centre line wavered for a moment and Gant steered delicately on the rudder pedals, his right hand hovering over the throttles. If the engines failed now, he could close them down . . . Without reverse thrust, they'd plough into the desert at the end of the runway.

'V-One,' he heard Vance call. Committed now. He moved his right hand to the control column as Vance assumed control of the engines. One-fifty knots, one-fifty-three, four, five — eight. 'Rotate.'

Gant pulled back on the column and the nose of the aircraft lifted towards the blinding, leached sky. Ten per cent, fifteen on the attitude indicator. He felt the undercarriage leave the runway.

'V-Two,' he muttered to Vance. 'Gear up.'

The undercarriage bay doors opened and he felt the slight increase in drag, then the bogies clunked home and the doors shut. He turned the aircraft into the wind. Altitude five hundred feet, the mountains diminishing in bulk, becoming manageable, dismissible. Twelve hundred feet . . .

He was sweating as Vance eased back the throttles to climb power. He dropped the nose to allow for the reduction. The miniature buildings of Vance Aircraft disappeared beneath the port wing and the mountains seemed to slip aside, leaving the emptiness of the air ahead and the architect's model that was Phoenix glittering on the desert floor, surrounded by reservoirs with mirror surfaces.

He was repeating the flight that had killed Hollis in every detail. Vance's presence behind him made the hair on his neck itch. Farther behind him were the two huge engines that had failed, and for which failure there was no answer . . .

The voice at the other end of the telephone, that of Michael Lloyd's only relative, an aunt in

Crewkerne, seeped coldly into her ear like an ointment. Lloyd's untidy handwriting on the single sheet of A4 paper lay on her desk, reminding her of his undergraduate essays when she had been his tutor in modern history. She sensed that even those memories were an escape route, one unplanned but quickly taken.

'Yes,' she murmured.

The aunt had fostered Lloyd as a difficult teenager, abandoned by a philandering father and a mother comatosed by her husband's desertion.

'. . . I never suspected, you see, Miss Pyott, that Michael was — that he took . . .' A gobbling, breathy silence. The intimacy of tragedy pressed against her, insinuating itself. It was as if the aunt were trying to catch her breath beneath a waterfall or facing a fierce, choking wind. 'Never once in my life . . .' Marian felt vile, like an eavesdropper.

An overdose of heroin — at least, of heroin that had been badly cut, insufficiently diluted. She had guessed, at certain times, from the heightened, dizzy manner of some of his phone calls, that there was the likelihood that he indulged some occasional cocaine habit. But heroin?

'. . . such a loving boy, when you loved him,' Marian heard.

'Yes, yes,' she replied eagerly, desperate to offer the aunt some sense of a shared sorrow.

'It was late last night — a friend of Michael's called at his flat, but couldn't get an answer, you see, and looked through the letter box . . . saw Michael just lying on the floor, not moving.'

'Yes . . .'

'The — what do they call it? The — the people he worked with, anyway . . . they're making the arrangements. For the — body to be returned. I thought here . . . ?'

'Yes.' There was nowhere, no one else. 'Yes, I think that would be right. I — please let me know if there's anything I can do — and of course, the funeral. The date —'

'There's some delay, because of the way — you know, the way . . .'

'Yes.' She felt her temples pressed by a drying thong, the sense of her clothes wrapped tight as a straitjacket around her, the heat of her body. The unfolded sheet of paper, the letter beside it, the little tub of undeveloped film, all were bold accusations on her desk. She could not understand why . . . then, of course, she did, feeling nausea rise in her throat. She had obviously forged some causal link between what he had done — those were the results lying there — and what had happened to him. And at once felt icily cold, perspiration chilly on her forehead. 'Yes . . .' she breathed.

'I'm sorry to have brought you bad news, Miss Pyott. I thought you would wish to know.' The aunt had moved on from sobs to the clarity of arrangements, of other calls, of the immediate future.

'Yes, thank you. I'll — I *will* ring, perhaps tomorrow. Just in case there's anything you feel I can do. Thank you for letting me know . . . I'm *so* sorry . . .'

'Yes. Good-bye, Miss Pyott.'

Marian put down the receiver with a clatter,

then gripped the back of her chair, lowering herself into it with the awkwardness she sometimes saw in her father's movements. Her elbows hurt as they took the weight of her head. The desk's surface was very hard, resisting her, as accusing as the items that littered it. She rubbed a hand through her hair, pushing it back on her head. It flopped back at once, blinkering her view of the items on the desk. She did not brush it away from her face again.

Eventually, she sniffed loudly and sat upright, shaking her head, shaking away the numb mood. Michael's letter offered itself at once to her new composure. It was a hasty note, no more, filled with anxiety and a heightened amusement, a sense of boyish adventure. He had been followed back to the Commission and they had practised a deception to discover who he was. *I think I may have exaggerated everything . . . security people are notoriously paranoid, aren't they?* Whistling in the dark? She could not now decide. Except that she did not believe in the heroin addiction, not even in a clumsy and tragic early attempt at the drug. Michael had bought a new car recently, and moved to a bigger, more expensive apartment. He had no money worries, no drain on his resources . . .

. . . guilt nudged, constantly returning her thoughts to her father's oldest friend, one of *her* oldest friends . . . Kenneth Aubrey. The undeveloped tub of film, the names on the page. There was no real surprise — the Euro MP whose constituency at Strasbourg included her own, the two EU Commissioners, the two planemakers. It was obviously Skyliner, and the urgency of the meeting and its secrecy had been demanded by the collapse of the Aero UK helicopter bid. There were no names attached to the people who had frightened Michael and followed him — and who . . .

She excised the thought. Sunlight streamed across her hands as they lay resting on the desk. Her diary was open; her notes for the Commons' afternoon business and the details faxed to her in preparation for her Saturday-morning surgery lay near it.

She snatched up the telephone and dialled. Eventually, she heard Mrs Grey's carefully modulated, slightly pretentious tones.

'Mrs Grey — is Sir Kenneth free this morning? It's Marian Pyott here, I'd like his advice —'

'I'm sure Sir Kenneth will be delighted to see you, Miss Pyott. He is lunching at his club — with your father and Sir Clive — but he will be here until twelve-thirty. What time shall I tell him you'd like to call?'

She glanced at her watch.

'Twelve — I can make it by twelve.'

'I'll tell him.'

Marian continued to study the receiver after she had replaced it. Somehow, having called Kenneth, invoking the spirit of his professional self, the names on Michael's sheet of paper seemed less innocent. Their contiguity troubled. Her own suspicions returned regarding the illegal diversion of EU funds for the development of the Skyliner project. The Transport Commissioner and the *Urban Development* chief . . . her attention underlined the title as Lloyd's pen had done. His was the wrong name, the broken bone sticking through the skin of innocence that clothed the meeting. There was no reason — none whatsoever — for his appearance at that hotel. He was British, there were other Brits there, including David and Coulthard . . . but he was *not* a Commissioner of influence, he was a broken-backed former Cabinet dogsbody who was enjoying his ride on the gravy train and his frequent appearances on TV. He enjoyed doling out largesse — and that was about the sum of it. And he never joined causes, especially lost ones . . . He wouldn't, of his own volition, offer to mop up the blood after Aero UK committed hara-kiri, let alone lend himself to lobbying.

Otherwise, all appeared quite normal, innocent. Would it to Kenneth? She must have the film developed —

— Michael. A friend's view of him, through the slit of a letter box, lying unmoving on the new carpet of the new apartment, dead of heroin poisoning. The Brussels Police Judiciare were confident that it was death by misadventure, nothing more. *The needle and the damage done* . . . but, unlike the ageing rock singer who had coined that song title, Michael hadn't survived. Had someone not wanted him to?

They were definitely professional, his letter said. *Not the sort of people the Commission employed and not just bodyguards, either . . .*

Then who were they? And would Kenneth have immediately asked that question — or was she simply caricaturing the attitude of an intelligence officer? Had Michael just messed up the dose? Or had someone decided on his eternal silence?

The sunlight ridiculed, but she could not entirely abandon the idea that Michael had set off an alarm somewhere and had, splashing carelessly and without heed in the shallows, summoned sharks.

The Grand Canyon swung beneath the 494 like a gaping wound, and he wanted to be able to study it with the impartiality of a surgeon. The repetition of Hollis' flight, minute after slow minute, had begun to unnerve him. He could find no detachment; assurance had seeped away, and his dead friend's voice kept on returning, like a phone call. It demanded things of him — answers, the airplane's safety, his own survival — but the increasing challenge of Hollis' recollected voice found him unprepared. He had no answers . . .

He imagined he could see the mules taking tourists from the top to the bottom of the canyon, pick out trailers and campers, even rafts on the Colorado's silver dribble. The vivacity of his imagination, the way it made the canyon rush at him, grow too close to the 494, unsettled. Behind his seat, Vance remained at the flight engineer's panels, his own bafflement as pungent and tangible as the sour smell of defeat. There was *nothing* wrong — nothing had occurred.

The short-duration flight that Hollis had undertaken had been a rehearsal for the full press flight. Views of the Grand Canyon, a river of champagne, small hillocks of canapés . . . and press acclamation in the following day's newspapers and on that evening's TV network and local news.

Hollis and his crew had fallen out of the sky less than another half-hour into the flight, making a final approach to Vance Aircraft — they had had no warning and he would have just as little. There had been nothing wrong. Gant had listened to the cockpit voice recorder again and again, at least as much of it as had survived the crash, and he'd read the drafts and readouts taken from the flight recorders.

And learned nothing new, found no clue. The small clock in the centre of the main panel in front of him ticked on . . . twenty-eight minutes to the point of impact, and the 494 continued innocently above the Canyon.

Vance had arranged that each of the centres, Phoenix, LA, Peach Springs, Flagstaff, that Hollis had contacted during his flight would respond as they had previously done. Just as he would fly every mile of the flight, perform every action of the dead man —

'Vance 494 — LA Centre. After leaving Peach Springs we understand you wish to head for thirty-point-five North, one-one-three-point-two West for some sightseeing, then rejoin at the GCN for Flagstaff and Phoenix at flight level three-zero-zero.

'Centre — Vance 494,' Gant replied, 'that is affirmative.'

'494 — Centre. Do you want to maintain your present level?'

'Centre — 494 . . .' His mouth was suddenly dry. Gant sucked his cheeks. 'We would like to descend to level six or seven thousand and make two or three orbits before climbing to level three hundred for rejoin.'

Behind him, he sensed Vance listening as anxiously as a possessive, vain parent to a child's performance in a Nativity play.

Brace, brace, brace —

— Hollis from the cockpit voice recorder. From the grave.

'494 — this is Centre. Your request approved. Don't descend below seven thousand feet on a QFE twenty-nine-ninety-three — we have local Canyon traffic below that altitude. We will advise local control of your intentions. QSY their frequency on one-eight-point-zero-five.'

'Thank you, Centre. 494 leaving level three-two-zero this time on a heading of three-two zero until clear of the airway.'

Gant eased back the power levers, cancelled the autopilot and manually flew the slow, controlled descent. The airplane slid through the flight levels. Speed, two hundred and eighty knots. The Canyon was below the 494, at the centre of his orbit. He was aware of the silence of the aircraft's passenger cabin behind him. Only the crew had died. Vance's dream hadn't caused a massacre of press and TV people —

We've gone from near stall to overspeed, godammit —

Hollis' voice again as the airplane betrayed him. What in hell did it *mean?* The 494 had fought him and won, caught him off-guard and killed him in minutes. *How?*

Gant eased back the power and dropped thirty degrees of flap. Watched the airspeed slow towards a hundred and ninety knots.

'Prescott Centre — 494 is with you at seven thousand feet. Starting our left-hand orbits.'

'Roger, 494,' he heard in his headphones. 'No known conflicting traffic. Be advised there is some local helicopter traffic in the Canyon. Quark seven-seven-four-six and keep me informed of your intentions.'

The Canyon rotated like a map being turned on a desk as he rolled the aircraft gently into its orbit. The shadows of the coaming and roof eased across the instrument panel in unison. Gant selected autopilot to maintain the turn at his present altitude, imitating the pattern designed to most appeal to the press and the cameras that would have been in the passenger cabin. The slow orbit was so gentle no champagne would have been spilt, no canapés would have fallen on the thick carpet along the aisle.

He glanced behind him at Vance. The man's expression was unsettled. It was as if he had come across its desperate fervency in a gloomy church, stumbling across someone in a kind of despair who wanted to snatch a fragment of hope from the incensed air, from the altar, the candles. The expression evoked memories of his mother and he thrust them aside.

Vance discovered his surveillance and shrugged angrily.

'Nothing — you want some coffee?' Gant nodded. 'I'll go get it . . .' Vance's voice seemed aware of time, as if each word he spoke marked off a second. They were maybe twenty-five minutes away from —

Vance opened the door of the flight deck, then his bulk hesitated. Gant smelt the sweetness of kerosene faintly on the air that flowed in from the empty passenger cabin.

Brace, brace, brace —

— near stall to overspeed . . .

'You smell it, too?' Vance asked hoarsely.

'Yes.'

'I — I'll take a look. Was there some mention . . . ?' He closed the door behind him on the remainder of the question.

'Prescott Centre — 494. Now leaving seven thousand for Flagstaff. Request an altitude for rejoining the airway.'

'494 — Prescott. Rejoin at flight level three-ten.'

Gant put the 494 into autoclimb and checked the power management system as it adjusted automatically to optimal power settings. He heard the cabin door open and Vance slid into the co-pilot's seat, shaking his head.

'It's gone now,' he murmured. His relief was as evident as his puzzlement. 'There's something I ought to remember about the smell of kerosene in the passenger —'

'Cockpit voice recorder. Check the transcript. Hollis referred to it somewhere —'

'Where?'

'Maybe around five pages in — where they go into the hold just prior to . . . descent back to Vance Aircraft. He wasn't concerned about it,' he added. It could have been something as simple as a faulty or badly cleaned filter in the cabin environment system.

Vance flicked through the typewritten pages. The Canyon slipped like a brown and silver snake away from beneath the airplane's belly.

'Is this what you want? Lowell had been in the passenger cabin and reported a smell of kerosene. Then it disappeared . . .' He flicked the pages dismissively. 'Just like now. Here and gone. It can't mean anything — can it?'

'Maybe not . . . There's a lot of detail missing from the recording. Maybe it wasn't the first time?'

'He doesn't say here that he smelt it earlier — something like *that smell's back again.* Maybe it hadn't happened earlier in the flight —'

Gant turned to Vance. There was a tension that enclosed them like an electric fence.

'It was there while we were in the left-hand orbit, over the Canyon . . . then it disappeared. Let's try to get it back —' He keyed the microphone. 'LA Centre — 494. We would like to stop our climb at flight level one-six-zero and make two left-hand orbits before resuming on track to Flagstaff at —' He glanced at the clock on the panel. It seemed to be the only clock now, on the flight deck. The only one that mattered. 'At six minutes past the hour.'

'Roger, 494 — you're cleared to do that. Contact AlbuK Centre at the boundary.'

As the 494 climbed, the landscape around the Canyon shrank like a memory.

'We're coming up to one-six-zero. I'll put the

ship into a left-hand orbit.' Gant cancelled the climb mode. The aircraft swung lazily into its orbit, like a bird adapting to a changed thermal. The Canyon came into view. 'Can you hold her in this orbit while I check?' Vance nodded. 'OK — take control. I won't be long —'

Gant slipped out of the pilot's seat and opened the passenger door. The scent of kerosene was palpable, though faint. The empty passenger cabin seemed somehow ominously deserted. Sunlight filled it, the landscape beneath the aircraft was visible through the windows. Yet there was something cold, even oppressive about the cabin as he moved along the aisle. He glanced to either side at the wings and the bulk of the two huge engines jutting from beneath them. Sensed the normal tremors of an aircraft in flight. The plane continued to swing through its orbit. The passenger cabin tapered towards the aircraft's tail. The smell of kerosene remained constant, from the flight deck door to the door of the rear galley. He opened the door.

Squeezed into the narrow space, he ducked his body in order to look through the tiny window, craning to stare behind the aircraft, then back along the fuselage towards the wing, off which the sunlight gleamed.

Nothing . . . He turned his head. Nothing . . .

. . . something? In the turbulence of the engine exhaust, he thought, but clearer behind the aircraft. What looked like a narrow, brief vapour trail, grey-white, easy to ignore or miss . . . He looked back again towards the engine. It was invisible, that close to the engine, it was only behind the aircraft that it condensed in the airflow into an unnerving pretence of a vapour trail.

Gant heard his breathing, louder than the engine note, louder than the tumult of the air passing over the fuselage. If Hollis or anyone else had even looked, they might never have noticed. It was fuel . . . being dumped from the starboard wing inner tank and condensing behind the plane. Fuel . . .

He closed the galley door behind him and hurried along the passenger cabin. He could see nothing as he paused at the window that looked out over the wing. He entered the flight deck and at once began reading the flight engineer's instrument panels. Fuel content as expected, fuel pressure — OK . . . dump valves *closed,* the transfer valves and pumps reassuringly normal. There was nothing wrong . . . there *was.*

Gant slipped back into the pilot's seat and put on his headset.

'Find anything?'

'We're dumping fuel from the starboard wing tank — I think . . .' He shook his head. 'We're *dumping fuel.*' He regained the controls and Vance, releasing his control column, squeezed out of his seat and settled himself in front of the flight engineer's panel.

Twenty-one minutes to the crash point . . .

'There's nothing here!' Vance exploded. 'Everything's reading normal — what the hell is happening? *Every* gauge is telling me we're not dumping fuel — are you *sure,* Mitchell?'

Hollis had made left-hand turns in the holding pattern . . . they had made left-hand orbits over the Canyon and now again. Each time, there had been the smell of kerosene . . . He'd *seen* it, streaming from the wing tank. And the engineer's panel, the whole fuel management system, was lying to them . . . as it had lied to Hollis.

'We don't know how much fuel we have left,' he murmured. 'And there's no way of knowing.'

'494 — Albuquerque Centre. Report your present position.'

The voice in his headset alarmed him. Nerves ached in his wrists, his fingers seemed numb on the control column.

'What do you want to do?' Vance asked.

'Centre, this is 494. Just by Flagstaff Victor three-two-seven. Flight-level-three-ten . . . Estimate Phoenix and Vance Centre at — twenty . . .' He felt his mouth dry and his throat constrict, then made himself announce: 'We have a slight distraction here.'

'Roger, 494. Do you require assistance?' The unemotional, machine-like voice of Albuquerque Centre failed to calm. Instead, it seemed to distance the offer of assistance, make it impotent.

'Negative at present,' he forced himself to say. 'We'll be looking for descent clearance in maybe nine minutes from now.'

He glanced down at knee level at the repeater dials. Aileron, elevator and rudder indicated normal, where he expected the settings to be. He turned his attention to the manual wheels, low down on the centre console where their readouts were difficult to see.

'Jesus . . .' he breathed.

There was no correlation between the two sets of instruments. The airplane was badly out of trim — possibly with stalled trim motors, an unknown fuel amount, and a monitoring system that was lying to them. They had no way of knowing even *where* the fuel was. The fuel management system moved the fuel around the tanks to keep the fuselage balanced about a constant centre of gravity . . . Otherwise, it would become uncontrollable and — fall out of the sky. Cold perspiration ran down beneath his arms, dampened the shirt across his back.

'Vance — we have problems. Call the company, get Ron Blakey on the horn. Tell him what's happening and ask him what we can do.'

In another moment, Vance was talking animatedly to his chief research engineer. *Near stall to overspeed . . . Brace, brace, brace.* There was almost nothing else, now, that he could recall of the cockpit voice recorder's transcript. It was all he needed to remember, he told himself.

He felt — or thought he felt — a tremor in the control column, as if what was being registered was the struggle of the autopilot systems against a violent, increasing instability in the airframe. Flagstaff looked like a tiny, gleaming clearing in the stain of the Coconino National Forest far below the airplane. The mountains that reared up ahead along their flight path, and which surrounded Phoenix, seemed to press against the flight deck's windows.

'Ron Blakey says all we can do is come out of autopilot, sort the trim on manuals, and — he said *good luck* —'

Gant's hand paused over the autopilot switch. Again, he sensed the unbalanced weight of the aircraft, the loss of fuel, the alien secretiveness of the 494. He was walking in a dead man's shoes down a road that a dead man had taken. His only advantage was that he knew the plane was losing fuel . . . Some advantage.

He cancelled the autopilot. Immediately, the 494 banked violently to the left and the nose reared like a wild horse's head. Vance slid into the co-pilot's seat and slowly Gant felt his supporting effort on the control column. Gant was able to reach for the elevator trim and adjust the nose of the aircraft . . . In moments, before he and Vance had regained control of the 494, it had turned almost three hundred and sixty degrees and climbed two thousand feet. Sweat ran from his forehead down his cheeks.

Slowly, as if coaxing a fierce and unpredictable animal into a cage, he brought the aircraft round on to its previous course. Phoenix glinted like fragments of a broken window ahead of them. The grey and brown flanks of mountains were unsoftened by heat haze or distance.

He called Albuquerque.

'Centre — 494. We're just coming round on to one-eight-six radial. This is part of the distraction notified earlier.'

'Roger, 494. We will clear a block of airspace, flight levels two-five-zero to three-two-zero in case you have further problems.'

'It has to be more than a spurious crossfeed, right? More than just fuel transferring from one of the fuller tanks to the port wing tanks. We're losing maybe most of — all — our fuel from the starboard wing tanks —'

'It feels like that?'

'I can't tell, dammit! The port wing's getting heavy, that's all *feel* tells me. Your fucking airplane has gotten a mind of its own from somewhere, Vance. You built it, *you* tell me what's wrong!'

'You want to die telling me I'm an asshole?' Vance snapped. 'Is that the extent of your ambition, Gant?'

'OK, OK!' Gant snarled. 'Tell me how we can cut the engines off from the fuel management computer.'

'It's in the computer?'

'It's the computer that's lying to us, Vance — the computer, *your* baby, that's dumping our fuel! Now, tell me how I can override it, cut it out before the tanks are drained!'

Vance's features adopted a strain of concentration, his eyes expressionlessly focused inward. Then he said:

'The only way is to close down the electrical systems.' Vance hesitated for a moment, then added: 'You have to shut down *all* the non-essential electrics and fly her —'

'Manually? On hydraulics and air pressure? Then *glide* home — right?'

'There's no *other* way. I can't isolate the fuel management system from the rest of the electrics. It has to be this way . . .'

'And when we get to where we've glided, I'll have to make a dead-stick landing,' Gant responded. Vance merely nodded. 'You sure know how to show a girl a good time, Vance — you really, really do!'

Non-essential electrics . . . It sounded simple, almost innocuous. Nothing dangerous in being without *all* the electronic displays and readouts and relying only on the air-driven primary instruments — All the radio and navcomms, except the VHF box, would also be out . . . the radar, the VORs, the ADFs . . . He'd be dropping in altitude with every second, navigating by means of features on the ground, sliding across the landscape, looking for the Vance Aircraft runway, a sliver of grey concrete in the dazzling miles of desert. Non-essential electrics . . . The 494 would go from a state-of-the-art airliner to a primitive glider in seconds once he took the decision. He had no need to climb any higher in altitude to allow him to reach Phoenix, he already had enough height to trade off against distance in the glide. He must make the decision now. Airliner to glider. Gant shivered . . .

. . . there wasn't a choice, just as there was no time-out for a debate with himself. There was only the one play he could make.

He contacted Albuquerque Centre. When he had finished informing them of the problem and his proposed course of action, the machine-like voice, still remotely calm, said:

'Roger, 494 — we understand your problem. Do you want to declare a Mayday? We'll patch through to Phoenix Approach meanwhile, clear conflicting traffic. We have you positively identified over the Verde River, range forty nautical miles due north of Phoenix.'

'Roger, AlbuK. We don't wish to declare a Mayday at this time. Out.'

The 494 was holding its altitude at thirty thousand feet. Airspeed, one hundred and ninety knots. His glide range — when the engines stopped — at that height was fifty nautical miles. He had ten to spare before the airplane ploughed into the Arizona desert.

He glanced at Vance, who seemed to be studying him.

'You ready?' he asked.

'You?' Gant replied.

The mountains ringed the city like huge, impenetrable ramparts. Phoenix gleamed like a spilt droplet of water in the brown desert. The Verde River twisted beneath them like a blue cord someone had dropped and forgotten. The control column strained against his fierce grip and Vance's supporting strength. Behind him, he sensed the empty plane like an assailant.

The airframe lurched in the air, weary and unpredictable as a drunk unable to support his own weight.

'Go for it!' Vance snapped. '*Do* it.'

Tim Burton and David Winterborne surprised each other in the grand foyer of the Club and were immediately affable, shaking hands firmly and without apparent reserve. Burton, taller than Winterborne, stooped habitually to the stature of other men, and did so now, even though Winterborne's Eurasian features always seemed at odds with his height. There was little else except the narrow eyes and sallow complexion of his

Chinese mother in him. His slimness was maintained without recourse to athletic exercise of any kind. Burton played squash and indulged in desultory bouts with shining bars and suspended weights. He brushed a hand through his long hair, summoning a cautious, uncertain grin.

'I — um, heard about your problems, but didn't gloat,' Winterborne offered. He and Aero UK had tried to press Skyliner on Burton and Artemis Airways, with great force.

'Thanks for that, anyway.' Burton's grin seemed again to have difficulty in precisely displaying itself, then at once it was entirely genuine. 'I don't mind telling *you* —'

'You wish you'd offered for some other aircraft?' The jibe was sharp.

They were standing before the grey marble fireplace, their images reflected in the Italian mirror above it. A Joseph Knibb bracket clock of ebonised wood and much gilding occupied the mantelpiece. Above them, the ceiling of the vestibule and foyer was wreathed with plaster vines and hanging bunches of pale fruit against an eggshell blue.

Burton shook his head ruefully.

'I *still* can't afford your monster, David — I told you and Coulthard that a year ago, when you were holding me down in my chair and practically forcing me to sign. No way, José —'

'And yet you can't afford to wait for the new Boeing, either,' Winterborne teased, glancing at the clock on the mantel.

'Balls, David.' The grin was now defiant. 'Vance's aircraft is a good one — *still* is. The

494's still the way to stuff the big boys. I'm not backing out of the deal, David —' For an instant, Winterborne's features clouded with something that might have been a frustrated anger, then smoothed themselves once more to pleasant imperturbability. 'Bad publicity, of course. But worse things happen at sea.' Yet despite his assumed air of confidence, he seemed to be like a dog worrying at a bone, and to be furiously enraged at the new precariousness of his position. Like Winterborne's own mood at moments. 'Think this place is grand enough to impress some Japanese bankers, David?' He, too, looked at the clock. 'A plane fell out of the sky — I'm not falling with it. Vance is going to get this right, David — I feel it in my water.'

'I'm to repeat that optimistic assessment, wherever I go, whoever I meet?' Winterborne chided.

'It wouldn't do any harm!' Burton laughed. 'Seriously, David, I'm not going down — I mean that.'

At once, he seemed to be practising his stance, his words, the expression on his face — everything that would be required to get him successfully through lunch. He was, all too evidently, suffering. Things were working as Winterborne had anticipated . . . though Burton refused to bend or break. At the moment. The Japanese banks were unlikely to underwrite large, earlier loans, perhaps no more than offer him scraps from their table. Burton would become increasingly desperate . . . But he had to turn away from the Vance 494 towards Skyliner *soon.*

'Good,' Winterborne offered. 'You always were a fighter, Tim.'

From Fraser's reports, the two 494s that Artemis Airways had shuttling around Scandinavia were almost empty, flying at a daily and increasing loss. People were frightened. Yet perhaps not sufficiently . . . Successful flights by the 494 would act like water on a stone, eroding doubt, smoothing confidence. Did it need *more* — would the strategy work? Doubt assailed Winterborne. Burton's determination, his large frame, his ebullient confidence, seemed to diminish the blows that had rained on him.

'Tim, I must be getting on. My guests are already here — almost all of them, anyway.'

'Lucky man, with time for *social* lunches. Pleased you're able to ignore the Footsie index, David. You're richer than I thought!' His laughter was without malice, his eyes were bright with understanding. Winterborne strained to retain the impassive smile he foisted on to his lips. Burton glanced across the foyer towards the Library and saw Sir Clive Winterborne and Giles Pyott, still slim and erect as a guardsman. 'I can see those who are getting hungry from here!' he joked. 'Old soldiers who might fade away through lack of nourishment. Enjoy your lunch.'

'And you yours. Good luck.' There was a seemingly genuine support in the voice, the liquid brown eyes, the hand pressed briefly on Burton's forearm.

Tim Burton watched almost with longing as David strode up the few marble steps towards his father and Pyott. Remembering, perhaps as an act of petty self-assertion, that same figure, thinner and just as tall but with sloped and apologetic shoulders, walking down the cloisters of the school. Though David Winterborne had been his senior by two years, and even though his father was a decorated soldier and the younger brother of one of the wealthiest businessmen in Singapore, David had always been *the Chinky.* Burton had been able to indulge a kind of patronising sympathy towards him, even though his own father had been a clerk who, by dint of night school and examination, had risen to the dizzy heights of company secretary, and his mother had managed a clothes shop.

David had muffled his pride and his temper in a cloak of assumed invisibility. Now, however, Burton envied him. His success might be rocky — the losses deeper than ever admitted because of Aero UK's recent disasters — but it was he who seemed more at home in the Club, more assured, the one able to rely upon his stable, elevated background. He might see himself falling like Lucifer, but David would never be ruined. For himself, the Japanese bankers just *had* to come through . . .

David, his father and Pyott went into the Library, and Burton remembered Charlotte's advice to be at his ease when his guests arrived, to make something of a parade and a minor difficulty of his coming to greet them. Charley — who wouldn't have been allowed to become a member, being a woman — would have been able to carry it off like a model on a catwalk. He, however, quailed at the atmosphere of the Club at that moment. It was as if he still only aspired to the world of power, influence and success that it symbolised, rather than truly belonged. David's father and Pyott had been members for perhaps forty years apiece. He felt like a parvenu.

A youngish barrister with political ambitions and the ability to trim like a racing yacht passed him with a confident nod in the company of an advertising executive. They mounted the steps like schoolboys . . . David in school, he remembered again. Carrying his hurt, his ruthlessness, his ambition inside a carapace of ingratiation and acquiescence. He'd paltered and shifted, tried to be inconspicuous — and, like a chrysalis, had turned into the iron butterfly he now was.

A judge and a Cabinet minister, a group of City people, a novelist past his sell-by date in company with a publisher. He felt them all as an admonishing, even mocking parade as they passed into the Club.

Where were the bloody Japs? He felt nervous now, as if he would forget all his carefully rehearsed arguments, the brochure-like confidence he must bring to the meeting. Come on, I'm drowning, not waving . . . And behind everything, there was Vance. *Come on, Alan, save my neck —*

Ahead and to port of the airplane, the Theodore Roosevelt Lake gleamed, as if flashing him a signal, one that was unable to distract him from the barrier of the Superstition Mountains directly ahead. Twenty miles to run, barely six minutes before he attempted to put the airplane down on the runway at Vance Aircraft. Airspeed one-ninety knots, altitude sixteen thousand feet and falling — but only slowly, deceptively, as if the airframe would stay in the air for hours yet. Instability tremored through the plane like the first symptoms of a return of malarial fever. Gant's hands and wrists, his forearms and shoulders, ached with the effort of keeping the unpowered airliner on course, in the glide.

The engine noise was missing. Air-driven pumps were maintaining hydraulic pressure in the flying control circuits. Once more, he nudged the nose up to maintain his airspeed for as long as possible. When he and Vance had made it, it had been a simple calculation. Altitude equals distance in a glide. They had enough altitude to make the runway at Vance Aircraft, more than enough . . . But he could not restart the engines in order to make the slightest adjustment in speed, height, direction. He and Vance had switched off all the non-essential electrics, to the point where they were wearing their headsets with one ear uncovered, so that they could hear one another. The fuel had been stopcocked. Cutting off all fuel flow had stabilised the airframe in its slow glide. The slightest alteration of course might unbalance the plane. He did not even know how much fuel — if any — was sloshing around in the tanks.

'494 — this is Vance Centre.' It was Ron Blakey on the horn, his tension palpable. 'QDM one-eight-six. You need to turn left five degrees to position for a straight-in. Inform us when you have the runway in visual range.'

The channel remained open for a second or

two, as if they expected him to reply. Barbara was there somewhere. He sensed her presence — concerned more for her father and the future of the company than for him. The pettiness of the thought made him wince. It revealed the strained, worn state of his nerves. It wasn't the slim, tiny form of a jet fighter behind his seat, it was the huge bulk of a long-haul airliner. He almost felt its great weight, its sluggish, resistant inertia through his hands and feet.

The runway at Vance was more than long enough, he reminded himself, unable even to glance across at Alan in the copilot's seat. It had to be, in case they lost the brakes. There would be no deceleration available from reverse thrust from the dead, unusable engines. It would be all brakework. His body tensed, as if the struggle with the aircraft's bulk had already begun. His forehead was sheened with sweat. The electrics for the air-conditioning had been switched off.

Phoenix's sprawling conurbation lay like a sand-coloured lizard, curled on the desert, surrounded by its silver reservoirs. The airflow seemed louder, poised to buffet at the plane in its helpless glide. He was flying on the trims alone, nudging the aircraft constantly to maintain its course, and saving the hydraulic power to the control column until he had to use the column to maintain the 494 on the narrow strip of the runway, which would blur beneath the rush of the airliner which wouldn't slow enough in time —

Stop . . .

Ten miles out, altitude nine thousand feet. His

hands shivered at the impression of them dropping like a stone towards the mountains. He still couldn't see the runway at Vance Aircraft, even though the city was bigger, its glass towers winking in the morning sun. Phoenix seemed to be rushing towards them, its ring of mountains suddenly like a huge, opening mouth — that of a shark.

Ron Blakey again. Gant was grateful that Vance maintained his grim silence beside him.

'494 — Vance Centre. Turn on to runway heading now.' A pause, then, almost apologetically: 'Emergency services are on full alert and standing by. Wind light and variable, QFE two-niner-niner-four. Call when visual with the field.'

The technical instructions were added in a rush of words, as if Blakey had become conscious that he had revealed his own fearful doubt and now wished to mask it.

'Vance Centre — 494. The field is not yet —' A dusty strip, thin as a pencil line in the desert, the tiny boxes of buildings nearby. His relief was huge. 'Correction, we have the field in visual. Two-niner-niner-four it is.'

Six miles out. A line narrower than the highways he could make out linking the suburbs of Phoenix. He looked at the altimeter. They were too high. He'd trimmed too safely, too well.

'Dump the gear!' he shouted at Vance, who was startled by his tone and urgency.

'Gear down?'

'Gear *down!*'

Two muffled thumps as the undercarriage entered the streaming airflow. The aircraft wobbled, tilted as if about to plummet, and he fought it back to level flight. A third, softer noise, less disturbance to the airframe. The lights confirmed all three sets of wheels were down and locked. The sudden extra drag pushed the plane's nose down and he struggled to trim again as the speed dropped. He had nudged the 494 on to the runway heading. Mountains seemed to brush like claws at the plane's belly, just hundreds of feet below them. The buildings of Vance Aircraft were thrown-away toys in the desert, shining in the sun amid hard, grey mountains. The runway was no more than a sliver of plastic placed on the desert floor, narrow and short as a slide rule. Dragged back by the undercarriage, the plane wobbled in the airflow.

He eased up the nose, further cutting the speed. Hollis' voice, which had followed him through the flight like someone saying the Kaddish, had vanished in the back of his mind.

Two miles out, he judged. Vance's hands reached for the copilot's column, in anticipation. Gant shook his head angrily.

'On my order!'

He dropped the leading edge slats and the main flaps. The 494 seemed to rear back from the approaching runway like a terrified horse. The hydraulic pressure reading dropped. Would the air-driven pumps replenish it before he needed to use the brakes?

The threshold lights flashed beneath the belly of the aircraft. The mountains reared up around them, the great mouth they had seemed to form reaching to enclose them. The six-thousand-yard markers were beneath them in another second, the impression of the plane's speed numbing Gant, overriding every other sensation. He saw the flashing lights of the emergency vehicles as they raced along either edge of the runway, throwing up dust in clouds. The runway rushed at them.

Gant hauled back on the column, wrists bulging with the effort, as if he were dragging it out of concrete.

'Now — !' he shouted, but Vance was already heaving on the copilot's column, his face squeezed and reddened with the strain.

No reverse thrust, no reverse — *Brace, brace, brace* — Get out of my head, Hollis . . . He continued to heave at the control column and it began to creep back towards him. Vance's eyes were bulging with fear and effort, his teeth set in a grimace. The runway was a blur beneath the nose, *so close beneath* — only the brakes —

Wheels touched concrete. The airliner bounced back into the air. Then the main undercarriage touched a second time and the nose butted down like the head of a charging ram and the nose-wheels thudded on to the runway.

'Feet clear of the brakes!' Gant ordered Vance as the airliner raced to overtake the nearest of the emergency vehicles, its flashing lights and red flank lost in a moment.

He couldn't burst any of the tyres and he needed maximum braking. No reverse thrust. The tyres howled on the concrete, the rushing air seemed to deafen. He hit the toe brakes. The nose of the aircraft shuddered as the nosewheels shimmied on the concrete. The landscape shivered like something reflected in a mirror the moment it was shattered.

Groundspeed one-forty-five knots. *No reverse thrust* —

'Three thousand feet to run!' Vance called above the din.

He could see the end of the runway. The airplane seemed to be *accelerating* . . . It was worse than making an emergency stop in a car . . . The hydraulic pressure faded and he felt the brakes slacken, become spongey. They were going to plough off the end of the runway into the overrun area —

— at sixty knots, he was flung against his restraints as the 494 hit the end of the runway and rushed on, throwing gravel and debris against the underside of the fuselage. The mirrors filled with dust. Thirty knots, ten —

Their speed died and the aircraft came to a shuddering, drunken stop. Dust boiled up around the flight deck windows, obscuring everything . . . Gant choked back sickness. Vance seemed to be yelling a stream of obscenities, somewhere at a great distance . . .

Quiet. For a moment, until the noise of sirens filled it. Gant dragged off his headset and then once more slumped gratefully, dazedly against the restrain of his straps.

The nose of the 494 dropped as the nose undercarriage leg slowly collapsed, as if he had ridden it like a horse to exhaustion.

The sirens began to wind down. The vehicles,

like a pack of small wild dogs surrounding a wounded buffalo, appeared in front of them as the dust cleared from the windows. At once, he made out Barbara's slight form climbing out of the 4WD.

'Shit,' Vance murmured, his voice thick with saliva. '*Shit* — shit!'

Gant rubbed his cheeks with his hands as Vance pounded him on the shoulder. He inspected the quivering in his fingers. Remembered Hollis. He shook his head slowly, repeatedly.

'Thanks,' Vance murmured.

'Sure.' He looked across at him. The man's features were shining with relief, with the vivacity of hope rescued from desperation. 'Sure . . .'

'The fuel management system. The assholes — they must have cut corners, shaved the costs, failed to check the circuitry . . . something.' He loosened his restraints, almost as if he were just awakening and about to stretch luxuriously.

Gant had done enough, apparently. Survived, unlike Hollis and his crew, and thrown Vance a lifeline. He'd be on the midday news, the networks by evening —

There was a TV camera, perched like a black parrot on someone's shoulder, pointing at them, then panning along the fuselage. A hurriedly poised, power-suited female reporter was already preparing to interview Barbara beneath the nose of the aircraft, amid the scenery of the emergency vehicles.

He turned to Vance and glowered at him. Vance shrugged and said:

'I knew you could do it, Gant — I just knew

it.' He grinned, waggling his hand. 'I couldn't pass up the chance to make headlines. All or nothing at all —'

'You're a Class A asshole, Vance.'

'Sure. Now, smile — you're on *Candid Camera*!' he pointed through the dusty windows. 'When they ask you questions, just keep it simple. A technical fault, but the airplane's fundamentally *safe*. OK?'

'And you get a Federal seal of approval, right? The NTSB speaks through me.'

'That's the way the game is played, Gant. Don't be a party-pooper. *Hero saves Vance Aircraft.* Don't you like the sound of tomorrow's headlines?' He waved towards the inquisitive camera, which had been joined by a second, then a third. 'Don't screw it up. I save my company, you get to be a celebrity all over again. Let's just play it as it lays, uh?' He paused, and a more vulnerable, grateful man looked out from behind the blunt planes and angles of his face. 'And, thanks. I mean it, Mitchell. Thanks.'

Eventually, as his relief and anger both subsided, Gant murmured:

'Yeah. Any time . . .'

'Am I being stupid, Kenneth? Tell me if you think I am.'

'My dear, you only ever ask that question when you're all but certain you're right.'

'And you only ever employ that patrician tone with me when your curiosity has been aroused.'

Marian blew cigarette smoke through the sunlight that blazed in Aubrey's drawing room. The green carpet and walls gave the room a dell-like privacy and invitation. Mrs Grey, who spent her time attempting to woo Kenneth from his occasional cigarettes, would disapprove of the scent of the smoke after she was gone, however privileged she was as a former don, present MP and always Giles Pyott's daughter.

Aubrey lifted his spectacles and rubbed his eyes. Their faded blue appeared childishly mischievous. He smiled at her.

'Am I curious?' he asked.

'I suspect you might be.' Then, as if brushing the banter aside like the last billow of smoke with her hand, she leaned forward and said: 'You know my suspicions amount to paranoia, Kenneth. At least, I know you think so. I just can't believe he overdosed on heroin.'

'Why not?' he asked, not unkindly. 'Many respectable young people do. It doesn't always happen in filthy public lavatories or on run-down housing estates.'

'I grant you that — but unless he had his hand in the till . . . Oh, I don't know! Perhaps he could afford a new apartment, a new girlfriend, a new car *and* a mainline habit . . . And perhaps I'm old-fashioned enough not to want it to be true. But it seems too coincidental to me. The very day —'

'Ah. Well, perhaps.' He replaced his spectacles, which had been catching the sunlight as he waved his hand airily, the thin wrist bony and skeletal, the flesh almost transparent. The dust motes slowed as he returned his attention to the sheet of A4. 'These names, you say, are not unexpected?' She shook her head emphatically.

'Well, apart from Laxton.'

'Laxton Not-so-Superb as he was known to Cabinet colleagues old enough to remember *real* apples,' Aubrey reminisced drily. 'He was always a denizen of the meaner realms of the body politic, I grant you. Why should his presence surprise?'

'Urban Development — his EU brief as Commissioner. He has no possible connection with Aero UK or Balzac-Stendhal. And before you ask, he is not a director nor has ever been. They were companies he must have missed out of his ample portfolio.' She smiled, brushing at the stray blonde hair at her temples. Her mane was pulled back from her face and held in a slide. She was soberly dressed in a cream suit. 'And I wouldn't gauge him to possess the clout to lobby effectively either at Westminster or in Brussels. Urban Development was the booby prize — or a slight to the new *British* Commissioner.'

'Otherwise, nothing?'

'Nothing.'

'Well, let me look at the photographs.' He flicked through the prints she had had rush-developed. 'Mm, I would not have employed that unfortunate young man on surveillance without an extensive course in the arts of photography. These are very poor, even allowing for the weather . . .' He studied the prints carefully, holding his glasses at slightly differing distances from his eyes, squinting. 'I recognise most of these faces, including dear David. But then, I presume you're not suspicious of David Winterborne in this, are you?'

'Don't be silly. Just because he was always pulling my pigtails, tying me to trees and leaving me for hours, putting frogs down my best frocks . . . ?' She tossed her head, laughing. 'No, I don't want to pay him back for his childhood cruelties to a mere girl five years younger than himself —'

'Who repeatedly invaded his boyish games, offered probity where there was inevitable cheating, and who accused him at every possible turn of unkindness to his younger brother, your playmate?'

There was a momentary silence as both of them remembered David Winterborne's long-dead younger brother. Then she said:

'I was going to describe a young girl, an only child, so loved that she had no sense of the cruelty children are capable of. But, Dr Freud, I'm sure you're right.'

Aubrey snorted with amusement, then continued to study the photographs, murmuring:

'A great pity he did not have the presence of mind to take some pictures of the men who so frightened him . . . Although, on the other hand —'

'What is it?' she asked eagerly, almost rising from her armchair.

'Patience is a virtue,' Aubrey remarked with mock primness. 'A face here, passing into the hotel. *Not* coincidentally present, I think. Here — this man.' She was already at his shoulder, leaning over the back of his chair. He smelt the slight, old-fashioned scent of her perfume and remembered that her mother had often worn the same. He patted her hand on his shoulder and she did not resent the touch, though he was certain she understood its motive.

'Who is he?' she asked, straightening.

'Bring me my magnifying glass. In the drawer of the desk there.' His request was almost reluctant, as if he had been forced to admit his age. She held it out to him. The faces in the photograph, through the rain and the slightly wrong focus, enlarged and distorted as if in fairground mirrors. 'Yes. Definitely,' Aubrey concluded.

'You know him — *I* don't.'

'My world, not yours, dear girl. *My* world.' His voice had an edge of asperity, even distaste. She took the photograph back to her chair and studied the face Aubrey had indicated. Rain-pallid, slightly blurred by the extra flesh of good living and poor camerawork. A tough, alert face; pale, dead eyes, set above large cheekbones, a long jaw, a shock of greying hair.

'His name is Fraser,' Aubrey was saying. 'He is a former field agent — quite a senior and experienced one — of my service. An erstwhile intelligence officer of particular, even peculiar skills.'

'You don't like him? He worked for you?'

'As little as possible. Others quite liked his — somewhat *direct* methods. Many agents wouldn't work with him, if they could possibly avoid it. You see, his survival instinct was capable of overriding all other priorities — including the lives of his colleagues.' Despite the chilliness of his account and the evident distaste of his tone, there was a dreamy, reminiscing pleasure on Aubrey's features. 'Patrick Hyde, of whom you may have heard me speak —'

'Endlessly. How is your long-lost son, by the way?'

Aubrey all but pouted, then smiled.

'I gather he prospers in the Penal Colony of Australia. Free of me at last, perhaps . . . But Fraser is our concern. Hyde would never, on *any* account, work with him.'

'Why not?'

'Fraser was a psychopath. *Is.*'

'In SIS?'

'Many of his skills were just what was required. He was also successful, efficient. Not all agents possessed the same abilities, nor the same personalities. Fraser was one of the truly bad apples we could turn to some account on behalf of Her Britannic Majesty's Government and in the further defence of the realm. Despite your disapproval!'

'Then . . . ?' she asked, still as shocked as a child might have been.

'Then it is possible that your friend did not acquire his heroin addiction until yesterday.' He shuffled in his chair, as if eager for activity, plagued by restlessness. 'I'll make some enquiries, Marian. I'll try to discover what the appalling Fraser has been doing in the way of gainful employment since he left the service.'

'When would that have been?'

'Two or three years — even as many as four. I must check.'

'And you think — ?' She paused. Michael

Lloyd's body, lying on his new carpet, seen through the letter box's slit, as if a scene from some wide-screen movie shown on television. She felt tears, and anger, equally.

'*Do* I think? Mm — perhaps I do. If Fraser's employers, whoever they are at present, felt that your young friend's presence was a threat . . . then Fraser would take just such a direct means to close the door with as much finality as he could. Yes . . . Fraser is certainly capable of killing your friend.'

CHAPTER FOUR

Ghosts in the Machines

His office was, for the moment, a dusty, cramped space in need of repainting close under the roof of the Commerce Department. The perspective from its one small window, jammed shut and wire-netted against the pigeons, was bounded by the Washington Monument and the White House. Since he was not a political animal, it had come as a surprise to Gant that he had been given the view. The office itself was much more indicative of his lowly status as a Federal employee.

Hands still in his pockets, he turned from the window and the morning sunlight falling across the Ellipse and its acres of grass, which made the Monument a dazzling and unreal white. There were reports on his desk that needed his attention, though none of them was urgent. Mostly they were filed copies of accident reports that had been forwarded to the headquarters of the Accident Investigation Office by the various state investigatory units which were only loosely linked to the

National Transportation Safety Board. He rubbed his hands through his cropped hair, his sense of frustration childishly acute, unreasonable. He had returned to a kind of sense-deprivation — the flotation tank of his daily existence — after the flight and the crash landing. He disregarded the newspaper and TV coverage, which Vance had milked and ignited in turn; that had all been Vance's prize.

The two 494s of Albuquerque Airlines were flying again, half-full, though the two planes Burton had in Europe were slower to be trusted . . . even though they were not fitted with the fuel computer system that had failed. Vance had, on TV publicly changed the subcontractor, reverting to an older fuel computer system which would be marginally less efficient but which had a track record. Also, he was very publicly suing the errant manufacturer for millions of dollars. The media had gone along for the ride; Vance was crowing again, like some overpaid sports star, and they liked that.

He didn't savour the exploitation of his own role, the images of 'Nam and himself in uniform and the scrappy accounts of his Cold War career. The MiG-31, the Firefox, sitting in the Skunk Works at Burbank, stripped down, its pieces of fuselage lying about its skeleton like the ripped-off shards of a giant beetle. Other images of MiL gunships, references to Winter Hawk.

He had turned off the set and gotten another beer from the icebox, regretting that he was being used by Vance; regretting more, perhaps, that he had broken open his new self only to find it the wrapping on a mummy's corpse and nothing more . . . Underneath the veneer of this office, his job, the secretary in the even smaller room next door, his paycheque, everything had crumbled into dust as soon as he had been exposed to flying, danger, his supreme skill with machines that flew. He could taste the dust in his dry mouth now. It had been stupid, so *stupid,* to have gone back, to have put himself —

The intercom blurted.

When you sold the farm, he thought bitterly, and moved on, you didn't return to it on Sundays and the Fourth of July. You forgot it.

'Yes?'

'Agent McIntyre from the FBI is here to see you, sir.'

Gant grimaced, then said: 'Show him in, Mrs Garcia.'

He took up his position at the window once more, hands in his pockets, shirtsleeves rolled, shoulders slightly hunched as if in anticipation of an assault from behind. There were grey squirrels on the lawn in front of the Commerce Department. He heard the door shut behind McIntyre, and sensed the enthusiasm of enmity that the FBI man brought with him into the cramped office.

'You're really appreciated by the NTSB, uh, Gant?' he heard.

The FBI Building faced the Department of Justice across Pennsylvania Avenue. They called that one of the ironies of good government.

'What do you want, McIntyre? I'm busy.'

'Sure — I can see that.'

A chair scraped on linoleum and McIntyre's

weight made its ricketiness creak in protest as he sat down. A lighter clicked and he smelt cigarette smoke.

'No, I don't mind if you smoke,' he murmured.

'Gant, you're a real cure.'

Gant turned to face McIntyre. The man's features, blunt and square, shone with the heat of the room and with some undisclosed satisfaction. The nose was too small for the size of the face, perched like a sculptor's first, unsuccessful attempt at proportion below narrowed eyes and amid hard, unimpressible lines. Gant sat behind his littered desk.

'OK — what does the Bureau want? You'd like to pick over my service career, my voting record — what?'

McIntyre shook his head.

'Something more recent, Gant. Something between you and Vance. Vance the crook.'

'I was doing my job.'

McIntyre waggled the hand that held the cigarette.

'And got well paid for it.'

Gant frowned.

'I didn't seek publicity. I just found out why an airplane crashed, McIntyre. As a public servant.'

McIntyre removed a folded sheet of paper from his breast pocket and smoothed it on the desk before turning it so Gant could study it. It was a bank statement.

'See what I mean about well paid? The latest entry . . . ? Drawn on the Vance Aircraft account at First Arizonan. A hundred thousand dollars.

Paid to you, *as a public servant.*'

Gant looked up bleakly. 'You mother.'

Again, McIntyre shook his head.

'It's no frame, Gant. Vance sent you a transfer for a hundred thousand yesterday. You didn't know? For getting him off the hook with his bankers — or is it your cut of the Federal funding we talked about earlier?' He was openly grinning now. 'Jeez, I wouldn't want to have to explain *this* on TV! You'd be even more coy than you were after you got that plane down.' He leaned forward. 'The Bureau can make a case out of this, Gant — one that ties you in with Vance. We'll begin by serving you with a subpoena — the *Senate Committee* will serve you with one, requiring you to give evidence at the hearing into Vance's affairs . . . while the Bureau keeps on digging. Your grave,' he added.

His eyes gloated. Gant knew his own posture was one of defeated truculence, that of the farm boy watching a storm flatten corn — defiant only out of complete lack of expectation. Vance always had to *prove* he had offered you his thanks and you understood he had. The hundred thousand was just that, done without thought of consequence or propriety; a thank you that enabled you to buy things that would remind you of his gratitude.

Barbara's attempt to show concern for him, enquire into his present life, had been just as intrusive, but less damaging. It didn't look criminal. The payment did.

'What can I say?' he bluffed. 'Maybe I've got the lottery ticket somewhere in the apartment?'

'A real cure, like I said.' McIntyre's satisfaction was complete; he could, for once, adopt a moral superiority. Gant had screwed up with a *bribe.* The man could taste his pleasure. He shook his head. 'It's a long way to fall, hero to cheapskate. To being on the take.' He stood up. 'You can keep the statement. It's a Xerox. Oh am I going to *enjoy* watching you fall, Gant!' he announced, his voice like his chest expanding with a kind of perverse pride. 'You'll land harder than you did two days ago — and you won't walk away from the wreckage, boy — you surely won't!'

He paused at the door, but there were no more words. His triumph was complete enough to ensure a grand exit. Gant watched the door close behind him, then slowly, gently lowered his head into his cupped, waiting hands. Between his resting elbows, the bank statement stared back at him.

'You stupid, stupid bastard,' he murmured. 'You made-in-America, top-of-the-heap *asshole,* Vance . . .'

The remains of McIntyre's cigarette smouldered in the tin ashtray which advertised Budweiser Lite, the smoke ascending in the still air of the room like a distress signal from a distant ship. Suddenly, the mummy's corpse of his present was not to be despised like a welfare cheque that would keep him going; help him subsist, together with the food stamps of football games and weekends in the mountains . . . They would even strip him of the remnants of this life; the job, the paycheque, the remaining reputation. It would all go. There would be nothing to hang on to, nothing . . .

'Yes, I understand. No, it couldn't have been anticipated,' David Winterborne concurred, the cordless phone against his cheek, Eaton Square below the balcony. The French windows were open and the air was still fresh after the early-morning rain. 'Absolutely. No, I don't think the suit has much chance of success, but you'd better talk to the lawyers. Thank you, Al. Keep me informed.'

He dropped the receiver on to the chaise-longue, richly carved and brocaded, against the back of which he was resting as he watched the traffic move through the square. One of his more elderly neighbours, the widow of a stock-broker, was walking her ridiculously small dog in the gardens; moving in and out of dappled shadow from the trees. He plucked at his smooth chin with one hand, the other arm folded across the chest of his dressing gown.

Des Moines Instruments, in which Winter-borne Holdings was a majority stockholder and which had supplied the fuel computer system for Vance's aircraft, had been calling with angering frequency for the past two days and nights. The untraceable fault in the fuel computer's chips *had* been found. His eyes narrowed in contemptuous dislike. Vance's former *son-in-law* had *just happened to be* a remarkable pilot. Once Vance had survived the crash landing and they had discovered that the fuel was being jettisoned on the computer's command, even though the instruments revealed nothing, Vance had removed Des Moines Instruments from the board, gone to another supplier, exercised his considerable charm and air of authority through the national media — and saved his company.

For the moment, at least.

Winterborne glanced at the maid who had brought his breakfast into the drawing room on a tray and was laying it on a table near the second pair of French windows. Beyond her was the door to the library — and the fax machines and the VDUs on which, at the press of a few buttons on the keyboard, he could play the newest, the ultimate video game. He could sit before the screen and watch his fortune vanish. Stock in Des Moines Instruments was down so far it might never recover. Shares in Aero UK were almost worthless and shares in Winterborne Holdings, *his* conglomerate, had been affected. Not merely scratched, but perhaps even fatally wounded. In forty-eight hours, the conglomerate's total worth had been diminished by seventy million, perhaps as much as a hundred million . . . and rising.

His aerospace interests in the UK, the US and Europe had, without exception, been damaged, perhaps beyond repair. Like some computer virus the doubts and the rumours had spread to contaminate the parent company and his other industrial and construction interests.

His hand shivered on his chin, but he stilled it through an effort of will.

Tim Burton's two 494s were still almost empty, shuttling around Scandinavia, but that was pitifully small comfort. His prospects were, albeit slowly, brightening. The 494 was a largely rehabilitated aircraft — and a *cheap* one, unlike Sky-liner.

He recovered the telephone and dialled a number as he walked to the table. Fraser answered almost immediately.

'You'll need to speak to our man again,' Winterborne announced. 'What he did for us with the fuel computer system was clever, but not clever enough.'

'Agreed. Couldn't have anticipated —'

'Perhaps not. It's still not good enough. I think our man should be on site on the next occasion.'

'Next? How — what?'

'There are two aircraft of the same type still flying in Scandinavia.'

'They don't have the same system on board —'

'I don't want the *same,* Fraser. Rather, something that is in truth undetectable. Talk to our man.'

'How long do I have? What kind of budget?'

'Two days. And what it costs — within reason.'

'OK. I'll be in a position to report this evening.'

Winterborne put down the telephone, already examining the exhilaration that had buoyed him as he spoke to Fraser. He was habitually nervous of the instinctual, as if such responses were immature or dangerous to himself. And yet there seemed — he buttered a triangle of toast — no other immediate solution. *Another* 494 had to fall from the sky, Vance *had* to be driven to bankruptcy. . . The shares he had recently acquired in two of the largest charter-flight companies would give him the necessary leverage to insist on their leasing a small fleet of Skyliners. Once the aircraft were in service, once the word-of-mouth spread, then Skyliner might yet be salvaged. *If* there was competition only with Boeing's new aircraft, due in another year or eighteen months, market share might mean something real, by then. *If* Vance's big, cheap plane had been removed from the board.

He crunched his teeth against the pleasant bitterness of thick marmalade as he sat himself before his kedgeree. *The Chinky playing at English gentleman again* . . . Another school taunt. They returned in his dreams, usually when he was stretched, uncertain, struggling.

He began the kedgeree the housekeeper had prepared. Opened the newspaper's pink, restrained pages. Prices had dipped further in Aero UK, Winterborne Holdings, a dozen other companies in which he had a heavy investment and a major influence. Events were a series of detonations under his fortifications — ones to which he had reacted too slowly and indecisively. He should have bought into the charter market much earlier, to protect the Skyliner. He should not have believed the protestations of politicians regarding the MoD's choice of helicopter. He had left himself dangerously exposed to the virus of lost confidence in the City and among the institutions.

Until now. Fraser must buy him the man who would buy him the time. And remove the 494, Vance and Burton from the game.

'Well?' She was as eager as a child, as he held up his hand in a mocking plea for patience.

'Come *on,* Kenneth — what have you got for me on our Mr Fraser?'

'My dear *girl* — how your father ever coped with your impatience I shall never know!' Then, mischievously: 'More coffee, Marian?'

'Hand it over! *Not* the coffee pot.'

'Ah.' He lit the first of the half-dozen cigarettes he allowed himself each day — and the first of the absolute maximum that Mrs Grey would tolerate in competition with the summer air through open windows and the constantly renewed cut flowers — then he opened a buff folder on his knees. 'Here we are. Everything to him who waits — or her.'

They were seated in two armchairs near the open French windows. Traffic noise was muted and there was, in reality or imagination, the scent of roses from the Park. Despite her impatience, she luxuriated in his company, in the room's familiarity and security.

'Our Mr Fraser has been quite busy since he left the service just a little more than three years ago. *Just* before the redundancy notice . . .' He ran his finger down the page. 'His positions have been among the usual ones,' he continued, shaking his head. 'The Gulf States, bodyguarding and pandering to the paranoia of unelected sheiks swimming in oil . . . Cambodia . . . the expected kind of godless association with the Khmer Rouge and other unmentionables the Foreign Office has sometimes sanctioned, or at least ignored.' His old features wrinkled more heavily in distaste.

'Were you always so moral?' she asked with some asperity.

'No. An old man's luxury — with a lifetime's witness that *im*morality doesn't begin to solve the problem.'

'*Touché* — a hit, a palpable hit.'

'Anyway, seven or eight months in Cambodia and neighbouring Thailand, then a stretch in Singapore. Living a very sybaritic lifestyle while apparently spending his ill-gotten Cambodian gains. Then a return to Europe perhaps a year ago.' He looked up, adjusting his glasses.

'To do what, exactly?'

'The usual. Contact or middleman for rather suspect arms deals, some industrial espionage . . .' He sighed. 'A man must go where the work is,' he added acidly. 'Even if he is going to the bad by the same road.'

'So, on the whole you're glad that Hyde's girlfriend came into money and saved *him* from this kind of thing?'

'On the whole, yes.'

'Who employs Fraser at present? The Commission?'

'Not as far as I can tell.' He smiled. 'Though it may be only a matter of time . . . No one seems to know. Obviously someone at that meeting. He is a director of a newish company, here in London — Complete Security. Industrial espionage, no doubt, and bodyguards to the rich, the crooked, the paranoid. Probably arms, too. However, that is speculation. His sphere of operations seems to be the UK and Europe. At present.'

'Who owns Complete Security?'

Aubrey shook his head. 'No one seems to know. In the main, it employs others of a like mind with

Fraser.' He paused, then said: 'These are not very pleasant people, Marian. I warn you to be careful. Very careful — if, indeed, Fraser was responsible for your young man's death.'

'There aren't many people to suspect, are there?' Again, Aubrey shook his head, flicking the ash from his cigarette. The net curtains moved gently in the soft breeze from the Park. The illusion of flower scents again. 'So — ? I ought to be able to discover which one it was without going anywhere near Fraser, shouldn't I?'

'Are you determined on this?'

'He was helping me.'

'You did not cause his death.'

'It's not that easy to dismiss. My *theory* got him killed — I think. Is that reasonable to you?'

'No. Fraser does not require a weighty reason before choosing to eliminate someone.' She shivered. 'I'm sorry, my dear, but my past is my past — the country's past in a small way. Things were done . . . Young Lloyd was merely *there,* that was enough —'

'But they must have had something very suspicious to hide — whoever employed him. Why not my version of what they're up to . . . ?' She paused, her mouth open.

'Exactly,' Aubrey said coldly. 'A British company, a childhood friend of yours, a powerful French planemaker, two senior European bureaucrats. One of them — or more than one — ordered a killing more ruthlessly than I ever would have done. Now, perhaps, you see your dilemma, and your possible danger. The police report says accidental death, as do the newspapers. The incident is closed. You have no reason to make enquiries of any kind. If you do, you will inform Fraser's employer that you possess information dangerous to him. Do I make myself clear?' He was leaning forward in his chair, his clawlike old hand gripping her wrist as fiercely as the talons of a hawk. 'I have no powers — no people — to watch out for your safety. Because of that, I warn you *not* to give Fraser or his employer the slightest hint of your suspicions. Because, my dear, if you are right and there is massive corruption and misdirection of EU funds, then *all* the people at that meeting may be involved, including David Winterborne!'

He released her wrist. As she rubbed it soothingly, she nodded and said: 'I'd already thought of that. But how can I stop?'

'I think you must, Marian. I really think you must. If it has been happening, it will soon end. The project is complete, even if a failure. This morning's *Times* expects Aero UK to collapse or be taken over —'

'That's no reason to stop!' she burst out. 'Not if they're crooks — surely?'

'*Fraser* is an actor in the drama. Stay away from Fraser, I beg you. Whatever you do — do *nothing!*'

It was late afternoon when Fraser halted the hired car a few hundred yards from the French farmhouse. He got out of the air-conditioned interior of the Renault into a balmy warmth that seemed to emanate from the small orchard, the slope of the land, the hills and dark, massed trees behind the house. There was no sign of Strickland.

'He is here, isn't he?' Fraser asked his companion.

The Frenchman nodded.

'I called him as soon as I finished speaking to you. He said he would be here all day.'

'He's probably watching us through a telescopic rifle sight,' Fraser muttered.

The youngish Frenchman brushed back his flopping, dark hair with one hand and laughed.

'Should he be quite as nervous as you suggest?'

'No. Come on, let's go and see him.'

They opened the gate in the wooden post-and-rail fence that surrounded the two or so acres that belonged to the property. Fraser was still stiff from the flight to Bordeaux and the hour's car journey that followed. Resentful, too, of the imperious, dismissive manner in which Winterborne had issued his orders, demanded success. The Frenchman, Roussillon, had been waiting for him at Merignac airport, having flown down from Paris. In effect, both of them were simply obeying Winterborne's command. Even though Roussillon was employed by French counter-intelligence.

Around the property, the Dordogne stretched and heaped away abruptly. The hills rose and pressed, the land fell away from them towards the thin streaks of meandering rivers. A litter of tiny villages was scattered across the landscape, nestling beneath hills crowded with dark trees, or hunched beside the rivers. There was the sense of gorges, of wilderness, too.

Then Strickland was in the doorway of the

farmhouse, removing a pair of wire-rimmed spectacles and squinting in the late-afternoon sunshine. He was weaponless but alert, until his myopic eyes recognised Fraser. The man's bulk was oddly at contrast with his patient silence and his mannerism of rubbing his eyes, head on one side, in a display of mild, innocuous curiosity. Then he stood aside, servant-like, gesturing them inside the house. The Frenchman's expensive leather shoes made clicking noises on the cool flagstones of the floor.

The scents of blossom, wood, polish. Strickland kept the farmhouse as neatly as any house-proud woman might have done. He followed them in, again gesturing without words to tall-backed chairs in a stripped, plain wood around the heavy table. The kitchen area flowed smoothly into a sitting room lined with bookshelves and prints. A heavy, fringed carpet covered the flagstones; the windows, tall and narrow, looked towards the closest village perched on a hillside. Fraser sat down and Roussillon, his dark features still amused, sat opposite him.

'Coffee — something stronger?' Strickland asked, already fussing to fill a cordless kettle on the kitchen worktop. His accent remained American, slightly southern in intonation, his voice as smooth and polite as a Mormon.

'Coffee for me,' the Frenchman volunteered.

'Beer.'

'Surely.' Strickland bent his tall, muscular frame to the fridge. He poured the beer into a glass as the kettle began to bubble. When he turned back to his guests, he said half-apologetically: 'I read the newspaper reports.' His smile was boyish, self-deprecating. 'I didn't take into account a pilot with that kind of insight. Well, truthfully, I didn't think of Gant at all.'

He made coffee for himself and Roussillon and joined them at the table. Fraser watched Strickland intently as if he might miss some sudden metamorphosis in the man. Yet Strickland continued to shrug apologetically, smile ingratiatingly. Fraser's various meetings with the American had all, without exception, left him more puzzled than before. The man killed people but behaved like a pastor — and there seemed no *evident* hypocrisy. Perhaps the explanation lay in the fact that Strickland always killed long-distance, removed people he had never even seen.

'What can I do for you?' he asked eventually, though not with any suggestion that he had tired of waiting for them to speak.

'A repeat performance,' Fraser announced, finishing his beer.

'Another?'

'Thanks.' When Strickland returned with a second can, he said: 'My employer needs another tragic accident.'

'How soon does he need it?'

'Quickly.'

'I don't usually follow the stock market, except as regards my own portfolio,' Strickland explained, 'but your phone call didn't take me off-guard. The price is two hundred thousand. Nonnegotiable.'

'It has to be done *on* site.'

Strickland appeared alarmed. A large black-

and-white cat appeared through the open kitchen window and lowered its forelegs into the sink in order to drink, its back feet still on the windowsill.

'That isn't the way I work.'

'Not normally no. But two hundred thousand isn't a normal fee, either. And there's the pressure of time, my friend.' Even to himself, he sensed his accent thicken as his voice darkened. Strickland seemed unimpressed by implicit threat.

'Why the rush? OK, don't answer that. Stocks and shares. Loss of blood, internal haemorrhage, even. Yes, there would be a desire to hurry . . . but I don't work in that way. It's too — messy.'

Roussillon murmured: 'There could be more money — perhaps as much as another fifty thousand.'

Strickland glanced swiftly at Fraser and realised that the two men were not engaging in some negotiating ploy. Fraser was surprised.

'Out of the petty cash, Michel?' he sneered. 'I didn't realise the DST were chipping in to bale my employer out or I'd have kept something back for myself.' He laughed. The French Intelligence officer smiled and shrugged.

'I wish Mr Strickland to feel we value him, Robert. Merely that.'

'And Balzac-Stendhal will, in any case, pay the price. *You* won't be left short.'

Strickland left his chair and walked to the window. He began absently stroking the cat, who was still half-immersed in the sink, licking at the drops of water the tap had spilt. While it licked, it purred. Fraser thought there was something reluctant about the man's posture, something like the merest suggestion of an internal argument, violent and intense. Then he turned to face them.

'Three hundred thousand. For an on-site operation — and one that is untraceable, even by someone as clever as Gant.'

'That was the pilot Vance used, right?'

Strickland nodded. 'Yes. An accident investigator, too. He could appear in the play again. I'll bear it in mind, this time.'

'You know him? Was he CIA, too?'

'From time to time. When things needed to be flown.'

'Oh, yes. I remember him now. Another of Aubrey's cowboy operators. I was working for Far East desk in those days. I wondered where I'd heard the name before.'

'You should try reading newspapers with information rather than bosoms,' Roussillon commented. 'One learns such things from such newspapers.'

'When must this operation be completed?'

'Two days — three at the outside.'

'That quickly?' Strickland pondered, his large hands knuckled on the knotted, scratched wood of the scrubbed table. After some moments, he announced: 'I've been working on some refinements to that fuel computer malfunction.'

'The copyright remained with you, according to the contract.'

'As always. I've had one or two other ideas since I got back. Perhaps you could make yourself comfortable? Give me an hour or two and I'll give you a definite answer. If I can do it, then I'll accept for three hundred thousand. But I'd like to make certain. Help yourselves to coffee, beer, anything else. You'll stay to dinner?' He walked to the door, then added: 'The work you bring is always challenging — I like that. I won't keep you long —'

Fraser watched his large frame disappear from the doorway. The early-evening sunlight spilt innocently into the kitchen, haloing the cat's fur as it followed Strickland towards a large converted barn behind the house.

'Shall I be mother?' Fraser asked, waggling the kettle at Roussillon.

'Merci, mon ami.' Roussillon stretched luxuriously. 'I feel so *comfortable* here,' he observed, yawning and linking his hands together at arm's-length above his head. 'As if the place belonged to my grandmother.'

'Instead of a psychopath with a genius for sabotage? I know what you mean —' The kettle began to steam. 'It was the good fortune of the private sector that the CIA could never *prove* he blew up his own Head of Station with a car bomb. I wonder what the guy had done to annoy him?'

'Probably the man did not like cats?'

'It would be enough,' Fraser agreed. 'I always feel around Strickland that I'm around a polite cobra.' He laughed. 'D'you think he'd be offended if we checked under the car when we leave?' He handed Roussillon his coffee, sipped at his own. 'Cheers. Here's to him — and to us. And to the *private* sector. Free enterprise.'

'Ah, Fraser — how could I join such a toast? I am a servant of the state.'

'First, last and always?'

'Of course.'

'If I'd worked for a service like the DST, I think I might have stayed in and waited for the pension.' He sipped again at his coffee. 'It's so much easier when defence of the realm — the *territoire* — and the national interest coincide exactly with what every businessman wants. When the security service can do anything it likes, just so long as another Froggie benefits!' Roussillon scowled. 'We had Protestantism, though,' Fraser continued. 'Puritanism, conscience, guilt. And however much you try to keep them out of intelligence work, they always turn up to spoil the party . . . unlike your lot. If you want to blow up the Greenpeace boat, you just go ahead and do it, for example —'

'That was the DGSE, not DST. Intelligence, not Security.'

'Sorry,' Fraser mocked. Then he asked: 'D'you think Strickland's a good cook? Worth staying for dinner, would it be?'

She paused in the Close and looked up at the three spires of the small market town's cathedral. The darkening air above seemed filled with wheeling swallows. Marian breathed deeply, unaffected by the meaning of the building, touched only by the swallows. One skimmed near her head. The choirmaster, whom she recognised, smiled in her direction as he hurried towards the west door. She walked on after a few moments, hands thrust into the deep pockets of her flared yellow skirt, her head bent as if to study her flat slippers or the uneven cobbles.

She left the Close and walked beside the minster pool. Children were being encouraged to feed ducks; the sullen, empty noises of early drunks echoed across the water. A winding street of medieval houses, mostly craft shops and cramped coffee houses, meandered towards the market square containing the banks, building societies, the cheap shoe shops and the church that had become a craft and visitor centre. She turned beside the pool, beneath darkening trees, her mood almost tranquil. Michael Lloyd's funeral was the middle of the following week and she could not attend. It had been awkward and guilty, the act of telling the aunt in Crewkerne that she would not be there.

The market town that was also a cathedral city — in a polite, impoverished imitation of one of the cathedral cities of southern England — was on the eastern edge of the constituency. Recently bloated by a small industrial estate and new executive housing — street upon street of declamatory triple garages and barbecue patios — it had become a commuter suburb for the raw, sprawling industrial conurbation to its west and south. Some of the poorer council estates and tower block encampments of the conurbation fell within the boundaries of her constituency, as did rural pockets of north Warwickshire.

Marian had won the constituency during a general election, inheriting it from a knight of the shire who had succumbed — they said — either to complete inertia or to an apoplectic fit brought on by the thought of the sheer physical and mental effort of continuing the Thatcherite revolution. She smiled at the recollected joke, first relayed to her by her party agent, Bill.

She had spoken to Bill before leaving the small flat she rented, in a building that clung like ivy to the cathedral close but which a local builder had bought up, knocked about and recreated as three *executive* apartments . . . that word again. She was on her way to meet that builder at one of the town's new, anonymous wine bars which catered for the influx of *executives* to the town's new estates.

The man had left a message on her answer-phone. He seemed both angry and hesitant, se-cretive and outraged. She had agreed that, since he could not *possibly*, under any circumstances, be in the town the following morning and attend her regular surgery, she would give him an hour that evening. After all, she quite liked the flat and the rent was not exploitative. His workmen came quickly to effect minor repairs. She only vaguely wondered whether, since he was a minor contrac-tor on the Urban Regeneration Project, it was something to do with that Venice of the Midlands grandiosity.

Gnats rose in slow, smoky columns above the still water of the pool. A duck followed her des-ultorily for a few yards along the bank on the other side of the low iron railings that fenced the water. Then she mounted steps and turned into a pedestrianised street of narrow, tall houses whose upper storeys seemed to rest uncertainly on a video hire shop, restaurants, an electrical retailer — and the wine bar.

Ray Banks waved to her from a window seat, climbing immediately to his feet, his stomach brushing the table, his florid tie almost draping itself into his glass of house white. He seemed eager and dubious as he took her hand.

'A glass of white would be fine,' she murmured, seating herself. 'There's only a trace of antifreeze in the bouquet.' Her smile was not returned. Banks seemed inordinately mortified, as if he had committed some serious social gaffe. 'Cheers,' she offered when he returned with the glass.

'Cheers,' he replied gloomily. There was the self-consciousness of a man seeking her good offices, even influence, about him.

Marian lit a cigarette and considerately waved the smoke away from Banks. Empty laughter from the street outside and the bark of a dog.

'Your phone call sounded urgent,' she prompted.

'Sorry I couldn't make it tomorrow — didn't want to put you out . . . Marian.' He always approached the familiarity of her name as he might have done an explosive device. His hobby was war-gaming; her father's military career rendered him deferential towards her — together with his lack of assurance when in the company of successful women. His wife and two teenage daughters seemed to Marian to have remained, mentally, in the back-to-back where the Bankses' married life had begun, when Ray had been a jobbing building with one workman, a decrepit truck and an overdraft. 'I — er . . .'

'Yes?' She tried to sound casually interested. Now, Ray had a dozen vans and small trucks, a building supply business, a successful industrial contracting company. 'Is there anything I can do to help?' She was reluctant to make the offer, but intrigued by his hesitancy.

'Dunno — I, well . . . I'm in trouble. The company, that is. I just don't know what's going on . . .'

Marian was careful to exclude all expression from her features. A youth stared at her through the window, then, probably assessing her age beneath her good looks, passed on with a shrug. The conversation of the wine bar revolved around money, football, barbecues, sunbeds, step aerobics and sex. Ray Banks wanted her intercession in some matter; a favour.

Her thoughts wandered to her conversation with her agent. The local party chairman had been badgered again by Central Office with regard to her profound Euroscepticism. The PM was — endlessly and yet again — calling for unity; which meant silence from all who disagreed. There was a women's coffee morning after surgery, an encounter with the remnants of blue-rinse loyalty and the fanatical devotion to whatever leadership was in place of the bottle-blonde, sunbed new generation of local committee-women who were the inheritors and perhaps even the daughters of the blue-rinse matrons.

'. . . bankrupt,' she heard, startled into attention. His features indicated that he understood she was inappropriately unheeding.

'I'm sorry, Ray, but I don't understand,' she recovered. 'Things have been bad in the construction industry, I know, but —'

'I didn't come for the party line,' he replied sourly, then immediately altered his expression to one of apology. 'There's *work,* but there's no bloody money for it. That's what's wrong — Marian.'

'Cash flow, is that it?'

'Cash *flow?* There's not a bloody trickle, I can tell you!'

'But you've work?'

He nodded vehemently.

'If you can call it that. I've got *contracts* is more like the truth.' He sipped viciously at his wine and drops spattered the florid tie and the lapels of his grey suit. She blew smoke at the ceiling. He continued: 'It's this bloody Millennium Project — the Venice of the Midlands crap! I won supply contracts, grants, contracts for construction . . . it all looked bloody marvellous on paper — which is where most of it stayed, on *paper!*'

'Money from Brussels hasn't materialised?'

'It did, at first. Trickle-down economics at its best — money trickling down from the main contractors, handed out to them by the appropriate officials and departments. *Wonderful* artists' impressions and architects' models, *great* site-clearance, lots of hype . . . We were all over the bloody moon, for months!' He paused, staring into his empty glass. 'You ready for another?' She shook her head. 'Won't be a mo—'

The Millennium Project was vast and crucial to the conurbation. Only a tiny fragment of the huge urban redevelopment fell within the boundaries of her constituency — some canalside prettifying, some executive apartment buildings from resurrected waterside factories and warehouses, a small part of the huge leisure complex around the canal basin. The rest of the development — the symphony hall, the conference centre, the office blocks and living and playing acreage, the new roads, the airport expansion . . . all lay outside the constituency. Thankfully, she had always thought, taking into account her own Eurosceptic credentials and the hundreds of millions that Brussels was pouring into the entire project. Wise old birds with long experience of Whitehall and Westminster murmured, out of the hearing of Whips and Permanent Secretaries, that it was simply a way of bribing the most sceptical electorate in Europe that the EU was a *good thing*, a source of endless bounty.

She was not disinclined to believe such judgements. Now — unfortunately, she considered — one of her constituents had brought the problem to her doorstep. What problem — ?

Banks returned to the table, making it scrape on the flagstoned floor of the wine bar as he clumsily, angrily sat down. This time, he had bought a bottle of the house white. He drank greedily and refilled his glass at once, waggling the bottle at her. She nodded, out of insinuation, and he topped up her glass. Marian lit another cigarette.

'What precisely is wrong, Ray?' she soothed.

'Bloody everything!' he announced in a hoarse whisper, leaning across the table at her almost in challenge. 'Look, I raised this matter' — his Midlands accent had become more pronounced, as if he was consciously reinventing a former self, the rough, pushy, relatively honest jobbing building from the Black Country — 'at the last meeting with the main contractors. Fat lot of bloody use that was!' He seemed to become distracted by his anger. 'I could have sold the business five years ago for over two million — you know that? I didn't. Bloody *my* business and it stays my business, I thought. Wish I bloody had, now!'

'What's wrong?' she insisted. The undisguised emotion, the sense of a long perspective of bitterness, intrigued her further.

'The main contractors asked me to be patient! The grants or whatever from Brussels had been delayed, they were in the bloody post or something!' Despite himself, he grinned. 'I told 'em I thought they were hanging on to the money and us small fry could get stuffed, just so long as the flash projects were on schedule! They didn't like that!'

'Neither would I,' she murmured, 'if I had a knighthood and an income of three-quarters of a million a year and sat on the boards of four other companies.' He returned the smile.

'No, not Sir Desmond only — the whole bloody gang of 'em. Banks, the local politicians, the main contractors, the architects. Yes, the bloody symphony hall's on schedule, and the most pricey apartments, the office blocks. That's the façade. There's bugger all being done on other parts of the project. Piles of bricks and mountains of conduits lying around. Bloody scandal! And us poor buggers not getting paid, not even being allowed to get on with the first stages. So *I'm* left hanging on by my balls with the bank manager trying to climb up my backside to pull my teeth out!' His features were crimson, then suddenly abashed. 'Sorry . . .'

'Could you really become bankrupt?'

'Two months — at most.' He refilled his glass. 'Two bloody months before they wipe out twenty bloody years. And I'm not on my own. There's dozens of chippies and sparks, all small firms, suppliers and fitters, carpet, lighting, double-glazing . . . I was speaking for them as well as myself.'

'How *much* isn't being done to time?'

'About twenty-five per cent, maybe more . . . half a billion? A third, anyway. There's local money, from the councils, not up front yet. But that's normal for those tight-fisted buggers. And the Brussels money. Fifty, sixty million that's not appeared — *months* late.'

'You want me to make a fuss, is that it?' His eyes glowed, as if he had somehow encountered a movie actress long admired. 'Questions in the House, see the Minister, invite someone in front of the Select Committee . . . ?' He was nodding as eagerly as if she were proposing a series of increasingly bizarre erotic fantasies.

'Could you? I mean — would you?'

'I don't see why not. I'd like more information before I do, though — and no, not this evening. I have a lot of preparation for my surgery tomorrow. Can I ring you next week?' It was as if she had whisked away the prospect of sexual gratification, and with it his wallet. His lugubrious disappointment amused Marian. 'I *will* ring you, Ray — don't worry.'

Reluctantly, he acquiesced, then burst out: 'You could try asking them to stop putting the frighteners on, too, while you're at it!' His voice was barely above a fierce whisper, his face close to hers, his breath rancid with cheap wine. His sincerity was not in doubt, nor was his sudden, unnerved fear. 'I don't *like* it —'

'What's happening? What sort of thing?' There was a momentary image, no more than a single, subliminal frame of film, of Lloyd's body. There was the same impression of endangerment about Banks' words, the sweat on his damp brow, his high colour.

'Two small companies — a sparks and an air-conditioning contractor. They've both had recent fires at their premises. Yobbos, the police say. Vandals.' He breathed noisily. 'A car followed my Sandra home from school the other day. She couldn't get the number because it was covered up with mud, she said. I believe her!'

Until that moment, the room their conversation had inhabited had been familiar, and furnished as she would have expected, with all the glossy appurtenances of graft, fraud, bribery. Banks seemed to have pushed her through a door into another, unfamiliar room, where arson had occurred and a schoolgirl had been terrified on her way home.

'Should *I* believe her?' she asked carefully.

'The car was there the next day, too!'

'When exactly was this?'

'*After* I ballocked the board meeting. *After* I threatened to write to the papers, talk to you.' His breathing was louder than his voice.

She pushed her hair away from her face. The place seemed suddenly hot and noisy with empty conversations. Yet it was the wine bar that should have seemed normal, Banks' accusations wild and improbable. Except for Michael Lloyd's body on the carpet, seen through his letter box, and a girl followed twice by a strange, anonymous car, and two cases of arson.

'When were the fires?'

'*After* wards.'

After I threatened to . . . talk to you, she remembered, her stomach fluttery. *Whatever you do, do nothing,* Kenneth Aubrey had pleaded.

Kenneth's world had been very real for forty-five years, for the duration of the Cold War. It had been her father's world in part, too. It had never impinged on her until that moment. Now, the sense of threat was palpable, as if she had become one of Kenneth's agents, and had placed herself in some vague but immediate danger.

'You bloody come and see what a pig's ear the whole bloody project is — behind the fancy façade!' Banks challenged. 'Come and see for yourself — *then* tell me where all the bloody money's gone!'

The office of the deputy director of the NTSB, Jack Pierstone, was on one of the middle floors of the Federal Aviation Administration building on Independence Avenue. Its windows looked towards the Smithsonian, then across to the Mall, the Washington Monument and the Ellipse. The view was like an enhanced, wide-screen version of that from his own cramped office. The Washington Monument was bathed in a reddish-gold glow and the part of the Reflection Pool he could see looked like the strip on the reverse of a credit card.

Gant stood stiffly to attention, as if before a military hearing of braided and bemedalled senior officers. He'd done that, too, more than once. Jack Pierstone was having more problems than those senior officers, floundering and blustering as he tried to find the words with which to fire a hero.

'. . . didn't need this kind of publicity-seeking, this idea we offer insurance and backing to failing airline manufacturers,' Pierstone was saying as Gant continued to stare over his head at Washington.

He offered no assistance, no mitigation, but stood as unmoving as when, all those years ago, a general had hung the Medal of Honor around his neck. He was waiting until whatever was to happen to him was over. His eyes were narrowed against the low sun, not against the situation. Vance had screwed up his life once more. The thought was as quick as the spurt of blood from a fresh wound. Then, almost at once, the cynicism of the thought *What life?* stilled any sensation of pain.

'You took totally unreasonable and unsanctioned risks. You played personalities with this thing.' Pierstone's voice was becoming stronger with the outrage of embarrassment and self-justification. 'The TV business — it was like an endorsement. You had no authorisation to interfere with a South-Western accident investigation or to wilfully disobey standard procedures. *All* of which come before the FBI's allegations . . .'

Once again, the engine of his indignation was on the point of stalling. Gant realised that Pierstone had looked at him and seen — again — the uniform and the medal, maybe even the flying suit. 'I — have to suspend you, Mitchell. These are serious charges, especially the FBI investigation. I can't do anything *less*.'

Gant allowed the silence to continue, to build like the approach of a storm. Eventually, he said quietly: 'I'll resign, Jack. It's easier all around.' He did not look at Pierstone's small, coiled frame behind the desk, preferring the images of the Smithsonian and the spike of the Monument and the reddish glow of the sun. The thin clouds above the city had moved away like slow fish during the minutes of the interview.

Pierstone cleared his throat, fidgeted with papers on his desk.

'I don't know —'

'Yes, you do, Jack. If this had been for Boeing or McDonnell, maybe a blind eye would have been turned. For an airplane-maker important enough to the economy, we'd have been there like locusts. And hell, why not? It's all for the country and we can wrap ourselves in the flag. It's our job, our patriotic duty, to help out. Unless it's someone like Vance, maybe —'

'That's unfair and you know it!'

'Maybe it is. Besides, Jack, you can't be expected to override the Bureau. The FBI could be waiting on Independence Avenue right now to make an arrest. Nobody in Federal employment needs that kind of publicity.'

Gant looked down at the desk for the first time.

Tiny images of the sun, the museum and the Monument were superimposed for a moment on Pierstone's forehead and cheeks like tattoos.

'I resign, Jack. I'll put it in writing and take my chances with McIntyre. He's not too bright — maybe he'll screw up the investigation, who knows?' His smile was wintry. 'He's just motivated by his own failings, after all. The only reason he didn't get to 'Nam was for *medical* reasons, otherwise he'd have been the first to volunteer. You know how the song goes, Jack.'

Pierstone himself had flown in 'Nam earlier in the undeclared war than Gant himself, flying bombing missions from offshore carriers. Before the US had gotten into defoliation and bombing Cambodia and the Ho Chi Minh trail. Pierstone, as if the past were some kind of bond between them, grinned sourly and nodded.

'Sure.'

'I'll go draft a letter.'

'OK, Mitchell. I'm — er, sorry . . .'

'I know.'

Gant turned away from the windows and the desk and the man behind it. At the door, he heard Pierstone murmur:

'You take care, you hear.'

Gant waved his hand without turning round.

'Sure.'

Even before the door closed behind him, he felt the awareness of another failure surround him like a sudden, thick mist. Another screw-up in a life with more past than future. He passed through the outer office and into the corridor with quick, somehow leaden footsteps.

As he waited for the elevator to the foyer, he felt he wanted to silently scream. He could not be certain whether its cause was McIntyre's malice, Vance's ox-dumb stupidity in paying money into his bank account, or the sensation of the empty apartment that waited for him. That, and the sense of the aimless days he would be spending there.

CHAPTER FIVE

Social and Anti-Social

The effect of money had worn away as easily as that of a sedative. Strickland once more confronted his fear of hurry. Because of urgency, he had had to fly into Oslo's Fornebu airport direct, rather than to Stockholm or Copenhagen, or even Bergen, where he could have approached the target obliquely and anonymously. He had disguised his departure from France by flying from Bordeaux to Geneva, then by changing flights and airlines again at Frankfurt before the journey to Oslo. But, somewhere, for someone who might look, there was the record of his arrival at Fornebu, the scene of his sabotage. Even with a false passport and identity, a stooping walk and greyed hair and a moustache that aged him a decade, he had *arrived* in Oslo.

He sat in the arrivals lounge, sweating in his crumpled linen suit, his cabin bag beside him, regretting with venomous bitterness the greed — so it seemed to him now — that had swept aside his habitual, talismanic caution, his profound resolve that he *did not work on site,* he must be *always hands-off.* It was his only, but his adamantine, rule of engagement; his code of professional conduct. It had been forged in the aftermath of a debacle when not only had his own bomb almost killed him but the opposition had been waiting for him. Since then, he had always created while others placed his devices in position. He should *not* have broken his own code . . .

His nerves jangled, his body temperature fluctuated as if he were passing through the rooms of a bath-house, from sauna to cold dip to sauna again. He glimpsed, like an arachnophobe might have seen in a shadowy corner a large and poisonous spider, his fear of Winterborne and his gofer, Fraser. It was the same fear that had broken in upon him after Fraser and Roussillon had left the farmhouse.

He'd cooked them a Dordogne peasant stew, served them wine and coffee, signed the contract, received the down payment, seen them from the premises. With the washing-up done and the cat on his lap, he had suddenly sat bolt upright in his chair as the last of the daylight darkened outside. The cat had scratched his thighs in surprise. Strickland had realised that he had been afraid not to agree, afraid not to take the money. Winterborne, using Fraser as his mouthpiece, had effectively insinuated that they would kill him without hesitation if he did not assist them . . . despite their knowledge that he stored, in a safety deposit box in Rome, meticulous and incriminating records of every assignment he had carried out. Against Winterborne, he was certain that evidence no longer offered a guarantee of his safety.

So, he had agreed. The price-hike had been a mere formality.

He glanced up. The long northern evening lay like a golden cloud over Oslo and the sloping land with the narrow Oslofjord beyond it. The panoramic windows of the passenger lounge let in too much landscape and seemed to expose him as the only still, fixed figure in the lounge's terrain.

Simple job . . . your own cleverness . . . The fragments of his self-assurance glinted like a window shattered by an explosion, but would not cohere. An airliner lifted into the evening, turning orange-red then golden then silver as it rose into the rays of the low sun, navigation lights winking. Beyond the main runway were the airport's maintenance hangars, liveried planes dotted around them. *Simple job . . .* The replacement fuel computer system circuitry lay innocuously inside his PC, in the cabin bag. *Simple job . . . your cleverness . . .* The papers that described him as an engineer with Vance Aircraft were in his pocket. One of the two Vance 494 airplanes was in a maintenance hangar for overnight checks before resuming its schedule of shuttle flights around the Scandinavian capitals . . . *Simple job,* then, to appear overalled beside it, to replace the fuel computer board with his own, which contained the redoctored chip which would jettison the fuel while the instruments continued to read normally . . . and which would *now* reconfigure itself on impact or engine-stop, declaring itself to be harmless, fully operative. This time there would be no trace, no ability to outguess him and recognise sabotage . . . *simple.*

He breathed a little more easily, his chest less asthmatically tight with the tension that Winterborne, his location, his immediate future all generated. It *was* that simple. One more appalling crash and the 494 would be consigned to aviation notoriety and history. Gant could not this time interpose nimblemindedness and experience between his design and execution. It would all happen with the functional reliability of an electronic component. Perhaps two dozen people would die, since passengers were reluctant still to trust the 494. The carnage would be minimal — stand-by tourists and commuters — but sufficient. The 494 would be grounded, Vance Aircraft would collapse, imploding under the pressure of the banks, the NTSB, the European politicians.

He admired Winterborne's ruthlessness. However, after this, he would walk away. Disappear for a time. One of his other boltholes rather than the Dordogne farmhouse whose tranquillity he so much valued.

Strickland glanced at his watch. Eight in the evening. They'd be working on the 494 for most of the night. He had time for a meal. Yes . . . his stomach seemed much less unsettled since he had refused the plastic tray of food on the flight from Frankfurt. He stood up, picked up his bag, and began searching the overhead signs for the location of the restaurant. *Simple job . . .*

The long Georgian façade of Uffingham was

floodlit against an orange sunset as her constituency agent's Land Rover came out of the avenue of oaks and the house surprised her, as it always did, with memories and its own beauty. It was, in Pevsner, the *most beautiful house in Warwickshire, perhaps the entire Midlands,* and to her it was utterly precious. She had spent many of her childhood holidays there, with or without her parents, depending on Daddy's postings and Mummy's eagerness or reluctance to accompany him. She had, in an important sense, grown up there, perhaps even more so than David Winterborne and his brother.

Clive Winterborne's family had owned the house for six generations — someone in their military, clerical and political ancestry *had been in trade,* she often reminded Clive, to have afforded such a house and estate in the middle of the last century; its building and inhabitation having bankrupted the gentrified Whig family who had created Uffingham. Clive had inherited the house from a bachelor uncle, having refused all interest — except his massive shareholding — in the Winterborne commercial empire, founded and web-centred in Singapore in the heyday of political empire. Instead, he had fallen into the role that nature, looks and habit seemed to have designed him for, that of paternalistic country gentleman. His Eurasian wife, whom Marian always had difficulty remembering — which saddened her — had returned to England with him after the army in Malaya and elsewhere. Just as he had wanted nothing to do with Winterborne Holdings, so he had disdained MoD, even against her father's blandishments. Instead, he had given himself, increasingly and with a seeming urgency after the death of his beloved wife, to good works . . . one of which had been to persuade her, so he always maintained, to first stand for the constituency.

Is it in your gift? she had asked. Laughing, he had replied, *Probably.*

She smiled now, remembering, as the Land Rover climbed the curving drive up to the house. A long stone balustrade, like a fortress' ramparts, contained the forecourt and the house as it looked southwards over farmland. The vehicle passed a huge urn sprouting a profusion of summer colour, and began threading its way across the gravel between the litter of Rolls Royces, Porsches, BMWs, Volvos and four-wheel drive executive weekend vehicles. Chauffeurs lounged against dark limousines.

Marian was grateful to breathe in the fresh evening air.

Swallows swooped about the house and she heard the screams of mobbing swifts. She caught a glimpse of them flicking amid the forest of chimneys. The Vanbrugh façade, cream in memory, was garish in the floodlighting. The doors beneath the portico were wide and lights spilled out. She could hear faint music, fainter than the rustle of Bill's wife's acres of taffeta and silk as she climbed from the high front passenger seat. The gorgeous redundancy of material in the gown, and its ladybird colours of red and black, rendered her own costume more mannish than ever. She had decided on her close impersonation of a man's dinner jacket and trousers, her hair tied back in a brief, bushed tail, her waistcoat shimmering like petrol in a pool of water.

'OK, Pat?' she asked as the central locking bleeped to Bill's satisfaction. His wife glanced up, as if the creases of travel in her gown were a matter of reproof from Marian, then she continued smoothing the taffeta and silk into pre-inspection satisfaction. She evidently felt Marian's outfit the next most obvious declaration of sexual orientation to dungarees. 'Good!' Marian announced brightly, wishing for a cigarette. She had not smoked in the Land Rover out of deference to Pat's intense hatred of tobacco . . . but perhaps the mannish suit might relieve her jealous suspicions of Bill's relationship with her. Poor Bill . . .

'You look gorgeous,' he dutifully informed Pat, who visibly brightened. Then they were crunching over the gravel towards the house, mincing between Jaguars, a pair of matching Ferraris, down the tall alleyways of off-road vehicles clustered as thickly as at some large agricultural show. More thickly, she observed.

Bill appeared nervous, Pat suppressed like a water main on the point of bursting. Two compliments at her gown, a peck or two on the cheek from the moneyed or notable, and she would become a swan, having been a self-conscious duckling. Then Marian saw Clive, hovering beneath the portico as if he was unsure whether or not he had an invitation to his own house. Once he recognised her — the smile at her outfit was immediate and gently sardonic, his widened eyes registering Pat's confection — he seemed enlivened, certain.

She kissed his drawn, leathery cheeks as she had so often done, then he was shaking hands with Bill and Pat. David Winterborne, his features less patrician than those of his father, his eyes less welcoming, stood just behind Clive. Yet he, too, seemed to brighten, even if only at the memory of an old antagonism, as he saw her.

'Hi, Davey.' The diminutive had always irritated him.

'Hi, Squirt.'

They embraced almost by instinct, warily and briefly, yet with the warmth of the long-familiar. Then Clive was fussing them into the cavernous main hall, which extended from the front to the rear of the house. The columns, niches, statuary, the matching pair of Daniel Quare longcase clocks were all so familiar to her that she almost turned off to the closed doors of the library or the drawing room.

'The band is on the terrace, and the tent is on the lawn,' Clive offered brightly, and she patted his arm. He, her father and dear Kenneth ranged themselves always in her imagination like great ancestral portraits, dwarfing the other men she had known, making them invidious by comparison. 'Kenneth's hovering somewhere near the musicians — perhaps one day he may learn to enjoy Mozart!' Clive added, shaking his head mischievously. Then: 'I'm displeased with that father of yours, my dear — why he needs to have a regimental reunion tonight of all nights, I do not understand!' Smiling, he shooed her onwards down the hall, towards the already apparent, slight and stooping figure of Kenneth Aubrey. Marian was struck, with a piercing sadness, by the age of the two old men, their decrepitude, as if it had been suddenly exposed by a bright, merciless light.

Almost in apology, she grabbed at Aubrey's arm and floridly introduced him to Bill and Pat — the latter returning her attention from the portraits, busts and ornate plasterwork. Aubrey's knighthood seemed to work on her like rough liquor, quickly animating. Then the cool air of the terrace at the rear of the house and a glass of chilled champagne in her hand from a subtly, silently offered tray. A chamber orchestra, to one end of the terrace, was playing one of Mozart's serenades. Some more elderly guests were seated on folding chairs, attentive. On the great lawn below the terrace, a huge marquee festooned with lights seemed to swallow eager guests. She heard ducks from the lake, disturbed by the people making last-minute checks on the firework display. She remembered from her childhood how the explosions would frighten the ducks, as the lights and flares and colours reflected in the lake. Beyond, where darkness gathered, Warwickshire fell away from the rise on which Uffingham sat proprietorially in rolling farmland, the first few hundred acres of which belonged to Clive.

The Millennium Children's Fund, Clive's anti-Lottery inspiration, had brought out the great and good of the West Midlands in force, she acknowledged, nodding to two businessmen of her acquaintance and a matron recently ennobled for charitable works. A hundred and fifty pounds per head, food and fireworks and a tantalising glimpse of the kind of property old money still inhabited — cheap at the price. There was even to be a disco after the fireworks, to the further perturbation of the wildfowl.

She gestured towards the marquee, squeezing Aubrey's arm and bending her head to whisper.

'You won't find the Tory party at prayer in the C of E any longer — more likely in one of those.'

'Mm — there did seem to be a great many *sports* cars arriving earlier, I have to admit. Margaret's real children, I imagine?' He glanced at her, his faded eyes alight with mischief.

'They're not in the Ferraris and the Porsches. Greed is still good only if it wears green wellies and drives an off-road vehicle,' she responded. '*No* politics. I warn you, Kenneth —'

He pressed her arm against his side.

'Like all pensioners, I'm already hungry and inordinately interested in what is on offer,' he said. 'You may help me down the steps.'

'Very well. I shall wear you like a crucifix, it might help ward off the vampires —' She waved to someone, then her hand remained aloft as she said: 'I've just seen the EU Commissioner for Urban Development — the old apple himself.'

'Laxton? Yes. I'm Clive's house guest, along with one or two other old decrepits. He arrived this afternoon, as a guest of David. Along with his fellow-Commissioner, Rogier, your Euro MP counterpart, Ben Campbell, and a few other specimens. My room overlooks the front of the house. I saw them arriving — what is it?'

'These same people keep cropping up —'

'— and always in connection with David. Quite.'

A group passed them, the women tottering on the highest, narrowest heels on to the steps down to the lawn, the men busily engaged with the first champagne and the rear elevation of Uffingham.

'I think I might have a word with Ben Campbell, if I can find him in the crush. He may be indiscreet, drop a few hints . . .' She paused and swallowed, then added: 'As to why the same men who were at the meeting observed by Michael Lloyd are meeting again. Mm?' Aubrey's face darkened with warning. Marian added brightly: 'Come on, I'll get you a bun and a glass of milk before I set off in search of him!'

Why, she thought, as they descended the steps, *are* they here? The men who met in Brussels. Her suspicions altered her mood and seemed to change the familiar terrace and the lawn more than the erection of the marquee and the presence of the chamber orchestra. Gales of noise rose from the marquee and she heard the futile little protests of the wildfowl. The barking of dogs.

'Did you discover who owns Complete Security?' His manner seemed suddenly, inexplicably furtive. 'Kenneth?' she demanded. Aubrey shrugged.

'It — um, it's a subsidiary of Winterborne Holdings, I'm afraid.'

'I don't believe in coincidence — do you?'

'I'd much rather you did, Marian,' the old man warned.

She ignored him, her eyes alight. 'I *wonder* . . .'

she breathed. But at once they were amid the distraction of a scrum of guests. The Lord-Lieutenant of the county and his large-bosomed wife, a scattering of local politicians and gentry like attendant lords swelling the scene. Small, louder-laughing groups of younger people, in gowns like modernist daubs that rustled of new money. The lights, candlelike though they were, seemed to affect her; they or the noise, so that she paused until she regained her equilibrium. No . . . She must not wonder anything of the kind, for that would mean making connections between Michael Lloyd's death and people she knew, had grown up with . . . Unforgivable; impossible.

Gales of laughter like contrary winds blowing between the kind of reddened, inflated faces that used to feature in the corners of old maps. *Here be monsters* — such warnings were imprinted for those who strayed out of the known seaways, the familiar trading routes. *Here be* . . . She craned her neck, trying to catch sight of Campbell. That would be somewhere to begin.

'I warned you, my dear,' Aubrey whispered, clinging to her like a child might have done, but anciently aware of her thoughts, like a sibyl.

'*You* wouldn't have listened to you,' she retorted. More laughter, callow and momentary, but now it seemed cruel, unfeeling. 'Should I?'

Acting was a skill at anonymity. He had always enjoyed the role-playing element of his intelligence career — the cover stories, the false identities, the disguise of himself. Standing in the great open doorway of the cathedral of the maintenance hangar, that sense of satisfaction returned, like the rediscovery of an old pastime.

'Sure,' he found himself easily announcing, 'girls in offices, they screw up. Alan Vance put me on a flight over here, and here I am. He's just making double sure, I guess.' Then he waited patiently, the smile retained like a credential, as the chief engineer subcontracted by Artemis Airways once more studied his papers. A few moments later, he offered: 'Call the number — make the check.' Even that invitation to be unmasked seemed to come easily, with hardly any constriction in his throat.

The Norwegian engineer looked up at him, and nodded.

'Your guy was lucky, *ja?*' he grinned. 'The Seventh Cavalry came to the rescue, and no mistake!'

'Sure.' Understanding that he was accepted as the deputy chief engineer of Vance Aircraft in Phoenix, he moved forward, nudging the Norwegian into turning with him. They began walking. 'The system we used on these two, this one and its twin —' As the Norwegian compliantly kept pace with him, he gestured towards the 494, the engine cowling bared like a striptease artiste's shoulder. The plane was surrounded by the metal cages of gantries and inspection hoists, fussed at by perhaps half a dozen overalled figures as ceremoniously as women arranging flowers in a church. '— not the same as the one in the accident. But Al Vance wants me *to make sure* — there's too much to lose if anything goes wrong.' He clapped his large hand on the man's shoulder. 'I won't get in your way. It's just the fuel computer I need to check over. Maybe an hour, maybe even less before I'm out of your hair.'

'You want coffee?'

'Great.'

'I'll organise it. You just go ahead —' He waved towards the aircraft.

Strickland grinned at the man's retreating back, then stretched small nerves out of his frame. He was now dressed in a check shirt, denims, high-heeled boots, a leather jacket. Maybe they would expect to see a stetson, but his sense of understatement had refused the notion. Idly, he walked towards the four-storey dock which was positioned halfway along the fuselage of the 494. Metal ladders, metal handrails, making the aircraft appear imprisoned. He watched it move on its rails, the motors whining, creeping like the shadow of an elaborate gallows along the liveried fuselage. For Strickland, there was the satisfaction of machines, the smell of oils, of metals, the single-mindedness of the service engineers.

It was eleven-thirty by his watch. After his meal, he had hired a car in the name under which he had flown in. He would be away from Fornebu by twelve-thirty, claiming that he was booked into one of the airport hotels until his return flight to the US the following afternoon. Then he would drive to Larvik and catch the ferry for Copenhagen. He could fly direct to Paris, then on to Bordeaux . . . then he would disappear for a while.

The huge flanged wheels of the dock ground along their rails and men moved purposefully around the aircraft. He clambered up the steps to the open mouth of the electrics bay of the 494, swinging his cabin bag into the hard-lit space, his head and shoulders following. An electrical engineer turned to him, at first surprised then rendered docile and accepting by Strickland's confidence and the voice of the chief engineer from the foot of the steps.

'You want your coffee up there — you ready to start right away?'

Strickland looked down from the hatch.

'Up here — and thanks. I'll get right on to it. It was a long flight and the movie was terrible!' He grinned confidentially. 'I don't blame you Europeans complaining about American culture — man, that movie!'

'We pretty much enjoy American movies,' the Norwegian replied, handing him the plastic cup. It burned his fingers and he set it down on the floor of the bay which lay beneath the first-class compartment. 'That's Jorgensen,' he continued. 'You need his help?'

Strickland smiled at Jorgensen, then shook his head.

'It's just a coupla panels — no trouble, nothing heavy to lift. Thanks, anyway —'

'Sure. I'll leave you to get on with it.'

As soon as his head disappeared from the open hatch, Strickland held out his hand to the Norwegian electrical engineer.

'Cal Massey,' he announced. 'Vance Aircraft.'

'Sure.'

Jorgensen took his hand briefly, then at once returned to his inspection of the auxiliary power unit. He whistled between his teeth, some low, crooning Norwegian dirge. Strickland sipped his coffee — too much sugar, but then he hadn't specified — as he sat cross-legged in the narrow, racked, luggage-compartment-like electrics bay. Thick bundles of wiring passed overhead and along the metal walls, ropy and multicoloured like the old diagrams in a school science lab of the human body's muscles, arteries and veins. Banks of switches, backup systems, relays, batteries in racked order, like a library of electronics. The slow, submarine growl of flanged wheels on rails came to him from the hangar as he sat, patient and absorbed as a boy brought there by some adult as a birthday treat.

Eventually, Jorgensen muttered: 'That's me finished.' He stood up in the cramped space and stretched. 'That's what the manual calls for,' he added, seeming to resent Strickland's silence, even his presence.

Of course, he was from Vance Aircraft . . .

'It's just a five-hundred-hour overnighter — I know that,' he soothed. 'I'm not here to watch you, fella. I'm here because of what happened back in Phoenix.'

'You know how that happened?'

'We do now — thanks to that pilot. He worked it out. I'm just here to check there's nothing wrong with the fuel computer system on this baby.'

Now that he was assured he was under no kind of examination, Jorgensen's thin features lost all interest. He yawned extravagantly.

'Maybe I'll catch the wife with her lover,' he muttered, looking at his watch. He seemed possessed of the kind of gloomy northern temperament that expected such surprises. As if to confirm Strickland's impression, he added: 'If the damn car starts. I had trouble with it this morning . . .' He was already descending the steps, then his shoulders and thin, narrow features disappeared through the hatch.

Strickland tossed his head in dismissive mockery, then swallowed the last of his coffee. He put down the plastic cup and dragged his cabin bag behind him as he crabbed on his haunches along the racks of boxes, batteries, wiring. He paused before the labelled rack holding the fuel management system.

Kneeling, he opened a small toolkit and began unscrewing the panel of the fuel computer, the twin of the model in his barn in the Dordogne. Familiar as an often-possessed body, supple and known under his touch. He, too, began whistling through his teeth as he studied the relays, chips and circuitry.

Simple job . . .

She was penned near one idly flapping wall of the huge marquee by the chairman of the local party, who conveyed to her with overbearing gravity and at great length the displeasure of Central Office. He had been rung at home by a party deputy chairman who was a former advertising executive. The chairman's wife, with fussy grace, was attempting to moderate her husband's effective impression of a patronising sexual chauvinist. Marian nodded and smiled and held herself erect with the intent vacuity of a mannequin, her wine warming in her grip, her plate of salmon and salad untouched. *It would be rude to stuff one's face while being lectured.* She forced the laughter from her eyes and made a vast effort to control her features.

'Absolutely, George,' she agreed, nodding vigorously. 'Absolutely.' The chairman was convinced that loyalty was something genetic, a measurement of the evolution of the species. The pressure of Central Office was mounting with each passing week of the summer, in anticipation of an autumn election. No one had decided a date, of course — except perhaps that political manipulist, *Events*. 'Of course, I entirely agree — *not* without proper consultation, not even when we're still thirty points behind in the polls.' Her election agent's features sagged at the jibe. Pat, beside Bill and slightly in awe of the chairman's wife — hers was older money and she was far better educated — was engaged in a pretence of interest in matters political.

The chairman was angry at an article Marian had written for the *Telegraph* on the European issue. His features were suffused with more than wine and food and the heat of the marquee.

'Just so, George,' she offered into another long, slow pause in his harangue. George was running out of steam. Not long now . . . There was already a general drift from the marquee to the lawns in anticipation of the fireworks.

Suddenly, as if his wife had decided that Marian's patience had been put to a sufficient test, she took the chairman's arm and murmured:

'Come on, dear — I'd like a *good* view of the fireworks.'

George seemed reluctant to let Marian slip,

then patted his wife's hand and nodded.

'Goodbye, my dear. Think about —' But his wife was already drawing him away, a smile of genuine affection, even admiration for Marian on her lips.

The marquee continued to empty, the long trestles of food and the copious drink temporarily abandoned for the lawns and the lake. The ducks and wildfowl had, with the wisdom of foresight, long since retired to more distant water. Marian swigged at her Chablis.

'Phew — crikey!' she said mockingly, smiling at Bill. Pat seemed puzzled, Bill irritated. 'I *listened,* Bill,' she soothed, forcing a nod of admission from her agent.

Ben Campbell, the Euro MP for the constituency that contained her own, was approaching, shepherding a group which included Bryan Coulthard, the CEO of Aero UK. *Another of the conspirators,* she thought, the notion changing from amusement to chill in an instant. She waved at Ben Campbell over Bill's head, but he seemed intent on ignoring her and his party passed out of the marquee. She had seen the two EU Commissioners, too, from time to time, glimpsing them across the crowded marquee. Pleasure did not seem their pursuit, but she may have been mistaken.

'Hello, Marian!' she heard, as Pat was attempting to move Bill out on to the lawn.

She looked down. Pat seized the opportunity to distance herself from Marian.

'Hello, Sam.' They shook hands.

'Sorry to mess you about — cancelling our

meeting, after ringing your office.' Egan almost purred.

'It wasn't important then?'

'No. Forget it.' He winked. 'Thought you could put in a word about . . . but the matter sorted itself out just after I called you.' His smile was eager.

Sam Egan was short, plump, apparently jolly. A great many of his business rivals had been disarmed by his appearance and been taken up the garden path at the same time by the shrewd brain behind the innocent, slightly myopic eyes. His wife was sunbed-browned to a crisp, and there was too much middle-aged flesh revealed by her voluminous frock. She disliked Marian, seeming to distrust her husband's association with her. Egan's lump of a gold watch and his gold bracelets caught the subdued lights of the marquee. His face was shining.

She remembered, Sam Egan's company, Egan Construction, was heavily involved with the Urban Regeneration Project — mostly beyond the constituency, though he and his wife lived just outside the cathedral city. Had he experienced difficulties with cash-flow, like Ray Banks? What *had* he wanted to see her about?

The remainder of Egan's party had already disappeared. One or two of the men, sleeked and coiffured, had glanced at her stature, her features, then seemed somehow disappointed at her mannish suit.

'Sam,' she murmured, taking his arm and bending her lips to his ear, to Mrs Egan's evident irritation, 'a little bird told me that there are funding problems on the Regeneration Project . . . Anything in it?'

His reaction surprised. A natural and comfortable assurance, a sense of his having eaten and drunk well but not to excess, was removed like a disguise. He was at once possessed of a suspicious, drunklike aggression towards her.

'*Who* told you?' It was as if someone had initiated a damaging rumour about his company or his sexual capacity. His hand gripped her arm, champagne spilling from his flute on to the sleeve of her suit. 'You don't want to listen to bloody rumours, Marian — there's always a couple of whingeing buggers in the construction trade . . .' The words seemed like a mantra, recited to recapture calm, confidence, repose. His smile faltered like a neon striplight, then came on. There remained, however, an edge of warning in his voice. 'You don't want to listen to gossip, Marian. I'm surprised. You want to see it, some time. It's going to be a bloody marvel . . . We don't need people running it down — sounds like a London attitude to the Midlands to me!' The smile remained like that of the Cheshire Cat, but around it Egan's features hardened rather than disappeared. His eyes studied her flintily.

'Well, that's good news, anyway,' Marian soothed and disarmed. 'Just what I was hoping to hear.'

'Who's been bending your ear, Marian?'

' "The isle is full of noises",' she quoted, smiling. 'Just something I heard — cash flow, late payments —' Egan's features distorted in a grimace of anger, then he masked it by raising his champagne flute to his lips.

The moment was tense, filled with suspicion, until it was defused by Egan's wife, who spotted a woman with a small role in a regional TV soap with whom she shared a hairdresser. Waving, she dragged Egan reluctantly away with her other hand. Little sparks of suspicion, even anger, played around his features like a dull St Elmo's Fire as he departed.

The marquee was all but empty. It was no more than a moment or two before she replenished her plate with prawns and more salad, had her glass refilled. The encounter with Sam Egan clung about her like a chill mist. There had been knowledge, and the attempt to disguise it, in his eyes; the sense of secrecy.

Marian wandered out of the marquee into cooler air and the anticipatory noises of the guests. A smile slowly spread across her face as she walked towards the house. She knew *exactly* where she needed to be to watch the firework display, a window from which she had watched such events as a child. Had Clive's Silver Wedding been one such occasion? The playroom window on the top floor of the house — the idea amused and attracted her. She'd watched the domestic rituals of the gardens, the loves and quarrels and hoeing and planting, from that window. In the company of David and his long-dead brother . . .

She climbed the steps to the rear terrace, pausing to look back at the floodlit guests like a corralled horde of peacocks and blackbirds. Then she entered the house. The housekeeper smiled at her with an old, affectionate familiarity, shrugging at the litter of abandoned glasses and plates obscuring the polish and inlay of eighteenth-century tables. Marian shook her head in sympathy.

The long hall was deserted, silent after the babble outside. Then she heard a voice she recognised, and another so recently familiar, raised in quarrel. She hovered, feeling exposed and foolish in the middle of the hall, standing on a faded Persian carpet that covered the marble floor. She had no real sense why she had paused to listen. She had heard no distinct words, only David's raised voice — and that of Sam Egan. Where — ?

In the shadow of the staircase, only yards from her . . . It cantilevered over her head towards the gallery on her right, its other branch, like some great upended railway junction, leading to the rooms of the west wing. She moved stealthily, startled by the sound of her own name. Except for the three of them, the hall was empty. She shivered as the first of the fireworks exploded to dutiful noises of acclaim and surprise. She pressed into the alcove on the opposite side of the staircase, hearing her name again.

'. . . Marian knows nothing!' That was David, the contempt clear in his tone. 'Whatever she's heard, or thinks she's heard, she knows nothing!'

'She's suspicious, I tell you,' Egan persisted. 'I know when someone's trying to dig up information. She thinks there's something in the rumours —'

'Who's been speaking to her?'

'Could be anyone —'

'Keep your voice down!' David hissed.

Marian felt heated. She had blundered into the conversation with Egan, disarmed by the occasion, and her own self-confidence.

'All right, all right. I just thought I'd better let you know.'

'Because you panicked, Sam?' David mocked. '*Panic* was why you called her the other day, wasn't it?'

'I thought —'

'— she could or would *help*. Marian? A blessing I stopped you before you went bleating to her! Listen to me — find out who may have talked to her. You know all the local subcontractors. It must have been one of them. Find out — and let me know.'

'I'll do that,' Egan reassured.

'Good. Now, go and see the fireworks — before that wife of yours thinks you've sneaked up to a bedroom with one of the catering staff!' Immediate footsteps. Then David added with contemptuous venom: 'The fireworks cost my father a small fortune. Try to enjoy them.'

Marian pressed back into the alcove and the shadow of the staircase. Egan passed her hiding-place without glancing in her direction, attracted by another explosion and a flash of multicoloured light that seemed to blow into the house like a stream of confetti. Weak-legged from tension, Marian sank on to a hard Caroline chair in the alcove and sipped furiously at her wine. More fireworks exploded.

Kenneth Aubrey tottered in from the rear terrace, his stick making severe tapping noises on the marble. He passed Egan in the doorway.

'Kenneth!' she whispered hoarsely, jumping from the chair, spilling the last drops of her wine.

Aubrey turned, half-startled, half-preoccupied. He was opposite the door of the library which she heard close with a heavy, comfortable sound. More fireworks, more exhaled wonder.

'Marian . . . What is it, my dear?' He glanced towards the library. ' "In close recess and secret conclave",' he murmured.

'What?' Her nerves made her voice sharp.

'Oh, Milton. Your friends are all foregathered — in there. I glimpsed them as the door closed. A tight little group portrait. Laxton, Rogier, the Transport Commissioner, Bryan Coulthard, David, of course . . . and that Euro MP, what's his name — ?'

'Ben Campbell. He is forgettable,' she smiled.

'You look shaken — inattentively so.'

'They were talking about me — David and a builder who lives in the constituency. I'd been talking to him a few minutes' before . . . What's going on, Kenneth?'

'What were they saying?' Aubrey asked heavily. 'About you?'

'Egan thought I was too suspicious about the possibility of fraud in the —'

'I warned you, Marian!' Aubrey snapped. 'You revealed your hand?'

'I didn't think — !'

'Then do so now.' He patted her arm as they leant together.

'Egan, the builder, thought I was trying to open a can of worms, that much was obvious. I asked him about cash flow, late payments. Things I'd heard — doesn't matter from where. He jumped to everyone's defence then rushed to tell David I was asking awkward questions.'

There was something more alert and houndlike about Aubrey as he listened. Concern for her, expressed as irritated anxiety, faded and was replaced by a voracious curiosity. He continually glanced towards the closed door of the library.

'There is knowledge they are afraid you may possess. Concerning —'

'My fraud theory? You don't believe me at last?'

'Something, anyway — and it involves money. Probably a very great deal of it.'

The firework explosions were more frequent now, as if heralding some climax. Flashes of coloured light were caught by mirrors, polished surfaces.

'Michael Lloyd . . . ?' she remembered. Then, clearing her throat as Aubrey glanced anxiously at her, she said: 'I spoke to a subcontractor yesterday, working on the Urban Regeneration Project. He believes he's being threatened, along with his family, because he complained. The money's dried up for the smaller fish. He wasn't getting paid by Euro-Construction —'

'— which is wholly owned by Winterborne Holdings, who are principal contractors for —'

'— as much as thirty per cent of the whole project. European funds are pouring in. Brussels thinks of it as a model for the future of the EU, price no object . . .'

'And the funds appear not to be flowing *out* again.' Aubrey took her arm. 'Come on, my girl

— I think another drink is called for. Clive's best whisky, I fancy. He'll not mind.'

'Where is Clive?'

'Rattling the tin under the noses of the richest guests by this time, I should think.' A cacophony of explosions; cheering and clapping after a momentary, stunned silence. 'We need to talk. Come!'

Twelve-sixteen. He looked up from the flight engineer's panel on the flight deck of the 494 as the Norwegian chief engineer's slight form appeared in the doorway.

'All finished,' Strickland announced.

'Good — you want more coffee? How is she?'

'Fine. No problems. Yes to coffee. I'll come out. The fuel computer's OK, so are the instrument readouts.'

'What did happen — the crash?'

'It's still being analysed, all the data. It looks like a rogue chip — not the one used in this baby — gave the command to jettison the fuel but there were no readouts that didn't say everything was normal . . . It was lucky the pilot spotted it. It won't happen again.'

Strickland closed the door of the flight deck behind him and followed the Norwegian to the main passenger door. The routine servicing of the 494 — all such effort soon to be wasted — continued at its unhurried pace.

'We've had no problems over the past six months,' the Norwegian offered. 'She's a good plane.'

'At Vance Aircraft we like to think so. And do

we need the *world* to think like you!'

'Come in the office, have your coffee there.'

'Sure. Thanks.'

He turned to look back at the 494. The huge dock had been moved back, away from the aircraft, and it sat in the hangar like some fabulous sea mammal thought extinct but utterly real, alive. He could regret what he had arranged for the fate of the airplane, even if the lives of its crew and passengers failed to impinge. It was, like all aircraft, proof of the beauty of machines.

There was a sardonic amusement in his situation. The chief engineer obviously wanted to grill him on the Phoenix crash. Professional curiosity. Who better than himself to explain in detail, after all . . . ?

There was bright morning light coming through the heavy drapes of the bedroom windows. Almost ten. The bed beside him was empty, cool. Charley had got up without disturbing him.

He fumbled for the telephone which had woken him. He hadn't slept well, endlessly rehearsing his meeting with yet more bankers and institutional shareholders, as if recollecting each move in a game of chess . . . a game which he feared, last night, he might have lost, despite his bravado and Vance's good news from Phoenix. That pilot, Gant — his ex-son-in-law — amazing . . . But the men in suits were cautious; soaked by a sudden shower, they seemed to expect another at any moment. TV in America, images of Gant and Vance and the plane, the initial explanations of a rogue chip in the fuel computer system, Vance's lawsuit against the manufacturer . . . none of it seemed to have borne them along. He decided, before he finally fell asleep beside an anxiously wakeful Charley, that his exhilaration, fed by champagne and a few necessary pills, had failed to convince them.

'Burton.'

'Tim — !' It was Stuart, his MD. 'Christ, Tim, it's happened again!'

'What?' He struggled upright in the suddenly heavy bedclothes, the entwining sheets and duvet.

'Fifty miles from Helsinki, no more. It went down, Tim — it went down!'

'One of our — ?' He could not, *could not,* ask.

'Oslo to Helsinki, early-morning flight. She was fucking *serviced* last fucking *night,* Tim —'

'How — ?'

'Nothing on that yet. Oh, Jesus Christ, Tim — we're *done for!*'

'How — how many died?'

'Everyone. Seven crew, forty-four passengers. She was running almost empty . . .'

'Yes . . . there's that, at least,' Burton replied, watching himself in a cheval mirror in one corner of the bedroom as carefully as if studying his performance on a television monitor. He would be doing that endlessly, later . . . 'Forty-four passengers, you said?'

'Yes.'

'God, it's awful. I mean — it's really *appalling.*' He felt shaken, made nauseous, by the sense of lives lost. It overpowered all other sensations, even those that already dragged at him concerning the immediate future. *Forty-four.* And the crew. And the plane had been almost empty . . . God, it was dreadful.

'What do you want me to do immediately, Tim?'

'What — ? Oh, yes. A bland press release — but emphasise the tragedy, our sorrow. We know *nothing more* at the moment. Get us both on a flight to Helsinki early tomorrow. I'll have to be here to field all the interviews today. God —' he breathed as the nausea and shock gripped him once more. 'It's not possible — not *another* . . .'

An immediate future of hysterical accusations, tirades that damned himself, Vance and the plane. Experts dragged into studios all over the world to pronounce judgement. The fall of the share price, the panic of the lenders . . . Forty-four people. And the crew. It was —

He threw aside the telephone and rushed from the bed towards the bathroom, the nausea overwhelming him, already bitter in his throat.

PART TWO

A Dark Philanthropy

My politics are the politics of honest folks . . . I'm grateful to the government when business is prosperous, when I can eat my meals in peace and comfort, and can sleep at nights without being awakened by the firing of guns . . . Now that we have got the Empire, everything prospers. We sell our goods readily enough. You can't deny it. Well, what is it that you want? How will you be better off when you have shot everybody?

Emile Zola, *Le Ventre de Paris*

CHAPTER SIX

Summer Lightning

The lights from the town of Tammisaari glowed as fitfully and hopelessly as distress maroons through the summer thunder storm that enraged the Gulf of Finland around the tiny islet on which they hunched against the howling wind. Burton felt his whole body numbed by the aftershock of the accident, as if he had been hurried to this place by plane, limousine, motorboat only to collide with the debris of his airliner — his entire airline.

Below the small, naked promontory on which he was standing, men scurried like crabs across sharp rocks and around the wreckage of the 494. Somewhere down there was Gant, authorised by himself and Alan Vance, who stood mutely stunned beside him, his daughter clinging to him as to an uncertain rock. The behaviour of the inspectors, the floating crane, the other vessels, bobbing and jolting in the waves, all seemed not only insignificant but desperate — the activity of a team of surgeons around an operating table when all the monitors showed flat, unvarying lines; no heartbeat, no brain activity, no pulse or breath. Forty-odd people had died, together with the crew, in that mockery of wreckage. Newspapers from Europe and the States he had seen in the arrivals lounge while waiting for Vance to fly in from Phoenix in his private jet showed another wreck. Headlines crying *killer airplane, deadly airliner* and the like . . . and stock market reports, graphs and indicators describing the terminal decline of Vance Aircraft and Artemis Airways.

The storm tugged at his long hair like a vindictive housemaster confronting him with wrongdoing . . . *Look at it, Burton, look at it, this is your doing.* He wanted Vance to say something, to assist by sharing the responsibility . . . but Vance, with Barbara clutched against his side like a spar, was contained within an iron maiden of failure. The FAA had immediately ordered all 494s grounded and a greatest-urgency enquiry into the safety of the aircraft. The banks and the DOW had responded by ditching Vance Aircraft. The company died that morning, in the press and on TV . . . and the creditors would distance themselves, call in the loans, pick among the rags of the few small subsidiary businesses for something to salvage. Vance and his company were finished.

Which made the *activity* down there on the shoreline, where the whale-like bulk of the main fuselage ground and screamed against rocks and one wing half-saluted from the rough water and the tailplane wearing Diana the Huntress stuck up to taunt him . . . *futile,* all of it. He could see men in diving gear, others in orange waistcoats, yellow waterproofs, all as small and pointlessly active as insects.

He had asked — begged — Vance to bring Gant, the pilot who had appeared to save them, like a phantom bugle-call now so obviously unreal. He had suffered a round of television and radio interviews and phone calls, newspaper assaults, with a weary and defiant determination, a black time in which Gant had appeared to be some kind of distant, but real, beacon. Confronted now with the wreckage, the body-count — they had already recovered at least two dozen bodies, including that of the pilot — and the howling, light-flashing storm, he knew that he had clung to the illusion of rescue.

It was a pathetic irony that Gant had been able to come, collected by Vance at Dulles airport in Washington, because he had resigned from the NTSB and was available for *freelance work.* The force of the wind made Burton's eyes water.

The floating crane, rolling awkwardly, lowered one of the big Pratt & Whitney engines on to its flat deck, and men secured it as gently as they might have fussed around a stretcher, tucking in a red blanket that covered a body. He glanced away from the scene, but Vance appeared still to inhabit another world, some inner nightmare.

Gant, glancing up at the low headland of the islet where the 494 had come down, saw two figures — Burton and the composite individual that was Vance and Barbara clinging to his side like an infant monkey. The sea roared around the rocks along the shore, sending another wave over him. Water ran off him, leaving his face and hands icily chilled, his waterproofs streaming. The noises of the airliner grinding against the rocks were deafening. The airplane had come down steeply, like the 494s towards the runway at Vance Aircraft, and tried to level too late to make a landing on the water. It had broken up on the shore of the tiny island off the Finnish coast, two miles out from the town of Tammisaari. The island was a nature reserve for wildfowl. He imagined their panic in the early morning as the plane had crashed and disintegrated.

Vance's private jet had gotten into Helsinki's Vantaa airport just ahead of the summer storm coming down from the Gulf of Bothnia. The sky had been luridly discoloured and threatening as they had driven west. He had been walking the pebbled, narrow beach studying the line of impact of the 494 when the storm broke, lightning all along the horizon and the waves rearing like grey cloud only fifty yards from him. The local investigation team seemed not to resent his presence. He was accredited as the technical expert representing the airplane manufacturer, and that seemed sufficient.

The flight recorders and the cockpit voice recorder had been recovered. He had listened to a cassette tape of the latter, chilled by more than the wind and the glare of the lightning. It had been like listening to Hollis die, like reliving the airplane's own attempt to kill him. Instability, growing like cardiac pains at a frightening rate, the airplane convulsing then dropping, its altitude spouting away from it like blood from a severed artery.

The sea rushed at him again from an angry cleft in the rocky shore, and he flinched away from the spume. Along the pebbled shoreline, across the rocks to the edge of the tide, there were gouges, splintered rock, great scars . . . *small* scorchmarks. There had been virtually no fire. The fuselage — he had leapt from a small boat into the main fuselage as it had wallowed in the tide — was crushed, broken, but hardly burned.

The 494 had been out of fuel, tanks virtually empty — and the instability had been because the fuel flow had not been computer controlled . . . and there had been no panic and no realisation because the flight engineer's panel had assured the crew that everything was normal, *normal.* But it had happened again, with a *different* computerised fuel management system. It had happened to an airplane that had encountered *no* problems with fuel management. Instead, it had been racking up the kind of fuel economy figures that both Vance and Burton required. Better than Boeing, *cheaper* than any other airliner . . . Gant glanced up again at the fuselage, tilted drunkenly towards the angry sea. The floating crane was limping away towards the harbour at Tammisaari with one of the big engines aboard. Smaller craft nipped and huddled between the surges of the sea, two of them marked with red crosses. Floating morgue wagons. The divers, now that most of the bodies had been located and marked with little bobbing flags anchored to them, were waiting for better weather, exhausted. The scene was already an aftermath, just a day after the crash.

Nothing but the fuel management computer

could have gone wrong, would have caused the same sudden loss of altitude, the same disaster without fire. He had hardly needed the accounts of eye-witnesses to confirm his analysis. *No, there was some flame, but not a big fire . . . No, there was no explosion.* One man, an ornithologist camped on the islet, had videocamera footage of the crash and its immediate aftermath . . . His eyes had been a good enough account. And his *nose.* No overpowering scent of aviation fuel.

Unless the routine overnight servicing of the airplane had created a fault, then there was no other explanation. Unless he or Alan Vance's technical people could find something wrong with the computer that controlled the fuel flow, then there would be no answer at all. He looked behind him, back along the track the plane had made along the shoreline, at the fragments of metal and perspex it had shed like old, flaking skin. He needed to talk to the Norwegian engineers who'd worked on the 494. And study the flight recorder readouts and computer realisations . . . like watching a movie he had seen before, one that had terrified.

He experienced a strange, new pity for Vance, and avoided looking up again towards the low headland on which he knew Vance would still be standing, immobile as if suffering paralysis. This broken machine was, quite literally, a broken dream; Vance's only dream during the years he had known him, had been his son-in-law, his pilot. Not money, not fame — just the plane, flying. The sea soaked him again, and the scene was once more lit with vivid, garish lightning.

Gant shivered, as if the emotion he experienced made him weak, sickly.

It was finished, for good. Vance, standing up there facing the storm like some old Indian chief calling on the Great Spirit in the face of his people's massacre, knew with a chilling, final certainty that it was over. The newspapers, the TV had pronounced. Wall Street would foreclose. Vance was bankrupt. The whole world was a repo man knocking at his door.

But, for God's sake, *why?* Airplanes were *safe,* they didn't fall out of the sky easily, regularly. Of all the accidents he had investigated, no *two* — no almost *three,* he reminded himself, in the space of a week — died in exactly the same way, unless it was during a war. Or unless . . .

He shivered violently at the magnified, shattering noise of the fuselage grating on rock. It was impossible. Only *terrorists* did things like . . . *Almost three — in a week.* The idea could not be blown from his imagination by the wind or burned out by the lightning.

Gant felt very cold.

Ray Banks' Mercedes, a vivid petrol blue in colour, was parked beside a large hoarding which proclaimed the Millennium Urban Regeneration Project. Beneath the grandiose boast were the gold stars on blue ground of the European Union and a list of the principal contractors and architects for what had become known in the region as the Venice of the Midlands. The larva of a marina scheme based around the city's old, polluted or derelict canal system had become the gigantic butterfly of the regeneration of perhaps a quarter of the entire city. Marian brought the Escort Cabriolet to a halt beside Banks' car and tugged on the handbrake.

Banks appeared gloomy as he got out of the Mercedes. He waved his arm to indicate the empty half-renovated warehouses and the stretch of recovered canal that was the site of Banks Construction's contribution to the project.

'This is it,' he said.

'Thanks for agreeing to show me round. On a Bank Holiday, as well.'

The site, partially ring-fenced, was silent. She could hear the distant sound of traffic on the breeze. Dust moved softly across the acres of concrete and earth — seemed to lightly coat the buildings, too, as if they were already part of some failed business investment.

'These three warehouses — they're my bit. Turn 'em into shops, offices, apartments. We're only a half-mile from the canal basin and the main part of the marina — oh, you'd better put one of these on. *Not* that anything's likely to drop on your head 'cause no one's working here any day of the week!'

He pulled two hard hats from the parcel shelf of the Mercedes and handed her one of them. She collected her blonde hair, worn loose that morning, and heaped it into the hat as she jammed it on her head. 'Dressing the part, I see,' he added and she caught the glint of attraction in his look, felt the study of his eyes.

'Don't all workmen wear denims?' she enquired innocently.

'My blokes don't look like you do in jeans.'

'Thank you, kind sir.' Her smile defused something that was a squib rather than a grenade. There were tiny black insects already settled on the bright yellow of her cotton shirt. She glanced at the hoarding. *Euro-Construction* were the principal contractors. Banks' small firm did not rate a mention. There were other names, European and even American . . . and she recognised two of them as familiar. They, like Euro-Construction Plc, belonged under the umbrella of Winterborne Holdings, David's conglomerate. She rubbed her arms as if cold.

'All right?' he asked solicitously.

'Just these tiny flies, or whatever they are.'

'Oh, right. Well, you'd better follow me, then.' He glanced at his watch.

She had rung him a little after nine and had immediately made herself sound eager to be of assistance to Banks. Kenneth had agreed, during their discussion at Uffingham, that she must be allowed to pursue her instincts . . . that the appalling suspicion that David Winterborne was some kind of crook must either be satisfied or dismissed. Besides, Kenneth Aubrey's legendary curiosity had, she had realised almost at once, been aroused, and it was fiercer than sexual desire and unabated by age. *Behold, I show you a mystery* — she, like everyone who knew Aubrey, knew his motto. It had not been difficult to persuade him that the danger was minimal, the possible outcome momentous.

She and Banks walked past a Portakabin with dusty windows, two of them broken. Concrete-mixers, a parked bulldozer, a dredging crane leaning over the canal like a still heron. Fishing a large bunch of keys from the pocket of his dark blazer, he unlocked the fresh-painted doors of the first warehouse.

'You'll see how far we've got — *and* what's still to do. There's no good reason why we're not getting on with it.'

It seemed no more cool in the shadow of the building. Perhaps it was the heat of the morning, but she felt a sudden and unexpected diffidence; the conspiratorial feverishness of her conversation with Aubrey had worn off, vanished like a headache. The shadow of the warehouse over the towpath and the canal was sharply black. Banks ushered her through the door.

A film set, she thought at first; then, merely a building site. Scaffolding, the smell of fresh plaster, dusty bootprints across the floor, hardened concrete on a board, a crumpled crisp packet that scuttled like a crab in the breeze that had entered with them. Sunlight burned through dirty windows and made the dust in the air glow.

'See?' said Banks, almost bullying her into sympathy. 'Nothing behind the bloody façade! And no money to go on . . .' His voice faded before her continuing silence. His imminent bankruptcy had been the goad her concern required.

'Are the other two like this?' He nodded fiercely. 'And this is to be — what, offices?' She waved her hand.

'That's it. Thousands of square feet of office space around a central atrium. See? Keep the tall windows that way —' He gestured towards the beginnings of flooring and a gallery. 'One of the others is supposed to become apartments, the third more offices. The other two are even less forward than this one.'

'How long have they been like this?'

'Stopped work a month ago — completely. Paid off the last few blokes, my best, out of my own pocket, too. Haven't had a bloody *penny* out of the main contractors since then — or for another six months before I had to down tools!'

His face was brick red with remembered arguments, recollected outrage and growing paranoia and anxiety

'And they just keep saying the cheque's in the post, is that roughly it?'

'Exactly it. Euro-Construction — with the other fat cats backing them because they don't have any cash-flow problems — just smile like my mother-in-law does when you try to persuade her that white is white and black black against her better judgement — !' He could not avoid grinning at his own waving arms, deep frustration. 'Honest, Marian — it's a right Fred Karno's army setup . . .' His eyes wandered the warehouse as intently as if he were studying a home that had burned down, then he snapped: 'Come on, I can't stand looking at this any longer!'

The shadow was cooler outside, at least for the first moments. Gnats swirled like smoke above the still water of the canal. Empty paint tins, the occasional condom, sodden cardboard and the inevitable mattress littered the towpath or stuck up out of the stagnant water.

'I even asked that bloody Euro MP of ours — toffee-nosed pillock! — to make a few enquiries. I never heard from him again, and his secretary can never get hold of him.'

'Ben Campbell, you mean?'

'That's him. Not much good for anything, is he?'

'I don't think he'd like to hear you say that.' She heard the bellring of a collar dove, startled by their presence, as its wings lifted it up to the roof of the warehouse. They passed beneath a narrow road bridge over the canal. She smelt the heavy unappetising scent of cooking on the breeze.

'The nearest streets — aren't they to be redeveloped or something?' She'd had letters and phone calls of protest, but had been able to do nothing other than make soothing noises. The city's councillors and planners had decided the old back-to-backs must go — not in favour of tower blocks, which was at least something, but to be replaced by a prettified, faked village-style development.

'Oh, the cooking smells. Sure they are — but no one's been moved out yet. The compulsory purchase orders have been served, the prices agreed . . . but that's the council, mean buggers. They haven't paid up yet because no one's ready to develop the place. I think they've pulled down two houses and a pub so far.'

'Are you — ?'

He shook his head.

'Egan Construction are down for that redevelopment.'

'Indeed.'

The other warehouses were on the opposite bank of the canal. A pair of new moorings had been excavated beside one of the buildings, there were even brass rails. A mattress floated where a cruiser should have been berthed, or a fashionably old-fashioned narrow boat. They turned a slow bend in the canal and she saw it stretching into the distance between other warehouses, beneath low bridges, amid the canyons of red-brick buildings, towards the canal basin.

'Are they working on the basin?' she asked. Banks' work was, after all, on the periphery, at the flippant edge of the whole project once it had moved its epicentre from the marina towards the regeneration of a quarter of the city. If money was in the least tight, then he'd be the first to suffer. She had, as yet, no sense of the scale of delay.

'Sort of — one or two blokes dithering about. A lot of it was completed with local funding — private and council — before the whole thing expanded. Not much lately, though,' he added. 'Most of this section of the development has shut up shop.'

She recalled the opening ceremony and the very public steering of a JCB by the PM — digging out the first rubble rather than cutting the first turf — two years before. The PM possessed a gravitational attraction towards the grandiose; a building site was a newly discovered country virgin territory for his classless society. Some colleagues referred to his *fatal attraction* for such schemes, and the hope that Glenn Close might spring up from the bath and stab him to death.

He had made one of his characteristically lame speeches regarding the redevelopment as the *largest urban regeneration scheme in Europe, perhaps the world.*

This part of it seemed to retain his fingerprints, she reflected sourly. Two weeks' enthusiasm followed by the remaining evidence of something in which interest had been lost. It was still a building site.

She deflected her thoughts from the familiar with a conscious effort. A figure dressed in a cap and uniform shirt and trousers was emerging from a small Portakabin sited on a stretch of weedy concrete. Beyond it, she could see the tired, cramped streets scheduled to disappear and hear the noise of thudding music and the screams of children. The man was in his late fifties, short, bowlegged, a mobile phone slung at his waist like a cowboy's gun.

'Oh, it's you, Mr Banks,' he offered, studying Marian with an intensity that belied his casual greeting.

'Hello, Stan.' On the man's cap and shoulder badges, Marian saw the blazon *Complete Security*. The surprise of memory must have been evident in her face.

'Anything wrong, Mr Banks?' He did not look at Banks as he spoke.

'Only the usual. I'm just showing —'

'I'm a relative!' Marian gushed.

'An MP in the family Mr Banks? You never said.'

'I apologise,' Marian offered quickly. 'We didn't want you to attach any importance to . . .

You were saying, Ray — funding?' She glanced at her watch. 'I need to be back for lunch, Ray. Sorry and all that. Could we — ?'

Snotty bitch. It was as if he had spoken the words, so clear was the sentiment in his eyes. *Nice one, Marian — after your classic piece of stupidity.*

'Oh, yes — take care, Stan.'

They moved away turning back to where their cars were parked. She sensed the security man's study of her as sharply as a lust. Bow legs do not a slow wit make, she recited, angry at her inept, unthinking lie. *Complete Security* . . . coincidence? The firm belonged to the Winterborne Holdings Group. Effectively, David owned the company that employed Fraser, who had, almost certainly, killed Michael Lloyd.

Not coincidence . . . She resisted the temptation to turn and look back. The security guard would be watching, without the shadow of a doubt. And knew she had tried to lie to him, and wore a mobile phone on his belt like a pistol.

'I want to see more,' she announced, surprising Banks. 'I want to know how *much* is not being done. Did you bring the plans?'

He nodded.

'Everything. Each site, the whole overview. What do you want them for?' His words were uttered with the kind of childish, resentful whine that attempted to wheedle adults about to redirect their attentions.

'*Because* . . . if you want my help, Ray, I want to know what is *really* going on!'

Or do I . . . ? She could not prevent the question. Conjuring images that mocked the PM, the grandiosity of this urban regeneration scheme, no longer seemed anything more than an insider's game, the irritating chuckles and giggles of people sharing an unimportant joke or piece of gossip.

'OK, OK — what do you want to see?'

What *do* I want to see? Evidence that David is a crook and one of his employees is a murderer — or evidence that Banks is paranoid and bitter and probably deserves to go out of business? *Damn* Kenneth's curiosity, she decided, it's infectious.

'The heart of the matter,' she announced. 'The biggest bits — are they dragging their heels on those as well? That's what I want to know, Ray.'

Because here, with these three warehouses and stretch of canal to be rejuvenated, she could only count in hundreds of thousands, perhaps one or two million. David could have easily sold one of his small companies, floated a minor share issue, cashed in some stock, if that was the size of the stake. There was no evidence that tens, hundreds of millions were disappearing.

The videocamera footage shot in the moments after the crash was replaying on a TV screen. The instruments that had thus far been removed from the flight deck were spread, like bones or runes, on a trestle table in front of Gant and Blakey from Vance Aircraft. As were photographs, weighted down with pebbles against the howling wind that blew through the frail canvas tent. Outside, the rescue and salvage work had been postponed until the storm abated. It lurched and bullied like an enraged drunk against the tent, which was erected in a hollow of sand and tussocky grass behind the low headland of the island.

'See?' Gant was saying, his finger pointing at the TV screen, where the videofilm flickered and swayed as if affected by the squall. 'There's little or no kerosene. The tanks must have been empty when she hit. You agree, don't you?' he added angrily. It was as if the storm had gotten inside him somehow, and was shaking his stomach and heart with great buffeting blows. Or maybe he was possessed by an idea he couldn't rid himself of — that the 494 had suffered sabotage.

Out of politeness, because he was already convinced, Blakey leaned towards the screen, removing his glasses, his bearlike frame looming over Gant, his thick fingers scratching at his beard.

'Confirmed. No kerosene. The lack of fire damage backs that theory up. She was running on fresh air . . . How?' he added sharply, plucking at the greying beard, his damp-looking eyes doubtful. 'We've been through that, Mitchell. There's nothing *here* . . .'

Ron Blakey had checked the fuel computer system on sophisticated portable monitors, and then rechecked on his instructions, angrily patient. And nothing . . . The fuel computer system, every last chip of it, *worked.* Gant *knew* there had to be something wrong with the fuel computer . . . instability, manual control, the uneven struggle against the pitching and yawing of the plane, the final loss of control *and* engine power when there wasn't enough fuel any more. It was all on the cockpit voice recorder, *and* what *he* had experienced with Vance.

More gently, Blakey said: 'I could have that system in the lab for a month and it would still read out the same. Sorry, Mitchell —'

Gant pointed at the littered table.

'Except that,' he said.

'I've explained what it does —' Blakey responded.

'But not why it's there,' Gant snapped.

'No . . .'

'It's not standard — it's not like the other components with the Microlite brand name. It's not like chips that I've seen that do the same job.'

'No, it isn't — but there's nothing peculiar about it except its looks. It's just another dumb microprocessor carrying out simple tasks, taking orders, passing them on.' Blakey shrugged.

'So, why is it different?' Gant persisted. 'Why is it *handmade* — your word?'

'Maybe it's a prototype — we can check with Microlite. It didn't cause the accident —'

'You say.'

'*You* say it did. The only thing that looks any different from normal, and that's your answer? That it's that chip? It isn't. I did the tests you asked.'

Gant looked up at Blakey. 'Ron — *please do the tests.* However many however long it takes. Take this back to Phoenix and find out why it dresses up different from the rest of the guys.'

Blakey nodded.

'OK — it's your call. And the old fella's desperate, right?' he added.

'Right.'

They looked away from one another. Both

Vance and Burton had been frantically engaged, by means of their mobile phones, in fending off armies of bankers, other creditors, the press, lobbyists, stockbrokers, the TV networks. The voices coming out of the ether were another storm, like the one outside, paralleling the one inside Gant himself.

Gant turned back to Blakey. When he had last glimpsed Vance he had looked ashen, buckled, Barbara at his side somehow drawing strength from him rather than supporting him. Lightning glared through the opacity of the canvas, then the thunder burst around them.

'Jesus,' Blakey muttered, and shivered with reaction.

Gant stared down at the trodden sand beneath his feet, the flattened tussocks of grass. The tent was as frail and insubstantial as the 494 would have felt to the pilot. Gant's head jerked up and he stared malevolently at the chip on the table, dwarfed by the fuel flow gauge with its lying needle. It *was* that unexpected chip, he knew it was —

The flap of the tent was dragged aside. Flying sand scoured across the instruments, the photographs, ageing them. Gant looked up and saw Vance posed for a moment, the storm behind him. Vivid lightning struck down from the heavy cloud towards the sea. Yet Vance's face seemed more thunderous, incandescently angry. Blakey assiduously dusted sand from the table. Barbara, her dark hair wild, was at Vance's side, pulling vainly at his arm like a child.

Vance lurched like a drunk to the table, leaning

heavily on Blakey a large hand clasping Gant's shoulder.

'Well? What have you got? What is it?' His breathing sounded hoarse as the rolling thunder died away The storm was moving slowly away along the Gulf of Finland. 'Ron — tell me what went wrong.'

Blakey, almost as bulky as Vance, seemed to shy from the older man, his hands gesturing vainly as if in supplication. Vance's features became ever more virulent, maddened.

'You?' He glared at Gant. 'Come on, boy wonder, *tell* me what happened to my airplane!'

'Alan, we don't know —'

'The hell you don't! I'm paying you way over the odds, Gant — and for answers, not apologies!'

Gant clenched his hands in the pockets of his anorak. Burton, dishevelled by the storm and his collapsed business, was standing in the opening of the tent, a stranger who had inadvertently walked in on some family crisis.

'Alan, I can't give you an answer — there isn't an answer. Not yet —'

'You told me it was sabotage, Gant! You sounded like you were swearing on your mother's life, for Christ's sake! Now you got nothing?' He turned contemptuously towards Blakey. 'And you, Ron — you got nothing, either? You still going along with this guy's theory?'

'We can't find anything. Not yet. But the odds against —'

'*Fuck* odds! I have had *odds* up to here! The company's dead in the water. I *know* the odds!'

'Daddy — calm down, for God's sake!'

'Barbara?' Vance seemed bemused, or stunned. Lightning made the canvas of the tent glow, as if there was some great conflagration outside. Then the thunder. Vance yelled above it: 'You taking *his* side? Something new for you, Barbara!'

'Alan,' Gant said levelly, 'it has to be sabotage. I don't know why and I don't know how — but it has to be.'

'Then *prove* it!' He banged his fist on the table. The instruments rattled, jumped, the malicious chip sliding across the surface. 'If you can't prove it, and prove it *now,* then you're no damn' use to me, Gant — no damn' use at all!' He was leaning heavily on the table, the litter on the surface quivering with the pressure of his rage and weariness. His face was shiny with sweat, his eyes protruding, his breathing loud and difficult. He seemed to be suffocating on his own rage.

'I will prove it, Alan —'

'But you'll prove it too late!' He waved a lurching arm towards Burton behind him. The Englishman's features were without optimism, expressing a withdrawn defeat. 'You think he and I have got the time to wait for you to *prove* anything? We ain't got *shit!*'

The man's entire career had subsided within him, Gant realised. The supremely focused, narrowly defiant ego had slid like a collapsing levee into the river of his rage. The 494 had been his dream, and it had turned on him like a wastrel child and betrayed him, leaving his whole business in ruins. He had clung to Gant's theory not because it was a way of surviving, but because it would keep the airplane pure, triumphant. It would *justify* the 494 and Vance himself. Now, the theory was unprovable — and to Vance it had become untenable.

'*I'll* get something on the move!' he growled, dragging his mobile phone from the pocket of his waterproof and consulting its memory. Then he dialled a number and waited. 'Yes — who's that? It's *Vance — !*' His face was freshly slick with sweat, his eyes and cheeks swollen. 'Is Olssen there? Olssen, your fucking *chief engineer — !*'

Burton seemed to awake from a light trance, eager to cling to his realisation of the purpose of the call. Gant presumed it was Oslo — the maintenance company who had performed the overnight service. 'Get that asshole Olssen to the phone, for Christ's sake! I know the guy is avoiding me! I want to talk to *Olssen* — now!'

He remained leaning heavily on the table, which continued to shudder under the pressure, the chips and screws and smaller instruments responding as to a distant earth tremor.

'What do you think might have — ?' Burton began with the eagerness of desperation, then fell silent.

Gant remained watching Barbara, who stood near Blakey as if she had retreated from the epicentre, and regarded her helplessness, her lack of influence over her father's rage, with evident guilt. Then:

'Olssen — Vance. I want to talk to you!' Vance was fiercely stroking his left arm as it held the mobile phone to his flushed cheek. 'Listen to me — you screwed up, Olssen! Your crummy little asshole company *screwed up!* My airplane fell out of the sky because of you!' Gant shook his head angrily but remained silent. Vance's lips were blue with rage, his face brick red. 'I'm going to sue the ass off you and your bosses, Olssen. You ruined me — I ruin *you!* Understand — *understand . . . ?*'

Gant did, catching Vance's weight as it lurched, one hand sweeping aside the litter on the table, the other dropping the phone to clutch at his chest, twist the waterproof down like a tourniquet that might stop the pain. Gant faltered under the weight, then Blakey held Vance, lowering him on to a folding chair.

For a moment his features drained of colour and his eyes stared wildly Then, as if a huge current had been passed through his big frame, he seemed to staggeringly leap from the chair towards the tent flap, then subside to his knees. Another jolting shock and he lay stretched on his stomach, Blakey and Barbara bending over him, gently turning him over, loosening his clothing. His eyes were open and staring, his mouth wet and working loosely as if with a foreign language of pain and dread.

Gant snatched up the mobile phone from the sand and dusted it brusquely. Burton retained shock like an anaesthetic. Barbara was murmuring, drying Vance's face with a handkerchief while Blakey placed a folded garment beneath his head, then glanced at Gant.

'. . . man from your own factory, your own *expert,* checked the fuel computer, where your trouble was supposed to have been . . .'

Gant's thumb remained on the off button.

'Wait,' he snapped. Then to Burton: 'Call for an air ambulance — *do it now!*' He realised that their shock was turning to puzzled contempt. Vance's heart attack — had to be that — had altered the tent's small universe, the physical and psychological laws that governed it. How could he, their eyes said, want to talk to Olssen *now?* He waited until Burton had begun dialling, then he turned his back on them. 'OK. Mr Vance wants me to talk to you. I'm FAA, got it? Please repeat what you just said — *what* man from Vance Aircraft? When? Where?'

'— did not wish to listen to what I had to —'

'I don't have time for all that, Mr Olssen. Just tell me about this man.' Vance was still breathing, struggling to swallow air like a fish drowning in it. Gant ignored the small, tight pain of pity in his chest. 'You claim there was someone from Vance Aircraft in Oslo two nights ago. What was his name? Who was he supposed to be?'

There was a groan from Vance, though it might have been some incoherent protest from Barbara or Blakey. Burton was talking urgently into his phone, describing symptoms.

'He called himself Massey. But, you mean he was *not* —'

'He was not,' Gant affirmed. 'Massey? There's no Massey at Vance Aircraft. What did he do? Why did he say he had come?'

He felt icily cold now, utterly detached from the scrabbling of feet in the trodden sand, the chirruping of alarm and comfort. He knew he was right.

'He had been sent to check the fuel computer

system, because of the first accident, he said. It was not necessary, since the system was a different one, but he had been asked by Mr Vance to make certain.'

'Sure. You saw him working?'

'No. Jorgensen did, for a while — one of the engineers. He was with us an hour. He was an *expert* — I spoke to him myself, he was definitely from Vance Aircraft, there was no reason to think otherwise.'

The slight singsong of the Norwegian accent was beginning to grate, as if it was the aural equivalent of the naivety of Olssen's opinions. The guy was an *expert.* He'd have had to be, to doctor the fuel computer . . . with another of *those.* Gant glared malevolently at the chip, which remained on the table even though the floor of the tent was littered with the stuff Vance had swept away with his hand. He had to speak to Olssen, face to face — he needed a description, a verbatim account of what the *expert* had said, how he had spoken, his nationality. And question this guy Jorgensen, who had also spoken to the *expert.*

'We'll need to talk, Mr Olssen. I'll drop by. My name is Gant — my real name.'

'But you are — ?' The tone was at once conciliatory, even ingratiating, then immediately defensive. 'But, how could we have known — ?'

Gant flicked the off button and put the phone in his pocket. Reluctantly he turned to look at Vance, a mixture of sensations invading him, making demands on him. The image was appalling, cold. Vance's mouth was open, loose, gulping air slowly. Burton waggled his phone, shaping with his lips, *They're on their way.* Barbara was sitting in the sand beside her father, holding his hand, murmuring continually. Blakey was seated on the chair as if studying a map drawn in the distressed sand. Gant stepped outside the tent without speaking to any of them. Vance might get over the coronary, he might not. He looked awful.

The sky was less lurid, the temperature after the humid claustrophobia of the tent surprisingly low. He shivered and hunched against the wind, watching the lightning, distant and toylike now, flickering over the tiny dark specks of other islets. The gap before the thunder was seconds long. The wind made his eyes water.

The man in Oslo, the unknown *expert,* had probably killed Alan Vance, along with fifty other people, and Hollis and his crew. Gant looked westward, out beyond the long, low headland on which Hanko perched, towards the Baltic. The grey sea was lightening, beginning to become fish-scale silver as the clouds broke. Over there somewhere was Oslo. The *expert* would be long gone, back into the shadows by now, leaving no trace. The wreckage down there held no clues, either. He stared at the fuselage as lightning seared on the edge of his retinae. It was almost dragged off the rocks by the storm, upended in suddenly deep water, like a damaged fish.

He would find him, the *expert.* For his own reasons, he had to find him . . . for being shafted by the NTSB and having to resign . . . for Vance . . . for the sake of *having been right too late to make a difference.* He hated that bleak, accusing thought.

'Ray, stop looking at your watch and worrying about your lunch!' Marian snapped, swiping a hand at hovering flies.

'Sorry,' Banks murmured insincerely. He was bored, truculently discomfited because she seemed no longer to be concentrating on *his* problems, *his* little patch of delayed work. 'We shouldn't be here,' he added.

'Oh, dear!' she mocked.

They had followed the canal as closely as possible towards the basin that had half-mutated into a vast marina. Crowded on to the banks were renewed warehouses, slipways, rows of shop-fronts, cafés, blocks of flats, iron-gated developments of new housing. It was a scene that was incomplete, like a child's puzzle where one compared two sketches and tried to decide what alterations had been made from one to the other — ladybirds now with six spots not five, a tree with a branch missing. They had played with such puzzle drawings at Uffingham, on rain-swamped days during school holidays.

Here, the marina was presented to her in a series of artists' impressions and computer images in a glossy brochure Banks had retrieved from the boot of the Mercedes, together with the maplike architect's drawings which now rested across her lap. *There,* around them, was the actual marina, and she had to glance from sketches to actuality several times before the huge site began to reveal its unfinished state. What had been a dazzling smile had missing teeth, plaque, carious decay. There was a warehouse still dilapidated there, intended as an office block. Farther over, across the still water that remained feet lower than it would eventually be, the wrought iron of high gates, behind which was little more than a building site rather than expensive executive homes.

There was millions in unfinished work around the canal basin, beyond which towered the blocks of two new hotels, built for American chains and completed on schedule. In the distance was the new symphony hall and the conference centre, the exhibition complex, the metro system's hub station and the new railway above it . . . and on and on, stretching west and south towards the present centre of the city.

And yet, this all looked no more completed, even if as substantial, than Bruegel's painting of Babel — except for the holiday absence of human activity. The dust around the spot where they had parked seemed unprinted, oddly settled. Babel . . . She always remembered that painting in Vienna whenever some particularly grandiose European scheme passed across her desk or her television screen. *Vanity, vanity, saith the Preacher* . . . But here, it might be crookery, crookery, she reminded herself.

'Seen enough?' Banks asked hopefully, unabashedly patting his stomach. 'There's an even bigger slowdown than I'd thought,' he added helpfully and in order to hurry.

'Is there?' she replied archly.

The signs of it were everywhere. A village-green project, surrounded by cheaper, cottagey housing, had not begun two miles away . . . two tall office blocks were merely empty boxes turned on end. Around their emptiness, more endlessly recurring building sites.

She slipped from the car seat and walked the few paces to the high fence that surrounded the marina, pressing her face close to its trelliswork of wire. Less than fifty yards away, vandals had pulled a short length of the fencing away from its stanchions. The metro station's entrance was on her side of the canal basin. It seemed dusty but complete, even to its *City Metro* blazon atop a flagstaff-like steel pole. Banks began sighing impatiently behind her.

'I'd like to have a look at the metro station, Ray. There's a gap in the fencing just along there.' She pointed exaggeratedly. 'Didn't you mention that, according to rumour, work on the tunnelling had been slowed down?'

'That's mostly the council's money, and private investment,' he replied, feigning boredom.

'And perhaps twenty million from Brussels,' she murmured. 'They like underground trains in Europe.'

'Look,' Banks began, 'we've seen enough, haven't we? I mean —'

'Ray, what do you think is going to happen if we engage in trespass? The canal basin isn't MoD property so far as I'm aware. Come on — let's see how advanced this advanced urban passenger transport system is, shall we?'

She strode eagerly along the fence, a broad smile on her face. It was as if the calculations she had made were of profits from her own investments . . . Someone *is* counting just like that, she told herself. David . . . ?

She ducked down and eased herself through the gap torn in the fence. There were pawprints in the dusty earth. Behind her, Banks puffed and wriggled his way in pursuit. Millions, she kept reminding herself, millions of pounds. To have kept everything on schedule would have cost millions more than was evidently being spent. And Phases One, Two and Three were, she remembered from the PM's unringing words at the opening ceremony, and from the architects' glossy handouts, intended to progress at the same pace. Now, large parts of those phases had seriously lagged, others had not even seen a sod turned in earnest.

Of course there were, dotted around the development, completed projects, new roads or stretches of road, whole new estates of houses, one of the shopping centres. She herself had been to concerts in the new symphony hall, addressed a gathering at the conference centre next door to it. But, like a city at night, seen from the air, the glaring blotches of light were balanced by areas of darkness. There were great pieces of the entire jigsaw missing.

And no one had noticed.

'You'll need this,' Banks announced smugly, holding up a heavy-duty lamp.

'Us women — so impractical,' she murmured.

'And you should have brought a camera.'

'Why, Ray? You imagine I could force people to tell me the truth by showing them a few snaps of building sites?' She immediately sensed the intemperateness of her response. 'Sorry,' she apologised. 'Right, let's have a look, shall we — ?'

She hurried down the steps out of the sunlight, into a warm gloom then a subtle change of temperature. The lamp's beam became stronger, more necessary for a moment or two, then the light, dusty as it was and somehow unused, increased as they reached the ticket barriers and a glimpse of the platform. There was a huge, greenhouse-like glass roof over the station's two platforms. The barriers were open, and she walked into disappointment. The station, beneath its light coating of dust, boasted tiled walls, mosaiced platforms, large steel notices. It was complete, awaiting its first train.

'I — I thought they hadn't got on this quick,' Banks faltered. Marian glared at him, as if he had been a subtle enemy, persuading her of David's guilt.

Marian's disappointment was vivid and ridiculous, even embarrassing. It reminded her of the mockery of some of her most complacent colleagues in the House who referred to her as Rent-a-Moral, because they easily tired of her obsessive, always challenged sense of justice. She *had* sometimes made herself ridiculous, her perennial outrage manipulated on sundry occasions by people who had no real claim upon it. As now, apparently.

The finished metro station, entire even to the awaiting, empty advertising hoardings. The succession of building sites through which she had travelled, and on which she had erected a castle of venality and fraud, had ended here, in these pristine, functional, *completed* surroundings.

'I —' She cleared her throat. 'I'm just going to have a look down the tunnel,' she announced. 'I'll borrow your lamp, Ray, if I may.'

'But it's all finished,' he grumbled.

'*Nevertheless* . . .'

'Oh, I'll come with you.'

'Good.'

She strode off along the platform. The hard hat was making her forehead damp; a headache encroached, but its cause was sheer bloody frustration, she decided. Her shoes clicked along the platform. She almost expected a sleek, blazoned train to sweep from the tunnel. She hesitated, staring into its darkness. The dry breeze of every underground station. The scent of concrete and dust, as the rails ran into the darkness.

'It's not live, is it?'

Banks chuckled, his masculine superiority comfortably worn once more.

'I shouldn't think so. Come on, then, let's get it over with.'

A sparrow fluttered against the glass roof, as if intent upon damaging itself rather than on freedom. The sight pained her.

'Right. Shine that lamp —'

A noise startled her, filtering down the steps and along the platform, echoing in the empty station. A car engine approaching, then the silence as it was switched off — then the slamming of a door . . .

He and Burton seemed the only heated and animate things in the aseptic hospital corridor off which were the doors to the intensive care unit. Windows looked out over Helsinki, now bathed in early-afternoon sunshine, appearing like a pallid ghost of Venice, with white buildings and open stretches of green and the grey sea beyond.

'If your theory's correct,' Burton was arguing once more, 'then you're making suppositions about motive and instigation that don't hold up — and I should know! These people *ruin*, they don't needlessly kill — they work by means of the rumour, the dawn raid . . . it's the letter that killeth.' He surprised Gant with a boyish smile.

Gant merely shook his head, holding his hands together in front of his knees as if to still them. He felt himself becoming more impatient; a truant listening to a homily while his adventure waited outside for him. Vance had suffered a second, and more massive heart attack in the air ambulance. Barbara's reaction had been a pallidity, an ashenness, that suggested she had suffered the coronary Vance had been unconscious for the remainder of the short flight. Mocking first sunlight had glared on his white face through the helicopter window. They had rushed him to intensive care . . . an hour ago. Gant believed that Vance must be dead. Twice in the helicopter they'd tried to jump-start his heart, as if he was a car with a drained battery. The body had shown the feeblest response, to which Barbara had clung as to the spars of a liferaft. Her grief washed her sunken cheeks and dead eyes with tears.

'It isn't like that — not anymore,' he said softly. 'They do what they have to . . . and the kind of people I know, who I've worked for in the past, they're looking for work now.' He looked up bleakly. 'You just don't get it, do you? You think yours is the world of grown-ups and you know the rules. It's the world I come from which has the adults in it — people who think nothing of walking *through* other people to be where they want to be. Not just walking over.'

'You're suggesting that intelligence people are involved here — in my business?'

'Why not?' Gant shrugged. 'Your membership rules say they can't join the country club?'

Burton glowered and was about to reply when his mobile phone trilled, as it had done a half-dozen times during the hour they had been seated in that corridor. He snatched it from his pocket. Gant stared down the narrowing perspective of the corridor, its walls and floor gleaming from the sun coming in through the glass.

'Yes?' Burton snapped wearily

It was Stuart, his MD. He turned away from Gant towards the windows and the view of the city which rendered the hospital corridor the comfortable anonymity of a hotel room. Gant's slumped, still form on the hard chair was too suggestive of defeat, of impotence.

'Tim — when are you flying back?' he heard. 'I think the sky's fallen in on us, sorry to have to —'

'What's wrong now?'

'We're being deserted in droves by passengers. Booking cancellations are into thousands for the Atlantic flights. Doesn't seem to matter which aircraft type — it's just having Artemis painted on the tailplane. And the big European carriers and the Yanks are making the most of it — *fly safely,* was one slogan in today's papers. I've managed to get that retracted by threats of legal action . . . Sorry to sound such a Job's comforter, but —'

'It's all right, Stuart,' Burton answered mechanically. Even to himself, his voice sounded remote, belonging to someone in the hunched, defeated-looking posture of Gant. 'We can't *give* tickets away, right?'

'Not without a lot of effort.'

'OK, I'm coming back as soon as I can get a flight.' He sensed Gant look tip at him, but ignored the tightness between his shoulder blades. 'Sure. Yes — no, I don't know what we can salvage . . . No, nothing here that helps *us.*' He paused, then added: 'It's gone to hell in a handcart, Stuart. But don't quote me.' There was no rally in his voice. 'See you —'

He switched off the phone and turned back to Gant, as if expecting his decision to be challenged.

'There's nothing you can do,' Gant said.

'Can *you* do anything?'

'Not fast enough to make a difference.'

'Think I'm finished — correct?'

'So is he in there — maybe permanently.' Gant's eyes were bleak, his cheekbones prominent, as if he was facing a hard, chill wind. Burton recognised an empathy with Vance, a remote kind of pity, emotions written in a tiny, minimalist handwriting on his features. 'There's nothing you can do. I'll tell her you had to leave.'

'Thanks —' Burton hesitated. 'I — if there's

anything you can do . . . I mean, I'm employing you, in a way I'll go on doing that, if you'll pursue —'

Gant smiled wintrily.

'I'll pursue. Someone did this to his airplane — just for money. The guy who planted the device got paid, and the guy paying *him* expects to turn a profit. That's all it is . . . I'll pursue.'

Burton nodded. 'Good. Let me know what you decide to do, what you need —'

'Sure.'

'Goodbye, Major.' Gant smiled. 'I must hurry —'

Gant watched him stride down the corridor, his steps threatening to become a fleeing run at any moment. When he had disappeared, Gant settled back on the hard moulded plastic of the chair and stared out towards the city. There were golden roofs down there, and neat parks, afternoon traffic, all of which remained ordinary.

It was almost two when Barbara emerged from the intensive care unit, the door swishing behind her, then sucking shut. When she told him that Vance had not regained consciousness and that they could not restart his heart and that she had given the instruction to switch off the life support, he did not look at her, but held her hand loosely, since she seemed to wish him to do so.

After an unmeasured time of sobbing and racked breathing as Barbara stared out of the windows down at the city, she quietly subsided into the chair beside him. Tentatively, he put his arm around her shoulder and she slid like a child against him, her head pressed into his chest. He felt her grief beat in her cheek and forehead like his own pulse.

As he held her, he stared at a perspective beyond the crashes of the 494, beyond the ruins of Vance Aircraft, and the sabotage that had murdered Hollis and Alan. The former had tried to be his friend and the latter his enemy, and both of them had failed. Just as neither of them had deserved to die so someone could turn an extra buck.

Out there, somewhere, was a man who doctored microprocessors so that they caused airplanes to crash. And beyond him, there was someone very, very remote, who had ordered it done. Someone with planes to sell, someone with planes to fill and fly . . . Someone he wanted very badly to find.

CHAPTER SEVEN

Economic Recovery

There were footsteps and voices from the platform which sidled into the hot darkness of the tunnel. They were out of sight of the platform because of a slow bend in the tunnel — to the point where the construction work had ceased. The track, the tiling of the walls, the lighting all petered out only hundreds of yards from the dusty newness of the metro station. Before Ray had extinguished the lamp, they had seen the roughly excavated workings, as incomplete and inhospitable as a coalmine.

To Marian it seemed too sudden, too decided. Petered out was the wrong expression. Work had been suddenly, quickly suspended . . . three months before by the date on the tattered, dusty copy of *The Sun* she had found. The newspaper had flapped against her feet as if alive, startling her until the light of the lamp had revealed a bare-breasted female and two lurid headlines expressing moral outrage at pornography on television and violence in films. Twelve weeks ago, work had stopped completely on this stretch of the metro line — and probably on the entire system.

'What do we do?' Banks asked breathily, his lips close to her ear.

'Who do you think it is — security?'

'Probably. Not day-trippers, anyway.'

Weak torchlight fell on the floor and walls of the tunnel. The footsteps were louder, the voices like murmured threats.

'What are we supposed to be doing down here?' Banks asked more urgently. They were standing in darkness, close together. She smelt the tense increase in the overpowering scent of his expensive aftershave, heard his breathing.

'Come on out of there,' she heard. 'Come on — we know someone's in there.' A looming shadow was washed along the tunnel towards them, as if it were pouncing. The voice was suspicious, but hesitant, too. The parked cars would not suggest local yobs, but would mystify. 'Come on — !' more impatiently, confidently.

'What are we going to — ? What are you doing?' Banks was startled by the noise of the zipper of her jeans, the rustle of the blouse as she tugged it free, unbuttoned it.

'Just follow my lead!' she hissed, grabbing hold of him. 'Turn on the lamp!'

She pulled Banks against her, feeling the pressure of his stomach. Their coupled shadows sprang out on the wall. *The beast with two backs* . . . Oh, dear, the things I do for England. She felt, with a curious repellence, his arousal. Hurry up, she thought, disliking the aftershave, the good-living roundedness of his jowl pressed against her cheek.

'Sorry —' he began to apologise.
'What the bloody hell are you — ?' she heard as her cue and pushed Banks away. His foot moved the lamp and their parting shadows danced on the walls. At once she began pulling up her jeans. 'Jesus Christ — !'
'I told you I didn't want to!' she snapped loudly at Banks in a passably local accent, her tone harsh with experience. 'Not bloody down here!' She buttoned her shirt as Banks ostentatiously rezipped his flies. Torchlight washed their faces, dazzled them. 'Christ, Ray — ! I didn't expect an audience! You and your bloody sex-drive!' Banks' features were stunned, half-amused, perspiring.
'Who the hell are you, mate?' one of the two figures asked.
They were no more than a few yards away. In the glow of the torch, she could make out the uniforms of security guards. Complete Security?
'You like watching, do you?' she challenged brazenly, tossing her hair away from her face.
'You're trespassing —'
'Ray hasn't got enough puff to do any damage!' she retorted, making as if to brush past the security men. *Complete* Security again, she realised. One of them grabbed her arm, restraining her. She smelt onions on his breath, and beer. She shrugged his grip away.
'Come on, fair's fair,' Banks began, dropping his voice, so that she only caught snatches of the male-camaraderie bawdiness of his explanation. She turned her back contemptuously on them. 'My secretary . . . down here just wondering about

one of the flats, you know — hot day . . . just seemed, took my fancy . . .' She wondered, so convincing was the performance as it reached her, whether Banks had experience in such matters. The wife was, at best, dowdy . . . Cat, she told herself. 'I mean, it's not a crime, is it?'

Banks had already begun moving them all towards the end of the tunnel and the platform. She snorted and tossed her head, more like a colt than a woman, and lit a cigarette; surprised at the ease with which she could adopt brassiness, the accent, the exaggerated walk as she went ahead of them.

'See what you mean — but you're still trespassing.'

'Look, I don't want any trouble, mate —' His accent, too, was thickly local now. 'I mean, you wouldn't be insulted if I offered —'

She glanced at the two men only once, to confirm their uniforms. Complete Security. Then kept ahead of them, her face averted. Stan at the building site of Banks Construction had recognised her, after all. These two — one in his thirties, the other middle-aged — didn't seem to know Banks, but just in case . . . *And wiggle your hips,* she cajoled herself. Her shoes clicked along the platform. Banks' tone was almost that of repartee now. She felt herself beginning to shiver with relief and stilled her body by an effort of will, wearing her new, brazen, adulterous self like a straitjacket.

The sun was hotter, it seemed. She ducked through the fence where it was damaged and hurried to her car. Hot leather seats, the hot paintwork. She dragged her sunglasses out of the glove compartment and put them on to mask her features. Then she sat on the uncomfortable heated leather, turning her face away from the two security men, who watched her for a moment, as if in recognition as much as desire, and one of them announced to Banks:

'You're getting too old to do it in railway tunnels, mate! I should put your name down for one of these flats, if I were you!'

'Ask him when they'll be finished!' she whispered urgently, as they walked off, laughing.

'When — when are they going to start selling them, then?' Banks called out.

The older of the two men, the one who had joked about the flats, turned back. His features were cloudy with a sense of having made some slip.

'It'll be in the papers, mate!' he snapped and the two seemed suddenly more reluctant to leave.

'That's it,' Banks admitted, his hand resting on the door of the Escort, the other waving acknowledgement to the two security guards. 'Time to bugger off!'

'Agreed . . . I'll see you then, Ray — at the office!' she called out, and started the engine.

Banks seemed nonplussed.

'Have you, er — ?'

'Seen enough? Yes, thanks — I'll call you. Don't hang around.' His sudden grin was lascivious, filled with memory. 'And that's the end of *that,* too!' she laughed. 'Well done — the character-acting, I mean!'

She waved her hand and accelerated away from Banks, hearing one of the security men call out something in a voice brimming with lewdness. The marina retreated in the driving mirrors, Banks becoming a stranded, tiny figure, the two security men ambling away, satisfied. She was sweating profusely, not merely because of the heat of the upholstery, not merely because they had been surprised. She felt dizzied with the success of her gambit, her personation of Banks' fictitious secretary. *Tanya,* she thought, would have been her name. She was hotter than the car, the day. The station was there — but there was *no metro system.* Just the excavated tunnels.

Millions . . . absolutely *millions* of pounds — ecus, rather — unaccounted for. As she drove along a new stretch of dual carriageway, raising the dust of disuse, the gaps in the jigsaw, the succession of unfinished, unstarted pieces of the urban regeneration project, struck more forcibly, imprinting themselves with the clarity of photographs on her memory. She was irritated and impatient that she would not be able to speak to Aubrey until he returned to London that evening. Because now she could not risk calling him at Uffingham, not with David there . . .

. . . David — *what are you up to?*

Lunch was to be late, by David's request. He remained ensconced in the library with his coterie of the great and the possibly-not-good — the two European Commissioners, Rogier and Laxton, the local Euro MP Campbell, Bryan Coulthard and Jean-Paul Bressier, chairman of Balzac-Stendhal, the French partners of Aero UK in the Skyliner project, who had arrived the previous afternoon. Which, as Aubrey reflected once more as he sat on a comfortably cushioned painted chair on the terrace of Uffingham, rather narrowed the field of suspicion. Whatever David was up to, it had to be connected with Aero UK and its disastrous recent experiences at the hands of MoD and the world's airlines. The whole gang of them had spent most of Sunday ensconced in the library. Incommunicado.

He was engaged in a second small Scotch and in conversation with his old friend, Clive Winterborne; and in the immensely pleasurable activity, now that he was well into his old age, of watching other people labour under a hot sun. The giant marquee was only now being dismantled, falling to the ground an hour since with the erotic grace of a woman's clothing. Clive had held a party inside it for the estate workers and their families on the Sunday. There was a rowing boat on the lake, with the swans and ducks, and two figures patiently fishing out spent fireworks. Volunteers, under the direction of the head gardener, were combing the lawns for the same spent bodies and the detritus of Saturday's festivities. *The vomit count was low, thank goodness,* Clive had remarked, his eyes bright with success and his habitual kind sense of mischief. *Broken glass tally minimal,* he had added.

Inside the house, Clive's secretary and a small team of volunteers were itemising the expenditure, the pledges, the cheques and the cash. The grand auction had been a success, after the gambit of the fireworks had increased the general sense of well-being and generosity. Swallows swooped and sewed the air around the house's eaves as they sipped their drinks and tasted their ease in each other's company. An ease which all but disguised from Aubrey his suspicions of Clive's son.

In Clive's company, on a grand terrace behind a boastful stone balustrade and overlooking a lake and hazy parkland, it was difficult to think of fraud on a giant scale, the misappropriation of European Union funds by *anyone,* let alone David Winterborne.

'You're thoughtful,' Clive murmured. 'Something wrong?'

Aubrey carefully shook his head.

'Just looking back over my long life,' he replied. 'It seems I can't achieve the trick of doing so without evoking a touch of melancholy.' Which was true, if not of the moment. An interrogator's ploy, he reminded himself, employing truth like a lock-pick. 'You've never had that trouble,' he added with a smile.

'No. My melancholic memories are quite specific, old friend — quite specific.' The death of his beloved Eurasian wife, the death of his charming, feckless younger son in a car accident . . . perhaps other occasions of which Aubrey did not know. Otherwise, Clive's army career and his later career in MI5 were a catalogue of success and esteem, as was his subsequent role as squire of Uffingham. Winterborne Straits had passed directly into David's hands while Clive continued his uninterrupted indifference to commerce.

And, in fifteen years, David had expanded it into Winterborne Holdings, breaking out of Singapore with the ferocity of an infantry assault, investing, acquiring, defeating competition, diversifying . . . creating a monstrous business behemoth. Clive had whispered, soon after Aubrey's arrival, that David was assiduously seeking US citizenship to facilitate the further expansion of Winterborne Holdings. Under David's stewardship, a trading house in the East had become a tentacular conglomerate in the West, something uniquely twentieth — rather than nineteenth — century.

Clive glanced at his watch. 'I've told David *two* is the latest I'm prepared to contemplate my lunch,' he announced gruffly but without irritation. 'It's almost that now.'

'So,' Aubrey sighed, 'you're well pleased with Saturday's junket?'

'Didn't you enjoy the fireworks, Kenneth?' Winterborne replied archly.

'Splendid. Marian thought so, too.'

'Ah, our shining girl.'

'Indeed.'

Aubrey felt uncomfortable beneath his panama hat, as if hotter within his old-fashioned cream flannel suit. The shining girl — almost as much his own child and that of Clive as she was Giles' daughter — troubled him; at least her suspicions did, plucking at his mental vision of things like a stye or mote. David's rapid, even cavalier expansion into aerospace, in Europe and the US alike, had exposed him to the banks and other lenders and investors. The recent history of Aerospace UK and its French counterpart — Aubrey glanced towards the tall windows of the library — threatened the various subcontracting businesses that Winterborne Holdings owned or controlled. The recession had afflicted his construction companies in every world market he had succeeded in penetrating. Winterborne Holdings, Aubrey had learned by a process of interrogation and compliation, was unsteady if not unstable; weaker than anyone liked, except its enemies.

The rowing boat had returned to the shore of the lake and was tied up at a pergolaed jetty, splashed with the pink climbing roses planted in ornamental urns that lined the small pier.

'Are you free for lunch on Thursday?' Clive asked. 'I'm up in town on some charity business. Shall we meet?'

'Naturally. I'll call Giles. Indeed, we can be his guests, since he so ungraciously failed to attend your fireworks party.'

'Good idea.' The lorry on to which the marquee supports had been loaded moved away along the drive and rounded the corner of the house. Clive sighed, as if he had that moment rid himself of unwelcome guests. 'Regimental reunions are all very well —'

'— but cannot be compared with fireworks!' Aubrey completed, chuckling.

'Giles probably had a precognition of Marian's encounter with George, our local party chairman,' Clive added. 'From all I hear, he would have been mightily embarrassed —' He grinned, his hawklike features softening, their leatheriness warming. 'She really does take all life head-on, doesn't she?' His admiration was undisguised.

'Though I shall have to have a quiet word with her about the height of her profile. Central Office is, I have it on the best authority, gunning for her.'

'They'll never manage her deselection!'

'Of course not. She could gain re-election in this constituency with an illegitimate child being breast-fed on the hustings!' When their laugher had diminished, Winterborne added more gravely: 'But it's this sometimes needless upsetting of people, her urge to trample on pretensions they have cultivated as carefully as rare orchids. Even someone with lights as dim as those possessed by dear George often knows when he's being patronised or mocked. It doesn't achieve anything — so why does she go in for it with such enthusiasm?' He threw his hands in the air in mock despair.

'Just consider the inordinate amount of time she must spend with the dim, the venal, the unprincipled and the boring,' Aubrey observed, enjoying their patrician dialogue. 'When she returns from the Mother of Parliaments, that choicest Palace of Westminster, you can't really blame her for bridling at a great deal more of the same.'

'I ask only for a little common sense,' Winterborne offered with a smile.

'Ah, our dear Marian was born not so much with common sense but with an ethical sense — a more combustible property altogether.'

'Exactly. It could blow her sky-high some fine day — and I would hate that to happen.'

'Quite,' Aubrey murmured, masking his features with the whisky tumbler. Clive glanced away towards the library windows and the door again — thankfully.

For Marian was engaged in one of her explosive experiments. *Light the blue touch paper and retire.* It served as a warning against Marian's curiosity as much as against the combustibility of fireworks. Her notion of the kind of fraud in which David could be involved — if it bore fruit — would indeed undermine her as well as David and Clive, and blow them all at the moon. Did she understand how dangerous her enquiries were . . . to her past, her sense of well-being, to some of the scaffolding of her personality?

He knew Marian well enough to experience a slight, unnerved nausea which he could not blame on the sun's strength or the second whisky. More immediately, there was a very real personal danger in her pursuing her investigation. Which was why he had told her little of what he had discovered since their last meeting. To have stilled her ardent intelligence would have been beyond him. He would have had to lie to her, and she would have known it. Nevertheless, she had little idea how close his own suspicions now were to those she held.

And that weakened him, in front of Clive, because the truth would destroy their friendship, would alienate Marian and her father from Clive and Uffingham. Marian, given free rein, would pull the whole edifice of their various relationships down. Aubrey's concern — perhaps his sole concern — was how he might mitigate the blow.

His nerves were startled as David and his guests emerged from the door on to the terrace, blinking in the sunlight like conspirators. Clive waved a lazy arm, then stood up, calling out: 'At last, gentlemen! Not a single healthy appetite among you, by the look of it!' The butler, as at a given signal, emerged to take their drinks order.

'Champagne, I think, Russell,' Aubrey heard David announce. 'Not premature, I feel.' He was smiling broadly, confidently. It was like sunlight after cloud, a sense of better weather; how could there be any villainy here?

Easily . . . In Aubrey's perspective remained something Marian's eager moral nose had scented then forgotten — Fraser worked for David, or at least he *probably* did, and there was a young man being buried in Somerset whom Fraser had *probably* killed.

'Champagne, Kenneth?' David called to him. He rose with an awkward hurry, waggling his hand in refusal.

'Not after Scotch, dear boy — thank you.'

David shrugged, his mood undisturbed. There was an ease among the group of men that had not been Aubrey's sense of them previously. There had been strain, an edginess. Perhaps Bressier, the chairman of the French aerospace company, had brought saving news? There was now tentative, and accumulating, interest in the Skyliner, albeit they were practically giving the aircraft away with boxes of cereal in their leasing arrangements. So someone had informed him at the Club, a leading economic journalist. Whatever had occurred, there was now the scent of relief, even success.

'Beautiful day, Kenneth,' David announced,

raising his champagne flute in an ironic toast. The swans glided on the still, glittering lake as if nothing could ever disturb them.

'Absolutely. I gather your self-satisfaction quotient is higher today than yesterday,' he murmured, watching the swans glide in and out of focus amid the gleam of the water.

'Ah — trust you to notice,' David replied carefully. 'I can admit to you, Kenneth, that things haven't been good the past few weeks and months. Culminating in the helicopter fiasco,' he added with deep vehemence. 'But Aero UK and Balzac-Stendhal have adopted my leasing policy and the planes are beginning to move out of the two factories. Once they're flying — well, who knows?'

'Indeed — who knows?'

'Come and meet everyone — most of them you already know, I should imagine.'

'Some, certainly.'

Aubrey shook hands with Rogier and Bressier, addressing them in his correct but fluent French. In their own language, he could detect more easily and certainly their relief, a certain new lightness of mood. Bryan Coulthard was bluffly, openly confident. Laxton, with all the assiduity of someone who learned nothing and forgot less, especially every petty enmity of his long and undistinguished career, was patronising; amused at Aubrey's old-fashioned suit and his remittance-man status at Uffingham. As a mere house guest of Clive, he did not merit the rank accorded to those who came to do business with David. Laxton glowed with the fleshiness of seized opportunities in Brussels, though drink seemed to be remapping his features as a chart of his veins. He perspired freely, but even that seemed suggestive of confidence.

Aubrey murmured of mutual acquaintances and recent deaths and the importance of Europe with Laxton, much to the amusement of Clive over the man's padded shoulder. A little business with Coulthard, whose replies suggested that he had emerged into a clearing. There was minimal sense of the pressure of creditors, of the stock market . . . Shares in Aero UK had climbed back slightly with news of Skyliners being leased. Aubrey, in his selfish wish to dissuade Marian and avoid the conflagration the truth would bring, began to feel more comfortable, affable even towards Laxton. If the *necessity* for villainy had ceased, if whatever they had been doing was an episode now closed, then perhaps, just perhaps, Marian would be satisfied with knowledge without action.

He found himself once more beside Rogier, who leaned deferentially over him. The man was well over six feet, still slim, groomed, narrow-featured, the gold-framed spectacles and bow tie making him seem more academic than his reputation suggested, less the skilful politician; a form of disguise, then. Europe, of course, moved from strength to strength, and Aubrey did not demur, largely indifferent as he was to Europhilia and Europhobia alike. He anticipated that the bureaucrats would, as bureaucrats always manage to do in situations where they do not possess the freedom to do wrong, make an unholy, scrappy mess of federalism. He nodded and smiled and allowed the Euroblandishments to vanish beyond his ears, towards the lake.

Then he said, as a sense of *ennui* assailed him, and almost to deflect the conversation: 'I imagine the suicide of that young man in your department was most embarrassing, Commissioner? I didn't know him personally, but a friend of mine did . . .'

Rogier's features were blanched. Aubrey made a huge effort of will to render his own face bland.

The real truth of the thing was murder — and this man knew it for what it was — and all possibility of dissuading Marian vanished in that hard light. Lloyd had been murdered by Fraser on David Winterborne's direct order, *in all probability.*

Russell, the butler, announced lunch.

'Ah!' Aubrey chirruped brightly. Thank God —

'Something wrong?' David asked sharply, seeing the expression on his face.

Aubrey shook his head, perhaps too emphatically. 'No, no — dear boy. A little giddy spell — hot sun, I expect.' David appeared not quite to believe. 'Shall we go in?' Aubrey pressed, mopping his brow not entirely in pretence.

'Is something *wrong,* Kenneth?' David insisted.

'No!' Aubrey snapped. 'Fine, fine . . .' He waved David towards his guests.

The heat of his body would not lessen, despite his effort of will. His thoughts, too, seemed heated. It was truly dreadful, *dreadful,* he realised. He glanced at Clive, whose expression was of concern. He smiled in a watery, assuring way and they walked together towards the house, away from the terrace and its now elusive and somehow darkened view of the lake's tranquillity. Clive took his elbow, as he had so often done, and Aubrey was grateful for the support. The group of confident men, their fraud probably already behind them, sauntered ahead of himself and his dear friend. It was utterly hateful to him, the knowledge he possessed and the frightening sense of what he must do with it . . . or how, for perhaps even deeper reasons, he must ensure that it remained hidden.

He must either help Marian destroy David Winterborne, and Clive into the bargain, or he must become an accessory after the fact of murder.

Vance's private jet waited on the tarmac, poised on the apron, nose towards the taxiway as if it had caught Barbara's mood of flight. A coroner's station wagon nuzzled beside it, and the metal casket which contained Vance was ceremoniously removed from its rear and loaded on to the airplane. Gant watched from a slight distance the results of Barbara's blackmail, string-pulling, desperation. Someone from the US Consulate in Helsinki stood with her now, watching the casket as if it contained the victim of some foreign war . . . Maybe it did, at that. Barbara wanted out and the Consulate had smoothed her way to that object. There'd be a proper post-mortem examination in Phoenix.

The evening was clear, high and light cloud goldened by the lowering sun. A Finnair Boeing rose from the runway and almost at once caught the sun, gleamed like a star. Kerosene on the breeze.

Reluctantly, Gant walked towards the plane. The diplomat was shaking hands with Barbara with official solemnity. She was nodding mechanically until he released her hand. Once he had done so, she turned and climbed the three steps into the fuselage of the airplane that had been the small dream of Vance's early years, his first ambition. It was — now — what Barbara thought he should have gone on doing, making executive jets for rich men.

In the hospital corridor, she had said to the air: 'Poppa, you should have gone on building toys for rich boys.'

'He couldn't,' Gant had replied.

'Then he was *wrong!*' she had raged against his death. Then, like a frightened, lost child: 'I want to get out of here.'

He really didn't want to board the plane with her. She had already returned to the idea of sabotage — and what he would do about it. It was not, yet, a plea or an effort at blackmail, but it would become so. And it had made him at once reluctant, recreating as it did a sense of obligation for the failure of their briefly shared past. She loaded him with guilt, with the sense that he needed to atone for something. What he had so easily promised Burton seemed impossible to offer Barbara. If he agreed to go on with it for the sake of her devotion to the dead idol he could never exorcise, then he would have to complete it, it would have to be finished.

He boarded the plane behind her. The casket was stowed in the cargo compartment. He thought of the co-pilot's seat as an escape, but the eager grief of her features dissuaded him. He was unable to abandon her. So he sat across the narrow aisle from her and fastened his seatbelt. She seemed satisfied, though it was no more than a moment before she blurted:

'You will go on with it?'

'I'll — take it as far as I can,' he replied levelly. At once in her eyes there was the sense of someone else who *would* have promised — except he was dead.

'You don't owe him anything?' she asked scornfully.

The flight deck door opened, but Jimmy, Gant's successor as Vance's personal pilot, assessed the situation in a moment and retreated.

'Nothing,' Gant felt impelled to reply.

'You were close to him. *You* believed, too.'

'Then we got divorced.'

After a long silence, where her hands twisted together and untwisted repeatedly and her features appeared thinned by some wasting disease, she said:

'I turned Poppa against you. I wanted all his support, his love. I had to make you the bad guy.'

'You must have wanted out very badly.'

'I did. I couldn't live with you, Mitchell. There's no *living with* in your case. I'm sorry I had to do —'

'It doesn't matter.'

And it didn't. It was like discovering that a teacher had marked down an exam paper in high school. How could you resent something so far in the past? They were, he realised, like two people in an Edward Hopper painting, almost devoid of colour and vitality, staring into the end of a situation in immobile helplessness, their bodies admitting it was long over.

'It doesn't matter,' he repeated more gently.

Vance had done what Barbara had asked of him, played the role of the wounded and outraged father. He and Barbara had been the figures in the Hopper painting long before Vance had badmouthed him. And it was he, Gant, who had put them there. In that, Barbara was right.

He didn't think there were any amends to be made any longer. But there was, he recognised, a dispassionate anger, a need to satisfy his suspicions. He felt disquiet, even disbelief, at Vance's death, but more urgently he could not live with the sense that he had been duped.

'Tell Jimmy to file a new flight plan — to Oslo,' he began. Her immediate sigh sounded almost sexual, climactic. 'Make a stopover. I'll look into this guy who posed as one of Alan's people. Maybe there'll be something —'

'Will it help?'

'It won't save the company. Who'd listen? Who'd *want* to listen?'

She could not hide her disappointment, her expression arranging itself in lines and planes that had so often expressed an easy, habitual contempt.

'Then I need to be back in Phoenix as soon as possible,' Barbara announced, rearranging her posture into an imitation of purpose. 'There are things to be *closed out.*' She was dismissive of him, suddenly. He couldn't save jobs, stock prices, investment — not even her father's reputation.

'You'll do what you have to. Just drop me off in Oslo.'

'Do you think — ?' she began, but the light faded from her eyes. To her, his surroundings were a kitchen, bathroom, bedroom, patio — anywhere they had quarrelled. He possessed no skill other than truculent, defeated argument. 'Hopeless, isn't it? You're right. Who would believe enough for it to matter?' Then, as if he were still wearing a last rag of the hero's uniform in which she had first seen him, she added: '*I* would like to know. For his sake.'

'Whatever I know, you'll know.'

He seemed about to add something, but the flight deck door opened again, distracting her. Gant watched her turn to Jimmy as if to the future.

'File the flight plan to Oslo, then on to the States,' she ordered. Jimmy glanced momentarily at Gant, who stared at his hands.

'Sure, Ms Vance. Won't be more than a few minutes, they're not too busy right now.' He closed the door behind him.

Barbara settled back in her seat, ostentatiously taking a laptop from the empty seat beside her, frowning at once at the screen's response to her impatient touch. Gant watched a stranger, studying her as he might have studied a map of some place he had once visited — but suspicious that he might only have dreamed the journey, the experience.

Oslo . . .

Charlotte Burton watched her husband put down the telephone and slump into an armchair in as slovenly and relaxed a manner as one of their sons might have done. It was nearly dark outside. Time to draw the curtains. She discovered herself more attentive to such matters from the moment the first 494 had crashed in the desert while Tim was in the States. She was almost eager to shut out Holland Park — not merely because of the occasional press encampment on the pavement but because the reporters and cameramen reminded her of her neighbours, even passing strangers, who would be mentally prying into their affairs.

Tim, only hours after he got back from Finland, had agreed to a visit from David Winterborne and Bryan Coulthard. They were messengers who need not be executed, they were bringing good news.

'Well?'

Burton was biting at his thumb.

'What — ? Oh . . . They want to put a deal to me. David says he wants to save Artemis.' He raised his arms in a huge, disbelieving, mystified shrug.

'A takeover — a buyout, what?' she insisted, sitting forward in her chair, hands gripping each other on her lap. 'Tim — what is it?' She was angry with him, almost as her mother would have been at her father for answering the door to visitors without donning his jacket. It wasn't the sweater and jeans he was wearing, though — it was the defeat they symbolised, the retirement from the whirl of meetings and suits and desperate efforts to save the business.

'I'm not sure. It's not investment — they haven't got the money!' He brightened, but it was a retreat into humour. He was afraid to believe the conversation he had just had. 'Maybe he wants to offer me some cheap leases on Skyliners . . . ? It sounded as if it could be that. Our mutual advantage, that sort of thing.'

'Will you? If that's what it is? Take his offer, I mean?'

'They'll have to be bloody cheap!' he announced loudly. 'But I suppose they might be interested in a deal like that. Mightn't they?' He was afraid to hope.

'Possibly. You're very high-profile at the moment — for all the wrong reasons. If you agreed to fly Skyliners across the Pond —'

'I could have them *this* summer — at least for July and August, catch some of the heaviest traffic. There'd be a lot of fuss about it, all the positive kind . . .' He rubbed his hands through his long hair, then looked up. 'Are there any drawbacks, Charley?'

'Not immediate ones. You'll have to be patient — grovel, I shouldn't wonder.'

'David likes that — grovelling.'

'You'll be dependent on Aero UK and the French for almost the entire fleet, for medium- and long-haul . . .' She plucked at her chin with finger and thumb. 'Pricing policy could be difficult, they'd be the tail wagging the dog, Winterborne and Coulthard . . . It could take years, Tim,' she concluded, looking up.

'But it could save the company, mm?' He almost pleaded for her concurrence. 'I mean, if you think it's all right —'

She smiled.

'Look at it this way, husband of mine, light of my life . . . The Skyliner was way too expensive for Artemis, so you plumped for the 494. Now, the 494 is no more and the Skyliner is — or should be — comparatively cheap. You could, if the deal is properly structured and you can beat the price down far enough, still undercut the competition, even with the most expensive aeroplane in the world!'

'Stuff BA and the European carriers, you mean! *Cor!*' He was grinning broadly, prompting the return of her own smile. It all sounded much too good to be true to someone not as eternally optimistic as Tim . . . not quite as convincing to her as to her husband, who had been plunged into gloom and all but silent since his return from Helsinki. Guilt and self-pity had battled for possession of his mood. 'I *wonder,*' he continued, 'I just wonder . . .'

He had made a few desultory phone calls, refused possible meetings, wanted to skulk in hiding at home. For the past few hours he had plucked at the sleeve of her sympathy, her identity with his mood, like an increasingly importunate child. He *was* a child, in so many ways — as now, with his mood elated. In moments, he would suggest opening champagne! Charlotte wondered at David Winterborne's true intent. Aero UK's own problems made Tim's suspicion feasible. Two men clinging to the same lifebelt — using each other as a lifebelt, more likely. It *was* possible —

She surrendered to his mood. She wouldn't draw the curtains, not yet.

'When are they coming?'

'An hour's time.'

'Then I need to change, make-up . . . And you, get out of that sweater and into some of the clothes I keep buying for you that you never wear! Come on, come on — Roman triumph or tumbril ride, you're going to be dressed for the occasion!'

The Rolls Royce drew to a halt in Holland Park, the evening sky holding a retinal afterimage of daylight. Bryan Coulthard got out of the car and Winterborne made to follow him when the car telephone began ringing. He waved a hand at Coulthard.

'Go ahead, Bryan — I'll just take this.' Coulthard nodded, closing the passenger door behind him. He stood on the pavement, hands on his hips, studying the elegant façade of Burton's house. Warm light fell on him from the first-floor drawing room. 'Yes?' Winterborne asked brusquely.

It was Fraser's voice, like an unpleasant reminiscence from a past acquaintance, recalling experiences he no longer admitted as his.

'Funny kind of reports on your friend,' Fraser announced without preamble. 'She's been visiting some parts of the Midlands you might not want her to.'

It was, at that moment, irritating to be the recipient of Fraser's clandestine humour. 'Do you mean Marian? What has she been doing?' he snapped. Coulthard glanced back into the Rolls as if impatient. Someone had opened Burton's front door; a door opening on to the future. 'I have an important meeting, Fraser — don't play games.'

'Sorry — sir.' The insolence was evident. 'She was with that guy Banks, the twopenny-halfpenny builder who's been getting uppity. They drove around the canal development, the marina . . . Two people who must have been them were surprised in the marina metro tunnel. She's cool, your friend. Pretended they'd gone down there for a shag —'

'What are you talking about?' But he knew. Why else had he instructed Fraser to be on the lookout for her? Egan's panic on Saturday evening, Marian's conversations with one or two other guests involved in the regeneration project . . . *Aubrey?* 'You're certain it was Marian?'

'As certain as one of our security men could be. He says he recognised her, and Banks. They were looking over Banks' site.'

'I see.'

Aubrey and Marian had been in some kind of collusion at Uffingham, he was certain. At lunch, Aubrey's questioning of his guests had appeared bland, conversational . . . but he had alarmed Rogier when he referred to Lloyd's death. Why would he have done so, other than deliberately? Aubrey had no connection with Lloyd, other than through Marian. And Lloyd must have been Marian's source inside the Commission. It would be his death that was spurring her on, not Banks' whingeing, and Aubrey was following her lead.

'Why must she persist?' he asked exasperatedly. 'What in God's name does she think she's doing?'

'She can smell something's gone off, that's for sure.'

Winterborne experienced a mockery of moral affront. Marian and Aubrey had no *right,* digging into his affairs. The matter was closed. Lloyd's death had been no more than an expedient necessity. It was in the *past,* over with.

'I — I'm not certain what should be done,' he admitted. Coulthard had already climbed the steps to Burton's front door and was waiting for him. Burton himself appeared, shaking hands with Coulthard. The moment of success was being made visible. 'What needs to be done?' he asked heavily.

'Can she still be warned off? You've always said she couldn't be bought —'

'No. How do you mean *warned?*'

'Banks needs attention, too. That would cut off all corroboration . . . The security man saw no camera. She won't be able to get back on site. Would she go to people with what she's seen, suspects?'

'I — no, I don't think so. It's not much, at the moment. Clues, nothing more. She'll go on asking questions for some time yet. Talk to Aubrey —'

'I don't like that,' Fraser offered. 'That old bastard having his finger in the pie.'

'I agree. I don't think we have any alternative there but to await his becoming bored. He'll come to see me, I suspect. Look, I have to go,

Fraser — have you any suggestion as to what we can do about Marian?'

'Surveillance tightened. *Proper* surveillance.'

'Anything else?'

It was as if he were prompting Fraser, nudging him into uttering the unthinkable, one child taunting another into hurting a cat, starting a small fire.

'Aubrey's hands are tied by his friendship with my father,' he announced with sudden, certain clarity. 'He's in a dilemma. I'm sure *he* would prefer nothing to emerge. But Marian —'

'Can she be frightened? Lots of the most unlikely people can be — moral crusaders quite often become easily unnerved.'

'Very well,' Winterborne replied after a silence. He sighed. 'If you think she could be frightened off, try it. But no *harm* to her.'

'To Banks?'

'I don't care what you do to keep Banks quiet!' Then he added: 'I must go. Handle this carefully, Fraser —'

'I always do.' Again, the professional insolence, the quasimilitary contempt for the civilian, the man whose hands remained clean. 'One other thing —'

'What?'

'Roussillon. Keeping an eye on the pilot, Gant.'

'Well?'

'Vance's pilot filed a flight plan for Oslo, *then* on to the States. That just came in.'

'Has Roussillon people he can use in Oslo?'

'Yes.'

'Then keep Gant under surveillance. You're

sure there are no leads to Strickland?'

'None.'

'Then he matters less than Marian. Good night, Fraser.'

Winterborne put down the telephone. It had been discomfitingly clammy against his ear. He paused for a moment to compose his expression, then got out of the car, waving instantly to Burton at the top of the house steps.

'Tim!' he called, taking the steps as eagerly as a lover. 'Thank you for seeing us at such short notice.'

They shook hands. He and Coulthard were ushered into the house. Everything was as it should be . . . The past had no authority, no right or claim to intrude.

She realised that she had fallen asleep in the armchair and that the notepad and the papers she had been studying had fallen from her lap on to the floor. She saw that it was after one in the morning and sensed her exhausted tiredness. She did not realise what it was that had awoken her. Perhaps just her leaden hand and arm slipping from the chair, tugging her awake.

She yawned and stretched. More papers fell from her lap. She vaguely glimpsed scrawled columns of figures, like a child's arithmetic, on the floor near her feet — her estimate of the vastness of the sums diverted from the regeneration project to . . . Aero UK, Winterborne Holdings, dozens of eager pockets —

— she held her head, which ached. Her vision was blurred; the room seemed filled with thick white smoke. She smelt something. As she tried to stand, she fell back in the armchair. Struggled upright again, pushing with her arms — smell? Burning . . .

She formed the thought gradually, and was shocked into wakefulness by her realisation. *Burning* — she could smell burning. The room was grey with weblike smoke — she coughed. A noise, low down on the scale like a tape-hiss played back in slow motion. She opened the door to the kitchen and flame roared at her, striking with the speed of a snake towards her head and arms.

'Are you sure about this?' Cobb asked.

The rear windows of the flat glowed with a lurid light. Behind them, the cathedral was massive against the stars and the minster pool reflected the string of lamps along its banks.

'What — ?' Jessop replied, adding: 'Sure I'm sure. I vos only obeying orders.' He chuckled. 'Fraser was told to frighten her. This should do it — vandals, someone cheesed off with her politics or the way she treated their whining, chucked a home-made firebomb through her window. Standard issue on most council estates these days, everyone knows how to make them.' Jessop studied the spread of the fire and nodded in satisfaction. 'If it kills her, so much the better. Fraser takes the blame if it isn't liked, anyway.'

'She will be frightened off, then?' Cobb asked.

'Wouldn't you be — if you were just a civilian, I mean?'

'Yes. Never did like fire.'

'Neither does she. She's still got the evidence

of a skin graft on her right arm, so the file says, from a childhood accident with a fire . . .' He paused, inspecting his handiwork, then he said: 'She doesn't seem to be coming out, does she?'

'The fact that you jammed the front door shut wouldn't help, would it?'

'I suppose not.'

'Shouldn't we — ?'

'Yes, I suppose so. Some member of the clergy might already have rung for the fire brigade. Come on, then — let's go and tell Fraser what good little Boy Scouts we've been. We should get our Firelighter's badges for this.' As he turned away, he murmured: 'She still hasn't come out — shame!'

CHAPTER EIGHT

Fire, Lies and Videotape

He stood in the passenger doorway of the small jet more as a gesture towards their past than anything else, in case she wanted to say something more, required further reassurance. When he was certain, by her expression, that all she desired was the continuation of the flight — her flight from the scene of the destruction of Vance Aircraft — he nodded to her and descended the passenger steps. That late at night, Vance's aircraft was cleared for almost immediate takeoff. He waved his hand at the smudge of white in the cockpit window that was the pilot's face. Then he walked away from the plane.

The engines wound up once more and he sensed rather than saw the plane move away towards the taxiway and the threshold. He deliberately did not turn back or pause in order to watch its departure, but continued walking towards the open-doored maintenance hangar. Oslo's airport was little more than a garishly lit island above the subdued glow of the city and the darkness of the Oslofjord and the Skagerrak beyond it. His sports bag brushed gently against his leg. He could already see the tailplane of an airliner being serviced, just as two nights before the 494 had been. And, just like him, someone had walked into this hangar and announced he was from Vance Aircraft and had been sent to check out the fuel computer system. One of maybe a dozen men, most of whose identities he did not know, with the dark talent to create a computer-generated piece of sabotage.

Behind him, he heard a four-engined airliner lift into the night. Jimmy would have put Vance's jet on to the end of the runway by now. He glimpsed in his mind Barbara's face at one of the windows, the features of a stranger seen on a passing train, drained, weary, tragic like those of a woman in a Hopper painting. Out of which he had again walked, probably forever. He blinked in the lights of the huge hangar. The dock gantry girdled the airliner like a whalebone corset. At once, but perhaps for no more than display, he was approached by a security guard. The man was in his early sixties, overweight, wary, the armpits of his uniform shirt stained by the perspiration of a hot night and nerves.

'What do you want?' he repeated in English as Gant shrugged at the Norwegian.

Slowly, Gant reached into his pocket and flapped Barbara's letter in the small breeze.

'I'm Gant. I'm here to see Olssen. I'll wait until you find him — or can you take me to him? It doesn't matter which.'

The security guard puzzled over the letter Gant had asked Barbara to write — *just in case,* he had said, *I need to enlist some official help . . . I lost my job, remember?*

Probably because it assisted the man in unpacking his responsibility, the guard said:

'Olssen told me you would be coming — I'll take you to him.' He handed back the letter. Gant took it and then turned quickly, alarming the man.

Vance's private jet — the one he had built and which now carried his casket — rose above the glow of the airport, into the night, navigation lights brighter than the stars. He watched it until it banked slightly out over the fjord, then dismissed it from his mind. The sense of Alan Vance's body on board the plane depressed him with obligation, and promises given.

'Sure. Lead on,' he murmured.

The scent of heated metal, fuel, oils restored an awareness of the immediate, the superficial. Work was evidently all but complete on the Sabena Boeing. Men were moving with the crispness of homegoing, or loitering to gossip.

'Mr Olssen — Mr Olssen!' the security guard called, waving to an overalled figure near the Boeing. 'This man has come to see you — you expected him!' His was the eagerness to pass something that burned. Olssen was at once studying Gant as he approached, as if matching his frame and gaunt features to some mental photograph. He held out an oil-stained hand, having wiped it on a rag.

'You're Gant,' he confirmed. 'Sorry you had to

come, that we meet like this.'

'Sure.' It was hotter in the hangar — or perhaps it was the remembered heat of Arizona, and that other hangar where the first 494 had lain like the rubble of a condemned building. 'Thanks for seeing me.'

'I understand that it is necessary. You must inspect our schedule, our records, on behalf of the FAA and the NTSB. I am not offended, it is routine.'

'Yes.'

'You will want to talk to others here, those who worked on the aircraft? They are about finished for the night . . .'

'I won't keep them — *just* those who saw the guy who claimed he was from Vance Aircraft. Then I'd like to talk to you — you spent time with him, I guess?'

Olssen nodded.

'Yes, of course. And Jorgensen — probably no one else. Like you, he came late, when we were almost finished on the aircraft —' His voice tailed away, as if he had suddenly become cautious, or perhaps merely reflective. His eyes suggested that he recollected their telephone call, his own protestations of innocence over the identity of Massey, as he had called himself. He blurted: 'There is no Massey, you said. Have you checked with Vance Aircraft? Perhaps —'

'There's no mistake on my part, Mr Olssen. Vance Aircraft never employed a deputy chief engineer called Massey. I have that from a man called Blakey, who *is* the chief design engineer.'

Blakey had remained in Helsinki to oversee the

further recovery of the wreckage, its investigation by the Finns, its eventual transportation, like the body of Vance, back to Phoenix.

'I am sorry, but I do not see that it is any of my —'

Patiently, but with a flavour of threat, Gant said:

'No one is blaming you, Mr Olssen, not right now. The man who called himself Massey — let's talk about him, uh? While you introduce me to your schedule, the other paperwork on the 494 service job you carried out.'

'Vance threatened me, this company! We have a good record, this hasn't happened — !'

'Sure,' Gant soothed. 'Vance was angry. His company collapsed around his head. He needed to blame someone.'

They were walking towards Olssen's office. Olssen was about the same height, slightly stockier, running to the first fat of middle age. His eyes kept furtively glancing at Gant, who appeared oblivious of his attention.

'Mr Vance did not come with you?'

'No.' Why tell this man, when he could read it in tomorrow's paper? 'He didn't. Now, Massey . . . ?'

Olssen opened the door of his glass-walled office. The old desk was littered with forms, other papers. Grey filing cabinets, a rickety table piled with books and manuals, the scent of dust, oil. Gant found the cramped place comfortable, familiar.

Olssen dumped a file in front of him as he sat down on the single hard chair on the visitor's side of the desk. The gesture was one of self-satisfaction as well as ingratiation,

'Here is the schedule for servicing on the aircraft. I dug it out when you told me you would be coming. You want some coffee?'

'Mm — oh, thanks.' He unzipped the sports bag and drew out a small tape recorder. 'First, just describe this guy Massey for me, would you? What did he look like? His accent, size, manner — take your time . . .' He placed the recorder on the desk between them. A family photograph lay on its back like a stranded insect amid the foliage of forms, regulations, a calendar. 'Take your time,' he repeated.

As Olssen cleared his throat, Gant leant forward with an eagerness that seemed to unnerve, even threaten the Norwegian. *This* man had seen him, the guy who had downed two aircraft and almost killed him in the third. This man had seen Massey, who had killed Vance — and over fifty others —

She was alone in the toolshed again, and her arm where the skin graft still showed *was burning. She had been trying one of Mummy's cigarettes. The toolshed in a hot, dry summer, had caught fire from the matches she had dropped when the cigarette made her cough violently. She couldn't open the door and her throat was too raw and choked for her to scream. Daddy* . . .

Marian sat slumped into a foetal ball in the hallway of the flat, unable to open the door . . .

She crouched in the farthest corner of the toolshed, her arm filled with pain — so badly hurt that she

could not relieve the pain by clutching it — watching the flames lick up around old seed bags, dry canes, terra cotta plant pots, herself. *Under the workbench, there were spiders but their clinging webs, filled with dead moths and flies, had to be ignored. Through a cracked windowpane, she could see the sunlight, the blue sky . . .*

The flames from the kitchen had reached the living room and flared garishly, orange-red, on the pale walls. The door wouldn't open, it was jammed somehow. The sound of breaking glass must have been what had woken her, when something burning had been thrown into the kitchen. She had seen the broken window in the moment before she had recoiled in sudden, recollected panic from the flames. Her arm ached deeply, to the bone. She could not move, could not get out of the flat. There was no one else in the building, the other occupants were away on long weekends or business. The burglar alarm was shrilling because of the rise in temperature. Someone would come, would come . . . She began coughing.

In the toolshed, she was coughing and her eyes were watering and she was screaming so loudly that someone must hear her, must, *it was only the back garden of the army house they occupied on one of Daddy's postings somewhere . . .*

Someone must come, the burglar alarm was so *loud*. Someone had to come, she couldn't move, her legs and arms and whole body were frozen with panic. She knew what was happening to her, the past coming like a massive injection of something that attacked the motor muscles, the nervous system. The panic was so enveloping it was no longer fear but paralysis.

Someone must come, Mummy would . . . was shopping, she had taken the car. Daddy would . . . was somewhere else, there was a barracks inspection she had heard at breakfast . . . someone must come . . .

The spell of the past, the straitjacket in which it held her, was too strong to be broken. She was helpless, the pain in her arm, remembered, overpowering her. The flames crept into the hall *and up to the workbench. Grass seed spilled from a bag being consumed by the fire,* the smoke from her smouldering furniture made her retch . . . Someone, *someone —*

— rough material, the smell of tobacco as when her mother pressed her against a blouse or cardigan she was wearing. Big hands clutching her up and out of the spiders' webs. The low mutter of constant cursing. The smell of soap pressed into her nose from the cheek against which her face was thrust, the sensation of bristles. Then the jolting passage through the flames and smoke, the squeezing of the hands and arms that did not allow her to breathe as she seemed buried in rough khaki cloth. Then the sunlight, the blue sky, and the scent of dry grass mingling with the smouldering smell of her clothes as she was pummelled. A big hand struck her burnt arm and she screamed again and then lost consciousness. . . . To wake up still on the grass, with big adult faces pressing chokingly close to her and among them, Daddy —

— woke up. The carpet in the hallway of the flat was smouldering, the living room was an inferno — the flame seen through boiling grey smoke. Woke up. She squeezed herself upright against the wall and grabbed the door handle, tugging at it until she remembered, with great, precise clarity, that it was jammed. By someone . . . She shook her head, the past nightmare slipping from her.

She blundered through the door of the spare bedroom at the rear of the flat, quite certain of her movements, her direction. Moonlight was coming through the window. The cathedral loomed across the Close. She thrust up the window and peeling paint flew off like white sparks. The glass reflected the fire inside.

Lance Corporal Davies had rescued her from that childhood fire . . . Just as he had rescued her every time the nightmare had come back, every time she had been terrified by fire. She climbed over the windowsill on to the fire escape . . .

Corporal Davies, looking down at her, his face as white as Daddy's . . .

Her feet touched the rung of the fire escape and she stumbled down it to the lawn behind the flats, coughing hard enough to make her want to retch. She slipped and fell on the dewy grass. Rolling on to her stomach, then rising to her knees, she looked back at the flat. The fire was visible at every window. She could hear the burglar alarm, and the noise of an approaching siren. Its noise gradually drowned the alarm. Her arm *hurt.*

It was almost two in the morning. Olssen's patience was gauze-thin, Jorgensen's indifferent contempt undisguised. His own tiredness was hard to conceal. The tape recorder remained amid the litter of the desk as if part of it and of no immediate concern to any of them.

Olssen's team of service engineers had long abandoned the hangar and the Boeing to the security guard. Gant had examined the service schedule with Olssen, out of routine rather than anticipation. Unless one of his people had screwed up, the answer didn't lie in the documents or their computerstored duplicates. But he'd known that anyway.

All that he had was the vague description of a tall, well-built man with an American accent — would two Norwegians know whether it was genuine or assumed? — who claimed his name was Massey and that he worked for Vance Aircraft. He had been wearing a check shirt, denims, a leather jacket, heeled boots. His hair was greying, he had a moustache, and maybe he was around forty.

It wasn't enough . . . not nearly enough.

'Can I go now?' Jorgensen asked Olssen, deliberately ignoring Gant but speaking in English so that he would understand his exasperation.

Olssen looked obsequiously, and with some impatience, at Gant.

'Sure. You're no help anyway, buddy,' Gant sneered. 'Maybe you'll do more good at home.' He smiled without meaning, other than a frustration of his own. 'You want to get some sleep, too, Mr Olssen? You want to leave me here — ?'

He wanted to rid himself of them now. They could be of no more assistance to him. Only these two had taken any notice, held any conversation with the saboteur, and neither of them could give him enough to recognise the man, or to be able to trace him. A stranger had walked in off the street, committed the crime, walked out of their lives.

'Look, I can hand over any keys, papers to the security guy. I may be some time yet.'

Olssen seemed relieved of caution and authority equally. Standing up, he said:

'Very well, Mr Gant — I will leave you the office keys, and you can lock up behind you. Hand them to Halvesson when you have finished. Come on, Jorgensen — oh, you know how to work the coffee machine?' Gant nodded. 'Then, good night, Mr Gant. I'm sorry we had to meet under —'

'Yeah. Me, too. Thank you for your help.'

'Do you think you will be able to identify this man? To think that it was a sabotage —'

Jorgensen was already out of the door and had begun whistling as he walked away.

'I don't think we have any evidence for saying that right now, Mr Olssen. Let's just keep that between us, OK?'

'OK. I — well, I wish you the best of luck. And thank you for understanding that there was no way that I could —'

'Sure. You couldn't have known. The guy had what looked like authority. I don't think anyone's blaming you.' He shook the man's hand quickly and sat down again, at once picking up a sheaf of papers. Keys rattled on to the desk, and he heard himself wished good night once more. ' 'Night,' he murmured. The door closed behind Olssen and Gant breathed deeply with relief, dismissing the last hours . . . But the disappointment leaked into the vacuum he created.

He was angry at the distractions of obligations, people, debts. Barbara had played on that. He had made easy promises as a consequence. Worse than that was the sense he had of being so easily reduced to impotence almost the moment he had begun something on his own initiative. He banged his fist on to the littered desk. The photograph frame jumped and the tape recorder moved; switched itself on. The button must have struck against something hard. He listened, as if transfixed, to the description of Massey with a fierce, renewed concentration.

But there was no sense of anyone he recognised. Presumably the man calling himself Massey *was* an American. Height, weight, features, dress . . . He switched off the recorder because it angered him like the buzzing of a wasp; it threatened his ego. Involuntarily, he got up from the chair and walked out of the office into the hangar. The Boeing sat like a promise on the oil-stained concrete. There weren't many men who could cause a plane like that to fall out of the sky without using a bomb. It was evident that the second 494 should have fallen into the sea and been lost, so the calculations were precise, the technology advanced. It was exactly the same pattern as the one he had encountered, instability succeeded by fuel starvation to the engines . . . He didn't know who, and he didn't know who had enough to gain. None of the big airplane manufacturers in the States would have sanctioned sabotage. The idea was crazy. So, *who?* The *why* had to be rivalry between manufacturers, not carriers. The 494 was flying only with

Artemis and a half-assed company in New Mexico. But Artemis was *small,* too small to worry the big carriers except with insect-stings. Irritation, not ruin. Vance was *small,* he couldn't have rivalled a big US planemaker.

Was it an ex-employee gone crazy, seeking revenge? Someone Vance had teed off even more than himself? He rubbed his hands through his hair angrily, lifting his face to the gantries, struts, metal beams of the hangar's roof. Was it just his intelligence experience that sought a strategy, a carefully organised *operation* in this, rather than a human motive?

Something at the edge of eyesight, high up among the metal bones of the hangar . . . Then the voice of the security guard distracted him. Irritated, he turned on Halvesson. The man was sweating, flustered.

'I . . . the telephone. My wife, she has been . . . I must go to the hospital, she is ill!' His terror was vivid, intense, as hard as a strong light suddenly shone into Gant's eyes. 'I cannot — the company does not have a replacement, I must *wait!*'

The woman might be dying or simply dizzy. Halvesson's shock could distinguish nothing except fear.

'The company won't let you go to the hospital, right?'

'No. I must stay here. My wife — I have just had a telephone call from the doctor who has seen her. He said I should *hurry.*' The man had aged, lost all volition, as if he had collided with the doctor's injunction. His hands flapped at his sides, his shirt was damp-stained across his chest, as well as beneath the arms. His face chalk white rather than flushed.

'I'm here,' Gant said. 'I'll be here most of the night. You'd better go. Nothing's going to happen here.'

'But you — you can't, you don't have authority . . .'

'Olssen left me his keys. He thinks I can be trusted. You want to see your wife, fella, you take off.' The quick sympathy he had felt was already evaporating. Halvesson was indecisive for perhaps half a minute, then he blurted:

'Yes, yes — I must go to her. She is not strong — she is often very depressed, you know — ?' He feared an attempted suicide. 'Thank you, thank you!'

He hurried away, scuttling rather than running. Moments after his stubby form disappeared from the hangar, Gant heard a car engine fire and then the noise of acceleration and the squeal of tyres. Then silence. He returned his attention to the Boeing, then —

— something . . . up above. He recalled an embryonic sensation of excitement, the moment before Halvesson distracted him. What — ? He scanned the ribs and shoulder blades of the hangar for something that had moved but had not been a bird. A slow mechanical, routine movement, something swinging from side to —

— camera. *Security camera.* Monitoring the hangar, its images projected on a screen in — Halvesson's office, its images *stored* there. A second camera, then a third. Routine, the dead, forgettable routine of machines.

Massey had walked into the hangar just as he had done. Into the camera's field of vision. Massey was *stored,* recorded, somewhere in Halvesson's office. Gant hurried.

'OK, I'll ask him what he wants done. Good move, *mon ami* —' It was not, on this occasion, meant to irritate Roussillon. Fraser rolled off the bed. Through the window, London's night-glow outlined Tower Bridge. 'No, I approve. Gant must be after Strickland. He knows it was sabotage — he survived it.' Fraser lit a cigarette, then blew smoke towards the open window. Two-thirty by the bedside clock. This was worth being woken for. 'He could easily have worked out the same trick was used in Oslo as Phoenix. How long's he been there? . . . That long? Talked to Olssen, yes . . . What's he doing now? You can't see. OK, hang on — I'll get back to you. Neat, Michel, I like it. The old hospital call to remove the only witness. I think the man will go for it. Gant's disappearance won't cause a ripple. Call you back —'

He switched off the cordless phone, then dialled the number of Winterborne's mobile, still smiling. Gant was a smart-arse, he needed taking out. He waited as the phone continued to ring. This was already turning into a tidying operation, its main phase already long completed — his only involvement had been surveillance, a bit of frightening, hiring Strickland. At least this way they could turn Gant off, another of Aubrey's fond memories. Marian Pyott — well, she was either dead, burned or terrified. Whichever would at least slow her down, probably stop her . . . and shitty little whingeing Banks was in for a surprise in the morning when his daughter walked to school.

'Sir,' without irony or insolence, 'Fraser. Just had a call from Oslo. Can you talk freely?'

'I've just got home. What is it?' The man's mood was easily identifiable; as satiated with self-admiration as if he had just come from a flattering mistress.

'Gant, sir. Roussillon's opinion — and I agree — is that Gant could become a problem. He's after some trace of Strickland, without doubt.'

'*You* don't know where Strickland is, Fraser. How is Gant going to find him?'

Fraser grimaced sourly and thrust the two fingers that held the cigarette savagely in the air.

'Maybe not, sir. But he must know it was sabotage. And he knows Strickland — *knew* him, anyway. At least, Strickland knew Gant at one time.'

'Where is he?'

'The hangar at Oslo airport. Roussillon is on the spot, has him under close surveillance. He's even got the security guard out of the way. Gant is alone,' he added seductively. He listened to the silence at the other end of the line. Eventually, Winterborne said, irritatedly:

'What about Marian?'

'Jessop and Cobb — a petrol bomb through her kitchen window.'

'And?'

'They didn't remain at the scene. Her file suggested it as the best way to make the biggest impact. Some childhood accident —'

'I *know* about her accident as a child!' Winterborne hissed. 'I want to know what *happened* to her!'

It was as if Winterborne was expressing regret for something he was certain had occurred. *Mea culpa.* All the guilt crap had infected him like a disease he had not expected to catch. He was afraid that the woman was dead; something was suddenly and surprisingly persuading him that he had *never meant it to happen.* Fraser mocked silently. Winterborne would get over it. It wasn't much more than a slight cold in his case, conscience — otherwise he would never have begun this, never have acquired Complete Security, staffed it with people like himself, gone as far as he had. In a couple of days, a week at most, he'd have persuaded himself of the necessity of the woman's removal. If it had already happened in the house fire, he'd soon see the sense of it.

'I'll find out, sir,' he replied obsequiously. 'But, Gant — I think I must emphasise that he poses the more immediate danger. A risk that is unacceptably high.' He added the last in deference to the evident self-satisfaction that seeped down the line.

'Agreed, then. Get rid of Gant. And do it quietly, with no traces. Tell Roussillon. Good night, Fraser.'

The connection was severed.

'And good night to you — *sir.*' Fraser scowled at the receiver. He switched it off and threw it on the bed.

One down for certain. There'd be tantrums if

the woman was already dead, or lying in an emergency bed, roasted to a crisp — that much was obvious. But none over Gant's demise. That was death at a safe distance . . . Made you sick, the ease with which they could order the disposal of human beings. *Look, my hands are clean.* Businessmen and politicos took to that easy kind of gangsterism with alacrity. The end of the Cold War had left people like himself lying around like weapons, ready to be acquired, ready to go off. The likes of Winterborne *enjoyed* an arm's-length relationship with people like him, it gave them a buzz. It provided them with simple solutions to problems. It was easier than most other ways of doing business.

He picked up the telephone and dialled Roussillon's number. As he had remarked to the Frog, his lot had always been up for the kind of thing the Brits were just learning . . . that you can run a conglomerate with the same methods and means as an intelligence operation.

So, good night, Mr Gant — and I mean good night.

It was a half-assed security firm. He'd known that after ten minutes of fast-forwarding the videotapes from the security cameras in Halvesson's cramped, dusty, somehow deliberately littered office. The tapes weren't labelled or dated. There appeared to be gaps in the recording, by the light and dark spilling through the open doors, by the identities of the airliners being serviced and their carriers' blazons. A heap of cassettes had fallen like a joke from a metal cupboard as he had tugged open the door.

It was three-fifteen in the morning and the bright inspiration of checking the security camera videotapes had evaporated like water in the desert sun. Gant rubbed his hands tiredly through his hair as the manic jerks and rushes of overalled men — like figures in a cartoon which no longer amused — passed on the television screen. There were four cameras covering the hangar, one of which he had already realised was unserviceable. Of the other three, Halvesson seemed to operate them more by whim than routine. Maybe he watched hired movies on his little bank of four screens, rather than the hangar. Maybe he was just a dead-end in a dead-end job. There was a bitter kind of life, or at least its after-images, in the airless office; photographs of a younger Halvesson wearing the kind of well-cut suit he couldn't afford on a security man's pay, beside an elegant wife. Children, too — a series of snapshots either framed or pinned to the wall which measured the ordinary suburban changes of any family anywhere. The measure of disillusion, loss of prospects. Children growing sullen and apart, the houses in front of which they were captured becoming smaller, less well tended. Scrubby lawns.

Halvesson didn't care any longer, maybe not about anything except the wife whose illness had caused him to panic.

Gant yawned. Halvesson's failed life was like a grubbiness on his clothing and skin. He rubbed his arms. He wasn't going to find anything, except by luck. Olssen's figure dashed dementedly across another unlabelled videotape, gesticulating like a puppet in conversation with Jorgensen and another man. Often, Halvesson didn't switch on the timer and the recordings didn't always carry a date or time. Daylight became darkness once again, as on a speeded-up film of clouds or plants growing. A Boeing became, almost suddenly, a McDonnell Douglas, then an Airbus. The timer came back into operation and Gant slowed the replay. The day before yesterday, darkness —

— something alerted him, a noise beyond the airless cubbyhole of the office. The skittering of something. A rat, probably. Two nights ago, and the Vance 494 was at the corner of the screen, undergoing its service. His finger paused at the buttons of the video machine. Too early, too late . . . ? The camera swung robotically and the airplane was displayed. He stopped the tape. Jorgensen climbing into the electrics bay. The gantry hugging the 494's waist like an old-fashioned corset. The time in the bottom corner of the screen read a little after eleven. Olssen walked out of view, towards his office. Gant's chair squeaked as he became more tensely interested in the silent movie of the recording. Outside the office somewhere, he heard rat noises again.

Ignored them . . . The camera's perspective included the entrance to the hangar. Through those doors . . .

'What's he doing now?' Roussillon whispered. Behind him, Oslo airport was silent, lit like a deserted sports stadium. He waited, then heard:

'Security office. He's watching the security

screens. Could be replaying the tapes — ?'

'Keep secure. Wait for my order.'

Roussillon switched off the RT. He had two men already inside the hangar. Gant was alone. He brushed his long hair away from his forehead. The night was pleasantly cool, outside. He turned and leaned his elbows on the high bonnet of the four-wheel-drive hydraulic platform, a Land Rover with a bent arm ending in the fist of the cage behind the driver's cabin. Through the night glasses, the hangar doors, wide open, were sheened with light.

Then he murmured to the remaining two members of the team: 'OK — move in. No noise. Kill him in there if you must and bring the body out.'

The two men slipped away, their dark overalls like assault garb in the night, their faces newly smeared with black. Roussillon watched them, as if they were moving across a monochrome television screen, dodging and scuttling towards the hangar. In another minute, they had disappeared inside. Was Gant armed? Unlikely. Roussillon smiled. There was something pleasurable, something one could taste on one's tongue, about the *known* identity of the target — that it was familiar by name, by repute, within the shadow pool of the intelligence community. Something satisfying, too, in that the body would be weighted and dropped into the Oslofjord as perfunctorily as they would have done any anonymous victim.

His own service, DST had given him *carte blanche.* He could *concur with* instructions from Fraser, from Winterborne. That was the nature of his freedom, that his actions could always be denied with utter conviction by his superiors, by the minister, the Elysée. The business of the state in this matter lay solely in preventing revelation. Balzac-Stendhal's dealings with Aerospace UK, the subornation of EU Commissioners, one of whom was a Frenchman and a possible future Prime Minister of France, the diversion of EU funds, must not be allowed to become public. There was no question of the moral rectitude or otherwise of the actions of a French conglomerate or a French politician.

Roussillon lit a cigarette and savoured the acrid smoke, sweet-smelling on the faint night wind.

A figure in the hangar doorway, his shadow falling darkly behind him as the lights caught him. Tall, broad-shouldered, a heavy face thickly moustached. The man was wearing a leather jacket, a check shirt and denims above high-heeled boots. He was evidently, somehow theatrically, American. What would be expected, looked for.

Gant watched the man move in slow-motion, watched Olssen approach him. Eleven-twenty, two nights ago. Olssen and the American-dressed figure spoke to one another. Gant leaned forward until the figures became grainy and unfocused as they slipped to one corner of the screen and then regained its centre as the camera followed its arc. Halvesson hadn't bothered with a close-up, maybe he hadn't even been watching the monitor. Gant pressed the button to halt the tape. American . . . ? An easy walk, the man's bag swinging loosely at his side. A confident actor already commanding his stage. Gant continued to stare at the screen for perhaps two minutes.

That was the saboteur, the man who called himself Massey. The frozen image caught him in half-profile, an anonymous grey face above a well-muscled body. He didn't know the man. He knew of maybe three or four people who had the skill to bring down the 494s in the way this stranger had, but he had no idea how many there really were. How many had been shown the door by the Company or the Bureau and who were out there, working for private companies and corporations, Vice-Presidents in charge of Industrial Espionage, V-Ps for Sabotaging Rivals. That was this guy's game.

Angry that the elation of discovering the right stretch of videotape had so easily vanished into the sand of the man's anonymity, Gant stood up and stretched. He'd have to take the tape with him — who'd miss it? — and watch it over and over, ask around, get still shots printed off it. His hand gripped the back of Halvesson's swivel chair and he leaned towards the screen, letting the images move in slow motion once more, then in real time, then slow motion . . . He caught, like the trace of cigarette smoke in an empty room, something familiar about the man's posture, his movements, but it was just like trying to grab at the dissipating smoke. He turned away from the screen as he returned the tape to real time, and looked at his watch. Three-forty. He was bushed, his body leadenly remembering that he had slept little or not at all for forty-eight hours. The littered office, the photographic measurement of

Halvesson's subsidence into failure, the TV screen, all irritated him.

He turned towards the windowed wall of the office that overlooked the hangar —

— movement. A flicker as if someone's shadow had entered the edge of eyesight so that he wasn't certain he'd seen anything.

He had. A darkly dressed figure hurrying, bent almost double like someone ill or wounded, vanishing beyond the Boeing. Rat noises . . . He'd heard, hadn't listened. He turned accusingly to stare at the screen and at Massey and Olssen walking side by side, slipping away and back through the camera's arc. Massey . . . *Who the hell was he?*

He shook the puzzle of the man's identity away like heavy, dragging bedclothes. Stared out across the hangar, tensed against sudden darkness or the glimpse of others. He heard his own breathing, then the quick patter of what had to be rubber-soled boots, but saw nothing. Two, at least. Massey . . . was being protected, the tidy-crew had come to make certain there was nothing left lying around —

— himself.

Lights . . . He stared wildly around the grubby, cramped space, aware of himself framed in the windows, backlit as if on a screen. Switch — darkness for an instant, then the hangar lights came flowing in as if on a breeze. Cord in his left hand. He jerked it and the dusty blinds rattled down across the scene. He stifled a cough as he crouched with his back to Halvesson's desk, seemingly mesmerised by the TV screen and the images of Massey, moving in real time, walking away from the camera — stopping. Gant listened intently, as if he expected Massey to whisper, expected he might just catch his words as his lips moved. Olssen must have called out to him. The office was hotter. He embraced his knees as he sat, his back pressed against the desk, the shirt dampening.

Rat noises again . . . Yes. His breath was loud as he exhaled. They knew where he was . . . Lights? The office was illuminated from outside, but the images on the screen shone out more vividly, in an etched, outlined way. He had to move. Take the videotape *out of the machine,* damn you, and *move* . . . Massey, facing the camera, Gant's heartbeat raised, senses heightened, sweat on his forehead in a narrow, cold line . . .

. . . *Strickland.* Behind the moustache, the greyed hair, the leather jacket and the boots. Something in the smile, the angle of the head as he paused, the whole posture. *The Preacherman* had been his codename, his soubriquet, his means of being known and insulted. The psychopath with the gentle voice and manners of a pastor . . . *Strickland.* He *knew* him, knew what he was —

Gant turned his head as the window-wall shattered and the blinds swelled inwards for a moment to allow something to roll across the floor, something that smoked comically like a bomb in a cartoon. It burst even as he turned his gaze from the blinding flash. The smoke was suddenly everywhere in the room and he was coughing. He lurched forward and on to his knees, head bent to the floor.

He rolled away from the shattered window towards the door. He crouched behind it, the videotape images still flickering, shining in his head. Strickland. They were here to protect Strickland. The smoke from the grenade obliterated the TV screen. His eyes watered, blinding him, and he could not stop coughing.

Door . . . ? His back was against the door. Other door *through* . . . ? He scrabbled across the floor towards the door which led into the next office. He opened it and blundered against heaped boxes which smelt of metal and protective grease. He slammed the door to the storeroom. An identical windowed wall with a blind, a desk, filing cabinets . . . He had *left the videotape behind.* He glanced wildly back but it was already too late. He heard a voice shouting.

All the rooms were connected . . .

He couldn't open the door to the third of the offices. Something was stacked against it. He realised it was blocked by the filing cabinet in Olssen's office . . . The smoke had followed him into the second office, slipping beneath the door. His throat rasped with it.

He gripped the handle of the door out into the hangar. They'd be watching the other door — only feet away — only *chance.*

He ran, crouching, hearing a shout and a reply. He hunched his body against the first shot.

'No! Do *not* open fire — under no circumstances!' Roussillon shouted into the RT, his whole body tensed as if he were on the point of running wildly towards the hangar. 'The grenade was *unnecessary,* Lucien — who fired it?' They had wanted to make a game of it, startle him out of the security man's office like a rabbit blinking in the light. 'The grenade must be recovered, every *fragment — no* shooting!' Gant must simply disappear, there must be no sense in which his death was declared or his vanishing a police matter. Gunshot scars would be like fingerprints. 'Is he armed? You don't think so — make certain! When you know, close in on him — !'

He flung the arm holding the RT aside, as if discarding the instrument. His hand banged achingly against the flank of the Land Rover. For the sake of God, how *difficult* is it to take one unarmed man by surprise? Don't let him get out of the hangar, *don't* —

'Lucien — what is he doing? Where is he?' he snapped into the RT.

'Sorry, boss — can't see him at the moment. There are vehicles parked down at the far end of the hangar. Pascal and Edouard are moving in on him from different sides —'

'Until they can be certain that they can hit him *and* the slug won't pass right through his body, no shooting. You understand me, Lucien?'

'Yes, boss — I've given the order.'

'A fucking smoke grenade! There was no need —'

'No, boss —'

'Can you *see* him?'

'No, boss —'

He crouched in the lee of a parked aerial platform, squashed down on its hydraulics like an abandoned concertina, smelling its small rubber tyres. He listened to their movements, their urgency. It was almost as if they were the ones panicked by danger, not himself — except that his breathing was ragged, trapped as he was. There had been no shots. They didn't want evidence left behind, shell cases, spent bullets. The smoke grenade had been to startle him into the open.

Lights . . .

He slid back from the parked platform to the corrugated wall as if only that moment remembering why he had bolted for this far end of the hangar. Red box on the wall. Main fusebox. His skin crawled with the anticipation of his exposure, the impact of a bullet. He reached above his head as he remained crouching against the wall, his hand scrabbling for the lever. Threw it — darkness.

Then the breath was knocked from his body, the noise of the collision rumbling through the corrugated wall. He rolled over, a heavier body pressing against his, hands gripping his arms. He gasped, the air expelled again as he collided with one wheel of the aerial platform. A hand over his mouth, his own hands striking as ineffectually as those of a baby as the dark-clothed, black-faced man sat astride him, his other hand against Gant's windpipe, pressing down with damaging force. Gant struck out at the black-streaked face with his hands, trying to hit, trying to hold. The man's breath smelt of food and triumph, sickly-sweet.

'Edouard — got him?' he heard someone call. English with a heavy European accent.

'Oui — ! Ici — !' His breath failed, gargled out, as the edge of Gant's hand struck across his throat. The pressure on Gant's windpipe was released.

He bucked his body, twisting it out from beneath the man as eager hands reached for his eyes. Gant struck sideways and upwards with his forearm, catching his assailant across the cheek and nose. He heard a muffled explosion of breath and the man's body jerked away from him, his hands feeling for his own face now. Gant rose to his knees, then into a crouch. Kicked twice, jaw, side of head as the man went down.

'Edouard — !' he heard, then: 'Where are the *lights!*'

'Fusebox — they're not working!' came a voice from near the hangar doors.

He hit the fallen man again as he struggled to get to his feet, bruising his knuckles against the man's temple. Something had skittered away in the darkness — gun? He stared wildly round but could not see it, then scrabbled at the man's pockets, looking for a weapon, an identity. Took what felt like a leather wallet.

'Edouard! Christ — find the fusebox! Claude — stay by the doors!'

Gant hesitated, trying to recall the dimensions, the points of the hangar's compass . . . doors, windows, equipment. Then he moved along the wall, away from the doors and the man who was guarding them, away from the man who had been calling for *Edouard.* French names, and the assailant had called in French, even though the language of the operation was English. Gant felt the angle of the wall with his hands, his back, continued to move away from the doors. A parked truck, passenger steps, a forklift . . . piled boxes and crates, then an open space. He could see the outlines of the vehicles now in the seeped lights of the airport. He could see well enough to know that they would see him.

'Here!' he heard. 'Bastard! Here — it's Edouard! He's alive —'

Gant saw someone move towards the aerial platform, and ran, his footsteps audible even above the racing of his pulse in his ears, above his loudening heartbeat . . . The shadow of the Boeing's nosewheel. He clung to the tyre as to a lifebelt. He could see Claude's form framed by the open doors.

In moments, one of them would locate the fusebox and the lights would come on. They were edgy, shocked into error, panic. That edginess meant they'd start shooting when the lights came on and he was exposed, even if their orders were to dispose of him elsewhere.

Gant looked up. The nosewheel's undercarriage rose above the huge tyres like an Indian rope trick . . . He began climbing, inching his way up, squeezing the undercarriage strut against his body, between his thighs. Then he clambered into the nosewheel bay as the lights flashed on bright as lightning. Claude moved a few steps from the doorway, the others he couldn't see . . . Yes, he could just glimpse the aerial platform shunted into the corner of the hangar, the man he had hit and the one who had found him. He couldn't see the fourth man as he hung from the bay, head down, arms already aching, his feet scissor-gripping the undercarriage strut at its root.

The fourth man walked beneath him. If he even glanced up, he would see Gant hanging like a paper kite above him.

'Lucien — I thought I saw something near the aircraft!' he called.

'Pascal, could he have got aboard?'

'Maybe. The passenger door's wide open — but there are no steps up to it. I can't see how.' Like a bad actor attempting the sinister, he surveyed the underbelly of the Boeing.

Gant stilled his breathing, sensing sweat drop from his forehead towards the man, like rain . . . Taking his weight with one arm, he savagely wiped at his forehead. His renewed grip was slippery. Lucien and the injured Edouard emerged from the shadow of the aerial platform.

'Where the hell are you, Mr Gant?' Lucien shouted.

His voice echoed around the hangar. Into the silence which followed, the rat-scratches of an RT and a tinny, indecipherable voice sharp with orders. The man below him, Pascal, seemed to take a firmer grip on the pistol he held, mocking decisiveness, determination. *Don't look up* . . . Even if he dropped on the man the instant his head lifted, there would be time for one shot at least.

'You can't get out, Mr Gant!' Lucien shouted. In the ensuing silence, the RT again. How many more of them? 'Give yourself up!'

He could see Lucien vigorously gesticulating. He heard the scuttle of footsteps. The doorway was empty now, presumably covered from outside. Pascal remained beneath him, alertly to attention beside the nosewheel.

Again, sweat dropped from Gant's forehead. They'd be slipping along the walls of the hangar, waiting for him to move, wildfowlers beating up a bird into their waiting guns. They would have been told they could kill him on sight now, too much time had passed and they would have started to fear their own discovery. Pascal would move in another moment . . . Shadow of another man in the hangar doorway. Just one.

No, Pascal wouldn't move, not yet. He was holding the sightline position. They were the beaters, he the sportsman. The pistol gleamed in his hand. Gant wiped at his forehead, his grip slipping, arms aching, legs beginning to numb. Pascal was rotating like a fairground sideshow toy, swivelling body and gaze across the expanse of concrete. He could hear the others moving in rapid, scurrying movements, almost hear their pauses as they checked equipment, machines, crates and pallets. They knew they still had him. Sweat dropped —

— the man's cheek flinched, his head turned almost incuriously, slowly. Gant dropped. His numbed legs buckled under him and his grip was slippery on Pascal's gun hand. The Frenchman's breathing was hot, surprised against his cheek as Gant lay on him, the gun waving at arm's-length as if taunting both his grip and Pascal's. Gant felt himself heaved away, his grip loosening on the man's arm. Felt himself struck numbingly across the shoulder with the pistol, heard Pascal shout. Butted at the face that was open-mouthed, feeling his neck go hot with the jarring impact. Sensed himself climbing Pascal's struggling body — legs kicking out at him, hips twisting — towards the gun. Explosion —

— deafness, a submerged roaring, distant, tinny shouts like a telephone ringing while taking a shower. He realised the pistol was in his hand, which then seemed of its own accord to strike down across the bridge of Pascal's already bloodied nose. Heard running footsteps, the first shot —

— lee of the nosewheel, momentary shelter, breathing stertorous. Two shots loosed off quickly towards men who suddenly realised they were exposed on a coverless killing ground. Shots from the direction of the doors of the hangar, the spitting snake noise of a silenced weapon. He was crouched behind the wheels, protected from them only until they encircled him. Pascal lay unconscious, his blood-masked face staring at the hangar roof.

The desire for survival was as urgent as his heartbeat. His mind raced — French *professionals* . . . protecting *Strickland* . . . videotape — evidence — *in the office* . . . He loosed off another two shots. The gun was a Beretta Mo92 — fifteen rounds. He fired once more, suddenly cautious, then ducked out of the lee of the nosewheel, darting across the lit, grease-stained concrete towards what he had seen as a slowly approaching shadow but which became the man who had last entered the hangar. He saw, in his joggling vision, surprise, hesitation, the close of the gap between them. Then the initial movement of the hand that had to be holding the gun, and the other arm jerking up in protective instinct. He launched himself sideways, cannoning into and off the man, stunning the breath from his body as he landed, rolling —

— they fired now because the man they might hit, their field director, was down and they had a clear sight of Gant. One bullet whined off the hangar wall just above his head as he reached the doorway, where the night air struck with unexpected cold. The side of his body was bruised and aching. He lurched to a halt against the open door and fired back at them. Three shots, scattering them.

Time gained. He ran towards their parked vehicle, away from the hangar lights, into the darkness, scrubby grass beneath his feet, the pattern of the airport's thousands of lights dazzling and disorientating him — and them, *and them* . . . He heard a couple of futile shots, then only his own blood. He was invisible to them now. Safe —

— for how long?

CHAPTER NINE

All My Sons

Giles Pyott, waiting beside the empty ticket collector's box at the end of the platform, glimpsed Marian coming towards him, briefcase at her side. She appeared worn, shocked. His customary elation at seeing her became a sudden terror of recognition; always she reminded him of Anne, but now her hesitant, slightly lost progress was too similar to that of his wife during her last illness. Giles felt enfeebled, even afraid, seeing Marian's haggard, weary features.

Marian halted, still without having seen him, and seemed to struggle with her handbag. Then he saw she was answering her mobile phone.

'Yes — Ray?' There was something breathlessly excited, deeply angry about Banks' voice. She felt physically assailed and weakened by its outrage.

'— nothing more to do with it — or you!' he stormed. 'My family comes first — !' It was the whine of a man who had been compromised by another, led into danger. 'She was on her way to school! Their bloody car just climbed the pavement and knocked her against the wall!' There was breathing, but no pauses; the anger was one fearful, long exhalation. 'She's all right, just concussed and shocked, a few scratches — no thanks to *you!*' His own guilt was evident, he was beating it towards her as if fighting off a swarm of bees that tormented him. 'Besides, the whole thing's been cleared up! They've paid most of the money. Cheque came this morning from the biggest firm I supplied . . . *plus* a cheque for the site work!' He did pause then, knowing he had admitted the nature of the stick, the nature of the carrot. She could not despise him.

'I'm glad she's all right, Ray, I really am,' she managed to offer. He seized on it like an admission of culpability.

'I shouldn't have listened to you in the first place!'

'No . . . probably not.'

'Just don't try to involve me again — in *anything!*' he threatened guiltily.

'No, Ray . . .'

Banks broke the connection. She felt dizzied.

Giles Pyott saw her sway with weakness and hurried to her grasping her — to her shock, until she recognised him and leaned against him like a drunk needing support.

'Are you hurt?' he asked as she looked up at him. They must, he thought, have looked like lovers — he ridiculously old, but certainly to be envied.

Marian shook her head.

'No. Just delayed shock or something,' she murmured vaguely. Then, the soldier's daughter, forcing a smile, she added: 'Corporal Davies *always* rescues me!'

She tried to mock the gravity of his expression, but he ignored her attempt at humour.

'What happened, Marian?' he asked sternly.

'Daddy,' she warned: *'Nothing* happened!'

'Someone tried to kill you. You were more confiding from hospital.'

'Must have been shock — didn't know what I was saying.'

Giles tossed his head. It did not serve to clear his features or shake off concern.

'Tell me what happened. Shall we go now?'

'Mm.'

He picked up her briefcase and ushered her towards the concourse. The other passengers on the InterCity Shuttle had vanished towards Euston's taxi-ranks or the tube, they were virtually alone on the platform, except for a clattering, towed caravan of parcel skips. Their noise startled her unreasonably.

'What happened?'

'Someone set fire to the flat — I told you.' He sensed her frightened attempt at secrecy.

'Who did it? Listen, my girl' — he ignored the arch, mocking glance she gave him — 'you weren't the almost-victim of an attempted lesson in smoking this time. Quite possibly, someone wanted you dead.' It seemed ridiculous, saying that to his daughter, the MP crossing the crowded Euston concourse, amid baggage and the announcement of delays. 'Tell me what happened.'

She seemed to revive in the fresh morning air as they reached Melton Street and he pointed out the Jaguar parked near the corner of Euston

Street. They crossed as gingerly as two pensioners on the zebra stripes.

'It was a petrol bomb, through the kitchen window. The fire officer told me that.' She was concentrating intensely as she spoke. Or perhaps simply studying her uncertain footsteps, he could not be sure. 'It took them no more than fifteen minutes to bring it under control — saved the bedrooms, the office . . . I wasn't burned,' she added with a perceptible shudder.

'Thank God,' he murmured involuntarily, unlocking the car, throwing her briefcase on the back seat amid newspapers and books.

He watched her brush her hair away from her face with a gesture that was defiant, but saw the almost cringing sense of fear in her eyes. As if she guessed his response, she said:

'Yes, they did frighten me, Daddy — they frightened me very much. If that was what they wanted and not, not —'

'Get in the car, Tig,' he said, and she immediately brightened at the use of his childhood name for her — short for the *Tiger* he always claimed she was. Giles remembered murmuring the pet-name over and over again as she lay on the grass, her arm burnt, her eyes filled with stunned, traumatic terror.

As the car pulled away from the kerb, up Euston Street towards Gower Street, she sniffed loudly and said:

'I must talk to Kenneth about it.'

She lit a cigarette. He wanted to disapprove of it, in his car.

'Why?'

She turned violently to him as he halted in traffic.

'Because only he can explain it!' Her voice cracked with strain. There were dark stains under her wide eyes. She stabbed at the air with the cigarette. 'It seems to be Kenneth's world, invading mine — doesn't it? It doesn't seem to be casual, *does* it?'

'Marian,' Giles said heavily, 'I don't know what this is, but I blame you and I blame Kenneth — in equal measure.' Suddenly, in his fear for her, he could not control his parental anger. 'How *can* you have stirred all this up? What the devil did you think you were *doing*, and on whose behalf? My God, you could have been *killed!*'

Marian stared ahead, her lower lip quivering. He was wrenched by guilt. She knew she could have died. Perhaps it was better to take her to Kenneth. Damnable Kenneth, who had no child to lose . . . Unfair, he corrected himself. Nevertheless, he could vent his anger more justly on Kenneth than on his daughter.

'Sorry, Tig,' he murmured.

Her hand covered his as it rested on the gear lever. He tried to ignore the hot waves of terrified gratitude at her safety which seemed to rise in his body like lava.

His complete lack of any luggage stirred the vague and momentary interest of a young Customs officer as he walked through the green channel. It was a small rehearsal which sharpened his senses so that when he emerged into the concourse of Terminal 2, he was almost immediately aware that they had already picked him up — two of them. Midday, Heathrow, and one of them was no more than ten yards from him, moving parallel and without concealing his interest, even signalling to the other man. They wanted him to know they were close.

Gant had shaken them off in Oslo by raising the alarm, swamping the maintenance hangar with airport police. It had cleared the area around him, giving him the time and space to catch the morning flight to London. He needed to see Burton, explain Strickland and the —

— pausing to catch their reflections in the windows of the bookstall, he felt as if struck by a fist. The newspaper headlines, the pink *Financial Times* bearing a picture of Burton and someone who looked Eurasian celebrating a new transatlantic leasing partnership between Artemis Airways and the Skyliner. Disorientated, he could not be certain if it was the headline that disturbed him most, or the smaller item on the front page of the *Herald Tribune* . . . *Hero's Arrest Sought*, and himself staring back at him from the newspaper.

In the reflecting window, one of the two men tailing him waved at him with a rolled newspaper, the briefest gesture, the clearest meaning. *We know you, we have you* . . . Gant suppressed a shiver. He felt rocked by tiredness and the news item, so that he snatched clumsily at the *Herald Tribune* and began reading it as if oblivious to the immediate danger. *FBI warrant* — McIntyre, then — *former Vietnam hero* . . . It was Vance's financial affairs, and the accusation that he had left America to avoid interrogation; charges of conspiracy, bribes . . . Yes, *Agent McIntyre added that Gant was* . . . He thrust the newspaper untidily back into the rack and turned away. The Burton story was emblazoned in other headlines — *Whiz-Kid Bounces Back* . . . *Delighted with Deal* . . . *Great Future Ensured* . . . *Burton and his lovely wife, Charlotte, pictured last night* . . . Turning away, he felt himself already struggling in deep water against a riptide, even before he glimpsed the tail who had waved his newspaper grinning at him.

Angrily, he snatched Vance's mobile phone from his pocket, swivelling on his heel as he did so — yes, the second man, no attempt at indifference, they were determined to pressure him, like another bill falling on his doormat the moment he was declared bankrupt . . . He punched out the number Burton had given him and waited. The concourse seemed airless, its crowds devouring his oxygen.

'Thanks for screwing Vance's airplane!' he snapped even before Burton spoke.

'Who is this?' he heard, but Burton already knew.

'It was sabotage, Burton. I know the guy, I saw him on security videotape. The name Strickland mean anything to you?'

'Gant? No, it doesn't — who is he?'

'One of the guys who's ridden off into the Badlands, Burton — just a nobody who downed two of Alan's airplanes. Maybe he was supposed to set you up for the deal you've just done? I wouldn't know!'

‘What the hell do you mean by that?’

‘Listen to me, Burton. You said you wanted answers. You were there when the guy died. I got the answer. The guy was *screwed.* Is that really what you wanted to know?’

‘You mean . . . it was deliberate? It was — ?’ Burton seemed winded. The two surveillance men had moved, but remained easily visible, unnerving Gant. ‘It can’t have been sabotage —’

‘I’m telling you it was!’

‘Look, Gant, I’m sorry you’ve had to read it in the papers — I don’t want you to think I turned my back on Alan easily. I didn’t. But, as you said, Alan is dead, his company and his airliner are finished. I had to do what I’ve done. I have thousands of people depending on me. I did what was for the best.’

After a long silence, Gant murmured: ‘Sure.’

‘Are you continuing to pursue this?’ Burton asked.

The two men were still plainly visible. Did they belong to French counterintelligence, like the team in the hangar, like the man whose ID he now carried in his pocket? *Edouard St Cloud, agent of DST.* DST — was it a French *government* thing?

‘Yes,’ he snapped, as if challenged.

‘Very well — I’ll pay your expenses, whatever they are. And I will listen to what you have to say, anything you discover. I — er, I must cut you off now, Gant. I have a waiting room full of people —’

‘OK — I’ll get back to you.’

He cut the connection, continuing for a moment to stare at Vance’s mobile phone, the one he had picked up from the sand on that headland overlooking the second crashed 494. The two-man team continued to hover about him like wasps.

Taxis. He saw the sign, a black arrow pointing the way. He moved — they followed. French counter-intelligence. He had tried to think it through on the flight from Oslo, but the ego had fought him, insisting on his scope for solitary action. The surveillance team, the newspaper headlines, had stripped him of that shallow confidence, and what he had entertained on the aircraft was now an imperative. This was *local,* it was European. He needed to talk to Aubrey, even if the old guy had retired along with Reagan and Thatcher, and the people who had run him in the Company. He needed *advice* and — maybe hard to admit — an operational controller. *Hero's Arrest Sought* . . . Screw you, Jack.

He followed the arrows, the two men behind but not moving in, content to wait, watch. He had made one call from Oslo, to someone who owed him favours who was still in Archives at Langley. *Where can I find Strickland? . . . Don't give me that, they always keep tabs . . . By midday British time.*

He hadn't called him yet. Maybe he had been warned off, or was just dismissive because he, too, had read the headlines. McIntyre had, on the surface, a watertight case against him. Vance had, damn him, wired him *money.* A Federal employee was on the take from big business. The *Post* would have put a half-dozen reporters on the story by now. He was news.

Gant grimaced as he emerged into the cool midday light. A queue of tourists and businessmen at the taxi rank, a line of black cabs. The two men kept their distance, unhurried in their movements. The place was too public for them to try anything . . . Maybe they just wanted to see what he did, where he went, who he saw. The roar of a big jet taking off, the slamming of taxi doors.

He joined the queue. The men hesitated, then hung back, as if they were determined to show him he was under no immediate physical threat. Just *contained,* controlled.

He had to locate Strickland, he was the key. The bombmaker for whoever. Could Aubrey help? He shook his head, not knowing.

The passenger in front of him, freshened with aftershave but with the back of his jacket deeply creased, got into a taxi, then it was his turn. He paused, his hand on the cab door. The two men smiled but did not move. He got into the taxi, a chilly sensation between his shoulder blades.

'Central London — I'll tell you where.'

The driver nodded and the taxi drew away from the kerb. He glanced back through the rear window. The tail-men were getting into the next cab. They'd follow him into London. He would have to lose them there before he made for Aubrey's place.

Aubrey — an old man, retired. What could he do? The people following Gant wanted him dead —

The signals of his success littered the ornately

inlaid side table, one or two of them scattered on the intricate Persian carpet. And yet he was unable to suppress a fury that he knew originated in anxiety, in the possibility of failure.

'Whichever shadowy master you are serving in the Elysée or the Quai d'Orsai or wherever, Roussillon, exposure is equally damaging to everyone involved in this affair!' David Winterborne stormed.

The Frenchman was seated uncomfortably, primly on a Sheraton chair. Fraser, Winterborne knew, was enjoying his discomfiture, even though he suppressed the signs of his pleasure.

'Twice — *twice!*' Winterborne continued. 'You let an amateur evade you — even as you assure me that you believe Gant knows Strickland was involved!' The videotapes lay near the newspapers that blazoned the deal between Aero UK, Balzac-Stendhal and Artemis Airways. His own photograph was beneath many of the headlines, standing alongside Tim Burton and Bryan Coulthard. Early copies of the French press were equally enthusiastic, chauvinistic. Boeing was already mounting a counter-campaign in conjunction with the big American carriers. A transatlantic price war was in the offing and Skyliner was in the forefront of it. 'And where is Strickland?' he continued, turning to Fraser, whose lolling posture on the chaise became the bolt-uprightness of a chastened schoolboy. 'You must find Strickland — he can't have just *disappeared.*'

'We're looking for him, sir.'

'Look *harder.*' He turned his back on them, as if preparing for an appearance on the balcony overlooking Eaton Square.

He had won. The daring of the fraud had kept Aero UK afloat for long enough, the sabotage had killed Vance Aircraft. Skyliner had saved Tim Burton, Europe's grand project had leasing orders beginning to flow in. Now these people — Gant and Strickland and perhaps Marian — threatened him. Somehow, Fraser and Roussillon had produced a whirlpool effect, drawing in people from their secret world. People opposed to him.

'Fraser, you say there is an FBI warrant for Gant's arrest — can that be used?'

'I've made some enquiries, sir. The agent of the Bureau most closely involved is a man called McIntyre. I've met him. He's dim and vindictive — former Company man. He's persecuting Gant, not to put too fine a point —'

'Can it be *used?*'

'If Gant returns to the States, McIntyre will put him out of harm's way. I'd bet on —'

He turned on them.

'Why has Gant involved himself?'

'Vance, probably. He was married to the daughter. He has a farm boy's view of the world. You know the Yanks, sir. They all hate big government, big business, out in the boondocks.'

'And he's dangerous?'

'He has no proof of anything,' Roussillon offered, brushing a dark lock of hair from his forehead.

'Hardly thanks to you!'

The Frenchman's cheeks reddened with affront.

'I do not work for you, M'sieur Winterborne.

I am not your *paid man!*'

'You would find it hard to persuade your service or your government that their interests differ from mine, Roussillon. Effectively, you take my instruction.' The Frenchman's eyes were polished with hatred. 'If Gant has no proof, then he can do little harm. Especially as a convict. But meanwhile, Gant is in London, *not* Washington. Can *he* find Strickland, Fraser? How well does he know him?'

'Not well. I don't think he knows where to start.'

'Not good enough. *We* do not know Gant well enough.' He was suddenly tired of his anger. In his study and his secretary's office, his calls were being held, his business suspended. He should not have to be concerned with this menial and degrading litter-collection. Gant and Marian and Strickland, blowing like infuriating bits of paper in the breeze of the affair, eluding his pointed stick. 'What do you suggest — Fraser?'

'Gant's still under surveillance — even if he thinks he evaded us using the taxi-dodge in Piccadilly. There'll be plenty of opportunity to settle —' The ringing of a mobile phone interrupted Fraser. Disconcerted, he removed it from his pocket. 'Fraser.' He listened. Winterborne watched his features feign a retention of the easy confidence with which he had spoken. Then, his cheekbones slightly reddened, he looked up as he switched off the phone.

'Well?'

'Gant. He — he's arrived at Aubrey's place.'

'*Aubrey?* What does he want with that damned

old man? Eh, Fraser — what does he want with *him?*' Like the two men in the room, Aubrey came to him in the moment of his triumph to remind him of something that already seemed as distant and unimportant as a childhood misdemeanour.

'Aubrey can't do anything, sir —'

'You have that in writing?' he snapped. 'You have it from Aubrey himself?'

He turned away. Aubrey would learn of the sabbotage . . . What could or would he attempt, armed with that knowledge? Surely the forces of inertia, euphoria, government would all weigh on him, rendering him silent. No one, no one at all, saving Gant and perhaps Marian, would *act.* And Marian was hobbled by the same pressures that would constrain Aubrey. She had to be . . .

. . . which left Gant. Only Gant. Looking for Strickland, just as they were. If the two found each other . . .

'Don't lose Gant,' he warned. 'Not for a moment. At the first chance, make certain you kill him.'

Aubrey's mood was almost that of a diarist, comfortable amid the flickering quarrel between Marian and her father. He was no more than intrigued by Marian's drama — once the initial shock at her appearance, her weariness, had diminished. She herself had shaken off trauma by means of defiant anger.

'Do you realise what you're saying, Tig!' Giles growled. 'You're talking about David Winterborne, for heaven's sake! Why — for what possible reason — would David take such risks, go to such lengths? Good God, you're practically accusing him of attempted murder with this story of some builder's daughter!'

'Daddy — they *are* behaving like gangsters! Is that what *you* would tolerate?' Marian threw back, her cheeks flushed, her hands flinging her hair away from her face. Her forehead was pale, the skin beneath her eyes dark. To Aubrey, she looked like some wild prophetess. Perhaps she was . . . And yet Giles must be correct, surely, despite his own suspicions and David's wariness of him and the clandestine meetings at Uffingham. Once one brought it all under Giles' honest, direct gaze, it did seem tinged with the fantastical. 'Well, Daddy?' Marian asked again, all but taunting her father. She had inherited all his moral sense and more; in her it had led to scepticism, rather than Giles' optimism.

'Children . . .' Aubrey murmured good-humouredly.

'I blame you, Kenneth, for much of this,' Giles snapped at him. 'You've always encouraged Tig's capacity for suspicion, for lifting up stones. And I think you're doing it now!' His features broke into a smile and he waggled his hand to fend off any witty riposte. 'You know what I mean, Kenneth. And I'm right, however pompous I might sound.'

'Is he?' Marian challenged. 'Are you about to dismiss Banks' daughter, the cheque in the post — Michael Lloyd's *murder?*'

'And Fraser,' Aubrey murmured soberly.

Giles, probably as an antidote to reflection, helped them to more coffee, then took his cup to the window, where he remained, looking out, statuelike. Marian's smile towards his back was warm, grateful.

'Well?' she queried. '*And Fraser,* indeed. And me.' At the window, Giles' shoulders flinched. 'Yes, Daddy,' she could not help triumphing. 'Even you think I've stirred *something* up.'

'But *not* David,' he protested without turning.

Aubrey waved her to silence, then said: 'We can't go that far, I agree.' Marian frowned, shaking her head. Giles visibly relaxed his posture. 'But there are all the signs of —' He broke off in irritation as the doorbell sounded. 'All the signs of a gigantic swindle for *some purpose or other.*' His voice sharpened, quelling Marian's contemplated outburst. He heard Mrs Grey's voice answering the video entryphone. A moment later, she entered the drawing room.

'I'm sorry to interrupt, Sir Kenneth.' She glanced deferentially towards Giles Pyott, her attention slipping at once to the cafetiere which, against her better judgement, she had been requested to use. 'There's a gentleman, an American by his voice, who wishes to see you urgently. He's at the door now — a Mr Gant. Do you — ?' She paused, ambushed by Aubrey's surprise and by the evidence that Giles' astonishment was as great.

'I — er, Mrs Grey, you'd better show him up,' Aubrey flustered. 'Yes, please let him in at once.'

'Very well, Sir Kenneth.' She was already suspicious of anyone who could ruffle the calm waters in which she habitually swam.

'Kenneth — ?' Giles began apprehensively.

'None of my doing. A coincidence worthy of a

Victorian novel, perhaps?'

'Kenneth, the man is in very great trouble. This isn't coincidence. If you had read your *Times* assiduously, you'd know there's an FBI warrant for his arrest on charges of —'

'— being on the payroll,' Gant murmured from the doorway. 'Hi, General — Sir Kenneth.' He shrugged childishly, self-deprecatingly, so that Aubrey saw him as a caricature of some prodigal son disclaiming any part in the wasting of the family fortune. He struggled to his feet with the aid of his stick. Marian's amusement was the equal of her curiosity, her glance studying Gant.

'Mitchell, my dear boy!' Aubrey's effusiveness was overdone. Gant's stare hardened.

'You look comfortable here, sir — I'm interrupting . . .' There was an edge of sarcasm to the remark. Gant turned to Pyott. 'It's just bullshit, sir. I wasn't on the take.'

'Just helping your former father-in-law?' He turned to Marian, whose arch expression disarmed.

'Yes, I was,' he replied with studied, affected politeness. 'He was being screwed, begging your pardon, ma'am.'

'I apologise, Major.' Marian stood up. 'I don't think you need score any more baskets — Marian Pyott,' she added, holding out her hand. He shook it perfunctorily but warmly.

'My daughter,' Giles murmured.

'Pleased to meet you, ma'am.'

'I take it this is not a social call, Mitchell — sit down. Mrs Grey, more coffee, please. Sit down, sit down —' Aubrey showed Gant to an armchair, on which he perched like some quiescent but alert hunting bird. He looked out of place, yet somehow self-possessed. 'You're looking well — if tired,' Aubrey added gauchely, as if he had forgotten his own self-assurance in Gant's presence.

Interesting, Marian thought. Intriguing. It was, in a strange way, rather like being shown Daddy's medals as a girl, romantic and also a potent reminder that her father had a past that stretched back for years before her birth. This was Aubrey's equally *real* past, personified by this confident American in his weekend clothes.

Aubrey studied Gant. It was as if the man rendered what had been, for Aubrey, a dispassionate debate into something altogether more interesting. He shook the thought aside. The sense of his professional life was uncomfortable, like a waistcoat become too tight or old-fashioned.

'I need your advice — your expertise,' Gant said. His shrug indicated an awareness of Marian as an intruder. Aubrey knew Gant required his peculiar skills. In connection with the Vance airliner, its spectacular failure, Vance's subsequent death . . . ?

'Marian is not an outsider, Mitchell.'

Gant glanced at her, then nodded.

'OK. I — it's this . . .' He drew something from the pocket of his jacket. Aubrey realised how dishevelled Gant's clothing appeared, stained and crumpled. 'Is it genuine?' He passed the folded piece of card to Aubrey, who immediately admitted surprise.

'Yes, I think it is.' *Edouard St Cloud, DST.*

'How did you come by it?' He handed the card to Giles, who nodded his agreement. Marian leant forward in her chair.

'Oslo. I went looking for a guy — I found *him*. Part of a team. They weren't waiting for me, but they found me fast enough.'

'Does this involve Vance Aircraft?'

Gant nodded. 'The second 494 to crash was serviced overnight in Oslo. There was a guy there who claimed Vance sent him, after the first crash, after Alan and I —' Again, he shrugged. Then he looked up bleakly. 'I need to know why the French security service is involved in this.'

'What was their interest?' Aubrey asked.

Mrs Grey brought the refreshed cafetiere, another Crown Derby cup. In an exaggerated politeness, Gant stood up. Mrs Grey at once warmed to him, poured him coffee. When she had gone, Gant said:

'Hostile action. They tried to take me out.'

'Why?' There was a tremor of excitement in Aubrey's voice. It was another moment like that on the terrace at Uffingham, or when he had discovered Marian in the hall of the house, having overheard David. Marian's moral outrage, Gant's intrusion, even Giles' protective fluttering, all like breezes exciting the calm lake of his old age.

'It was sabotage — each time,' Gant announced.

Aubrey heard Marian's easy, immediate shock in her breathing and the rumble of Giles' disbelief. For himself, the past had bullied its way in.

'You're certain of this?' he said.

'Yes.'

'And you know who?' Aubrey blurted, realising an angry excitement about Gant.

'A guy called Strickland. Former Company man. It's his career. I recognised him on video-tape — they have it now, I guess. I didn't retrieve it.'

'You mean' — Marian burst out — 'Alan Vance was the victim of sabotage, that someone employed this man Strickland to make certain the 494 was a disaster?' Her eyes were drug-bright.

'That's about the size of it.'

'Who?'

'I don't have the answer. French security is protecting Strickland in some way. It's a cover-up.'

'Kenneth!' she exclaimed. 'Kenneth . . . ?' Her voice tailed away into sombre reflection. Her hands were agitated in her lap, amid the huge flowers of her full skirt.

'Wait, Marian, wait,' he urged. 'Mitchell — tell us what happened to the first aircraft, then to you . . . Please. Take your time.'

As Gant's brief narrative concluded, Giles was the first to speak.

'You're certain of everything you've told us?'

'I am, General. Burton wants me to follow up, but I don't think it's anything but polite interest. He doesn't want to know what's *really* going on —'

'Do we?' Aubrey asked sharply. 'Not you, Mitchell, not you — we three?' Gant's sense of wrong was primitive. His motive had been evident in the way he spoke of Vance, or perhaps more accurately, of his aircraft and his ambition. But this . . . ?

He was afraid of Marian's keen intuition. It was much like his own. Would it lead her to — ?

'You think this effort to discredit — ruin — the Vance 494 originates in Europe, don't you, Major?'

'I'm not sure. Does the French security service freelance, sir?'

'Infrequently,' Aubrey admitted.

'Kenneth — stop dragging your feet,' Marian said, her brow creased, her eyes staring at the carpet as if reading some hieroglyphic text. Her hands made small, decisive chopping motions as she spoke. 'The two things *have* to fit together. The consequences of what the major has discovered have been of the greatest benefit to Aero UK, to David.' Gant's attention was hungry, fixed. 'No, don't interrupt me . . . Tim Burton has been won over, Skyliner is on the brink of worldwide acceptance when it was a dead duck only a couple of weeks ago. Aero UK flourishes, when a fortnight ago it was about to collapse.' She looked up, her eyes hot. 'Two plane crashes have made all the difference in the world!'

'You mean you know — ?' Gant began. Marian nodded, but Aubrey protested.

'We *know* absolutely nothing, Mitchell — nothing!'

'Kenneth, that's just obfuscation —'

'Marian, you're letting your imagination run away with you,' Giles warned. He glimpsed the realities, but they made him only more determined to avoid them for his daughter's sake.

'Am I? Well, Kenneth, am I?' she challenged.

'We know Aero UK has been kept afloat by fraud. Perhaps it needed murder to make certain of the eventual outcome!'

'You're talking about business rivalry, not some vendetta!' Giles objected angrily. 'This is all nonsense.'

'Well, Kenneth?' she asked again. Aubrey merely shook his head. He appeared old, somehow uncomprehending, and her disappointment with him was mirrored in Gant's expression. She added: 'They killed Michael Lloyd for the sake of his silence. What would a few aircrew and some passengers — all total strangers — *matter?*'

To Marian, Aubrey's complacency seemed little more than slowness of mind, her father's defensive tactics and dismissal of what was so glaringly obvious merely tiresome; even Gant was no more than a messenger bringing confirmation of her own insight. The French security service was involved because of Balzac-Stendhal, obviously. The sabotage had been a kind of violent asset-stripping, a dawn raid with real weapons. She fumbled her cigarettes from her handbag and lit one, puffing furiously, waving her hands as she continued to berate the men in the room.

'There are just too many coincidences, too many common factors. There's Fraser and the death of Michael — there's *my lucky escape* — there's Tim Burton changing sides, if you like — the two sabotaged 494s — the attempt on the major's life — *everything!* If you can't see that it all forms *one* design, not two, then you're being wilfully complacent, Kenneth!'

The silence that followed was charged. Aubrey

dissembled, she realised, in maintaining his lack of expression. Her father's nervousness was apparent, an admission that he agreed with her and was afraid of the consequences of the truth. Gant asked:

'Can you explain — what's the problem over here?'

Leaning intently forward, Marian jabbed her cigarette in his direction in accompaniment to her hurried explanation. She felt her cheeks flush, her body quiver with her unsuppressed anger. She had been right all along! David had *planned* this, he had employed a professional saboteur to remove the rival to Skyliner. Following the collapse of the helicopter project, it had been ever more urgent that he display some kind of success. He had had to bring down a *second* 494 to make certain.

And he'd done it, just as easily as he might have ordered dinner in a restaurant.

'I'm certain the fraud and the sabotage are linked,' she repeated. 'Both companies would have been ruined, the fraud would have come to light, if Artemis had bought 494s and then other airlines had followed suit. The helicopter cancellation was the last straw. They *had* to act, and act quickly!'

She sat back, stubbed out her cigarette and immediately lit another. She poured herself more coffee, her gestures as theatrical and calculated as those of an actress. She had to persuade Gant — and Aubrey and her father — that this must be pursued. Its scope, its daring, its moral vacuum affronted her. Her father and Kenneth could have all the comforts of claiming that it was none of their concern, that it was *civvy street* to them and bore no relation to the battlefield or the intelligence world of the Cold War — but *not* at the price of denying the facts. Her father's expression pleaded with her, as if she could will a self-imposed amnesia. Kenneth was owl-like, patricianly dismissive.

'Nothing to do with you, Kenneth?' she taunted waspishly. 'Other side of the street, someone else's concern?'

'Marian!' her father snapped in the voice with which he had upbraided lapses of good manners during her childhood.

Gant's expression was thoughtful. She suspected that he was more than half-convinced. Looking challengingly at Aubrey, she asked: 'What do we *do?*'

After a long silence, Aubrey sighed heavily.

'Very well,' he admitted with as bad a grace as he could muster. 'Very *well.*'

He was irritated, as if woken from a nap, having missed the fall of two wickets after a too-good lunch. Marian realised that she had hooked his curiosity like a fish. Her father appeared infuriated that Kenneth had been won over. He wanted nothing more than her safety . . . Marian suppressed the shiver that threatened to reveal her nerves. That fire . . . they had tried to kill her. She breathed slowly, deeply. Even so, Giles was aware of her disquiet. His expression pleaded with her to give it up.

'Kenneth —' he warned.

'Yes, old friend, I understand,' Aubrey murmured. 'But these two young people have *already* excited the curiosity of interested parties, even their counter-activity. We cannot now leave things as they are. *Twice* they have tried to kill Mitchell and —'

'— once in Marian's case,' Giles said heavily, and then immediately burst out: 'But we're talking about *David* here! How can we be discussing the son of our oldest friend in this way?'

Ungenerously, deliberately, Marian snapped: 'Who *else* could be behind it, Daddy?'

'The French — Coulthard . . . ?'

'Hasn't the brains for it,' she retorted.

'Then the French.'

'It isn't primarily an intelligence operation, Giles,' Aubrey smoothed, waving Marian to silence with an angry little flap of his hand. 'They would do it for *la France* or *la gloire* or reasons of state, even for *business* . . . but they don't appear to be the prime movers here. They have no direct involvement with the city regeneration scheme and the massive fraud. *David's* companies do. David is involved in Aero UK, *David* has met the European Commissioners Marian suspects — Lloyd's former superior among them — and *David* is concerned at any and every interest shown, whether by myself or Marian. *David* . . .' He shook his head, more sorrowful than enraged.

'You mustn't, Kenneth,' Pyott pleaded.

'Giles — I must help if I can.' He assayed an ingratiating smile. 'You, after all, couldn't forbid her.'

'Clive must never, *never* be involved, Marian.

Or know that any of us are involved.' He turned his back on them the moment he finished speaking, as if to disown them, and stared out at Regent's Park in the midday sunshine.

Aubrey asked quickly: 'Why do you wish to pursue this, Mitchell? Why are you here, precisely?'

'Are you asking me why I need to do it, or if I can do it?'

'Perhaps both.'

Marian was shocked by Aubrey's bluntness, his sudden recovery of concentration. Gant was aware of her surveillance of him, more challenged by her than by Aubrey.

'Vance built a good airplane. Someone decided they couldn't compete and changed the odds by killing people. Some of them were — friends of mine.' His admission, to Marian at least, seemed more like a duty than an affection. Then Gant added: 'The pilot of the first airplane, Hollis . . . I couldn't be at the funeral. I should have.' He looked up at Aubrey, his eyes hard. 'When you've taken the bones out of that, yes — I can do it. I *know* Strickland. He's just one of the psychopaths I've run across. He did these things. For *big business,* right? So the stockholders aren't disappointed at end of year.' Marian saw the utter contempt, his narrow, upright suspicion of politicians and businessmen in suits with manicured hands and dead eyes.

'I can find him. I called a guy in Langley, someone who owed me. They always keep records, especially on people like Strickland. He called me back when I was on my way here. I have an address — in France.'

'If you have the address, so do they,' Aubrey remarked.

'I guess so.'

'I'd like Strickland alive.'

'I'll try for that.' Gant seemed to dislike the idea. 'Strickland is like someone off religious TV. Big business would like him. He would make it easy for them to go down his road. Any suit who needs an edge can have Strickland call by his office, in a jacket and tie, and the arrangements are easy.'

Marian realised there was something compulsively moral about his disdain, and it strangely thrilled her, such was its lack of compromise.

'You think your man is using Strickland, right?'

Heavily, Aubrey replied: 'Possibly. It does seem so.'

'If I bring you the proof you need, you'll just do the *English* thing, you and the general, and tell him to lay off. Right?'

'There isn't another way, Mitchell. This hasn't entirely crossed the border into our country. There are different priorities —'

'Your *man* crossed over.'

'Yes, I think he probably has.' He felt suddenly invigorated. He clapped his hands together, startling them, eyes alight. He cleared the fug of moral and emotional considerations as quickly as Mrs Grey would clear away the crockery that lay on the coffee table.

'To work then,' he beamed. 'You, my lady, are to maintain a low profile — no, I mean that.

David is already suspicious of you — he must not be *alarmed.*'

'I'm not going to sit on my backside, Kenneth —'

'You *must!*' he snapped. 'Mitchell, where is Strickland now?'

'He has some place in France — a farmhouse. The Dordogne?' He evidently did not know the area.

'You know exactly?' Gant nodded. 'Very well. We'll discuss the details in a moment. Will he be there?'

'He's owned it for some time.'

'I remind you again — *they* will know that.'

'Sure.'

'Then we must prepare. I think —'

'Kenneth,' Giles said quietly, 'I am quite sure your flat is under surveillance.' He turned casually from the window. 'They must have followed Gant here. What do you recommend we do, in the circumstances?'

CHAPTER TEN

Festung Europa

'Well, where's the charabanc?' she called with an attempt at gaiety that was utterly at odds with the last, draining effects of shock.

The members of the Commons Select Committee for European Affairs were gathered near St Stephen's Porch like schoolchildren, awaiting the transport that would take them on their eagerly anticipated outing. Indeed, there were two members of the Committee old enough to remember having been evacuated as children during the war. They were the ones whose smiles were broadest at the joke she intended to lighten her own mood.

Cromwell's statue seemed to frown at the little group in Old Palace Yard as they waited for the liveried minibus that would transport them to Waterloo and the Eurostar high-speed tram. The air of holiday that hung about the party of ten — two researchers had managed to wangle their way on to the junket to Brussels — failed to infect her. Her colleagues had murmured soothing, anodyne sympathies regarding the fire and her escape from it. Remembering it was still like touching at new, painful skin over the childhood burns.

It was not the fire, however, that preoccupied her. There was another terror, more slow and acidic, that she wished she could put at a distance. Only a few minutes before leaving her London flat, she had discovered that it had been expertly burgled while she was in the constituency. Someone had broken in without leaving any trace and stolen the scribbled notes and the photographs that Michael Lloyd had sent her. Her computer had been wiped clean of everything she had transferred to it concerning —

— *David* . . . the fraud . . . her suspicions . . . Michael Lloyd. No shred of proof, or evidence, had been left behind. She wished she had not checked the hiding-place before leaving for the Commons, for then she would not have known how completely and expertly they were moving against her . . . Her long fingernails were hurting her palms as she squeezed her hands into fists. *Pull yourself together*, she instructed herself sternly. *But all the proof's gone . . . Then you'd better find some more.*

She shivered, alerting the attention of a senior Opposition MP, a Eurosceptic ally on the Committee. She smiled disarmingly at him. He was as unpopular with his party's leadership as she was with the government. The old man turned away and she felt the memory of the burglary press at her again . . . This time, she was able to fend it off. She breathed deeply, calmingly.

Another sceptic from her own party was very obviously consulting his watch.

'Typical! I don't doubt the champagne will be too cold, too!' His adopted squirearchical manner was a better joke; his parents had been teachers, he an estate agent in one of the larger London firms.

'Typical of you, Roger,' offered one of HM Opposition's most vociferous and unquestioning Europhiles. His *nom-de-guerre* throughout Westminster was Ethelred the Undoubting. Some — the irredeemable — called him Euro-Jew. A darkness passed over Roger's narrow features. An irredeemable? She rarely made common cause with Roger, even over Europe.

The familiarity of the company, the mere prospect of the trip to Brussels, was working on her like a restorative. She did feel calmer.

'Settle down, children,' she offered, smiling with an almost polished brightness. 'The time for squabbles is on the way back, when you're all tired out — ah, here we are!'

Suitcases were at once snatched up with that eagerness she only ever witnessed among Honourable Members when they were travelling first-class and without payment and heading towards a fleshpot or a trough. Brussels offered almost everything your average MP could desire, except a permanent posting! That had not been one of her jokes. The Eurostar livery gleamed in the morning sunshine on the flanks of the stretched minibus as it pulled up in Old Palace Yard as near to the group as was respectful.

She picked up her own small suitcase and, as she straightened and was saying in an ironic tone:

'I see the boys are pushing to the front as usual — !'

— saw David Winterborne crossing the cobbles in the company of the Minister of State at the Department of Trade and Industry. Her suitcase felt awkward, heavy in her grip. The members of the Committee pressed on to the minibus, their cases loaded at the back by the uniformed driver, the bright, empty chatter of the hostess merely bird noises. David's features darkened stormily for just a moment, then his carefully nurtured aplomb was recovered.

'Marian! How wonderful — !' His hand was extended towards her. The junior minister, knowing their long acquaintance, noticed no tension between them. She took his cool, slim hand.

'David — as you see, you've just caught me off on a jolly. Another freebie!'

Aubrey's last words to her were in her mind. *There has been no crime because the reason for the crime no longer exists. Such matters are known by the soubriquet of business ethics. But they will be all the more determined to act against* anyone *who even threatens to remind them of the fact that there* was *a crime, that people* died . . . *Be careful, I beg you.* He had addressed Gant as earnestly as herself.

'David,' she repeated with a great deal more self-confidence. 'How nice to see you — and to see you have the time to spend cultivating business in our little banana republic!'

David was forced to chuckle. The minister, whose gravity was that of an undertaker rather than born of confidence or sincerity, scowled at her levity. As if in further rebuke, the Chancellor of the Exchequer, emerging from the official limousine, waved to David before brushing his tie straight across his ample stomach and flicking a cowlick of hair away from his forehead.

'Flavour of the month,' she murmured.

'Ready, David?' the junior minister intruded.

Marian was relieved rather than irritated with the man's pompous assumption of superiority. David's unwavering gaze was a withering light beating on her nerves.

'What? Oh, yes . . . Marian, have a wonderful time in — Brussels, I presume? You're all right? I mean, after that fire — ?'

The question was dazzling in its innocence.

'Fine!' she replied with as much ingenuousness.

He leaned forward and pecked at her suddenly cold cheek. She held herself rigid so that she would not flinch away from his kiss. He was smiling as he drew back from her, then his attention immediately embraced the junior minister. At St Stephen's Porch, the Chancellor still loitered, waiting for a word with Winterborne. *There has been no crime,* Aubrey had said. Damn you for being so *right,* Kenneth!

She felt bewildered until the elderly Member took her arm and began to guide her towards the minibus with its ridiculously grinning hostess. She was unable to suppress the shiver of nerves, alarming the Opposition MP.

'All right, lass?' he asked in his broad Yorkshire accent. 'You're not sickening for summat, are you?'

She smiled. His tone was as normal and reassuring as the traffic as it jerked from light to light along St Margaret's Street; as familiar as Parliament at her back. Marian shook her head.

'I'm fine, Henry — fine. Wrong time of the month — you know.'

'Aye. And I've heard that excuse cover a multitude of sins in my time, too.'

They had reached the bus and she patted the hand that still lay, gnarled and blue-veined from coal, on her arm.

'I doubt it was ever used to resist your advances, Henry. Thanks.'

Shaking her hair away from her face, she climbed aboard the minibus and plumped aggressively into a vacant seat. The male MPs seemed infected with the atmosphere of a holiday. What else was it? She kept her briefcase on her lap, opening it determinedly to remove *Private Eye*. She turned to its parliamentary gossip, 'HP Sauce', and almost at once called out:

'I see you're in the *Eye*, Roger — *again!*'

Roger appeared mortally offended, but knowledgeable.

'Everything there is already declared on the Register,' he snapped.

'You hope!' someone else called. Another commented good-humouredly:

'I see Marian's up to mischief — as usual.'

And she was . . . She had left Aubrey's flat late in the afternoon, with Giles, having promised *to be a good girl.* Giles had taken her at her solemn, pretended word, but Kenneth had been suspiciously anxious on her behalf . . . And now she knew why. She frowned as she scanned *Private Eye*'s already widespread gossip. She even knew the source of most of it.

Gant had stayed behind with Aubrey for some kind of briefing; perhaps he had stayed overnight. He seemed contained, but like a pressure cooker filled with boiling water and steam. She understood his motives, even though his intent had a primitive, violent end in view. Strickland had caused a chaos in his world, just as David Winterborne had done in hers. The minibus pulled out of Old Palace Yard into traffic, towards Waterloo and the train to Brussels . . . where Michael had been murdered.

Her briefcase was full of the morning papers, each of which celebrated, in its own particular manner, Aero UK's success, Tim Burton's expansion plans and the coming transatlantic price war. Boeing was already engaged in furious counter-hype. Air France was about to lease a dozen Skyliners, with a promise to buy at least six of them by the end of the year. Europe was vigorously thumbing its nose at the States and its planemakers.

She looked up as Ben Campbell sat himself next to her. His smile was engaging, self-regarding. His *Times*, as he unfolded it, observed in a headline *Success for Skyliner at eleventh hour.* It had been close, the line between success and failure, threadlike. David had merely tilted the balance a little, slightly moved the goalposts, so that he, Aero UK and Balzac-Stendhal were now standing on the other side of the narrow line. Success and failure . . . all it had required was a few instructions given in a high office overlooking the City — after receiving best advice — and the consequence had been one murder in another country and two remote aircraft accidents. For those small and obscure events, the reward could be a difference of hundreds of millions, eventually billions. How could David *not* have taken the course he had?

'You all right?' Ben Campbell asked. 'You looked a bit off-colour out there.' The Euro MP's enquiry was brightly, incuriously made.

'Fine,' she replied, glancing up — then quickly down again as she met the hot penetration of his stare, sensed the weighing, the judging that was occurring behind it. 'No, I'm fine, Ben,' she repeated. 'Thanks for asking.'

'That fire business, I suppose?' he murmured.

'I suppose,' she snapped ungraciously, then added: 'Sorry — it was a bit unsettling . . . You know.'

'Yes, I'm sure.'

Campbell, a Euro MP for the last three years, a Commission functionary before that, was their *duenna* for the junket to Brussels. It was a PR role he seemed formed by destiny to fulfil, his thick hair, white teeth, firm jawline offering the necessary assurances concerning the rectitude of everything European. *Campbell's Eurosoup,* many Members unkindly called him.

'We *will* be out to change your mind, Marian — I give you fair warning,' he announced with an ingratiating smile. 'Throw off our ogre's clothes for something more attractive to you.'

'I don't doubt it.'

His eyes seemed filled with a piercing enquiry, but she could not be certain that it was not her own nerves that made his proximity and interest suspicious. There seemed to be another role, besides that of expert PR man. Of course, Ben Campbell had long been a lobbyist for Aero UK and Balzac-Stendhal . . . and an associate of Winterborne. With surprising ease, she could imagine herself and Campbell as prisoner and escort. She rubbed her arms involuntarily. Ben Campbell was a professional, fully employed smoothie . . . it was just his manner. Wasn't it . . . ?

'Did your mum make you up some sandwiches for the train?' she managed.

His smile was warm, reassuring: it disarmed. Yet his presence discomfited. London slipped past the window of the minibus, but despite herself, she could not help feeling once more that she was under threat; even from Campbell.

The minibus crossed Westminster Bridge. She glanced back towards Parliament as if expecting David to be standing there, monstrously enlarged. The sunlight made the Palace of Westminster a gingerbread house, biscuit-coloured. The Thames was flecked with pleasure craft — other junkets, corporate entertainments, business as usual. Had it been at some cocktail party or reception that David had first decided that Michael Lloyd must be silenced . . . that she should be burned alive?

She shivered and Campbell noticed the involuntary spasm. Waterloo loomed as darkly as some Victorian prison-house. *Come on, come on,* she told herself, but there seemed no defiance available.

His eyes moved from the map strapped to his knee to the landscape four thousand feet below the Cessna. He was above Périgueux, Limoges behind him, Brive a smudge away to the east. The land ahead of the aircraft was beginning to crumple like a suddenly ageing face into the worn folds and creases of the Dordogne. Soon he would need to find somewhere quiet to land.

He had walked out to the plane Aubrey had hired for him, into a glad-to-be-alive summer morning through which he had had to pass as if it was no more than a stage set. Dew still on the grass. A young woman in the office had completed his paperwork and glanced casually at his pilot's licence. There had been no more to it than that before he had unlocked the Cessna, done his external checks, climbed in, started the engine. Even the name of the place, Biggin Hill, had impinged without any sense of its history. The hours he had spent with Aubrey, after the general and his daughter had left and before he had briefly slept in the old man's spare bedroom, had sapped like leeches. Until this flight over southern England, the Channel, then northern France had seemed no more than a getaway, some kind of temporary escape.

The woman had grasped at him like feverish hands, her determination greater than his, her sense of urgency more vivid. His search for Strickland wasn't just a wild card to her, it was something like a solemn promise. He felt the weight of her indignation, her demand for the truth, press at his back. She was uncomfortable to be around, even to remember.

The Channel had been filled with shipping and white wakes, an impression of slow, inexorable purpose and of certainty and destination. His flight was more empty than that, the plane's unfamiliar slowness suggesting drift, aimlessness.

He checked the map again. The clock on the instrument panel showed ten-forty. French air traffic control was on a go-slow, not answering his calls since he had first contacted Paris. An Air Algérie flight, picking up one of his calls, had offered to relay to Paris Control on his behalf, but that hadn't been what he wanted.

There was an airfield at Périgueux, already behind him, another at Brive and a third at Sarlat about eighteen miles south of his position. Sarlat was ideal — had he wanted to use an airfield. He didn't. Almost certain that he had left Aubrey's apartment without detection, and that his taxi hadn't been followed out of London, he still sensed that they would be waiting for him — French Intelligence, the people from Oslo — at Bordeaux, which his flight plan claimed was his destination. Any diversion to another airfield was traceable and a matter of no more than an hour's drive from Bordeaux. He needed to disappear, temporarily, and to have a secure, undiscovered airplane to return to . . . with Strickland. *If* Strickland was at his farmhouse —

Doubt was pointless. He cut it off and eased the throttles back and put the Cessna into a gentle, descending turn. His altitude was four thousand feet above sea level, the country was three thousand feet below him. He had seen narrow river valleys that were possible landing sites, but hedges and clumps of trees were scattered across their slopes like traps. Most of them were narrow gorges anyway — too narrow for him to ensure a safe landing. It should only *look* like a forced landing, the airplane had to stay in one piece, its flimsy undercarriage usable for take-off.

He dropped lower still in a left-hand orbit. His right hand reached out to grasp the fuel mixture control. He made the mixture leaner, his fingers almost stroking the control, until the engine banged, popped, became fragile and insufficient to support the weight of the Cessna against the air. The wind noise intruded into the engine's coughing. Nodding, he returned the mixture to normal running.

Someone would have heard the first failing notes of the engine. When he repeated it and seemed to drop more quickly out of the sky, eye-witnesses — as they invariably did — would embroider what they saw. Smoke, maybe an engine fire, a wing coming off . . . People did that, trying to help the investigation. He smiled briefly.

The land was dotted with villages, some of them clamped like mussels on to rock outcrops, the roofs of the buildings biscuit-brown. Dark paint-spills of forest and cultivated orchards and groves. The threads of rivers like bright woollen strands accidentally plucked from a complex tapestry. He continued to toy with the mixture control, producing a rough-running engine note. Fifteen hundred feet below, a tractor, seemingly immobile, was tilted on a sloping field, earth crimped darkly behind its plough. The field looked free of fences, ditches, bushes. Dotted with old, broad trees, it sloped in such a way that it would provide sufficient approach and landing distance. He allowed the Cessna to sink leaflike towards the field, as if the plane was turned only by the wind. The engine continued to cough and bang convincingly. The man on the tractor seemed to be staring skywards, the vehicle unmoving on the slope of the field. A few sheep were grazing on part of it, but already seeking the shade of the trees against the heat of midmorning.

Eight hundred feet . . . A double bang, felt through the controls as much as heard. He pushed the mixture to fully rich, alerted the pitch of the aircraft, as it seemed to wobble for an instant, as if about to tumble from a cliff-edge of air; levelled the wings. He checked the instruments furiously, unnerved. The controls responded normally. *What in hell — ?* There was a crimson and white stain on the starboard wing strut.

A bird strike. A bird had flown into the propeller. There were dark specks on the cockpit windscreen, a smear on the starboard wing. The engine coughed and choked now without his interference. The Cessna sank towards the trees and the sloping field. The man on the tractor watched him, posed in imperturbability. The wind direction was right. He reduced power and lowered the undercarriage. A rabbit hole would be enough to fling the light aircraft violently tail over cockpit, send it tumbling to fragments down the slope of the field. He lowered the flaps a notch, his attention focused on a point perhaps two hundred yards beyond a small knot of trees and resting sheep. He closed the throttle.

He dropped the flaps fully and tensed himself against the first touch of the wheels . . . *now.* The plane seemed to float for an instant, as if it had encountered water which buoyed it up. The wheels thumped, bounced, began to roll. He switched off the fuel. The engine's noise was replaced by the clatter of running over the rough pasture. He passed the tractor, glimpsing the driver's surprised expression. The plane slowed as if running through mud. Then it came to a gradual stop, the gradient of the field rising in front of the nose, the tractor in the mirrors abandoned by the farmer, who was stalking towards him.

The engine ticked as it cooled. He opened the cockpit door. The gyros whined down into silence. He heard birdsong and then the shouts of the farmer. The sheep had bolted from the shade out into the sunlight. Gant waited for the Frenchman to reach the plane. Looking down at his reddened, perspiring features, his evident outrage, he shrugged and said:

'Sorry, fella. Engine trouble —' He climbed out beneath the wing, tugging at a rucksack, and dropped to the grass. The Frenchman was gesticulating angrily at the Cessna, at his field, at the already nibbling sheep — even at the sky and the country around them. 'Sorry — can't *parlez Français,* fella.' A shrug of incomprehension as he continued: 'Engine trouble.' He spoke as if to an idiot child. 'I need a *garage* — got to make some repairs . . . Understand?'

His relief had become amusement.

'Garage?' the Frenchman replied in heavily accented English. 'The aircraft — your engine? I heard —' He pointed at the sky, at his ears. Gant nodded.

'That's right —' He looked at his watch, already possessed by a sense of the small scene as an interlude, something put in a Hitchcock movie, just before someone got killed or the audience, taken off-guard, was shocked in some other way. Strickland's farmhouse was no more than a couple of miles from where he stood. 'I can leave the plane *here?* While I go for spare parts?' He banged his hand on the engine cowling. 'Repairs? Can I leave the plane *here?*'

The farmer nodded furiously.

'*Mais oui, m'sieur* . . . You are OK?'

He should be making final approach to Bordeaux's Merignac airport in another ten minutes. He was overdue to contact them. Time was already being wasted, evaporating in the morning heat.

'Thanks, fella — I'm fine.' He locked the door of the Cessna. 'Where's the nearest garage?'

'St Amand-de-Coly, maybe.' He shrugged. 'What do you need, m'sieur?'

'Just a couple of parts.' He studied the map, pointing out the village the farmer had named. It lay in the same direction as Strickland's farmhouse, maybe a couple of miles farther southwest. He wouldn't create any suspicion by suddenly heading off in the wrong direction. The farmer's blunt, earth-browned finger tapped the map in agreement. St Amand-de-Coly. 'I'll be maybe two hours, three — ?'

'No one will steal your aircraft, m'sieur!' The farmer laughed. Gant slung the rucksack across his back, waved to the farmer, and began walking towards the gate of the field. Time began to hurry in his head. *They* would be waiting at Bordeaux airport, they would soon realise he wasn't going to show . . .

There was more champagne, more canapés, then the sudden harsh lighting of the Channel Tunnel as the train sped into it like someone dashing for shelter from the rainclouds gathering in the blue Kent sky. Marian concentrated with a deliberate effort on the remnants of her constituency postbag, the tickle of her claustrophobia raising her temperature, making her body wriggle uncomfortably in her seat. The table in front of her was littered with the ordinariness, the seductions of Parliament; submissions from researchers on half a dozen matters, her tape recorder and notepad. Roger and one or two others had already mocked her Goody-Twoshoes attention to Commons business as they wolfed the canapés, downed the champagne. Attentive stewards glided and poured and offered as brazenly as hoardings. *Come to sunny Brussels for the Good Life . . .*

She rubbed her eyes, and looked up as Campbell slipped into the seat opposite her. Ben Campbell again, as if to dispel the comfortable talismans she had drawn around her. The lights of the Tunnel flashed past the windows like some hypnotic and virtual reality.

‘Looks fast, mm?’ he murmured, nodding at the window. ‘Wait ’til you try Skyliner — you’ve never flown on her, have you?’

‘No — looking forward to it.’ Was it his presence or simply the nag of claustrophobia that made her feel heated, almost menopausal? ‘Something to celebrate,’ she added.

‘Too true! To think that a couple of weeks ago —’ He shook his head. ‘Skin of their teeth, Aero UK and the Froggies — not to overstate the case.’

‘Are they all out of the wood?’

He waggled his hand.

‘Let’s say the Commission is still uttering collective sighs of relief.’ He grinned.

‘Grandiose project back on the rails? Almost Napoleonic, one might say.’

He seemed puzzled for a moment, then: ‘Ah, you’re grinding your axe, Marian.’

It was her turn to shake her head. Her hair fell across her face. There was a moment of purely sexual interest in Campbell’s brown eyes, then their interrogative, assessing expression was back. She brushed her hair back ostentatiously, teasingly, but he remained unaffected.

‘Not really. I’m *pleased* that Skyliner has a future. So are a lot of my constituents — not to mention the shareholders . . . people like David who must have stood to lose a fortune. He is a major investor in Aero UK, isn’t he? And he’s a subcontractor in a dozen ways . . .’ She expelled a relieved-sounding breath. ‘A damned close-run thing, as someone else once said in Brussels.’

‘Quite.’ Archly, he added: ‘Does this signal a

change of heart. You'll go easy on poor Bryan Coulthard in future?'

'I was always keen for Skyliner to succeed, Ben. It was the *cost* that was close to being obscene, nothing else. Not even the dreams of bureaucrats, however wet.'

He smiled a moment later.

'A hit. But you'll see — it's a wonderful aircraft. More luxurious than this train, business-class level of comfort for every passenger, first-class sleeping compartments . . . and the food's out of this world!'

'I'm not in the market for one of my own,' she murmured.

He seemed suddenly irritated by her mockery, and snapped:

'Perhaps you should try giving it a rest, Marian! Let people who *care* have a say for a change.' His dark complexion was suffused with irritation. It was as if his role discomfited him, attached him to a stubborn, recalcitrant child he detested.

'Ben, I didn't know you cared —'

'Marian, yours isn't the only commitment in town.' Then, with an effort: 'Sorry . . . But it is important for Skyliner to succeed. The whole future of European planemaking *was* at stake, you know.'

'I know. Apart from millions, even billions — government fundings, private fortunes.'

His eyes narrowed momentarily and she was angry at her overconfidence. Campbell only looked like a male model, she should not underestimate his intelligence. He was a highly attuned political animal.

Their glasses were topped up once more. Marian refused yet another tiny sandwich or sliver of toast and caviare. Around them, the noise of their companions was entirely convivial, the laughter hearty and uninhibited by party or personal antagonism. It was as if the scene had been arranged as a temptation. *Why not join in, have fun, ignore the dark corners? It's all over and done with now — why make a fuss?*

If only it were that simple, she answered herself and the joviality.

'Did you know Michael Lloyd, Ben? Ever work with him at the Commission?' It was asked carefully, almost gently, yet it startled him like blatant honesty might have done.

'Er — yes. Couple of years back, when he first arrived. We were together in the Transport Commissioner's office. I — heard about his overdose.' There was a slight emphasis upon the word, the shadowy mark left by an eraser. He shook his head. 'Great shame. Bright young man. Bit independent-minded, leftish where the Commission wasn't. Still, I'm sure he'd have gone far. Did you know him, Marian?'

'A little. Mutual acquaintances, interests. You know.'

'Ah, I see. I thought you were closer than that.'

'No . . .'

Campbell glanced at his watch, then along the aisle of the compartment. She felt he seemed satisfied with the assiduity with which other Euro MPs and one or two Commission functionaries were soothing and smoothing, flattering and flannelling.

He murmured: 'His current partner seems to have been at a loss to explain it — I mean, it must have been a terrible shock.' The embarrassment was almost instantly drained from his features by an effort of will. He leaned back. 'I heard she was in a terrible state, poor thing.'

In her notebook, on a disk, they had been Marian's own words . . . *at a loss to explain it* . . . There was no reason on earth why Campbell should have knowledge of the young woman, or have taken anything but the most cursory interest in Lloyd's death. Michael and he, she knew, had never liked each other. Campbell had either read, or been told of, the jottings from her PC. *After* the burglary.

'I expect she was. It's always so difficult to deal with that sort of death. Such a waste. Almost as if Michael was rejecting her. And she had no idea he had a heroin habit . . . Strange, that.'

'I — er, I suppose so.'

The lights of the Tunnel sped past. Her awareness of the train's bulletlike velocity increased. It seemed to be rushing her headlong towards risk.

'And my girl *is* safe?' Giles Pyott asked from his position at the window, from where he had already announced the renewed presence of the surveillance on Aubrey's flat.

Aubrey wanted to be open with Pyott. Instead, his busy fears closed him like a mussel's shell, separating him from his oldest friend. What was there, after all, to make David stop now? Marian had not told Giles of the burglary, and now he could not do so, either. David had proof of her certain knowledge. He should *not* have allowed her to travel to Brussels, not without taking many more precautions than merely a repeated *Take care, be careful* . . .

'Yes, Giles. Public places, in constant company — I'm sure,' he answered sweetly, almost with conviction.

Giles, for the stilling of his own fears and perhaps out of a pride in his daughter's competence, seemed to accept his reassurance.

'Very well. But — Gant? He is our agent, but can he do anything?'

'I hope so.'

Gant had left unseen at dawn. A light aircraft had been hired, a flight plan to Bordeaux filed. He had papers other than his own. Even so, it did not seem adequate, to pit one man against Fraser, French security, David. With no certainty that Strickland, the saboteur, was sitting calmly in the Dordogne, just waiting for Mitchell to collect him like a parcel.

'Very well, then,' Giles announced. 'Us? What do *we* do?' The old man who turned from the window with grave impatience was as erect as ever he had been as a serving soldier.

'This,' Aubrey sighed, gesturing at the littered desk behind which he was seated, wedged into one corner of the flat's drawing room. He had, he realised, been sitting there, almost without stirring, since six-thirty. 'I think we might make a start here.'

Pyott picked up the file and wandered nearer to the window, at once an old man again as he slipped on his reading glasses.

After Gant had left, Aubrey had attempted to sleep, but the effort had been futile. Instead, he had risen, dressed and sat at his desk as the early-morning joggers had passed beneath the windows and pigeons and crows had busily inspected the grass beyond the railings of Regent's Park. He had heard mockery in the bird calls, out of which had arisen an anger at his age, his lack of office. And a fear that he had sent Gant on a mission that might prove fatal . . . and failed to prevent Marian from sailing off towards the reefs and disaster in her characteristic mood of utter self-confidence and moral invulnerability. He had written the bitter thoughts in his diary, something he rarely did in recent, retired years. The exercise had not helped to calm or reassure.

'We shan't have much time, Kenneth — Johnny Laxton's flying to Brussels today. Marian told me. The European Commissioner for Urban Development has to show his face at the various bashes Tig's attending. Stands to reason.' The last phrase was delivered with the snort of a soldier contemptuous of civilians and their petty corruptions.

'Yes — I anticipated that. I've invited him to lunch with us at the Club, as a consequence. I have a brief board meeting — one of David's companies, I have to confess,' he added with a kind of soiled shame. 'But I shall be there before one.'

'Fine. I'll be waiting for the two of you.' He smiled in a hard, anticipatory expression. 'I don't want to pour cold water, Kenneth — but are we likely to get anything from Johnny Laxton? The man was so stupid as a Cabinet minister I have to wonder whether he knows anything at all that would be useful to us.'

Aubrey laughed, the sharp barking noise of a fox.

'Oh, I think Laxton knows, Giles. I think Laxton's allowed a great deal of the money to pass through his hands, across his desk.' He hefted himself upright from the chair with audible noises of breath and old joints, but his step was firm and urgent across the carpet. 'Come on, old friend. We must frighten Johnny Laxton as he has never been frightened before!'

He grabbed Pyott's arm with an eager, young man's grip, as if to sweep him, girl-like, on to some imagined dance floor. Pyott, looking down at Aubrey, grinned.

'To horse,' he murmured. 'And towards the sound of the guns.'

Aubrey watched Giles' fears for Marian swallowed by his awakened enthusiasm. His own — for her and for Gant alike — remained bubbling like volcanic hot springs.

The track up to the farmhouse and its single barn was deserted. The house itself seemed even more silent and lifeless. From the knoll where he lay, studying it through field glasses, he was certain Strickland had gone. Not merely to the local store in the nearest village — but gone, period. The previous evening and night, and the hours of the flight, collapsed behind him like a derelict building, leaving an empty lot. The mission was rubble. He had just the one address, this single lead to Strickland. There wouldn't be any more, not for him, not for a fugitive from justice.

The Dordogne noon was heavy with the noises of insects. A small tractor inched across a distant field, and cattle were dotted like specks of soot on sloping meadows. There was the high contrail of an airliner that had taken off from Bordeaux's Merignac airport, where his flight plan had claimed he would land. He was overdue . . . He could make up the lost time by leaving now, there was nothing down there for him.

He swung the glasses impatiently across the landscape. Dotted farmhouses and barns, scattered villages in folds of the land or on limestone outcrops, the buildings brown as coins in the noon sunlight. Stretches of dark holm-oak forest, groves of walnut trees, open fields of yellowing cereal crops. Châteaux and hunched, brooding castles like watchtowers marked the Dordogne valley to the south of him. His gaze moved back to Strickland's farmhouse.

Stillness . . .

He waited another half-hour, then slung the rucksack across his shoulders, rose to his feet and began jogging gently down the slope towards the grey-white track leading up to the house. Nothing moving . . . nothing. He climbed one fence, then another. Butterflies rose from the long grass, he startled a bird but nothing human. The midday was hot. He slowed to a cautious walk as he reached the track a hundred yards from the house. His shoulders slumped to casualness, his gait suggested he had already walked some distance. Strickland might have recognised him . . .

but then, Strickland wasn't home.

The shutters, small rectangles of peeling green paint set in the golden limestone block of the farmhouse, were closed on each of the ground-floor windows as well as the first floor. Three smaller windows jutted like snouts from the steeply pitched roof of flat brown tiles. Beyond the house, the weather-peeled doors of the barn were similarly closed. The place didn't seem out of keeping with Strickland's personality. The Preacherman possessed a diffident, hermitlike introversion — he was the man who had been the boy who spent day after day in his bedroom, building, dismantling, reading, brooding. Gant halted, studying the house and his reflections on Strickland.

The guy was mad, certifiable . . . and too much like himself. He shrugged but the recognition would not be dismissed. Another lonely, maybe brutalised kid who had retreated into himself, kept out of sight of parents, neighbours, the whole world. And finally poured everything bottled up and unused into flying. Gant shook his head. It didn't matter, except that this was just the kind of place Strickland would have chosen.

He reached the door of the house and knocked innocently, checking the pistol Aubrey had given him, thrust into his waistband in the small of his back. The sound of his knocking died away somewhere inside the empty house. He tried the handle of the door. The place must be locked up —

— the door opened slightly. As if the worn, clumsy door handle had burned him, he shut the door, moving away from it towards the nearest window, perspiration breaking out on his forehead.

The door shouldn't be unlocked . . . It was unlocked *deliberately*. Strickland made *bombs* . . .

Roussillon closed the flap of his mobile phone and turned in the front passenger seat of the big Citroën estate car.

'He's reached the farmhouse. For a moment, they thought he was going in through the front door —'

'But no such luck?' Fraser interrupted, a lack of surprise on his features. 'I told you it wouldn't do our job for us, Strickland's booby-trap device.'

'You did indeed, my friend.'

Roussillon shrugged. His men had searched the farmhouse early that morning. A minute visual inspection had revealed the front door rigged to explode a small bomb when pushed open. He had ordered the device left in place and the farmhouse put under close surveillance. There had been the chance that Strickland — who had obviously disappeared — would take care of his fellow-American for them. Now, they would have to do the job themselves.

He flicked a lock of dark hair away from his forehead. Through the rear window, he could see the small town of Beynac huddling at the foot of the hill on which its castle stood. The second car was fifty yards behind the Citroën. They were half an hour, at most, from Strickland's place.

Gant would find no clues as to Strickland's whereabouts. The place looked like a *gîte* awaiting the first tourists of the season rather than a place where someone had lived until very recently.

The main road followed a loop of the Dordogne River. Limestone cliffs, dark oak and chestnut trees crowded down to the road. Sunlight gleamed on the river.

Fraser's manner and tone had been lacking in affability. He was imitating, like the good messenger he was, the displeasure of his master that Gant had escaped his hit-team in Oslo. Beyond his irritation with failure and Fraser alike, Roussillon felt a resentment at his increasing collusion with the former SIS agent and Winterborne. His immediate superiors had instructed him to continue the association. Balzac-Stendhal, wrapping themselves in the *tricolore,* had borrowed him and certain elements of his service, the DST until such time as all possibility of scandal had receded. Effectively, he was taking his orders directly from Winterborne rather than from Paris. What had begun as the protection of secret funding to the French planemaker, in contradiction of EU principles, had become a manhunt for an American agent, the concealment of two acts of sabotage, the hunt for the bomber. The *affaire Winterborne* had become distasteful, demeaning. *Le diable* was always in the world, at one's elbow . . . The devils with which he was forced to consort because of this operation were not those he would have chosen.

The road dropped once more towards the river as it slid between limestone outcrops like a silver snake slipping into a crevice between boulders. The village of Domme stared down at the car from its crag. *Pour la France* did not seem an adequate or satisfying description of what Roussillon was being called upon to perform. It was a bandage around his eyes that was becoming threadbare. The trees lining the road became mesmerising, flickering dappled light on the windscreen.

'How did he get here?' Fraser asked incuriously.

'A light aircraft was seen earlier in the area. He may have landed it somewhere close to the farmhouse,' Roussillon replied, adding with a certain, relished malice: 'You have no idea how he left England this morning?'

'If it was his plane they saw flying around, get your people to look for it. It'll need putting out of action. How much bloody further is it, anyway?'

'Twenty minutes.'

'Let's hope he's still there when we arrive.'

'He can't leave again without being seen — and stopped.'

'Good.'

'I think this Gant is not M'sieur Winterborne's big headache, *mon ami*. I think he has to decide how he can dispose of an English MP if he is to feel secure. Don't you agree?'

The shutter was loose and he angrily dragged it open. He squinted into gloom, his breathing hard and dry, the blood still quick in his ears. Strickland made *bombs* . . . He fumbled at his waistband, locating the Smith & Wesson revolver Aubrey had removed from a small wall safe and handed to him as he might have presented a dead rat to a hotel manager. He could make out the lifeless outlines of furniture. He moved further along the wall, turning the corner to another shuttered window. The shutter resisted his efforts, but its neighbour did not. There were flecks of green paint and dust on his fingers. He looked into the same big room, this time towards the door.

He adjusted the field glasses, focused them against the glass of the window and studied the door frame. Eventually, as his eyes became accustomed to the dim light, he discovered the snailtrail of wire and the small box that had to be the trigger mechanism. Open the door, trigger the device — wherever it was hidden, maybe up on one of the exposed beams? — and by the time it took a man to walk carefully to the centre of the big room, his head would have been blown off, his torso ripped to shreds. It would need only an ordinary frag grenade with a substituted time-trigger for a pin . . . Strickland could do that in minutes, with his eyes closed and his hands in mittens.

He studied the window and then broke the small pane nearest the catch. Pushed it open, then eased it up on the sash, holding his breath. Waited —

— exhaled loudly. There could be a dozen devices, a dozen ways to set off one device . . . Gant climbed slowly over the windowsill and stepped into the room. He listened to the undisturbed, unalarming silence, then crossed to the door.

Another six inches open and the wire would have parted from its contact and . . . yes, the tiny box was a transmitter. He looked up, towards the beamed ceiling, low and near his head. Taped to one of the beams was a short tube. Six steps into the room from the door, perhaps a five-second fuse, or even ten to account for any intruder's caution, then the detonation.

He stood for a moment studying the dull metal of the tube, the colourless tape, the grain and knots of the beam to which the device was attached. Strickland might have assumed that no one local, no one innocent, would push open his door — but it didn't matter anyway. The message would have remained the same even if French security or anyone else had read the item in a newspaper. *Don't come after me, stay out of my back yard.*

He looked around the room. The sunlight through the two sets of shutters he had opened revealed an orderliness, a contentment. An old dresser, better than the one in the house in Iowa he had waited years to escape from, was vivid with heavily decorated plates, china cups. There were paintings on the whitewashed walls that bulged pregnantly with the history of the old building. Sofas covered with bold, stylish cloth, a deeply polished dining table.

He moved warily through to the kitchen . . .

. . . found an animal's bowl, empty of food, the crocks washed and slotted into a plastic drainer, little dust. A neatly folded newspaper in the trash can, no wiring on the rear door. No IR boxes, no wires that disappeared beneath rugs. Strickland had left just the one clear message. Where was the animal?

He looked through the window towards the

barn, then returned to the big room, out of which a staircase creaked to the first floor. He climbed the worn treads carefully, pausing at each one.

A narrow corridor, two bedrooms, neat in the gloom of shutters, a bathroom. There was nothing in the bathroom cabinet or the shower cubicle.

He returned downstairs, checked his watch, listened to the continuing silence. Then he began his search, turning out each of the kitchen drawers, opening all the cupboards. A packet of sugar, coffee — the icebox was empty. No calendar, no notepad. He searched the big, gnarled dresser, polished almost to dullness, removing each of the drawers, emptying the cupboards. Strickland evaded him like a wraith, like smoke. Either there had never been anything personal that wasn't on a laptop or it had been methodically cleared from the house before Strickland had left. Check the garbage —

A sideboard yielded nothing. He heard the ticking of an old, thick-waisted, big-hipped clock that stood against one wall. It became louder and louder, mocking him. Time going, time wasted. Clock — ?

He opened the door in its belly and checked the weights. The pendulum flashed dull brass, the lead weights were near the floor. The key, shaped like a pump handle, was inside the door on a string, but there was nothing else. Had Strickland come back here after Oslo?

He opened a small desk using a kitchen knife to break the toylike lock. It was empty. He opened each drawer and replaced it, his frustration a hot anger. He thrust the last drawer back violently, meeting a small resistance. He pushed again, and something crackled, like stiff card being folded by the thrust of the drawer. He yanked it out and bent to look into the shadowy space. Carefully, he withdrew the small obstruction . . . a creased snapshot. He smoothed it on the inlaid leather of the desk.

Strickland stared out at him, a severe, hardly permitted smile on his face, his eyes narrowed against the sun. It was some years old, by his appearance. He was the age he had been when the Company still employed him. He was standing with one foot raised on a fence — no, it was the railing of some kind of jetty. There were mountains, still snow-tipped, in the distance, and the water of a river or lake rather than the ocean blearily behind the figure.

It was the only tangible indication that Strickland had ever been in the house. Gant put the snapshot in the pocket of his windcheater. The clock ticked, the only other sign of recent habitation.

He looked around the room again. He had been there for almost a half-hour. He listened to the silence that stretched away into the distance, interrupted only by the noises of birds, the occasional lowing of cows. There was nothing else downstairs, except maybe a garbage can in the yard. He'd better check upstairs first.

Fifteen minutes later, he knew that the snapshot was the only thing Strickland had overlooked, except some hair in the drainhole of the shower. He'd either had little there that was personal, or he'd been as thorough in removing all trace of himself as he was when bomb-making. Again, the sensation that the man was lost to him assailed Gant, maddening him as hornets would have done. He crashed a fist against the old plaster of the bedroom wall, hearing its thick hollowness, sensing the blow's force die away in the heavy stones of the house. He'd returned to this room, the larger of the two with the better view over the countryside, after checking the cramped rooms in the roof-space. Dust, dead insects, the rustle of swallows building or feeding young. Nothing else.

He leaned back against the wall, his face raised to the beamed ceiling. The room smelt of old plaster and abandonment. The bed was neatly made, with the mocking suggestion that Strickland planned to return. He opened the window. Gradually, the scent of grass and flowers and the afternoon heat wafted towards him. Gant's breathing calmed. It was impossible now. Strickland was gone, *period* . . .

Eventually, his hands pushed him away from the wall and his line of sight fell across the window. The land dropped away from the house towards the Dordogne valley where limestone outcrops were raised like a ragged dyke against the afternoon sky. The specks of cattle, the orderliness of walnut groves, golden houses . . .

For a moment, the dark clothing made Gant believe he was seeing a scarecrow. A figure was walking towards the farmhouse, moving with a caution and slowness that was not entirely caused by the slope of the land. He crouched beside the window. The figure came on, unaware of him, almost bent double at moments, frequently pausing. Then one arm was waved and Gant saw a second figure rise above some sudden contour of the land. As he watched, the two figures began scurrying the last hundred yards or so towards the house. White faces, hands . . . He made out the shapes of weapons.

Gant hurried towards the door, across the corridor into the second bedroom. Pressing against the wall, he peered round the window frame. Another figure was on one knee, weapon trained, two hundred yards away.

Three — at least. They knew he was there. The house had been under surveillance and he'd failed to spot it. He'd walked right into the trap.

PART THREE

Familiar Midnight

Rich rich the Emperor's desmesnes
And all the palaces, how resplendent
The imperial road emerging from the wood
The palace roofs all brandishing bright flags.

But our prime longing lay in the blue hills
And to keep the company of the white clouds . . .

Wang Wei, *Poem of the Melon Garden*

CHAPTER ELEVEN

Innocence and Experience

Aubrey, Laxton and Pyott sat with their sherries near the great chimneypiece of coloured marbles in the Library of the Club. Three men of years, distinction and some renown who might have been taken by an observer to be comfortably at one with their surroundings. Intrinsic to the pageant of power, privilege and patronage in the high-ceilinged room; suitable additions to the lines of grand portraits or the murals of victories in foreign wars.

Yet to Aubrey's sharp, rather sour inner eye, they were simply three old men, two of whom were rendered ineffectual by lack of office and the third a political trimmer who had gone to the bad, dirtied his hands in a massive fraud.

A spy and a soldier pretending to the moral heights while their companion complacently walked the valley of the shadow of avarice . . . amusing, in another context. They were, perhaps, a frieze for the times.

'Your health, John,' Aubrey proposed. Laxton smiled sleekly in response, with a glance at his watch suggestive of the preciousness of his own time.

Pyott sipped his sherry, frowning at the gesture.

'Kenneth,' Laxton purred, looking around him, measuring the living against the portraits of the dead, against his own prestige. He seemed eager to exchange nods of familiarity, to give and receive deference. 'Very good of you to offer me lunch — a light one, though, I think, in the circumstances.' The smile appeared indelible, recently painted. As a politician, he had often seemed harassed on television or in the House. As a Commissioner, he was Olympian.

A present member of the Cabinet passed with a friendly nod. Laxton responded as eagerly as he might have done to a callgirl.

'The trough is likely to be laden this evening, then, is it?' Pyott asked gruffly, as if the murals had suddenly reminded him of the sole relationship it was possible to have with Europe. Wellington on horseback, his army behind him, clashing with the French at Salamanca.

Laxton remained unperturbed.

'I heard your girl's not above accepting the Commission's hospitality, Giles,' he murmured. Pyott's momentary scowl was as sharp as if Laxton's mention of Marian contained an open threat. 'Doubtless we shall all be treated to another seminar on the iniquities of Brussels, over the canapés.'

'A hit, Giles,' Aubrey soothed, smiling with a dazzling innocence. 'I suggest the sole, John, if you wish to preserve your appetite — and I think a Corton-Charlemagne to start. You can continue with the bottle while Giles, who so evidently feeds exclusively on red meat, will probably join me in sharing the claret.' He leaned back in the deep, high-backed leather armchair, innocence becoming a look of limited intelligence and great complacency on his cherubic features.

Laxton sighed in anticipation.

'Do you know, Giles,' Aubrey announced, 'I found our old companion-in-harness, dear Gilbert, in rather liverish mood at the board meeting this morning.'

'Liverish? That young wife of his hasn't upped and left, has she?' Laxton's attention seemed satisfactorily drawn, as if Aubrey were opening a small leather moneybag which contained that most priceless of the metals of government, gossip. In this instance concerning a former Permanent Secretary at the Department of Trade and Industry.

'I think not. I merely enquired as to whether there had ever been any interest at the DTI, during his tenure, in Marian's suggestions of misplaced funds and dubious payments over this' — Laxton's features allowed a purplish suspicion to spread like a stain over his self-satisfaction — 'um, Millennium Regeneration Project, in the Midlands.' The sherry at his lips seemed to tickle the back of Laxton's throat. Pyott glanced warningly at Aubrey, who persisted: 'I just wanted to be clear whether there had been any form of internal enquiry into the rumours that were current in the House and the press —' His eyes sharpened their glance the moment Laxton interrupted him.

'Surely that was just *Private Eye*-type nonsense, designed to embarrass?' he insisted, adding as he glanced at Pyott: '*Just* the sort of thing to get your daughter aerated!' His chuckle was thick with confidence.

'*Exactly* what Gilbert said, in much the same tone of voice — dismissive,' Aubrey demurred. 'There you have it, you see. Anyone who so much as raises the subject is laughed at as a fool.' He shook his head, as if reproving Pyott. The gesture deflected Laxton's suspicion. 'But surely the net was spread a little wider than *Private Eye*, John?'

A steward approached. Aubrey glanced at the lunch menu and the wine list on his lap, then closed the heavily leatherbound volumes with a snap. Laxton stumbled his order to Aubrey.

'. . . and for General Pyott and myself, the smoked salmon to start, followed by the Beef Wellington. A Corton-Charlemagne and the '83 Château Palmer. Thank you, George.' Aubrey rubbed his hands in anticipation. 'Splendid. Now where were we — ? Ah, yes. John's stout defence, echoing that of Gilbert, of the probity of the funding for the Millennium Regeneration Project —'

'What is your interest in this, Kenneth?' Laxton enquired, his eyes hooded, his sherry glass on the low table between them. 'Mere curiosity?'

Aubrey shrugged expansively, smiling at a passing former Permanent Secretary at the Foreign Office, a man affable by nature, seized with enmity in all his dealings with Aubrey and the intelligence services, until their mutual retirement. Apparently, a moral distaste for espionage and subterfuge — when not the private fiefdom of the diplomatic service — had inspired his antagonism.

'Probably. You know how it is, the smell of the battle afar off, the old warhorse thing.'

'You're wasting your time, Kenneth, you really are!' Laxton assured.

'As Gilbert affirmed.'

'Seriously, Kenneth — I *am* the Commissioner for Urban Development, after all. I would *know!*'

'Did you?' Pyott asked abruptly, exact in his timing. Laxton was disconcerted.

'Did I *what?*'

'Know.'

'There was nothing *to* know.'

'When questions were asked? You did enquire?'

Laxton's features were blustery with suspicion.

'The DTI felt that the press rumours ought to be confronted, and confounded. The then President of the Board of Trade —'

'Whose office is reputedly the largest in Whitehall!' Pyott barked.

'— contacted me. I was able to assure him that he could, with the utmost confidence, refute the allegations of —'

'Fraud? Misappropriation of funds?' Aubrey interjected. 'You're certain? There are all sorts of rumours, you know, John. We'd just like to be certain.'

'You? Why should *you* require reassurance?' There was a cunning in Laxton's expression. His wave in response to the mouthed greeting of a former Cabinet colleague was perfunctory, distracted. Contempt for their superannuation mingled with a desire to probe the depth of their suspicion. 'Tell me that, Kenneth. Whatever can it be to do with you?'

Aubrey's past confronted Laxton, giving birth to the suspicion that he might be on some kind of temporary assignment. His questions might be being asked on behalf of . . . ? It had been the tactic which had suggested itself to Aubrey, and towards which he had guided Giles. Laxton could not know, with any degree of certainty, *who* in reality was the originator of the questions put to him by a former Chairman of the Joint Intelligence Committee — did old spies, after all, ever really *retire?* Laxton's confusion amused.

'I'm not at liberty to divulge,' whispered Aubrey, leaning forward in his chair. 'You know how these things work.'

'*What* things, precisely?'

'Word to the wise . . . could you just check something for us, that kind of thing,' Aubrey murmured. Indeed, the Club was exactly suited to the conversation. The chimneypiece dwarfed even tall men, suggesting conspiratorial groupings, activities. 'Nothing to worry about, John. Just an assurance sought.'

'Assurance of what?'

'That there is nothing to come out — no detonations to be anticipated.' Laxton evidently regarded Aubrey as a potential ally, Giles as an intruder. 'It's why Giles is here, principally,' Aubrey explained. 'We want to be able to assure Marian — quieten her. Soothe.' Again, he leaned forward. 'There are some rather alarming instances of work curtailed, of late payments or no payments at all . . . and your department at the Commission, we know, provided the funding, passed on the grants . . . mm?'

'There's nothing in all this, Kenneth!' Laxton protested, his forehead heated and pink. 'The money has been disbursed by Brussels — by my authority, I suppose — and the project is —'

'— *not* on track!' Pyott snapped. 'No, it's no good soothing *me,* Kenneth. My girl's not the only one to have heard rumours. You may think you can cover up —'

Aubrey raised his hand in warning.

'Giles, *please!*' he demanded with mock exasperation, 'I'm sorry, John. You were saying — ?'

'The project's own complexities account for any delays there may have been, Kenneth. David has assured me —' He appeared to have startled himself. 'You'll see. Go and look for yourself, why not?' His confidence returned like blood-flow released from a tourniquet.

Aubrey felt disappointment like a stone in his chest. After a moment's insight, Laxton was sufficiently confident to become dismissive. He really did have nothing to fear. The diverted river of funding had been restored to its proper course towards the Millennium Regeneration Project.

'Was there a *proper* DTI investigation?'

'So far as I am aware, there was. As there was at the Commission.'

Giles, still in character, harrumphed loudly. Aubrey's smile was bland, retentive. Laxton, their best, weakest target, could not be shaken. The recent past held no ghosts that would come back to haunt him. He felt safe.

It depended, then, on Gant and Marian.

The line of perspiration along his forehead was like an old branding mark, claiming ownership. His palms were clammy against the old, white-washed plaster as he pressed back against the wall of the smaller bedroom. A man kneeling, rifle raised, drawing a bead on the house, the slight movements of the barrel caused by his telescopic sight's surveillance of each of the house's windows.

With a great effort he pushed himself away from the wall and across the polished floorboards. A bright rug was disturbed by his clumsy steps. He crossed the narrow landing and crouched his way to the window of the main bedroom. Slowly, he raised his head at the edge of the window. His heart was pounding, like panicked footsteps hurrying away from there.

The two men were no more than forty yards from the house and only a few yards apart. Gant smelt the must, age, wood of the house. The afternoon was heady in the empty, closed farmhouse. Both men were dressed in black, accustomed to this kind of encounter. Gant's hand scrabbled for the loops of the rucksack and dragged it across the floor to his side. The two men, seeming to have communicated some silent decision to each other, came on quickly towards the shadow thrown by the house.

He heard the first of them collide gently with the wall beneath the bedroom window, then a further, softer detonation of flesh and clothing against the house. They would know about the booby-trap, they'd come in via the window he had prised open. He wiped angrily at his forehead. He touched at the revolver Aubrey had supplied. Sweat under his arms, hands clammy. The stigmata of the old game, he realised, his lips parting across his teeth in a feral, threatening expression. Three, four — how many? He withdrew the revolver and checked the chamber, listening beyond the glass to the noises of birds, the rustle of a slight breeze, the sound of footsteps — maybe — along the wall of the farmhouse. He replaced the Smith & Wesson in his waistband, this time nestling it against his stomach. Its stubby barrel and no-snag front sight were unfamiliar only for a moment. Wood creaked in the afternoon silence.

There was no one between himself and the barn. If he dropped from the window and ran, he would be exposed for no more than thirty yards, a matter of a few seconds . . . while he ran headlong, enlarging all the while in a telescopic sight, falling away as if kicked by a horse when the first bullet struck. There was no one between him and the barn because they wanted him to go that way, if he had seen them at all.

Gant, still crouching, edged his way across the polished floor, sensing rather than hearing the tiny scuffs and irritations of his rubber-soled shoes against the wood. Then he straightened on the landing and tiptoed towards the head of the stairs, aware of the dry, crumbling texture of the plaster as his left hand stretched out to steady his unnaturally slow movements. The rucksack was slung across his shoulders. On a table at the head of the stairs was an old oil lamp. Gant could smell the fuel, the burnt wick. It rested on a clean, neat cloth of lacework, the kind his mother might have made. Strickland's mother, too . . .

. . . shadow across the room, short and stubby with the early-afternoon sun, pausing after having climbed through the window. He listened and could hear the unseen man breathing, and perhaps another's breaths beyond that. One still outside the window. He waited, reluctant to draw the gun, to fire it.

The shadow moved, precisely, carefully. It possessed a bunched hand from which a tiny, stick-like accompanying shadow protruded. They would even *expect* this one to get blown away, but it would serve to locate him exactly, narrow the field of fire . . . He was sweating profusely. The revolver remained in his waistband, his hand instead touching against the polished brass of the old oil lamp, a pattern of leaves etched on its clouded glass bowl.

Three or four more steps and the shadow would be at the foot of the stairs, they would be visible to one another . . . His grandmother had worked by the light of lamps like this one, his mother had kept one as a memento . . . He had picked it up as the memory drifted through his awareness, had replaced it like a reluctant purchaser, had opened the box of matches that lay beside it on the lace, had watched the shadow take one step, then another . . . Had held his breath as he eased off the clouded glass and crooked it against his stomach with a bent arm, had turned up the wick, had — struck the match, a loud, slowed-down sound, watched the wick flare up, before —

— foot of the stairs, the first man, his hand on the banister. Gant threw the flaring oil lamp towards the stocky, square-faced man, who ducked aside. The lamp broke, spilt its oil. The flame ran after it hungrily.

Even as the fire began behind him and the curtains burned as quickly as rags, his gun was aimed at Gant. He drew the Smith & Wesson and fired twice, ducking back against the plaster that splintered from his attacker's shots, stippling his cheek with fragments like small stones. The man lay sprawled back across a flaming rug, his clothes already smouldering. The crackle of an RT stronger than the crackling of wood catching fire. The second man was still outside the window. Gant launched himself down the short flight of stairs, not pausing to glance at the window, turning instead towards the kitchen, running —

— colliding. His breath deserted him, his body was shocked into vulnerability as he lurched back against the heavy table, seeing the man he had collided with arched against the sink, as if they were two fighters resting. Through the window, a fuzzy image of men running. He thought he recognised the figure and stride of one of the team from Oslo. The man against the sink was coughing air back into his lungs. Gant struck him across the temple with the stubby barrel of the revolver, the foresight cutting the skin open. Even as the man fell aside, Gant was opening the door and running towards the barn.

His ears pounded. It was difficult to snatch air into his lungs, the knowledge that he was running towards a marksman compressing his chest. Someone shouted as the first shot whined away near his shoulder. A window shattered behind him. He plunged through an open gate in a low stone wall into the dappled shadows of trees. A small orchard. Old nuts, empty shells, cracked beneath his feet. A tree was white-scarred by other shots as he surged through the orchard bent almost double. Sunlight, shadow, sunlight —

The land dropped sharp as a grassy cliff away from the orchard towards a grove of dark trees, towards fields dotted with animals and fringed with lines of holm-oak. Beyond the nearest field, gleaming through the trees, the glint of water. He saw the immediate landscape like an aerial map, from the vantage of the Cessna.

He glanced back. Flame licked from a window, pale in the afternoon light. Puffs of smoke. Three men running after him into the orchard, the one he thought he had recognised from the hangar in Oslo waving his arms, directing the others into flanking movements.

He skittered down the steep slope, the long, lush meadow grass brushing against his knees. He stumbled, falling. Two shots whined over his head, the flat cracks of the rifle startling a grazing cow, which lumbered away from him. He scrabbled to his knees, looking back. They were already coming quickly down the slope. The trees and the water were still a hundred yards or more away.

Gant ran, weaving like some manic footballer evading invisible tackles. There were two more

shots. He swerved left, right, right again, left —
— crashed into a thin branch, then through tough, restraining bushes. Lost balance, stumbled forward, then rolled. Water drenched him. The banks of the stream were high and close, the water no more than a couple of feet deep. He was holding the revolver above his head as if frozen in a desperate waving action. Trees leaned heavily over the slow water. For moments only, he was hidden from them.

David Winterborne's office looked down on Poultry's narrow street, and across towards the Bank of England and the Mansion House. He could also see the Royal Exchange and St Mary Woolnoth, the oblong Hawksmoor tower which struggled to symbolise faith, surrounded as it was by the highrises of banks. David had selected the location for his corporate headquarters years before, when the view from the windows had seemed more necessary; an attempt to suggest that Winterborne Holdings truly belonged in the City.

He looked now at the church, imagining its ornate, baroque interior, its columns and *baldachino* reredos. It was Marian who had first taken him inside, made him look properly, lectured him. Marian, *naturally* . . .

Irritated by the recollection, or even the pigeons on the windowsill, Winterborne turned to face his desk. The screen of his PC held the e-mail letter he had drafted to Strickland.

It could be sent anonymously, without trace. It contained a proposal for a commission. A target for one of Strickland's bombs. The letter purported to come from a third-party fixer on behalf of some shadowy, extremist Middle East group. The target was not specific, but Strickland would be able to deduce that it was Arafat . . . *The traitor to the dispossessed people and to God, the puppet of the Zionists* . . . Winterborne had enjoyed creating that description. Hamas and Hizbollah, or Islamic Jihad, were never subtle in their condemnations.

The proposed fee was half a million US dollars. Strickland would be tempted not by the money, but by the fact that he had once, years before, *failed* to kill Arafat. He had probably been employed by the Israelis on that occasion. The Chairman of the PLO had left the bathroom in which the device had been placed ten seconds before it was remotely detonated. Strickland's failure had humiliated him. He would be unable to resist another chance. His pride in his infallibility was the glue that held him together.

Strickland would respond to the e-mail via his own PC. He would have no idea to whom his reply was being addressed. Even if he had a suspicion that it was a trick to draw him out into the open, he would still come. The prize was too tempting to resist, Winterborne was certain of that. Strickland would offer a meeting on neutral ground. However careful he proved to be, he would come — and then he would be eliminated.

Winterborne would transmit the enticement in another moment or two. Meanwhile, there was the Bach on the CD player. The B minor Prelude and Fugue filled the office. The music seemed appropriate to Hawksmoor's church, to the elegant cornicing and ceiling rose of the room and the heavy bookshelves, and to his mood. Reflective intimacy in the prelude, the profound yet strict order of the fugue which followed. He listened for a few moments, remembering that it had been Marian who had given him his appreciation of music. Effortlessly clever Marian . . . He shook his head and scrabbled the remote control from his desk, switching off the music almost savagely.

He studied his desk, supporting his weight on his knuckles. His application for US citizenship moved smoothly, oiled by lobbyists and tame Congressmen . . . The leasing deals for Skyliner lay like raked leaves . . . Other businesses prospered. His staff, in other offices, busied themselves with sublime confidence, skating on newly thickened ice that bore no resemblance to the thin, dangerous crust on which he had been moving with so much caution only weeks ago.

Now, he was poised. Once the citizenship was settled, he could move on the microprocessor firms, the construction and other companies he needed to weld together to form the hull of what would become Winterborne Holdings in the US. He would be raiding, soon. The US banks were *now* eager to lend and CEOs of companies were keen to sell out to him, for the appropriate golden balm.

It still unnerved, like a recollected nightmare, the thought that it might all have fallen into ruin because Aero UK could not sell Skyliner and Euro-funds had had to be diverted to prop the company up. The discovery of the fraud would have ended — everything.

What was necessary had been done. It was over.

He thought of Marian again and of a withering description she had offered of him after an early piece of stock manipulation had outraged her. *You're a mixture of Buddhist fatalism and European imperialism, David, a contradiction. Because of the one you believe it doesn't matter what actions you take, and because of the other your actions are those of a bandit . . . Why?*

He had answered her mockingly, quoting from one of the Chinese poems she had introduced him to when she was still a teenager. Li-Tai-Po, the drunk, the revelling hedonist . . . *Dark is life, so is death.* She had hated that — because it had been true. Nothing really *mattered.* Contempt for life *made you a Buddhist or a bandit, OK, Marian?*

That, perhaps, had been the day when they had finally seen the gulf between them, each on opposite sides of a deep canyon.

He smiled, re-reading the e-mail, then turned back to the window. A pigeon continued to strut aimlessly along the windowsill above the traffic, occasionally thrusting out its wings as if uncertain of its ability to fly or woo. He returned to his desk and abruptly pressed the transmit key, sending the e-mail to Strickland's PC, wherever it was on the planet. Days, perhaps a week, and Strickland would come out, blinking like a mole in the sunlight — to be beaten on the head with a spade.

The still-green buds of rhododendrons were like spearpoints at the edge of his vision as he sat hunched in the concealment of the thick bushes that leaned out over the stream. He had moved upstream for perhaps half a mile. The bushes were dusty and old. Insects buzzed outside, suggesting that the rhododendrons were impenetrable, that he was safe. Sunlight dazzled beyond the outermost bushes, through the gold, red and pink of opened flowers.

He studied the map, checking the location of the Cessna. They would have found it, he insisted to himself. There'd be someone waiting for him . . . or, just to make certain, they would have emptied the fuel tank or damaged the controls. His finger traced the stream towards the nearest village. Maybe there — ?

He recollected the tiny village from the air as the Cessna banked over it, a curl of water around it, the old *lauze*-roofed houses crouching beneath the abbey church, fortified and threateningly large in its surroundings. The slopes of the land, the narrow valley emptying into the Vezere, parked cars, hot sunlight and dark shadows in the cramped streets. Should he make for the village? Beyond the rhododendrons was a small copse of trees, then open fields dropping away towards the village. The Cessna sat in a field he would be able to see from the edge of the copse.

The dust from the bushes, the heat of the afternoon, irritated his throat. One man had passed noisily along the bank of the stream above him ten minutes before. The crackle of his RT and unheard instructions interrupting birdsong. Gant was becoming stiff in his hunched position, he needed to move. He listened beyond the hum of insects and the birds to the heavy afternoon silence. The distant noise of a cow, of a vehicle on some hidden road.

He turned on his stomach and began wriggling through the undergrowth, catching at his breath with each movement as a cough threatened. He emerged into the copse of holm-oak and poplar and rose to his knees, listening again as his heartbeat died back to quiet. Then, standing, he slung the rucksack across his shoulders and began moving through the shadows, avoiding the splashes of sunlight as if they were irradiated.

Crackle of an RT, an answering, harsh whisper. Off to his left, perhaps fifteen yards. He moved behind the bole of a tree. There was more sunlight, the ground was beginning to drop away. He moved his feet gently, gliding from the cover of one tree to another.

He raised the fieldglasses to his eyes. The lenses misted, then cleared. He scanned the fields to the west of the village, where the Cessna's livery was suddenly bright and incongruous amid grass, near the shade of trees. He could see no one, not even the farmer to whom he had explained his engine fault, his need to seek parts, his return in no more than three hours . . . Around the Cessna, like an exaggeration of the afternoon heat, a haze he at once realised was evaporating fuel. They'd drained the tank rather than more obviously damaging the airplane. To the left of the Cessna, no more than a hundred yards away from it, a momentary gleam of sunlight on metal.

Disappointment wrenched at his stomach. He leaned back against the rough bark of the tree, staring up at the canopy of leaves, letting his breath exhale in an expression of defeat. Sweat ran into his eyes . . .

Minutes — whole minutes — had been wasted. He felt drained, raising the glasses once more with weak arms. The Cessna, but only for an instant, then cows and sheep sweeping through the lenses, trees, and lines of willow and poplar that marked streams, ditches. To Gant the landscape became more covert, military; a map of trenchworks from a long-forgotten war, each hedge or screen of willow and poplar marking water or a ditch where he could move unobserved. He traced the lines carefully, fixing each stretch of cover, each exposed area.

A hundred yards to the first parade of poplars . . . another seventy yards before he had to break cover again . . . fifty yards to a belt of oak, then another long field, then more trees that had advanced like a besieging force up to the fortified walls of the abbey church. Two cars and a pickup moved like bright, carapaced insects along the winding, shadowy street of the village, sunlight flashed from windscreens on a minor road. He listened behind him. Someone was blundering with slow, elephantine caution away from him.

He tensed, then began hurtling down the slope towards the first line of poplars, which waited like a still troop of men for his assault. He heard shouting, and his blood racing. The grass was noisy with his passage, a cow veered away from him. He ran brokenly at first, then in a straight line, despite the first shots away to his left. Sheep that had discovered the shade of the poplars moved away in truculent panic as he blundered into shadow, and reached the rivulet the trees had marked. He jolted himself to a halt against the bank. The ditch was no more than four or five feet deep, the water just inches. He splashed along its slippery, stony bed, his breath roaring. He remained crouched as he scuttled rather than ran, hearing shouts of pursuit.

He collided with something, was struck. Then something grabbed him, even as it shouted for support. He smelt food on the man's breath, arms pushed him off-balance, his feet slipped, hands closed on his throat. A face, as distorted as if it were garbed in a stocking mask, pressed against his eyes. Gant struggled, shaking his head to rid his throat of the man's grip. His vehement denial seemed impossible to transmit to the rest of his body. The man pressed him back against the bank, his hands still tightening around Gant's throat. He tried to snatch at air, his mouth twisted wide, but he was unable to swallow. Breathing became almost impossible . . .

. . . Black lights flickered before his eyes, blocking out the sunlight streaming through the tracery of poplar branches. The man's stubbled, rounded face was contorted with effort. His hands were tight on Gant's throat, whose back was arched against the bank, his hands scrabbling with dirt and grass and roots as if he were frantic to escape underground. The RT was somewhere close, dropped into the water or in a pocket, and it was urgent with exhortations to hold him and with promises of immediate help.

He couldn't reach the revolver, didn't know

where it was, dropped or still thrust into his belt . . . His hands still clawed the dirt of the bank, panicking at the encroaching loss of consciousness, his feet shuffling in the water. Scrabbling . . . as if he was being pulled into a narrow space . . . black lights, flecks big as fragments . . . scrabbling . . . the man's face filled with effortful blood and triumph . . . His arms came up together, threading through the man's arms then flinging them wide, breaking the grip around his throat —

— breath . . . coughing — breath . . . He brought his arms together again as the man lunged back at him, striking with one forearm, then with the flat of his hand to the throat in what seemed a palsied effort. Coughing, he punched twice at the midriff, once to the head, then struck again with his flattened hand, then with a thrust of his knee, slipping on underwater stones. He hit the man again and again, beating him to his knees then into a prone lump, face down in the inches of clear water . . . No coughing. He staggered, leaning back against the bank . . . A shadow amid the dappling of the poplars, twenty yards along the ditch. He struggled for the revolver, still in his waistband, drawing it out exaggeratedly, like a drunk. The shadow glanced aside behind a narrow tree bole.

Gant struggled to run, one hand massaging his throat, the other holding the gun as if he wished only to drop it. He turned wildly and fired behind him, the weight of the rucksack across his shoulders unbalancing him. Then he staggered on before launching himself at the low bank of the ditch and scrambling out. Oaks next . . . oaks. Then another field, then trees . . . Shots. He dropped.

On one knee he watched a man in a check shirt and denims hurry from beneath the poplars into the afternoon sunlight. He fired twice, holding the revolver stiff-armed, his left hand clasping his right wrist. The target was clipped backwards, to lie prone, as quickly and non-humanly as on a practice range. Gant got to his feet and ran brokenly down the field towards the oaks, blundering into their shadow, hurrying through patches of sunlight and shade, out into the long, sloping field above which a skylark poured a song that rippled outwards to encompass the whole field. The song seemed to fill his ears.

More trees . . . He dragged himself to a halt, gripping the trunk of an oak, staring wildly back up the field towards the other clump of trees. There was a figure kneeling beside an invisible something, and another man hovering at the edge of the oaks, uncertain now that he was exposed. He had, perhaps, two or three minutes. The noise of traffic, the hoot of a horn and the acceleration of an engine, urged him to move.

The ground rose in a hump, as if there was a mass grave beneath, then dropped towards the abbey church's squat, frowning tower. He realised he was walking over buried fortifications. He emerged from the trees at the end of the village street. Hot, shadowy normality. The yellow limestone wall of the church flung its afternoon shadow over him. Two men, unsurprised by his sudden appearance, were talking beside a Citroën pickup. One of them wore a beret, the other a black soutane — parishioner and priest. There was a smell of sun-warmed vegetables from the back of the truck. Its engine remained idling; the only noise of which he was aware. He glanced behind him. There was still no sign of his pursuers, the killing had slowed them, as if they were the next terrified cattle to enter an abattoir. He controlled his stride, walking with the casual dislocation and curiosity of a tourist. The priest and the pickup's driver remained engaged in their own rapid conversation, aware of him, anticipating that they would have to struggle with English or German or some other language in order to set him on his course.

He half-raised his hand in polite enquiry, apologising for interrupting them. The young priest seemed less reluctant to acknowledge his existence . . . his face altering its expression as surprise seeped into it. Gant had climbed into the cab of the pickup. The gears clashed, harsh as the owner's cry of protest. He let off the brake and accelerated the Citroën, skidding as he oversteered, then righting the truck, its engine small-sounding as a sewing machine, the protests of its owner fading behind him, like his diminishing figure in the rearview mirror. The priest stood with his hands on black hips, bemused. Then there was a third figure beside the two, then a fourth —

He wiped sweat from his forehead with the sleeve of his windcheater. His hands were clammy on the steering wheel. Relief made him weak. He struggled the map from his breast pocket. He needed side roads, they knew what vehicle to look for —

Already, champagne flutes together with the odd crumpled napkin or bone-china plate carelessly decorated the tops of the illuminated glass cases which displayed engravings. A little of modernity in the first-floor room of the Musée des Beaux-Arts which austerely celebrated Bruegel.

Marian was standing in admiration before the painting known as *Landscape with the Fall of Icarus.* White, thrashing legs sticking out of the green water as a peasant ploughed unconcernedly at a stubborn headland's soil, a shepherd rested on his crook, and a third man fished, ignoring the tragedy. A ship sailed unaware towards a white port. She felt as if she had foolishly snatched a moment in which to reassert her bluestocking credentials amid a noisy, headlong party; and her vanity was making her parade her intellect and taste.

There was, of course, a fourth man in the picture, almost hidden by bushes, at the end of the ploughed land. His head, white-haired and balding, stuck out from the undergrowth; he was dead, unexplainedly so. No one noticed him, either. She shivered, as if she had moved apart simply in order to be afraid. She rubbed her arms beneath the stuff of the scarlet jacket. That and her blouse ought to have been sufficiently warm — the temperature at which one viewed priceless paintings in museums was stifling. Nevertheless, she felt very cold. As she had tried to nap in the suite at the Amigo, take her shower, make-up carefully in the bedroom mirror, their faces had continued to appear to her like a troop of ghosts in a dream.

She, the soldier's daughter, could neither discipline nor defeat her fears. So, she continued to stare at the painting, the noise of the cocktail reception behind her solid as a wall, while the images of David, Campbell, the lout Fraser, Rogier, Laxton, others, continued their effort to take form within the canvas. Her attention could be distracted only by the waving, drowning legs and the sticking-out head of the dead man.

Later, they would dine at the outrageously expensive La Maison du Cygne in the Grand' Place, but this preliminary was cultural Brussels — almost as if designed solely to seduce her. Her colleagues, for the most part, glanced at the paintings as if they were passing through a room in a museum of anthropology amid the flotsam and potsherds of a lost civilization. To her, the room whispered *Come and join us, we're civilised, too . . .* but in the voice of the Commission.

The feeble joke palled. The dead man was still there in the painting, Icarus had still fallen into the sea for flying too high, not knowing his place and *showing good sense*. Just like her. Campbell and Rogier, the Commissioner who had been Michael Lloyd's superior, seemed aware of her unsettled fears, and too aware of their complicity to be quite natural in their manner. It was as if they were waiting for David to arrive to pull their puppets' strings. Icarus the boastful, his *hybris* punished in one small corner of the canvas, was surrounded by indifference . . . *Her* demise would be just like his.

She twitched visibly at the sound of a drawling voice beside her.

'I take it I *was* reading your habitual Leveller preoccupations again in last week's *Economist*, Marian? Fittingly anonymous, of course.' Peter Cope, nudging at junior ministerial office — head-butting at the door, some preferred to observe. Small, neat, expensively suited and coiffured; blameless, lifeless eyes. Someone had said of him that they had *never known utter lack of ideas and beliefs could be engaging until they met Peter Cope.*

'Yes, Peter, you were,' she drawled in riposte. '*Mea culpa*, I'm afraid — again.' Even Peter Cope had his uses. She rallied because of the banter. The article was one she had contributed to a continuing debate on the future of the British constitution, hers under the title *Who is Represented?* Even Peter Cope had heard of the seventeenth-century Levellers.

'You're becoming in need of a new tune, Marian,' Cope ridiculed. 'No one's going to bring back the Civil War just to please you.'

She smiled faintly, mockingly. 'And my father would certainly have been a King's man — I know. But the party has to do *something*, Peter — even the Barbours and the green wellies are deserting us in droves and at high speed in their off-road vehicles,' she added.

'Drop it, Marian,' he snapped in exasperated dislike, dimly sensing he was punching well above his weight and the effort was wearying. 'God, it's hot in here,' he flung at the room and shuffled away.

Her cold stare had been little more than a further attempt to ward off her fears, Peter its unfortunate recipient. She felt a sudden desire to hurry back into the knots and cabals of the reception. Commission civil servants moved as assiduously as the waiters, topping up bonhomie, confidence, complicity, as quickly and certainly as the champagne flutes were refilled. Rogier still remained conspiratorially close to Campbell, beneath the canvas of *The Fall of the Rebel Angels*, a painting more like Bosch than Bruegel, filled with the energy of tangled limbs, great flying wings and damnation. Butterflies, birds and weird fish represented the metamorphosed damned while God's team flew above them, blowing great trumpets; above Rogier and Campbell too, though they seemed supremely unaware of the fact. Or perhaps they still numbered themselves among the unfallen, righteous angels?

They were, however, curiously diminished by the painting above their heads, and she found herself able to breathe more easily. Rogier, especially, as Campbell was distracted from his side by his tour-guide's duties, seemed deflated, even guilty. She watched Campbell dive into a small scrum of her colleagues and Commission functionaries with the eagerness of a sportsman. Rogier's glass was refilled and he seemed self-consciously aware of his momentary isolation. She hurried towards him.

Her features must have declared her sudden, invigorated determination, for the tall, slightly stooping, elegantly slim Frenchman flinched from her approach as if she was armed.

'M'sieur Commissaire,' she murmured. 'Marian Pyott.' She thrust out her hand. He was reluctant to take it; his eyes revealed his anxious knowledge of her. Nevertheless, he bowed formally.

'Of course, of course — one of our most formidable opponents,' he rallied. 'A pleasure to welcome you to Brussels on behalf of the Commission.' His eyes seemed to seek support from the others in the room.

Marian pounced with: 'We have a mutual acquaintance, M'sieur Rogier — that is, until recently. Michael Lloyd. We spoke of him over the telephone after his death —'

'Yes, of course. So unfortunate — tragic . . .'

She felt her body heated with eagerness. She knew she must force the pace.

'I had a word with someone at the Police Judiciaire —' Marian offered. Would Rogier recognise the lie at once? His eyes narrowed with calculation before adopting a purported concern. 'On the advice of someone in London — in security . . . You see, knowing Michael as I did, I just couldn't believe the overdose theory.'

'The police? I understood that they were satisfied with the cause of death, that it was not suspicious . . . ?' Rogier murmured, stooping close to her face, his eyes darting once more over her shoulder, presumably towards Campbell.

Marian sipped her warm champagne, 'I think I managed to create a little doubt in that quarter.'

'They will re-open the case?'

'I hope so.'

She was fiercely satisfied with his anxiety, the

evidence that he was at a loss. Rogier's features seemed burdened as well as furtive. He probably knew, and had diplomatically filed and forgotten, the cause of Lloyd's death. He remained silent, an actor who had dried on stage.

'Marian — !' It was Campbell, interposing himself like a bodyguard between them, one hand lightly on her shoulder, the other on Rogier's forearm, steadying the man. 'Not cornering the Commissioner, surely?'

Angered at the bluff emptiness of the tone, she snapped: 'We were talking of Michael Lloyd, nothing controversial!' Exhilarated at his evident rebuff, she added wildly: 'It was absolutely nothing to do with my dangerous theories on the subject of Aero UK, Ben — no need to worry!'

She suppressed a shiver of tension. The charged atmosphere between them was like a cone of hot silence. At the edge of the painting, the frogs and fish gaped, tumbling from heaven. Then Campbell's features were lit with pleasure. His hand waved.

'David!' he called like a threat. Rogier's relief was shiny on his high forehead. Marian turned.

Winterborne had entered the room accompanied by Laxton and the President of the Commission, the three of them trailing a comet-tail of minor functionaries and assorted businessmen.

She swallowed carefully. Winterborne's gaze focused on her. Rogier was whispering to Campbell, whose hand was making denying motions. The Commissioner was being assured she was bluffing. She moved away, smiling. Winterborne and the President received champagne as reverently as the Host while acolytes seemed magnetically drawn towards their group from every part of the room. The President at once engaged the Chairman of the Select Committee, his hand cupping an elbow, his ear still half-bent to the aide who had identified the man. Henry, the senior Opposition MP, was openly amused as their chairman actually blushed at whatever compliments his dignity was being paid. He grinned at Marian.

'We meet again,' David murmured.

'You didn't expect me to be here?' she asked.

He raised his glass as if to toast her.

'I *knew* you'd be here, my little bluestocking. The art is too good for you to miss.'

'True.'

Campbell was with them, drawing David instantly aside with little pretence at subtlety, whispering urgently. Deliberately, she wandered away towards the napkin-littered glass cases which contained the engravings on loan to the *musée* from the Bibliotheque Royale. She peered down at *The Festival of Fools*, her neck tickling with the sense that Campbell was reporting her bluff. She shivered as she moved along the row of cases. Small landscapes, then *The Poor Kitchen* and its companion, *The Rich Kitchen.*

David appropriately rejoined her as she pretended to study *The Battle between the Money Banks and the Strongboxes.* It suddenly seemed as dramatic as the painting of the angels in combat.

'Ah — the perfect allegory for your taste, eh, Squirt?' His tone was warm and she hated the memories it at once evoked.

'You know me, Davey,' she responded as innocently as she could. 'And look, a sleeping pedlar being robbed by monkeys — and there, *Luxury*, and here *Justice* and *Prudence* . . . I had no idea this trip would be so educational!'

'Marian,' he sighed, shaking his head. His eyes glanced towards Campbell. 'Always stirring things up, Squirt. 'Twas ever thus . . .' His gaze hardened. He snatched at her arm and drew her to his side, huddling them away from seekers and purveyors of influence alike. Gales of laughter at a poor witticism, a mood of enjoyable sycophancy, and the mutual acknowledgement of elites. 'Marian, *please,*' he whispered. She stopped, turning to him.

'What?' Her innocence was pronounced, provocative. His lips narrowed, his eyes flashed.

'For God's sake,' he warned without disguise. 'Just *stop* whatever it is you think you're doing!'

'What *am* I doing?'

He had pleaded with her like this as a boy, in his better moments. Begged her to desist, to accept, to *agree* . . . before he hurt or excluded her. His hand was gripping her arm painfully, like pincers. She drew away, rubbing her arm.

'Will you stop?' he asked. There was the shadow of a plea in his voice.

After a long moment, she shook her head.

'I can't,' she said softly, hoarsely. *His computer, his computer,* she heard in her head like the chanting of a mantra. 'I can't, Davey — !' she blurted as if in pain, remembering his childhood cruelty.

He nodded stiffly.

'I didn't think you could. I — had to ask.'

Voices were demanding his presence. As he turned from her, she sensed his well-being at once restored, his awareness of his power seep back. They were adults again. Campbell hovered, waiting to direct his master towards the most necessary handshakes and pleasantries. David's shoulders were set, his expression evidently threatening, by the mirror that was Campbell's face.

You fool, you *bloody, bloody fool,* she told herself. She was, indeed, very frightened. However, she gradually calmed herself by concentrating on her mantra . . . *His computer, his computer, his computer* . . . Tonight or tomorrow morning she must gain access to David's laptop. It would be in his suite. She had to get hold of it, there'd be proof abundant there . . .

David, she tried to convince herself, was a superstitious creature, a character of habit and custom. He *had* to be — he *had* to still be using those old passwords. Robbie was long dead and he couldn't possibly know that she knew them too.

However stupid and far-fetched, she had to try.

CHAPTER TWELVE

In the Machine

The morning sun haloed the Gothic turrets and spires, and the baroque roof statuary of the Grand' Place. From the windows of the suite's lounge, David Winterborne saw them as the back of a movie set. There was gold, pinked marble, stone, the flickering of birds. The murmur of traffic was fended off by secondary glazing.

Seven-fifteen. Fraser sat on the sofa, an impatient, barely restrained machine. Winterborne had chosen to sit at the desk, in the leather swivel chair, toying with his fat black pen with his long fingers, his bathrobe closed primly over his knees.

'. . . must have gone Stateside, on an early tourist flight. That's the best Roussillon's been able to do, trace him as far as Schipol. He's going home —'

'After Strickland?' Winterborne asked quickly.

Fraser shrugged. 'Could be.'

The man's features were pinched with anticipation, and something like resentment. For Winterborne, Fraser's presence obscured the vista of the day's anticipated successes. The Skyliner flight, the publicity that would attend it, the assiduousness of EC officials . . . Fraser had come to his suite with dirty moral hands, informing him of Gant's escape, and demanding that he commit himself irrevocably regarding Marian. Strickland had not replied to the e-mail, had not taken the bait. Fraser did not believe he would. He had another way —

'You're positive that an approach to this man McIntyre is the way to proceed?'

Fraser nodded, shifting slightly on the sofa, to greater comfort.

'McIntyre is the man looking for Gant, just as seriously as we are. Gant's gone home —'

'You think.'

'I think — we know. Sir . . .' Winterborne waved him to continue, the permission of a sultan. 'He's a vindictive sod . . . ex-CIA, joined the Bureau in the early nineties. I *know* him, sir. *And* he was Strickland's Case Officer in the field. They did a lot of dirty things for the Company and Washington, *none* of which McIntyre would want seeing the light of day.' It was a rehearsed, carefully offered argument. Persuasively complete. 'I'm certain he would help us, in order to keep Strickland quiet, if he thought he could get his hands on Gant by doing so. And keep his own nose clean . . . If not, *you* can offer him a security vice-presidency. Fat salary, big title, key to the executive bog —' His nose wrinkled in contempt. 'They like that sort of thing, his sort of Yank.'

'So you've reiterated.'

'He'd be likely to know Strickland's boltholes, aliases, the sort of detail *we* don't have.' It was seductive. The shadow of a flitting bird crossed the windows. The e-mail stratagem might not work, this could be more certain. A pigeon settled on the windowsill.

'I see that.' He leaned forward, adding: 'You and Roussillon should have stopped Gant yesterday, Fraser.'

'There have been underestimations all round — sir.'

Winterborne could not keep the faint, momentary flush from his cheeks. He snapped back: 'Stopping a rogue accident investigator who's already wanted by the FBI is, I would have thought, easier than disposing of a high-profile MP!' He instantly regretted his loss of control. 'I still don't see how you avoid the danger of involving the FBI in this.'

Fraser seemed mollified. The whiteness that had appeared at the sides of his nose vanished.

'Offer him the choice, sir. If Gant finds Strickland before McIntyre finds Gant, then maybe all the dirty tricks will pop out of the box. To prevent that, *and* to secure a prosperous future . . . which would you choose, sir — if you weren't already you?' His hands opened in a gesture of conclusion. 'You can get rid of Gant and Strickland at the same time — and have the resources of the FBI to do it for you.' It was the voice of a tempter. Or was it simply that of a machine holding the recorded voice of inevitability?

Winterborne wrapped the bathrobe around his legs as he refolded them. He sensed himself as shuffling indecisively before a subordinate, of having been dragooned into choice.

'McIntyre isn't popular or liked — maybe not even trusted — by the Bureau. He could be shaken out any time. And he's greedy . . .'

'Tell him nothing!' Winterborne felt impelled to insist.

'Of course not, sir.'

'Very well. Take the earliest flight to Washington you can get. Persuade McIntyre —' He stood up. 'I have a breakfast meeting at eight, I need to —'

'Sir — the woman?' It was a demand rather than a question, and Winterborne was reduced to the sensation of himself as a boy about to leave the headmaster's study, half-escaped from punishment, and then called back to face more accusations.

'What?' he snapped. 'What about the woman?'

'You have to decide, sir — you have to give a clear instruction.'

'Now? Why now?' He felt heated, unnerved. He did not turn to face Fraser. The pigeon lifted away from the windowsill as if not wishing to become a co-conspirator. 'Not *now* . . .' he murmured.

'I *watched* her, sir,' Fraser insisted. 'Watched her deal with Jessop and Cobb when they put the frighteners on late last night. Dark street, a man following her . . . She *won't* be frightened off, sir!'

Winterborne whirled round on Fraser, his features compressed with a violent anger. Gant and Strickland — yes. The situation had become unstable to the point of explosion, he must take a risk there . . . but *this?* Fraser was applying the perspective. The man thought Marian's death a simple matter, something expedient and hardly to be debated. *But this is Marian.*

'Strickland, Gant, Marian — anyone *else?*' he attempted.

Fraser grinned. 'It's not much . . . It's not out of control,' he soothed. *Not yet,* his eyes declared. 'But you need to watch Campbell, sir. She'll work on him and he's an invertebrate at the best of times —'

'Ben Campbell *now!* For God's sake, Fraser!'

'I'm not suggesting anything specific, sir. Just tell Roussillon to keep an eye on him. If you get rid of the woman, there'll be no need. He'll have been involved. The Judas-goat. That will shut him up. But you have to instruct Roussillon to eliminate *her.*'

'Not *now!* I do not intend to be late for my meeting, Fraser. Make your arrangements regarding Washington. I'll talk to you before you leave.'

He turned away, his body once more heated, quivery with a sense of being cornered. Marian was, indeed, his enemy — yet how could he consign her to the dark? How could he — ?

As he walked into the bedroom to begin dressing, he heard Fraser telephone the hotel desk to make his flight reservation.

Yes, that certainly would be achieved, the elimination of Strickland and Gant. But, *Marian — ?*

She woke in the old-fashioned hotel bedroom, startled; as if she had expected the comfortable familiarity of other old houses, Uffingham especially, only to find herself betrayed by memory. She felt shaken from thin, fitful sleep. Her dreams had been filled with faces peering down at her which did not quite disappear whenever she roused. Grey daylight struggled through the heavy curtains. Marian sat bolt upright, rubbing her right arm with her left hand . . . just as she had done after the light-footed man, his single breath hot against her cheek, had collided with her on the dark, cobbled pavement outside the hotel.

She had been walking back from the restaurant, replete, her fears and senses dulled with food, wine and bright conversation. He had appeared from a narrow, unlit doorway, clumsy as a drunk, and had lumbered into her. She had exhaled a small scream of surprise. She had been half-attending to the footsteps clicking in a magnified way off the high walls and façades of the Rue de l'Amigo, wondering if someone was following her, when the second man had blundered against her. His weight had been sharp, heavy, before he had staggered away and she stumbled into the hotel entrance.

There had been no more to it than that — footsteps clicking out like the exaggerated ticking of an ominous clock, a momentary collision . . . but she had understood the message as clearly as if it had been delivered by hand to the door of her room.

She squinted at the illuminated bedside clock in the gloom. Seven-twenty. In the night, too, there had been a drunk or purported drunk knocking at her door, demanding entry. She had, eventually, persuaded him hers was the wrong room, that he should go away . . . in somewhat obvious language. Reluctantly, she swung her legs out of the bed, at once lighting a cigarette, coughing, drawing the smoke in deeply, her hand shaking once she took the cigarette from her mouth.

'God . . .' she heard herself breathe as if there was someone else in the room with her. The cigarette began to relax her, working against the new buffeting of her nerves when she realised what she had decided to do. The thought made her queasy, even blundered against her like the man in the street, the other man against her door.

She thrust herself off the bed and dragged open the curtains. The unfamiliar, comforting nightdress swished with the anger of her movements. Traffic noise, the early summer morning blue after rain over the rooftops, the tower of the Hôtel de Ville, the tiny minarets and upthrusts of the other heavy buildings of the Grand' Place.

David Winterborne — his features flushed with drink and confidence — seemed to stare into the room from just beyond the window. He would soon be at a power breakfast with EU officials, Aero UK and Balzac-Stendhal executives, and representatives from Sabena and other European carriers. She had overheard a time of eight bandied between table companions at the restaurant the previous evening. Already it was only a half-hour away. By ten-thirty, she and her colleagues, together with Winterborne and a tribe of officials and executives, would be at Brussels' Zaventem airport, boarding the Skyliner. The breakfast meeting would last for perhaps an hour. David's suite would be empty for no more than that.

His PC . . . Silly idea now. And yet the image tugged at her like a hangnail caught in cloth. David, creature of habit, the boy who avoided the cracks in the pavement, walked the borders of the carpet, checked the light switches obsessively . . . there *was* the slim chance that he would still, like touchstones, use the old passwords.

She began to hurry, stubbing out the cigarette in a cut-glass ashtray, scrubbing her face into wakefulness in the bathroom, dashing her make-up on, choosing her outfit. Eight . . . eight-five. They would be about to eat breakfast in the private room now, comfortable, assured, the windows slightly fogged with power, arrogance. Snatching up her handbag and the camera she always carried on jaunts, she closed the door behind her and stood for a moment in the corridor that smelt of thick carpet and dry air. Her heart was thudding against her ribs; she was already jogging against time.

She went up two floors in the lift. There had been an open door on her own corridor, a maid bent over a bed, tugging off linen. She rounded the corridor —

— another housemaid, pinafored, tinily Oriental and almost hidden by the trolley of linen and cleaning materials she was pushing from one door to the next. David's suite was —

— two doors closer to her than the maid . . . Time, *time.* Eight-nine . . . A strange and ludicrous image of waiters clearing away grapefruit, melon, the scent of kedgeree, and bacon and eggs. David loved kedgeree, always had. The maid looked up with the shy, almost flinching incuriosity of her race and occupation. Marian clicked her fingers exaggeratedly, after fishing in her handbag, attempting to appear panicked. The maid seemed troubled on her behalf.

'Do — you — speak — English?' *God, I hope so . . .* 'English?'

The reply was precise. The girl was, on closer inspection, young enough to be a moonlighting student.

'Yes, madam.' Not even the French appellation. Nevertheless, Marian continued her impersonation of Anglo-Saxon patronage towards foreigners, speaking slowly.

'I am Mr Winterborne's personal assistant —' She gestured towards the suite's double doors. 'He needs something from his room. He didn't give me the key. It is urgent. Can you let me in?'

'Mr Winterborne?' She consulted her list, nodding daintily, precisely. 'Yes,' she confirmed, looking up at the doors. Then she studied Marian — and seemed satisfied.

Her pass-key strained the material of the pinafore outwards as she tugged it towards the door on its brief chain. The lock clicked. Furiously, before the girl could turn, Marian wiped her finger along the sudden wet line on her forehead.

'Thank you — thank you!' She lurched into the suite, still scented with David's aftershave. The maid remained in the doorway. Marian turned and said peremptorily: 'That's fine — I won't be long. You can continue with your duties.' It was insultingly dismissive and the maid turned away, letting the doors close behind her. Marian heard her own loud breathing in the spacious sitting room. The bedroom door remained half-open. A suit hung against the door of a dark old wardrobe like a hanged man.

Eight-twelve. Croissants, preserves, waiters gliding like unhearing ghosts between the extravagant dollars, the dates, the counter-proposals. David at the head of the table, his slim hands on the white cloth, patiently still, stirring only slightly whenever the discussion moved in his direction. His presence was almost real enough to be in the bedroom next door.

She was startled by the noise of a vacuum cleaner blurting awake in the next suite. She had miscalculated, the maid was only one room away . . .

Nothing on the writing desk, the armchairs or the chaise. Small items of David's — a fat black pen, his cigarette case, silver and initialed, a comb. Eight-eighteen. The bedroom, then —

The vacuum cleaner growled like a dog beyond the wall, occasionally lurching softly into furniture. The unmade bed, the discarded shoes and underwear, the hanged suit. Files, the open suitcase, a guide book, rolled fax messages. She touched at them but did not read . . . Eight-twenty . . . The satisfied, male clatter of knives and forks against crockery, the more desultory conversation, as the power breakfast consumed its allotted time. Eight-twenty-one . . . The wet line was back across her forehead. Her hair flopped over her cheek and eyes and she brushed it violently aside. She glanced towards the bedroom window. A pigeon, staring back, shocked her like an enemy.

It must be in the wardrobe. She held the suit over her arm, removed the small, flat crocodile leather case which contained the PC, rehanged the suit against the wardrobe door. With harsh, thankful breaths, she carried the case to the writing desk and flipped the locks. They sprang open. Another pigeon — perhaps the same one — watched her from the sitting room window with red-eyed surveillance. She opened the lid, exposing the screen of the PC, its keyboard sliding smoothly into place. Tiny, delicate . . . The handbag's strap seemed to bite into her shoulder. She would have to photograph the screen, once she gained access . . .

Her fingers trembled as she poised over the keyboard. The pigeon's beak tapped on the thick glass of the window, as if to encourage her. David's fat black *executive* pen lay beside the cuff of her blouse. *Oh, David,* she couldn't help but think. He had pleaded with her in the Musée, there had been exaggerated glances of entreaty over dinner, as if she had wounded or disappointed him.

And a bleakness in his eyes.

The PC came to life under her fingers. *Hello, please tell me your name,* it ingratiated itself. She hesitated. The request disappeared, then reappeared. That would happen only once more.

Shadow, she typed.

Hi, David, the machine replied. Marian wrinkled her nose. Her own computer was severely English, restrained in its responses to her.

'Hi, David,' she murmured, as if she was reading a headstone, and sighed.

The memory remained clear to her, ten years later. After Robbie's death, David had presented her with a battered cardboard box. His *brother would have wanted you to have some of his books,* he had offered with savage, tearless restraint. The gesture had, nevertheless, touched her and was meant to indicate emotion. In a moment of recollection a few days later, she had opened the box and examined the books — from Robbie's childhood, adolescence, student days. Most of them unread, some of them even given to Robbie by herself.

And there was the well-thumbed copy of an anthology of Chinese poems of the eighth and ninth centuries in translation that she had given to David, not Robbie. In his late teens, David had been reacting with unexpected, oversensitive ferocity to the prejudice of his fellow pupils, and she had bought him the book partly as a salve to wounded pride. A leaf of paper bearing Robbie's scrawl had fallen from between the pages. The poem it had marked was annotated in David's neater hand. A poem by Tu Fu, *To a Younger Brother.* From the handwriting of the two brothers, she had worked out that David had evolved the passwords into his first computer by using lines from the poem — and that Robbie had discovered the trick . . . and had betrayed the tenderness implicit in David's choice by breaking into the computer.

She had never forgotten that small betrayal, nor the affection that had made David, years after she had bought the book, use that poem for his passwords.

Eight-twenty-eight. Time stunned. The way into the PC's menu was *Rumours,* the first English word of the poem. The *Shadow* might have been David himself, or Robbie. Now it was herself.

She felt very heated, her hands quivered. What did she want to know, what did she need? *Wind in the dust prolongs our day of parting,* the poem said, a metaphor for war. This was a different war, the one between her and David.

The menu unrolled on the screen. The vacuum cleaner, she realised, had ceased unnoticed in the next room. Towels changed, duster wiped over surfaces. She strained to hear, but there was only a murmur. Come *on* —

She summoned *Millennium* because it was obvious. The fraud was upon the Millennium Urban Regeneration Project.

. . . a list of charities? She had fumbled the camera from her handbag, but the screen seemed to mock her as she held it. She scrolled the information forward with a jabbing, angry forefinger. Contributions, schemes, the names of dignitaries . . . Eight-thirty . . . The clearing of breakfast plates, the sense of coffee being served as sharply as if she had caught its aroma. The damp line across her forehead, at the roots of her hair . . . The *Millennium* file she had opened rolled to its enragingly innocent conclusion. Ceremonies, fundraising, invitations, monetary gestures.

She returned the menu to the screen. Jabbed at *Skyliner.* She could hear the ticking of her blood's clock, accelerating. Investments, involvements, negotiations, the narrative of failure, the hurrah of recent success . . . innocent, all of it. *Winterborne Holdings,* she summoned. There was silence from the next-door room now. Briefly, registered only subconsciously, there had been the noise of a radio or television. The maid would be entering David's suite any minute now. All the companies, the investments, the shareholdings, the details of boards, chief executives, salaries, pensions. Her finger jabbed the key endlessly, furiously, scrolling the useless, *useless* information up the grey-tinted screen and back into oblivion. It was as if she was reading some gangster's accounts, the ones prepared for the tax man. The *other* accounts were hidden somewhere in the computer but she had no idea, no inkling, where they might be. Filed under *what — ?*

She returned from the brief history and assessment of David's empire to the menu, hurrying through it more and more violently, carelessly. Blood's clock — eight-thirty-five . . .

'Oh, bugger!' she breathed aloud. David's fat black pen seemed to mock her like a complacent expression.

The name almost vanished before it registered . . . *his* name. Curious. Her forefinger hovered above the key, to be joined by other fingers, her other hand. Her breathing was very loud. Her temples throbbed, as if all thought was an effort. It was like finding an old love letter, written by a parent one had always thought incapable of love, when clearing out drawers after their death. David and Robbie. Perhaps there was some surviving sentimental element in David's nature, within the deep, suspicious tomb in which David had always buried feeling. Robbie had been dead for a decade, killed when he crashed his latest red Porsche. He had been a stranger to David for a long time before that

R-o-b-b-i-e, she typed slowly, hesitantly. Then at once gasping with relief and success. *Fraser,* she read. Then other names . . . Roussillon — who? — the chief executive of Balzac-Stendhal Laxton, others . . . dates of meetings, sums of money, as if David had been intent on itemising some Dutch treat at an Indian restaurant. The camera clicked twice. She scrolled on . . . The Urban Regeneration Project, the EU funding . . . the beginnings of the careful, precise balance sheet of theft, of Aero UK's failure. The dates measured, like a financial ECG chart, the crucial cardiac arrests the company had suffered . . . *and the injections of diverted EU funds into the company to keep it afloat.* She was shivering with excitement, the camera's eyepiece was becoming fogged with her delighted tension. She was terribly hot. *Steady the camera —*

'I am sorry —'

Marian straightened in the chair as if she had been electrocuted. Whirled around. The maid was standing in the doorway, apologetically surprised. Seeming not to recognise her. Marian clutched the camera against her stomach like a weapon designed to disembowel her.

'I — yes! Come in, yes — I've finished. Come in — !'

She exited the computer and shut the lid of the PC as if a snake was inside. She experienced almost a sense of bereavement as the keyboard slid out of sight and the screen disappeared. She closed the catches and stood up, hiding the camera at first then thrusting it into her handbag. She walked stiffly into the bedroom and replaced the leather case in the wardrobe. The arms of the empty suit attempted to arrest her. She brushed wildly at her hair. The maid watched her passage to the door with a dull, respectful stare, her eyes blinking once like camera shutters. Marian slammed the doors of the suite behind her, leant back against them. Eight-forty-two . . .

She was perspiring freely. Her whole body seemed to tremble with weakness . . . and for *nothing,* she castigated herself in a fury of frustrated failure. *All for — bugger-all!*

'Damn,' she breathed aloud. 'Damn, damn, *damn!*'

She had been panicked by the maid's appearance. Just like a silly girl at her first sight of an erect penis — a stupid *virgin!*

'Damn, damn, damn — *bugger!*' she breathed.

Her hands were slippery on the doorknobs. It had all been there, begging to be photographed. She could have simply told the maid to wait, that she mustn't be interrupted. She had had it all in her hands and had just thrown it away! She had nothing but some names, the first few snippets of the gigantic fraud . . . fishscales from David's leviathan crookedness, nothing more.

She would have to try again . . . The idea appalled her.

Winterborne listened to the scattered words, the tapping noises on the keyboard of his PC, her breathing, her shocked, delighted surprise — none of them were able to shatter the deep pleasure of his mood. The breakfast meeting had been replete with the rich diet of deals, leasings, promises to purchase. It had been like arriving somewhere long desired after a strange and perilous journey. It had *worked,* the whole desperate strategy.

'. . . Come in, yes — I've finished,' Winterborne heard. 'Come in — !'

The tiny, amplified noises of the PC being closed, the sound of the wardrobe door in the bedroom, the movements of the maid who had interrupted her. Winterborne stood at the window of the suite, staring blindly through the glass, as if rain had dissolved some magical vision.

He turned and glowered at the tiny tape-recorder he had almost nonchalantly removed from the desk drawer, expecting to hear only the sound of a vacuum cleaner. The fat black pen, uncapped so that its noise-activated microphone could function, seemed to mock him. Such had been his eagerness for the breakfast meeting and his sense that it would go well, he had almost forgotten to uncap the pen. Habit had saved him —

— and condemned Marian. His features twisted in an expression of pain as much as rage. He silently cursed himself for continuing to use those old passwords that Robbie had discovered so long ago. No one else knew them *except* Robbie. How *could* Marian have known? From Robbie?

It did not matter *how,* he told himself angrily. She *knew.* She had broken into his PC. She must know *everything* . . .

He heard a snarling noise, strangled in someone's throat. His own, he slowly realised. He rubbed furiously at his throat as if he suffered a kind of moral laryngitis, an inability to curse her; then he rubbed his cheeks and eyes. Sunlight slanted across the desk, the recorder, the black pen.

He punched his fist down against his thigh, hurting himself. Again and again.

Then he began smoothing the bruised place rhythmically, as if using some healing ointment. Marian had — sealed her fate, as a melodrama might have expressed it. She had engaged in enemy action, *she* had persisted after his warnings, refusing to let the matter rest. She had flouted their mutual past, the very thing that had held him back in front of a subordinate. Very well . . .

He moved round the desk and thrust the recorder back in a drawer. Glanced at his watch. He needed to speak to Fraser immediately, before he left for America — and to Roussillon. There must be some kind of accident . . . ? At once, it was there as brilliantly and quickly as a light being switched on. A mugging that went terribly wrong, perhaps . . . Ben Campbell would be with her, he might even be injured. But Marian would be killed. A victim of mindless, motiveless street crime. Campbell's cooperation in the incident would silence him as effectively as Marian would be silenced.

He snatched up the phone and dialled Fraser's room. He had ten minutes before he must leave for the Skyliner jaunt, for more success; the seal on the enterprise. He smiled.

On board the plane, he would introduce Marian to Roussillon. She was a perceptive woman, perhaps she would even recognise her assassin.

'Fraser — come up at once. Find Roussillon for me and bring him, too. I've made up my mind.'

She concentrated on the traffic on the Brussels ring road, then on the interchange with the E10 autoroute to Antwerp, as if the ordinary, the meaningless, would remove all thought of David.

Yet the knowledge that she had obtained no real shred of proof against David and that she must try again bobbed on the surface of her mind like a body she could not drown. Campbell's mood, as he sat beside her in the back of the chauffeur-driven limousine, was strained, quiet.

The ramps and twists of the motorway interchange were left behind and the panorama became a flat expanse dotted with buildings whose windows reflected the midmorning sun. The light gleamed from the tailplanes and flanks of dozens of aircraft. One lifted from the runway as she stared from the window almost lurching into the sky by an effort of will.

Ben Campbell had been engaged in a brief, furious conversation with David in the foyer of the Amigo as she had come out of the lift. She was wearing her brightest clothes, a black and yellow spotted skirt and a bright-yellow jacket — the insect-colours of warning and defence, a deliberate choice. However, she could hardly summon the willpower to sustain its defiant humour.

Because David had known what she had done, she was certain of it. He had glowered at her in the moment before he had changed his expression to a bland smile and had pecked at her cheek. Somehow, he had discovered her interference with his PC. She could not dismiss her impression. Campbell, dumb with some weight and mood of his own, confirmed her sense that she had increased her danger.

'There she is,' Campbell murmured as the car ran beside the high perimeter fence. His hand pointed eagerly but his voice lagged, as if he were weary of his own enthusiasm.

'Oh — yes.'

The Skyliner seemed bulbous, even ugly, beside the sleeker European and American airliners that surrounded it. A great bottle-nosed dolphin of a thing, its front section bulging like a deformed head, its waist thick, its wings and tailplane earthbound. Then she lost sight of it as the car turned into the main gates, her last impression that it was liveried in the colours of the European Union, blue, white and gold-starred. The grandiose European dream that it represented seemed diminished by her sense of a small provincial airport, a cramped, dowdy collection of buildings. The new terminal, built to handle international flights, seemed inappropriate; a superstore sprung up in a quiet residential district.

'You'll be impressed,' Campbell offered, his salesman's manner somehow crumpled, under pressure. 'It's a very good airliner. It was just too expensive — until now.' He rallied more by habit than excitement.

Marian nodded. The limousine drew up on the concrete apron in front of the terminal. Airliners in a dozen liveries nuzzled like piglets at the pier's airbridges. She got out of the car, even thankful for the overpowering scent of aviation fuel on the warm breeze, and the sense of bustle, after Campbell's desultory, drizzling conversation in the car. As he began marshalling the occupants of the little fleet of limousines that had driven from the hotel to the airport, Marian studied him.

Throughout the short journey, Campbell had seemed uncharacteristically preoccupied, even brooding. His talk was mere soundbites left out in the rain to spoil. He seemed wary of her. Nervous of being near her, as if she carried some raging infection. Almost as if she made him feel guilty.

Another aircraft flashed in the sunlight as it lumbered into the air. Then, calming as a doctor, Henry was beside her.

'All right, lass? You look pale.' The elderly Opposition Member was a thankful distraction. 'Bloody funny-looking aeroplane, has to be said!' His raised voice teased the smooth, ushering Commission civil servants. David, she saw, was watching her intently, until Tim Burton dragged at his arm like a small boy filled with enthusiasm, pulling him towards the airliner.

She saw Bryan Coulthard, the chief executive of Balzac-Stendhal, Rogier and Laxton together, all of them supremely cheerful. A select band of European press figures, from the broadsheets and the tabloids, were marshalling their photographers, buttonholing MPs and EU officials alike.

No one seemed to want to interview her, thankfully. Perhaps she was the skull at this particular banquet? It was David's day . . .

There was a general movement towards the Skyliner, something as natural and irresistible as a tidal swell. It was sleekly fat close to, its girth Victorian-boastful, reeking of luxury.

'You all right, Ben?' she asked waspishly as she found Campbell once more at her side.

'What — ?' He seemed uncertain for an instant, then he added: 'Oh, yes — just don't like flying all that much. Never really taken to it —' His sickly smile irritated her.

David was surrounded by reporters and officials, his hand firmly grasping that of the President of the Commission. The smooth Belgian was inclining his head towards David in the manner of an obeisant or that of a fellow conspirator. The little tableau increased her annoyance.

'Ready, Marian?' Campbell asked uncertainly. He had watched her studying David.

'Yes!' she snapped. '*Ready*. Are *you*, Ben?'

'What? Oh, yes. Let's go then.' He gestured towards the passenger steps.

Once they were in the first-class cabin, Campbell left her side, hurrying away into a scrum of journalists. A glass of champagne appeared magically in her hand as she surveyed the lounge, spacious as a hotel foyer.

'Big bugger, eh?' Henry said at her elbow. 'Like a bloody cruise ship. But then, I suppose that's the idea, eh, lass?'

She managed to nod in a mimicry of enthusiasm. That, after all, had been the principle on which the Skyliner had been created. First class as an imitation of a liner's stateroom, the seats scattered as casually as in a club's library. Business class, the remainder of the cabin space, was narrower, but still huge-seeming, stretching away from her. Wide aisles, groups of seats, computer workstations, desks . . . The carrier of choice for the global marketplace. Other cabin variants offered luxurious charter flight facilities, one even provided lounges and a cinema. The latest, or so she had heard, proposed seating in excess of the new Boeing, now that price was a factor. Tim Burton would put that type into operation on the Atlantic run.

The aircraft seduced. There had been an unfairness about its previous lack of success. It was big, quiet, luxurious — affordable, now — and the logical next step beyond Airbus. It did indeed seduce . . . She shook her head.

'Summat wrong?'

'Ringing in my ears, Henry.' She smiled.

People had died for this occasion, this display. To place her here, with the influential, putting champagne to her lips amid the joviality of power and money. The innocent had died.

'Hello, Marian!'

It was Tim Burton, grinning like a boy with a new train set. She knew him as someone she had encountered at parties or occasionally scouring the House for a tame lobbyist.

'Tim — your new toy? I like it.' She raised her glass to the downlighters in the cabin's high ceiling. Henry had drifted away towards a knot of civil servants, bent on mischief. 'Congratulations.'

'Damn close-run thing, Marian — I can admit that now.'

His grin was infectious, his too-long hair suggestive of innocence. 'Poor Alan Vance, of course. You heard about that? Mm. Well, thanks to your friend David and Bryan Coulthard, I'm off the hook! My version won't be as luxurious as this, of course — hi, David!'

He was as grateful — and innocent — as a puppy. Gant would not have wasted a moment suspecting his involvement. He had been all but ruined. *Hi, David.* It was what his computer had said to her — and David, she was certain, knew of its infidelity.

The man with David was in his late thirties, taller than David, slimly elegant, dark-haired, brown-eyed. Deeply attractive.

'Marian — my friend Michel asked to be introduced to you,' David murmured. At the same moment, his hand was proprietorially on Tim Burton's shoulder. '*Mizz* Marian Pyott, one of our most colourful Members of Parliament . . . I warn you, Michel, Marian doesn't like foreigners. Michel Roussillon, who is in charge of our security.'

They shook hands.

'David exaggerates my bigotry,' she flirted. 'My prejudices *are* capable of being disarmed.' Her smile was dazzling. Roussillon was remarkably good-looking.

Roussillon . . . *Roussillon.*

She released his grip, too quickly not to alert him. His name had been in David's computer under the *Robbie* file —

The lake was all but empty of canoes and tourist sailboats in the late afternoon. Anyway, it was too early in the season for there to be more than a few people renting cabins.

An otter's head broke the water thirty yards from the pebbled shore along which he was walking. When the scout camps and the fishermen and the playacting tourists came, the otters retreated to secluded pools. For the moment, trout and salmon were theirs for the taking.

Smoke drifted above lodgepole pines from the invisible chimney of an occupied cabin. He heard the faint noises of children.

He was walking to the store for supplies, and walking to think the thing through. In the lodge, even in the dense forest around it, it was difficult sometimes to see matters in any clear light. It was all too comfortable and familiar, too much a refuge; and it prompted his sense of control, suggested he accept the offer that had come via the e-mail. A fundamentalist splinter group wanted Arafat killed — just as a fundamentalist Jew had killed Rabin last year. It seemed a simple, if challenging, proposition, one which oughtn't to disconcert. It did, though.

Strickland's large hands were thrust into the side pockets of his windcheater, as if he were attempting to imitate an even larger man. His head studied the pebbles along the narrow beach as if reading runes. The pines crowded towards the shore and the mountains were reflected in the still deep blue of the lake. He ignored the familiarity of the scene and its congenial sense of wilderness. He raised his head once, attracted by the puttering noise of the mailboat returning across the lake towards the jetty and the scramble of wooden cabins and lodges that were the only settlement for miles. Then he returned his attention to the pebbles, to his own long afternoon shadow, the images of snowcaps and glaciers fading from his retinae.

The middleman had placed the asked-for, non-returnable deposit in his Swiss account. The bank had faxed him the confirmation two hours ago. Now a meeting had to be arranged. But he had come here, to the wilderness where he was known by another name, because he had been certain, after Oslo, that Winterborne would turn Fraser and the Frenchman on him, just to clean house. Only days later, an offer that challenged ego and invited greed had appeared out of the blue . . . because they'd lost track of him? Was it *them,* or was it genuine and coincidental? Even Winterborne — or Fraser or Roussillon — could have guessed that he'd find Arafat an irresistible target. Rabin had been a clay pigeon by comparison. *One of the most difficult men in the world to eliminate,* the e-mail had offered like a tempting menu. *A traitor to the Palestinian cause,* or something like that, had revealed the target's identity. Arafat.

Winterborne could easily have discovered that he had been hired once before to kill Arafat in North Africa — and had failed when Arafat left seconds before the device was detonated. And *everyone* knew how much he hated failure . . .

. . . a meeting, then. Could he risk it? And if he did, where? He paused in his stride, looking up. The familiar mountains, spilling frozen snow and ice; the still lake, the mailboat's wake fading as it bobbed beside the jetty, its engine off. An otter's head, then that of a second. A mule deer appeared confidently from the pines, maybe aware the tourists and sportsmen hadn't yet moved into the wilderness. The animal watched him, unafraid. A canoe rounded the flat, tiny, sparse-treed islet in the middle of the lake. Strickland breathed deeply.

The afternoon temperature had begun to drop. His indecision remained with him, a solid, indigestible lump in his stomach. He *was* challenged by the commission . . . and he *was* suspicious. The walk had resolved nothing.

The shuttle flight from Miami dropped towards Phoenix's Sky Harbor airport as the desert evening purpled. The ground was a sodium-lamp orange-yellow, scattered with the crucifixes of giant cactuses. Gant watched the ground rushing towards the airplane and Phoenix's lights spring out of the dusk, as if someone had just created the city. He was dog-weary, unshaven and unwashed. The wheels touched, skidded, settled and the whine of deceleration filled the cabin of the medium-haul Boeing. The terminal and the hangars slipped by as if half-remembered.

The plane slowed, the airport became more real, the desert and the cactuses now unreal as the Boeing turned on to the taxiway. It was darker amid the neon, a sudden night. He yawned behind his hand but even that small politeness seemed to irritate the blue-haired matron at the window seat, her permanent Sunbelt tan having worked on her skin like heat on old leather. His whole appearance, perhaps even his unwashed smell, had offended her throughout the flight from Miami.

He felt little or no anxiety as the aircraft came to a halt on the apron and the transfer bus rolled towards it. He had felt none when he had landed at Miami International, passed through the transfer lounge and eaten a meal while waiting for this flight. Perhaps he had left all such feelings behind him in France, or perhaps weariness had eroded them like rain on soft stone. He had reached the airport at Toulouse by backroads and without hindrance. By evening, an Airbus 320 had flown him on a shuttle service to Amsterdam, where he had spent the night in the departure lounge, attempting to sustain a sleep interrupted by the noises of tired children and worn adults. The first Stateside flight out of Schipol in the early morning had been a Delta tourist flight to Florida by Boeing 767. He had been lulled, amid the Dutch, German and British tourists, by the American accents of the flight attendants, the American movie. He felt he was the only one on the flight uninterested in Disney World as his destination.

He had thought, momentarily, of returning to London. But Aubrey's idea had gone down the toilet with Strickland's disappearance and the French counter-activity. Aubrey wouldn't have any more ideas. It had been time to come home . . . like Strickland?

The snapshot was in his breast pocket like a talisman. If Strickland was running from the same people who'd tried to kill him — and Gant was certain he was — then maybe he, too, had come back to the States.

Besides, he needed to talk to Blakey, even to Barbara. There were resources at Vance Aircraft he could use. Just maybe he could find Strickland alone, he reaffirmed with a lack of conviction as he stood up and allowed the matron to drag her cabin bag from the overhead locker and to brush unapologetically past him. He shrugged, pulling down his own sports bag, one he had bought at Schipol along with a clean shirt. It was just sufficient luggage not to arouse interest. He stepped through the passenger door behind two fractious children and a pregnant mother into the mobile lounge, scissor-lifted on its hydraulics. He stood at the far end of the vehicle, strap-hanging, idly watching his fellow-passengers. Then the lounge was lowered on to its chassis and accelerated towards the main terminal building. The first stars gleamed high above the glass roof, and a sliver of moon seemed as abandoned and unnecessary as a nail-clipping low on the horizon.

The pregnant woman and her two children, were, he realised, Apache. The matron, seated a few feet from them, seemed to dissipate her disapproval between himself and the Native Americans. The Sunbelt had seen another landrush, this time of new businesses and early retirement. There wasn't gold or cattle country out here now to take away from the Indians, just golf courses.

The doors of the mobile lounge sighed open at the terminal gate and he filed off behind the other passengers, hesitant for perhaps the first time.

Then the automatic doors embraced him and he began to trek towards the exit and the cab rank.

He was unaware that, together with the other passengers on the flight, his photograph was taken as he had entered the concourse. The FBI agent was bored, impatient for his shift to end, and certain that Gant would not return to Phoenix. He was therefore uninterested in visually inspecting the passengers; but because McIntyre in Washington had insisted, and he was a hard-nosed, unforgiving sonofabitch, he dutifully photographed all arriving passengers at Sky Harbor that night.

Gant walked out of the terminal into the fresh cool of the evening, confident of his continuing anonymity.

CHAPTER THIRTEEN

Accident and Design

Reluctance remained on her wearied, drawn features like a mask. Blakey, too, seemed older, misplaced. It was as if both of them had moved on in time and resisted being drawn back into the situation. Gant stood in the doorway of the executive suite, sensing Alan Vance's absence from the big room like a visible, black hole. Barbara watched him warily, as if he had declared some intention of reviving their marriage and of hurting her further.

Gant shrugged and said: 'I didn't intend to cause trouble, Barbara.' Then he turned at once with evident relief to Blakey. 'Hi, Ron.'

Blakey grumbled something into his unkempt beard, his dark eyes looking at a loss and aged, his whole manner that of an actor learning the role of a derelict. Gant moved forward into the familiar pine-panelled room. Barbara was seated behind Vance's big redwood desk, Blakey on a long sofa against one wall.

'I need your help, Ron. Some computer stuff —' Then it was as if he, too, succumbed to the invisible nerve gas of defeat and bankruptcy that had replaced the room's habitual energy, its atmosphere of effort and confidence.

Through the windows, their blinds still raised, the dusk was uninterrupted by the glow of lights, the sense of business, the light-map of hangars, workshops, runways. Vance Aircraft, he had realised as the cab had approached it, had become a vacant lot. The banks and the other major creditors had foreclosed. The company had been declared bankrupt, without the benefit of Chapter Eleven or any other saving delay, as the business had been asset-stripped as effectively as if by locusts. He'd read the obituary in *Newsweek* on the flight from Amsterdam. He could read it even more vividly on Barbara's face. For the first time in years, he felt an ache of sympathy for her.

'I had meetings, Mitchell — I didn't need to be interrupted,' were her first accusing words. They were, however, delivered in a very worn, husky voice, as if she had finally tired even of insult and her dislike of him.

'Sure. I realise what's been happening.'

'Do you?' Then her features softened; crumpled, rather. 'Maybe you do at that. What is it you want?' She waved him to a seat. 'Drink?' He shook his head and she shrugged, sipping at her own large bourbon. There were stains of tiredness under her eyes, the make-up was disguisingly heavy.

He turned to Blakey, as if embarrassed. He took out the snapshot of Strickland, posed on a jetty of some kind, where there were mountains, pines, a lake; somewhere in the world. He, at least, felt refreshed after the shower he'd had in his motel and was determined to shake off the room's mood, its air of defeat. Strickland was his sole concern.

'This is the guy who made the rogue chip,' he said. 'His name's Strickland. He's ex-Company.' Blakey seemed nonplussed, his features with that empty concentration of a wino.

'There's nothing more I can tell you about the chip, Mitchell. My guess is it reconfigured itself — it's wearing a disguise, or maybe it's gotten amnesia after it did what it was intended to do.'

'It's not the chip that matters, Ron,' he replied with a patience that surprised him. 'I want to trace this guy.'

'Can he make things come out right — like in a story?' Barbara asked derisively.

He looked at his ex-wife and shook his head. 'No, he can't. Look, Barbara, there are people out there who hired him —'

'Who?' she demanded.

'Not yet. There's no proof. It's to do with Europe, with airplane companies, even security services — it's all still vague. Except for Strickland. I saw him on a video in Oslo. He was there. He did it. And he'll know who hired him.' His eyes hardened. 'They want him too. I don't have a lot of time.' He looked up, glowering at Barbara. 'I need this blown up, examined on a computer. There has to be a clue, somewhere in the photograph, as to where it was taken.'

Blakey was turning the creased snapshot in the light from a lamp, squinting as he did so. Barbara seemed to move in and out of interest as she might have done a mild hypnotic state.

'Could be anywhere. You think it's America, somewhere?'

'Strickland is American — it could be. Or Europe. He had a house there.' He sniffed. 'Those buildings in the background. Maybe there's a signboard —' He became angry with himself. 'It's all I have. I can't go to Langley and ask at the door!'

'You took a risk, coming back at all,' Barbara offered.

'I had to. They tried to kill me — twice. I needed to lose them.'

'And that's why you're here?' she mocked. Gant understood her vengeful frustration. Over the telephone, when he had eventually demanded and received her attention, he had sensed a desire being awoken that he could only disappoint; as in their marriage. 'Sorry,' she added suddenly. He waved the apology aside. Failure was eating her away as surely as a cancer, and he could not avoid his empathy with her.

'I can scan this to transfer it to computer. We can maybe play with it, Mitchell . . . but don't hold your breath, fella. It doesn't look all that much to me.'

'Nor to me,' Gant replied without turning to Blakey, his gaze still on Barbara, who shifted uncomfortably under his intense, even unwelcome compassion. 'It's all there is, Ron — all there is.'

'Then let's get started,' Barbara announced, standing up with a jerky movement. 'It's getting late, and I have to go on supervising the disposal of what's been salvaged from this disaster — keep on running the fire sale.' She managed a brief, wintry smile.

'What *is* left?' he asked.

'Oh, some small component work — some of the avionics stuff.' She shrugged her thin shoulders. 'We can maybe keep on five per cent of the workforce — in cheaper premises. We won't be building any more airplanes!' Invigorated by something close to hatred, she snatched the snapshot from Blakey's fingers. 'This is him, is it? The bastard who killed Alan?' Gant nodded. 'And you know who hired him? *Who?*'

'Not yet,' Gant replied. 'Not yet. First, I have to find him.'

The air-conditioning needed fixing, forcing him to leave the windows open against the clammy warmth of the early-summer night. He could hear the noise of music from the Ethiopian restaurant two doors down the street, African drumming from another bar, the laughter of the ethnics and the noise of traffic. Adams-Morgan as a place to live was the antithesis of everything McIntyre would have chosen.

His estranged wife, May, with ambitions to become an artist, had moved them there because the narrow old house's top-floor apartment possessed a studio. She'd enjoyed the bars, the bookstores, the galleries and the sense of the exotic that was the tourist impression of that district of Washington.

For a time. She couldn't paint or sculpt, despite

all the lessons that had cost him so much hard-earned money. It might have been the discovery of her complete lack of talent that had caused her to run off with an Hispanic jazz musician two years earlier; on the rebound from the untidy, unused studio that mocked her every day. Or maybe it had been from his ridicule, his conservatism, his smug certainty that she would never cut it in art like in everything else.

McIntyre stared at the letter he had had from her a week before. She was bleating about the delay in the alimony. The African drums and the whining Ethiopian reed instrument reminded him forcibly of May, reinvoking his contempt and anger. The Hispanic jazzman wasn't getting gigs — too bad. May was waiting table in a diner — too bad . . . He threw the letter aside on the cluttered desk that occupied one corner of the studio. May's potter's wheel, her brushes and canvases, littered the remainder of the room. May had walked out on him and left him without the money to move out of a neighbourhood he despised and in which he felt an exile.

His blunt hands flicked at the heap of unpaid bills, then rubbed his broad face in a washing motion. He yawned, then lifted the bourbon to his mouth.

He stood up and walked to the tall windows of the studio. Beyond the streetlights of Columbia Road was the hard glow of Washington. May's letter was just another hassle. There was pressure from everywhere. He'd forced Gant into a corner, making him a fugitive from justice, now the Bureau wanted to know why he hadn't caught up with him. Fuck Gant . . . fuck May and her Hispanic. Fuck his chief, who didn't like or trust him.

The telephone buzzed like a trapped bee and he snatched up the receiver. It was the English guy, Fraser. Fuck Fraser, too . . .

'Mac? Well, here I am in Washington — just checked in to the Jefferson Hotel. Very nice suite.' It sounded like a come-on line. The guy was so *obvious* — the fucking Jefferson Hotel, one of the best, for Chrissake!

'You've had a wasted journey, Fraser,' he growled. The man had once been a kindred spirit. They'd cooperated on a couple of ops when he'd been Company and Fraser was in MI6, the British intelligence outfit. But who did the guy think he was, calling him earlier in the day, flying all the way over here? His free hand rubbed his stubbled cheek. 'A wasted journey,' he repeated sullenly.

'Just hear me out before you make that judgement,' Fraser replied, his confidence undiminished.

'You don't pull any weight any more, Fraser. You're in the private sector. You talked horseshit this morning — you woke me up, for Chrissake — !' Fraser's chuckle was angering.

'Private sector — I like that. You'd like it, too, Mac. We want the same things — don't we . . . ?'

Strickland's name was an itch he could not scratch. Gant was after Strickland. That much Fraser had told him . . . *Why don't we pool resources, get together on this one?* The guy had a real neck. All he wanted was the Bureau's cover and assistance while he went after Strickland on US soil. There was nothing in it for McIntyre, personally.

'Do we?' he responded almost involuntarily. *If Strickland talks to Gant, what else might he say — about the Company, about you?* Fraser had asked him when he rang. It hung in the air of the studio like a blackmail threat, like May's paint smells and her rage at her lack of talent. 'What in hell do you *want,* Fraser?'

'To help you, Mac. To find Gant with you, to . . . find Strickland. That's all —' He broke off. 'Ah, room service. Champagne, canapés —' He laughed. There was no attempt to make the deception subtle or convincing. The bribe was as vulgar as soiled notes on the desk in front of him.

'Fuck you, Fraser,' McIntyre snarled, turning again to the window and raising the bourbon to his lips.

Drops of the liquor stained his shirt front. The humid night moved against his body like heavy, sullen drapes, smelling of memory — and defeat. Strickland had been used in the Company's dirty campaigns in Latin America in the eighties. Some friends were helped by having their opponents removed — car bombs, house fires, the usual range of wet solutions that had called for Strickland's special, psychotic skills. He'd run Strickland, given him his targets — for two years. Neither the Bureau nor the government would touch him with anything but a long stick if any of it came out. They'd make him a leper to prevent themselves being tainted with the disease of the past.

His glass was empty and he refilled it with one hand, the glass making a wet ring on the scuffed leather top of the desk. Fraser seemed content to wait in silence; as if he expected a favourable decision.

It wasn't that easy, he thought, swallowing the bourbon. He returned to the window above the loathed thoroughfare.

May's letter flickered in his imagination like a mocking salute. If Strickland started shooting off his mouth, the Director would personally throw him out on the street outside the J. Edgar Hoover Building and his hat after him. He needed to think . . . But not dismiss Fraser out of hand. He could be useful.

'OK — let's talk. In the *morning.* I'll call at your hotel, early.'

'I'll be waiting, Mac. Good to talk to you —' The receiver was at once replaced, leaving McIntyre listening to the tone. He slapped his own receiver down.

He was in a bind, he admitted. He needed money — May could take him to court for the back alimony and the Bureau's puritans would want him out for that reason . . . Strickland could blow his ship out of the water, or Fraser could spread the word anyway, if he didn't co-operate . . . The bourbon burned the back of his throat. If Gant got to talk to Strickland —

— fax machine. He turned at its fourth ring. Then the telephone rang.

'McIntyre — it's late.'

'Sorry, sir.' It was Chris, still at the office. 'I'm sending through a photo we just received' — there was an edge of excitement in his voice — 'from Phoenix.'

McIntyre, his breath somehow lost or disregarded, stood over the fax machine as if he might bully or interrogate it. Slowly, like oil seeping out of the instrument, Gant's features, in three-quarter profile, emerged.

'Got it?'

'Sure.' McIntyre grinned. 'It's him. When was this?'

'This evening — early. Sky Harbor airport. He got off a shuttle from Miami International.'

'Where is he?' McIntyre breathed.

'I checked the surveillance at Vance Aircraft. Vance's daughter and the chief research engineer, Blakey, both arrived less than an hour ago — out of the blue. He must be there, mustn't he?'

'Maybe — but why? Why come back? What does he want with his ex-wife?' Gant must hate her like he hated May. 'OK — tighten up surveillance. I'm coming by the office right away. Get yourself ready to take a trip and get a Bureau flight organised to Phoenix by the time I arrive.' It was difficult to catch his breath, as if he had been running hard. The Ethiopian pipe and the African drumming seemed like his breathing, his heartbeat. 'Warn those hicks in Phoenix what they're dealing with — no one leaves Vance Aircraft without being arrested!'

'Sir —'

McIntyre put the phone down on Chris's eager compliance and excitement, the latter like a theft of his own feelings. He whirled as if in triumph towards the studio's tall windows, glanced up at the glass roof. He had Gant — he watched his hand close into a fist, fascinated. The guy had walked into a surveillance net like a four-year-old. Beautiful —

He hurried into the bedroom and dragged the always-packed suitcase from the back of the wardrobe. His sober suits hung to attention above his row of shoes. The wardrobe, despite all he could do, still smelt of May's perfume, which she had lavished on her clothes as well as herself.

He closed the studio windows on the street noises and locked them. He turned to the door — and remembered Fraser. He hesitated for a moment, then picked up the telephone.

It wouldn't do any harm to take the guy along. He could be useful . . . there was a fix in, Fraser had offered him a brighter future. Maybe they could work something out. Meanwhile, why upset the guy . . . ?

Out of the warm spread of the lights, he could look up through the glass roof of Blakey's office suite and see big stars hanging in the desert night. He felt no impatience. Blakey had put the snapshot through the computer, scanning its creased surface, and had then begun the process of blowing it up in sections. Mapmaking. There was a curious, angering sensation that lingered as the elements of Strickland's large, pale features grew, inflated, became more inscrutable. His one hand, resting on the rail of the jetty, was now the size of a baseball mitt, his shoulders huge, the brand name of his windcheater large as a neon sign above a diner.

Gant listened to the computer keyboard responding to Blakey's fingers like a small, excited bird; to the hum of machinery, the occasional purring regurgitations of the printer and photocopier. In a few more minutes, there'd be a composite enlargement, big as a map, to spread on a worktable and examine. The process of discovering where the picture had been taken was in the hands of machines, and that satisfied him.

The mountains behind Strickland were volcanic in origin, and there were three of them. From the shadows, the angle of the sun and Strickland's squint, the time of year was spring and the mountains stretched away north of the small lake into which the jetty thrust like a stick. There were pine trees in the background, on the slopes and around the tiny cuticle of shoreline that could be seen. Northern hemisphere or New Zealand — not quite anywhere in the world, but you could still take your choice of the two hemispheres, outside the tropics . . . Gant still felt that Strickland had come home, that it was a snapshot taken in America.

The main computer at Vance Aircraft had produced, at Blakey's instructions, a relief map of the area in the background of the photograph, then a section outline of the landscape. There was a vague, newsreel-like familiarity about the rise and fall of the volcanic land, the lake, but nothing more concrete. The map and the section lay on the large table on whose edge he was perched, waiting.

'His clothing doesn't look new,' Blakey called out without looking up from the huge image he was assembling delicately on the plate of the colour photocopier. 'Like he's worn it a lot. Maybe he wasn't a tourist at the time the picture was taken.'

He seemed not to expect any reply. There was a high vapour trail at the edge of the sky in the snapshot. From its altitude, it was a civilian flight, Gant estimated. But then, most wilderness areas in the world were overflown by charter flights, red-eyes, shuttle services.

'The clothing's American —'

'You can buy American in any part of the world,' he replied to Blakey's observation.

'Yeah.'

'Anything in *writing?* On the jetty, one of those huts or lodges or whatever they are?'

'Another few minutes . . .'

He sensed Barbara close beside him and turned to her. Her tiredness looked just as strained, less to do with the hour than with the defeat of dreams, the loss of Alan.

'You OK?'

She nodded.

'You?'

'It's going to come out right — this, I mean. I feel it. Every picture tells a story — and this one will tell us where Strickland lives.'

Barbara seemed to dislike her eagerness. 'Is it dangerous — I mean, *how* dangerous is it?' she asked huskily.

'Some. Maybe a lot. Strickland has killed plenty of people. He's been perfecting his talents for a long time.'

'Could you — I mean, when you find him, can

he be persuaded to talk? To tell you the truth?'

Gant shrugged. The machines continued to hum and chirp. Blakey was murmuring a tune as he concentrated.

'I can only ask the guy.' He made as if to smile, but Barbara shuddered. He touched her arm, which jumped but she did not move away. 'I have to find him first.'

'The truth won't bring Alan or the company back to life.' Her features arranged themselves into the now habitual grim planes that somehow sullenly refused to catch and reflect the warmth of the room's lights. She was toying with a glass of whisky but not drinking it. Then, throwing her dark hair away from her face with her hand, she stared at him. She expected — *demanded?* — as she had so many times before, something she already doubted he could give. 'But it will save *your* career?' He realised there was no unkindness in the question.

'Maybe. That's not important. It will save Alan's reputation. It's the truth, that's all.' He was aware his gaze was bitter as he added: 'Strickland killed innocent bystanders on the airplanes. He was hired to do that by *big business.*' The contempt of his tone was venomous, embracing. 'For dollars and pounds and D-marks.' He studied his hands as he spoke. 'The things I did, the things I was ordered to do . . .' He sighed. 'Well, they weren't for the dollar — at least, they weren't supposed to be. There seemed to be some point in it.' He looked up. 'I'll find him . . . then whoever hired him.'

Her hand brushed his, then the moment was

broken by Blakey's voice.

'You guys want to come see the Incredible Hulk?'

Barbara followed Gant to the long worktable where Blakey was smoothing the huge, photocopied enlargement of the snapshot, as if it was cloth-of-gold. The computer's jigsaw blowups had been made whole again. The creases in the original were like swordcuts across Strickland's body and the sky. Barbara hovered at a slight distance, as if threatened by the man in the photograph.

'He doesn't quite look the part,' Blakey offered.

'He never did.' Gant leaned forward over the photocopy the size of an airplane blueprint. His fingers traced, as if longingly, the faint vapour trail in the sky, the volcanic peaks retreating northwards, then the dark mass of pines and individual trees.

Blakey's blunt forefinger tapped at some point near Strickland's temple, against the brown squareness of a wooden building — perhaps a hunting lodge, a rural motel. 'See?' Gant peered. It wasn't a place name, not even that of a person. On a shingle hung on the eaves of a verandah was the word TACKLE in capitals. Above it was a blurred sign. BUD LITE. 'Here, too,' Blakey offered, his hands moving. On the corner of the building, which looked out over the lake from the shore end of the jetty, was a notice. All the print was illegible, even at that magnification, except for two headlining words. FISHING LICENCES.

'Back in the USA,' Gant murmured.

'Got to be the Pacific North-West, somewhere — Washington state, Oregon, northern California . . .'

'Can we narrow it down?'

Barbara's breath was warm against his cheek as she leaned between them to look, somehow emboldened by the identification of the place, It wasn't foreign, unknown — which made Strickland less dangerous, less impervious.

Blakey, by way of response, collected the relief map and the section from the other table and placed them over the enlarged snapshot.

'Three mountains in a kind of line, south to north,' he muttered. 'This has to be a National Park or Wilderness Area, I guess. Give me time to run through the atlas on CD-ROM, see if I can pick out some likely locations. It could also be Canada — I'd better check.' He looked up at Gant, smiling. 'Hang loose just a little longer, Mitchell. I think we can put ourselves in this guy's backyard!'

'What if he was there on vacation, nothing more?' Barbara asked.

'Let's hope he wasn't.'

'Does it seem like his sort of country? You said he had a house in France —'

'He did. That was out of the way, too, in the boondocks. Strickland likes privacy.' He studied the enlargement once more. Blakey was already hunched over the computer keyboard, scrolling through the vivid images, the colours, contours, highways and mottled towns, of an atlas' computerised maps. 'I think he lives here, Barbara — wherever *here* is.'

'Where are we going, Ben?' she demanded.

The night air was cool on her cheeks after the heat, smoke and semi-darkness of the jazz club in a basement under a narrow row of shops. As they emerged from the quiet sidestreet on to the Boulevard Anspach her patience, rubbed almost raw, vanished. Campbell looked at her as if stung.

'I — er . . . You didn't seem to be enjoying —'

'The jazz was fine, Ben. It was the company that was the problem.' She positioned herself confrontationally, arms folded across her breasts, purse jutting like a flat weapon, feet planted squarely in the high-heeled shoes that were beginning to pinch. The care with which she had dressed for the reception seemed days earlier.

'Oh, that —' He assayed a grin that a streetlight made into a purpled rictus. His arms flapped in an approximated shrug, as if he had lost all orientation.

It was after one. He had collected her at the Amigo at seven-thirty to take her to the reception, during which he had whispered to her that *they must talk, it was vitally important . . . dinner somewhere, after this?* She had nodded vehemently, letting surprise and irritation form all her volition. She had excused herself from a group of colleagues intent on fleshpot-crawling and Campbell had taken her to a supper club, then the jazz cellar.

As they had left the reception together, she had seen David watching them, in company with Roussillon. Her anger had finally determined her.

Campbell was the weak link, Campbell must aid her. Then nerve had failed her and she had drunk too much wine, as Campbell had, and they had both seemed to subside into a mutual gloom. The sense of her danger had been dulled. Now, the effects of the wine had gone as certainly as her patience.

'Where next, Ben? Somewhere preordained?' she challenged, her mouth dry with too much alcohol and too many cigarettes. She lit another and puffed angrily at it. Then she refolded her arms belligerently.

'No . . .' he sighed. His eyes had seemed to throw back the denial more vehemently before he shrank into a kind of whining schoolboy slouch in front of her.

'What is it, Ben? Why did you ask me out — for a date, for God's sake?'

'Don't be *stupid — !*' he snapped, his hand waving her away from him. Cars passed, headlights washing over them and catching the gleam and sparkle of goods in grilled shop windows. 'Why do you have to always be so *stupid?*' It was the fearful rage of a parent who had recovered a child after hours of anguished absence. He moved closer, drink on his breath, his lips wet. His eyes were narrow, hateful. 'You're always *right!* You always have to be bloody right! Christ, you've really blown it this time, Marian, my God but you have!'

Candour seemed to momentarily exhaust him and he leaned against a darkened shop window like a sullen drunk. Behind the glass, weary fish swam slowly in a huge tank. Crayfish and bound-clawed lobsters, too. Revolting and appropriate.

'What have I blown, Ben?' She felt a weakness move up her body. Instinctively, she glanced around them. There were still a good number of pedestrians, a fair amount of traffic. The boulevard was alive with lights. Her hotel was a ten-minute walk away. 'What?'

'Everything, you stupid bitch!' His voice was a quiet scream. 'Everything . . . Why do you think I asked you to come to dinner? Because I *fancied* you?'

'I know the outfit's a bit creased and I'm showing every one of my thirty-eight years, Ben . . .' The forced humour vanished on her tongue. 'Why, then? Because you loathe me?'

'It's not *you*, it's the whole bloody *thing*, woman!'

'*What* thing?'

The traffic noises faded as she ground out her cigarette with the sole of her narrow black shoe. The fish continued to swim slowly, leadenly, the lobsters scrabbling at the bottom of the tank.

'*The* thing — !'

'What do they want you to do, Ben? *When?*'

'For Christ's sake, what will they do to me?' he murmured, seeming to catch sight of the captive shellfish for the first time. He rubbed his eyes and forehead furiously, as if he thought himself trapped in a dream. Perhaps he was. 'I wanted to say . . . couldn't —' He turned to face her, eyes gleaming, his handsome, assured features crumpled like a page torn from a priceless illuminated manuscript. 'I've kept you alive, you stupid bitch — *alive!*' He yelled it like an accusation. Then his hand covered his mouth as if he had been caught out.

Marian brushed slowly at the beaded jacket, feeling its roughness, then touched the pearls at her throat. She smoothed the hair at her temples; all as if anticipating being photographed. 'I see,' she murmured.

A young couple passed, seemingly amused at their parody of some minor marital quarrel.

Campbell looked at her intently, as if he sought some kind of guidance. His breathing was louder than the traffic. Changing lights turned his features from sickly green to shamed red. The masks he had discarded and replaced during the evening were all gone. His flesh was as white as bone as he moved his head.

'All right, Ben,' she announced. 'Tell me what you're supposed to do for them, as far as I'm concerned.'

'You don't think I wanted to, do you?'

'Probably not. But David owns you — sorry, *employs* you, and this is just another of the favours you do for him. What, exactly, was it?'

'It doesn't matter . . . it's over now. It was supposed to be earlier.'

'What do you mean, over?'

'I kept you off the streets, in company, away from dark places! Does that answer your question? I didn't *do* what I was supposed to do — hours ago . . .' Again, the effort at something akin to truth seemed to exhaust him. 'I just — oh, *shit* . . .'

'Thank you — whatever you did. Thanks for not being the Judas-goat, the one with the bell.'

'I tried to warn you off — before.'

'I know.'

Marian lit another cigarette and drew on it slowly. Traffic, pedestrians, the long street of shops beyond which jutted incongruous church spires. She felt sorry for Ben Campbell; for his weakness, his ambition, and his present violent fear. He had failed David.

'I — can we get in the car, just drive?' he asked, as if he had become newly afraid of the open street, or of other people. His BMW was parked no more than a hundred yards away. He looked ill in the purpling light of the nearest streetlamp, as she must have done herself. 'Just drive for a bit . . . ?'

'Yes,' she nodded.

He walked like a quick marionette to the BMW and got in, slamming the door. She got in beside him, fugging the interior with cigarette smoke and nerves almost immediately. He seemed to resent the intrusion of both. He started the engine and pulled out with a squeal of tyres into the thin stream of vehicles, heading north. Traffic lights were against them at the Boulevard Baudouin. Marian exhaled smoke that rolled back at her from the windscreen.

The misting of the screen was erased at once by the air-conditioning. Her mind was clearing with much greater reluctance. Ben Campbell had colluded with David, then lost his nerve. Because of that, of *him*, she was alive, and for no other reason. The car moved away from the lights, across the intersection and along the Rue de Brabant, towards the port and the Laeken park.

The anger came back again, like a recurring bout of malaria, making her head ache, her body tense against her situation, against David. She had to *do* something, *any*thing.

Traffic lights at the junction with the Avenue de la Reine. He had switched on his left indicator. He was heading for the park, it seemed, as if towards a wilderness where he might lose himself.

Suddenly, she flung open the passenger door. He turned a stunned face to her.

'I'm getting out now!' she snapped at him. 'David can find me for himself —'

'No, please — !'

The lights changed.

'I can't *trust* you, Ben — I have to watch out for myself! This could be a trick —'

'No!' he all but wailed, shaking his head. The first horns had started behind them, impatient even at that hour.

'Get in — for God's sake, get in the car!' he bellowed, his features drained and desperate, pleading with her.

'Will you *help* me, Ben? Will you talk to me?'

His face was ashen, his eyes furtive, moving rapidly like those of a dreamer. The car horns were louder, like the sounds of threatening creatures in the dark. Ben Campbell was utterly unnerved. His lips were wet as he nodded. Cars pulled out and passed them, faces glaring at the BMW. Campbell flinched at each one, as if seeing enemies he recognised.

She climbed back into her seat, closing the door.

'Will you tell me everything?' she asked quietly.

He continued to nod like an automaton, something clockwork. David had asked too much of him. Broken him, the butterfly on the wheel. She could feel no anger towards him, just pity.

'He shouldn't have asked me . . . he *shouldn't,*' Campbell muttered as he put the car into gear and the BMW screeched away from the lights.

'What do you know about the aircraft sabotage?'

He looked at her as if she had asked the question in an unknown language.

'I don't under—'

She waved it dismissively away. 'It doesn't matter. Tell me about the fraud with the regional redevelopment funds. Everything you know.'

'I know *everything,*' he confessed mournfully.

She removed a tiny recorder from her purse and switched it on.

'Never mind, Ben,' she sighed, exhausted. 'Just talk. The fraud. Begin at the beginning . . .'

It was probably because of his heightened, strained nerves, Winterborne decided. His mood lit his imagination like a succession of flares over a battlefield at night. He could not stop thinking about her. Marian kept coming out of the shadows of the large bedroom of the hotel suite, announcing in her careless way that he was wrong — wrong to think, say, act as he did.

There were new leasings, firming-up purchase enquiries, acres of beneficial newsprint and television reportage. Skyliner and Artemis Airways were in the process, like Hilary and Tensing, of planting the flag on the summit of the mountain they had had to climb. The banks were like eager children pursuing them, desperate to become part of the game with debt rescheduling and new loans alike. The European Commission was dining to bloating on the turnaround that *he* had achieved.

And yet there she was, in his imagination, her expression quizzically mocking and long familiar.

David Winterborne brushed his hair back with long fingers, then rested his hands once more on the duvet of the bed. He studied them, watching them curl involuntarily. They were like those end-of-pier machines, a pair of clawlike grabs which hovered over but hardly ever held small and useless presents. However many times you put pennies in the slot and the arms moved out and the claws grabbed, nothing ever seemed to be won, picked up —

He smoothed the duvet with straightened fingers. That was an image Marian would have used and enjoyed. The cranes, the diggers and the grabs were working again on the Urban Regeneration Project sites. The parliamentary rumour machine was in high gear, whispering that no one was any longer making disapproving noises concerning Winterborne Holdings or European funds. Except Marian — who would be warned off, told to keep her lips firmly together. The Whips' Office had promised —

— and if you could see your way to making a contribution to Party funds, with a General Election in the offing . . . ? The knighthood remained unmentioned — but palpable. Unless it came soon, of course, it would never come. American citizens did not qualify. He smiled, as if a bout

of indigestion had passed. The last General Election had cost him a quarter of a million. It had bought him much gratitude, latitude and influence. This one might well cost him a half-million in contributions. More if he hedged his bets and contributed to the Opposition's campaign. The money would buy him immunity —

— there again. Like a tormenting ghost, walking towards him across the litter of faxes, newsprint and notes that were the confetti of celebration. He had dined Coulthard, Tim Burton and a dozen movers and shakers after the formal reception. It had gone well, spirits were high. It had been whispered to him that even the old irritant — *dear* Kenneth — had been warned off, his palm read for him by the Cabinet Secretary, no less . . . and at the Club, too. That news had especially delighted him. Aubrey, like some ancient Lear-figure, had been shown a kingdom of friends, influence and self-satisfaction in danger of forfeiture. He had been *humbled* —

— and yet Marian stood at the foot of the bed like one of Scrooge's ghosts, damn her, so palpable was the sense of what was to happen to her. Campbell had tried to thwart his intent, keeping her safely in public places. It had been wise to alter the strategy and include his demise. He glanced at his watch. Soon, very soon now —

The value of Winterborne Holdings had risen seven per cent in three days, and the conglomerate's worth was still climbing. And yet it was not that which ran through him like a sexual charge, it was what was imminent for Marian. The gold-strapped watch had been a crystal ball, showing the future, the point in time that was — he looked again — less than five minutes away. The smile she still smiled in his head would soon disappear — for ever. *Miss Priss the Puritan* he had angrily called her when they had been children one summer afternoon of bickering and rainclouds.

'Why is it so *difficult?*' he breathed aloud, startling himself and looking quickly round as if he feared discovery.

Campbell had to be got rid of. He would be just another accident victim to be added to the list of names that had appeared in the press when the two Vance 494s went down. Yet something in him kept reciting, like a prayer without content, *but this is Marian . . .*

Roussillon had telephoned only minutes before. She and Campbell were in the car, heading towards the port and the Laeken park. Campbell, so the Frenchman seemed certain, was in poor shape. Winterborne looked at his watch again.

In two minutes, give or take, a truck would plough into Campbell's BMW while a van sandwiched it, providing the anvil against which the hammer would strike. There would be few witnesses — Campbell's delay had been both futile and helpful — but two people in a car would pull over and dash to assist . . . and ensure there were no survivors in the BMW

Simplicity itself, the soul of efficiency.

He felt the dampness along his hairline, as if the pressure of the impact he envisaged so vividly had squeezed the cold droplets through the pores of his skin. The seconds ticked precisely, steadily in his mind. In one minute, metal would tear, cry out and then crumple, glass would shatter, leather rip. The BMW would implode like a squashed beer can between the truck and the van.

He listened to his slow, deep breathing and felt his shoulders relax. *Kismet.* It could not be undone, it was already almost accomplished, the vehicle's shrinkage to the proportions of a coffin-sized box. A road accident, a statistic — this is *Marian* . . . It possessed a great deal less force. Her features had all but faded from his mind.

He looked at the gold watch.

Now —

She glanced out of the passenger window. A white anonymous van was beside them as the BMW crossed the Rue Marie-Christine, beyond which rose the Gothic Eglise Notre-Dame. They crossed the sea canal and she glimpsed long, dark barges as lifeless as oil spillages on the flat black mirror of the water. Ahead of them were the beaded lights along the Avenue du Parc Royal.

Campbell's monotone had hardly varied or diverged, except to react to other vehicles or his own fears. The traffic was heavier, with trucks making for the port and its ocean-going ships. What she was recording seemed no more real, and offered no more excitement, than a description of a book he had read. Somehow, they were not things that had actually happened, his dead voice insinuated. Perhaps he could only deal with it by making the whole account sound like a police statement in a courtroom; dry, matter-of-fact, uninflected, monotonous —

'Look out!' she cried, her throat tight, eyes

wide. 'Ben, for God's sake, *look out — !*'

She heard the metal of the car begin to scream. Saw Campbell's terrified, betrayed face turn to her as the shadow of the truck blotted out all light, all other movement. She felt the passenger door torn off and the impact of her body with —

'There . . . what did I tell you?' Blakey breathed, as if he had been present at the birth of his first child.

After a moment, Gant murmured: 'Surf's up.' Blakey chuckled in his beard.

The relief map that Blakey had produced on the computer, the guessworked map of the snapshot's scenery, had been transferred to a transparency. It lay over the printout from the CD-ROM atlas that Blakey had chosen. Layers of geological strata, pages of a book. The relief map was almost a perfect twin of the atlas layout . . . the Three Sisters Wilderness Area, Oregon.

'This lake's called' — Blakey raised his glasses away from his eyes — 'Bonner Lake. A couple of miles south of South Sister, right between that peak and Mount Bachelor.' He let his breath whistle out between his teeth, as if someone else had performed the magical trick that had made the guess and the atlas match. Gant gripped Blakey's shoulder, the tremor of his hand displaying his excitement.

'The snapshot is looking north, so . . .' Gant said, studying the map by peeling away the transparency, '. . . this place is Squaw Camp.'

'Tourist season place. Just a collection of necessary stores and accommodation. Strickland — if he's there — probably has a lodge somewhere in the woods.'

'It would suit him.' Gant remembered the farmhouse in the Dordogne, its isolation, the sufficient proximity of the small village. Another tourist area. Strickland would be away off the backroads somewhere, a couple of miles or more from Squaw Camp —

— telephone. He needed a telephone, fax, computer link. *To run his business.*

'Ron, you got the telephone directory on computer?'

Blakey grinned.

'You'd better believe it. Oregon, right? Coming right up, sir!' He almost ran towards the keyboard.

Barbara came back into the room, carrying a tray with three coffee mugs on it, sugar and milk.

'What is it?' Her features struggled with disbelief, as if ashamed of her conscious choice of scepticism.

'Oregon. Strickland's in Oregon,' Gant said, taking a coffee, sipping at it.

'Where? Three Sisters . . .' She sounded as if she had become lost in the Wilderness Area, plunged into some forest.

'What is it?'

'I went there once, on summer camp. I was just a kid. Alan sent me there when Momma died —' Her hand flailed at his movement of sympathy, and he retreated carefully. She shook her head violently. 'I'm sorry. Just surprised me — the name, the place.' She sniffed and looked up, brightly dry-eyed. 'Is he there — really there? *Now?*'

'I think so —'

'You could be wrong, Mitchell. There's no Strickland listed,' Blakey called out.

'It's no surprise,' Gant murmured, apparently without any real sense of disappointment. 'But it was worth trying. His number's unlisted.'

Blakey tugged at his beard.

'If it is, then no one's going to give it out.'

'Then I'll have to go up there and *find* him, won't I?'

To Barbara, he seemed suddenly filled with a nervous energy he could not expel. Then his demanding eyes turned to her. 'You must have something on the plant that I can fly up to Oregon? To save time?'

'There's . . . ? Ron?' His demand angered her. 'For Christ's sake, Mitchell, we're bankrupt and now you want an air-taxi?'

'There's the Vance Executive you used to fly the chief around in,' Blakey offered apologetically. He was, Barbara realised apologising for his continued enthusiasm.

'Then call in a crew and get it ready, Barbara.' It sounded like a threat.

'*Your* priorities — !'

'Look, Barbara — it might take me days, a whole week, to locate this guy.' His attempt at mollification was amateurish, unpractised. 'I need to get up there by the quickest means. I don't think I should take too many more civilian flights. Do you?' His features and his voice had altered. Reflection had shown him his own danger, flagged the FBI wanted posters in front of his eyes.

'OK, OK,' she grumblingly agreed, as if they were enacting yet another of their interminable domestic squabbles. She brushed her hair away from her face. 'I'll get to it. Take *care* of the airplane!'

She moved away from them towards a telephone. Blakey shrugged conspiratorially with Gant, who waggled his hand. Then he rubbed at his worn eyes. It *would* take a week, maybe more, combing the Three Sisters area, all of it wilderness, sparsely populated, poor roads, mountainous . . . Even then, he might never find Strickland, especially if the guy was living there under another name . . .

'Aliases,' he said. Barbara was speaking into the telephone, obsessively businesslike, demanding in her own way. 'Strickland had aliases, maybe four or five . . .' He held his temples in his hands, applying pressure. 'When I ran into him he was called . . . ?'

Barbara watched him retreat into an intense abstraction, trying to remember. All too often during their brief marriage when he had employed the same posture it had seemed more like absenting himself from their situation, a protective, defensive stance.

'Yes, Bill,' she said into the telephone. 'It *is* urgent — yes, the men will be paid a bonus . . . Thanks, Bill. A half-hour? Good.' She put down the telephone and turned again to watch Gant. His face was chalky with the effort of recollection.

'He had various OpNames like *Preacherman*,

Mechanic — *Fireball* was another one —' He clicked his fingers impatiently, as at some invisible waiter. 'His codenames . . .' He reached for a notepad, scrabbled for a pencil. Scribbled furiously, shaking his head, roughly scrubbing out whatever he was writing.

Barbara wandered towards Blakey, as if choosing his more comfortable, bearlike appearance. She stared casually at the printout of the Oregon map, and at the hugely enlarged sky and the man's forehead and eyes beneath it. Strickland seemed as distant as any stranger in other people's snapshots.

'Try this — !' Gant offered urgently. 'It's one of his names, I'm sure . . . then this one.' The pencil tapped on the pad like insistent morse.

'Christianson,' Blakey murmured. 'Ford —'

'They're based around *Preacherman* and *Mechanic.*'

'OK — let's see.'

At the command of Blakey's blunt, quick fingers, the telephone directory for Central Oregon scrolled up the computer's screen, the Cs flicking past as casually as an eye might glance across the columns of names of some war memorial . . . The Christiansons, dozens of them. Blakey slowed the movement to the speed of movie credits.

'No initial, given name?' he asked.

Gant shook his head, as if to loosen the tension that Barbara was feeling as they pressed at Blakey's shoulders, staring at the screen.

'I don't recall —'

Blakey glanced quickly, repeatedly between map and screen, checking unfamiliar names, ignoring the towns like Bend, Redmond, Oakwood . . . Eventually, shaking his head, he set the screen in flickering motion once more. Then slowed it as *Ford* appeared. The list moved as sluggishly as diesel in the Arctic. *A. Ford . . . Arthur J. Ford . . . Bob Ford.* Eventually, the screen became still, frozen. *Peter Ford, Sun Bear Lodge, Squaw Camp, Three Sisters . . .*

'Well?' Blakey asked very softly.

Barbara listened to Gant's breathing. It was like that of a tense, roused animal. Blakey's face expressed the pain he must have been experiencing from the ferocity of Gant's grip on his shoulder as he stared at the screen. Blakey had isolated the name and address, so that it sat enlarged in the dead centre of the otherwise empty screen.

Eventually, Gant nodded.

'It's him. Hello, Strickland — *hello*.'

CHAPTER FOURTEEN

Flight and Rest

He sat in the swivel chair that had been Vance's, his back to the large desk, watching the dawn begin to leak into the desert sky and dim the stars. The scratch ground crew that Barbara had gotten out of bed were almost finished now. He was just waiting for the ground engineer to call him down to the hangar. The ship was fuelled and had the range to reach Bend, Oregon, without landing. His flight plan had been filed in the name of the pilot who had taken over his job after he resigned; the guy who had flown Barbara back from Oslo after Alan died.

When the phone on the desk rang, he swivelled round in the chair and picked up the receiver.

'Mitchell? We're through down here. You want to take our baby for a drive? We can talk about the monthly repayment plan and the insurance . . . ?' The humour was tired but refreshing.

'OK, Bill — just give me a minute.' Barbara

had been at the edge of eyesight when he picked up the phone. She was still there as he replaced the receiver. He shrugged at her in a way that he hoped would discourage talk. 'They're ready . . .'

She was poised like a rain cloud near the door of the executive suite.

'Time to go,' she replied. He felt her press against his temples like an ache.

She seemed reluctant to let him go, not out of anything that resembled affection, but as if she would be adrift once they parted.

'Try to bring my airplane back in one piece, uh?'

He sensed a twisted well-wishing beneath the bluntness.

'OK. You need it to fly to DC next week.' He grinned. She was subpoenaed to appear before the Senate Committee that was continuing its investigation of the affairs of Vance Aircraft, despite Alan's death and the company's collapse. Whatever scams and frauds he had perpetrated weren't going to be allowed to die with him. There seemed a Federal vengefulness towards Vance much like that of McIntyre towards himself. *You stepped out of line, now you take the consequences,* that kind of thing. Just one of the recurrent bouts of malarial righteousness they suffered on Capitol Hill. Screw them. It was all mostly irrelevant now, as far as Vance Aircraft was concerned — just another shovelful of earth on the company's coffin.

He turned away to stare out of the windows. The dawn was purple along the horizon, the first crags and outcrops coming back to silhouetted life.

'Will you be able to find him? *If* you find him, can you —' Looking at the back of his head, his set shoulders, she remembered that he meant only to kill Strickland, not bring him back. 'For God's sake, Mitchell — !' she was impelled by desperation to shout at his back. His shoulders flinched. '*Help* me! God, I *need* the sympathy vote his confession would give me!' She could say no more. It hurt so much to have uttered the words at all.

Gant remained watching the slow seepage of the day, the first faint outlining of a small cloud with pink against a blue-black sky. He could begin to pick out the hanged-men silhouettes of cactuses beyond the perimeter fence. The taxiways and the main runway were the slightest difference of shading from the desert sand. He imagined a flicker of light for an instant, out beyond a clump of rocks. His chest felt tight, his shoulders cramped with too many muscles. Then he exhaled noisily.

'OK, Barbara — OK. I promise I'll try and get him back alive.' He sighed with what might have been disappointment, a sense of having been disinherited. 'I — promise.'

He sensed her about to say something else, then was aware, through his tense shoulders, that she had gone and the door had closed behind her.

Out beyond the fence, there was another glint, like that of sunlight on a piece of mica. Flickering like a signal. There was someone out there, he realised. He stood up awkwardly, quickly, and grabbed up the rucksack and the other equipment from the sofa. He had to hurry.

Fraser sat across the aisle of the Learjet from McIntyre, his sense of being an unwelcome travelling companion undiminished by the hours of the flight. The FBI agent regarded him with a hostile suspicion that seemed to increase in proportion to the crumbling of his professional loyalties. Fraser was adept at patient silence and was prepared to wait McIntyre out. Gant lay ahead of them, and Fraser was almost certain that Strickland was tied to Gant by an invisible thread. He was sure that McIntyre knew Strickland well enough to be able to locate him. That was information that would have to be bought . . . McIntyre had not yet opened his shop for business.

The great plains over which they had flown, sprinkled with the occasional lights of cities and towns, were giving way to the western mountain ranges; that bulldozed rim of the continent beyond which lay the fantasy of California. Kansas City's lights were long behind the aircraft and Colorado loomed, together with the deserts of the south-west. Chris, McIntyre's young, naive assistant with the shining face and clear eyes, sat ahead of them, poring over maps, keeping in telephone contact with the surveillance team around the Vance Aircraft factory complex outside Phoenix. He was drinking prissily at a glass of 7-Up. Fraser was sharing McIntyre's bottle of bourbon. The cramped passenger cabin was dim-lit.

Fraser glanced through the tiny porthole beside him, back towards the first faintness of dawn which seemed in pursuit of them. Ahead of the plane, the blackness was filled with bright, frozen stars.

He realised McIntyre was studying him from beneath heavy eyebrows, his eyes narrowed, folded into the creases of flesh around them. Fraser had murmured the temptations of a large salary, a bright future . . . in exchange for Strickland, at the same time fending off McIntyre's intense curiosity regarding his prospective employer — Strickland's employer. He'd had to shrug in voiceless admission at McIntyre's realisation that both he and Gant wanted Strickland because of the two downed 494s. McIntyre's value and the price of the information he could supply had risen in moments, like some wild stock exchange barometer in response to rumours of tax cuts. McIntyre had realised his true worth.

The man smiled conspiratorially. Greed was working in him like an acid. Fraser was satisfied.

The handset in Chris' armrest warbled and the young man snatched it up. At once, his shoulders were tense with alarm and surprise, alerting McIntyre. The melting ice in his glass spilt on to his lap as he lurched upright. He picked up his own telephone as Chris gestured earnestly.

'McIntyre,' he snapped.

'Sir — we have kind of a problem here,' he heard from the surveillance team's leader.

'Tell me,' he growled.

'There's an airplane being prepared — flight checks, that kind of thing, refuell—'

'Where's Gant?' McIntyre sensed his own shortwindedness, as if he had exhausted himself in a race, only to lose at the tape. He glanced heavily across at Fraser, who continued to sip like a woman at his bourbon and feign no more than mild interest. 'Where is the *asshole!*' McIntyre bellowed.

'Sam picked him out, in the people around the airplane. He went aboard, we think —'

'Why didn't you *call* me?' This time the shockwave of his rage seemed to unsettle Fraser. Chris was staring at him over the back of his seat, his phone still pressed to his cheek, like a man watching his house burn down. It was slipping away. 'You just *watched* while all this was happening?' Spilt 7-Up from Chris' glass bubbled like acid on the aisle carpet. 'While the guy just walked on to a *plane?*'

'Sir, we couldn't be sure what was going down! You ordered us to wait for your arrival —'

'Your ass is in the fireplace, Kennedy!' The asshole even had the right name to be a genuine, made-in-America prick! 'Get in there — *now!* Arrest Gant and anyone who gets in the way!'

'Sir.' The response was pinched off by urgency and dislike.

McIntyre slammed down the handset. He *had* wanted Gant to himself, had told them to hold off until he arrived. He'd wanted to grin into the asshole hero's shocked, defeated face as he read him his rights.

He quashed the perception of his error and the momentary flush of its possible enormity as if it had been a glimpse at a foreboding X-ray plate. Then glowered at Fraser, whose features at once settled into immobility. Chris turned away. McIntyre looked out of the window.

They had to stop Gant, stop him flying out, getting away —

The Learjet seemed, to his boiling impatience, to be suspended in some geostationary orbit between night and the pursuing day. There was nothing he could do . . . They *had* to stop Gant —

For Kennedy, sweeping the binoculars across the Vance Aircraft site, there remained a moment when McIntyre's panic seemed unwarranted, even ridiculous. The morning breeze whirled dust, the runway was empty, the first windows to catch the rising sun gleamed back innocent light.

Then the nose of the small jet sniffed out of the hangar below him. Kennedy watched the airplane emerge, easing itself into the first dawn sunlight. Its movement mesmerised.

'— anyone who gets in the way!'

'Sir.'

He heard McIntyre break the connection. The sun was climbing into the wing mirror of the car against which he leant. Dazzled he flung the carphone away from him as if it burned his hand. Suddenly, the situation was slipping away from them, accelerating like the airplane below; it was fully visible now, turning on to the taxiway, making for the main runway.

A noise startled him into issuing orders. Someone shunted a round into a Bullpup shotgun close to his ear.

'Move it!' he shouted, plucking up the car intercom. 'Go, go, *go!* Biles, get *your* car down there, head him off — block the runway!'

He climbed into the passenger seat of his car as it accelerated wildly over the lip of the outcrop from which the surveillance team had watched the Vance Aircraft site for most of the previous night. The windscreen in front of his eyes seemed to possess its own urgency, joggling and eager, breaking up the landscape as if he was seeing it reflected in the broken fragments of a mirror. The two other cars followed him down the slope.

He tugged the pistol from his shoulder holster and checked it. Don, the driver, was flinging the steering wheel from side to side like a kid playing a video game in an arcade. The executive jet was sliding as smoothly as if on ice towards the main runway. It seemed to be moving in a different element from the car, with greater confidence.

The mirrors were blind with dust. The car lurched and flew for an instant as it hit the road, then Don swung the wheel viciously again to right it, the tyres screeching. It was no more than a hundred yards and a few seconds before they turned into the open main gates of the site. If he screwed up here, he knew McIntyre — a *continentally* renowned bastard — would make him pay for the rest of his career.

The other two cars skidded and lurched through the gates behind them, and immediately Biles' car peeled away, making directly for the runway. Don was heading their car towards the main administrative building.

It could all be too late —

'Head for the runway, Don!' he bellowed, changing his mind. Gant must be kept on the ground, the runway had to be blocked. The car swerved and then shimmied off the paved road on to desert sand. Ahead of them, Biles' car was streaking forward, seeming to tow behind it an impenetrable cloud of dust. Kennedy lost sight of the airplane's ghostly whiteness in the shadow of the surrounding mountains. His disappointment was as violent as if he had already seen it lift away from the ground. 'Come on, Don, for Christ's sake — !'

Had he seen it turn on to the end of the runway before the dust concealed it — ? The third car was invisible as it continued towards the office buildings. Then his car swung out of Biles' dust cloud and he saw the executive jet once more.

In the same instant, he heard McIntyre's voice again over the carphone. Kennedy pressed it to his ear and cheek as if it was the means of a self-inflicted wound.

'What's happening? Kennedy, have you stopped the airplane, dammit?'

Gant turned the executive jet on to the runway, nose pointing towards the two racing cars. Biles' sedan slewed on to the runway, maybe a little over halfway down.

'— almost!' he heard himself shouting back at McIntyre. 'We got the runway blocked *off* — he's going nowhere!'

'Make sure of that!'

'I'm making sure — dead *sure!*'

Biles had swung his car across the centre line of the runway. As the dust cleared in front of his windscreen, Kennedy saw the airplane clearly, and realised that it had begun to accelerate.

'Get across the runway!' he screamed at Don.

Biles and his driver were out of their sedan, shotguns sticking up, but their immobility suggested a growing fear rather than confidence as the executive jet roared towards them.

'Across the *runway!*' he wailed at the driver, the carphone still clamped against his cheek.

The white airplane was growing larger and outrunning them as the car seemed to move more and more slowly . . . Biles had parked *too far down the runway* . . . Then the whole scene froze for an instant, the only movement being the slow, very slow upward movement of the undercarriage . . . Then there was a lurch of acceleration and the jet screamed away and over them, the dust enveloping him and the car, Biles' car . . .

. . . Barbara saw the cloud of dust, anticipating the moment of impact between the plane and the cars. Then, as she heard *his* voice over Alan's intercom system, loud in the room, the Vance Exec lifted clear. The plane seemed to stagger with the effort of retracting its undercarriage too soon and the severe angle of take-off.

'— *up!* Jesus . . .' she heard over the intercom, the relief evident in his voice.

Then there was only his breathing and the ether. The plane winking in the lightening sky. It was as if he remained in the room with her as the plane diminished; the dangerous, somehow cornered animal she had often felt him to be. The dust settled, exposing the two stranded, purposeless cars on the runway. The plane was no bigger than a star, then it was gone.

The third car had already drawn up outside the administration block. Bill and some of the ground crew were watching the disappearing plane from the gaping doors of the hangar. Beside her, Blakey only now seemed to breathe a sigh of relief. The throat-clearing that immediately followed was more like an anticipation of problems. Barbara impulsively patted his arm.

'Had to be,' she murmured. 'Thanks, Ron.'

'Sure.'

The two cars on the runway had repossessed their occupants and had turned, like blind, squat insects, towards her and the buildings, as if they scented another source of sustenance. They accelerated in mutual frustration across the desert sand, throwing up dust that caught the sunlight and sparkled like cheap jewellery.

The plane had vanished southwards, towards the city and Mexico as if fleeing. Mitchell would turn north only when he was certain he was out of visual range. Leaving her to answer their bullying questions, confront their anger . . . even face arrest for assisting a fugitive from justice.

As the strange elation of his escape subsided, she recognised her own situation, for the first time. The other two cars joined their companion below her window. *She* was the one left hanging out to dry.

The phone rang on the desk and she snatched it up.

'Honey?' It was Tom, her husband.

'Yes?' She could not keep the impatience from her voice, and he was at once brittle and defensive.

'When are you coming home, Barbara — or do *I* have to wait until the babysitter gets here? I have to meet important *clients* today!' Even the emphasis of his unpractised anger was wrong. She hated the cold judgement she made of him.

'I'm sorry, Tom, I may be tied up here for some time yet —'

The men getting out of the cars below the window were grim-faced with failure.

'That's not helpful, Barbara —'

'For God's sake!' she almost screamed. Blaming Mitchell now, almost entirely. 'I'm busy, Tom — OK? I can't just drop things!'

'OK, OK — just be as quick as you can, uh? I'll try and reschedule —'

The intercom buzzed.

'I have to go. Sorry . . .'

She put down the phone and answered the intercom. It was Bill, the ground engineer.

'The FBI, Ms Vance. They want to talk to you . . .' The embers of self-congratulation still smouldered in Bill's even tones.

'Right. Send them up, Bill.'

'You want me to stay?'

She glanced around the room, shaking her head.

'No, Ron. Just take all the stuff you did for him, and shred it. Don't let them find it.'

Blakey nodded and left the room. As Barbara sat down in Alan's swivel chair, she glimpsed the moon, hanging by forgetfulness above the desert in a pale-blue sky. Carefully, she posed herself behind the large, impressive desk, the daylit window behind her.

She feared she would have to tell them, eventually. She did not want *them* sitting on her, along with everyone else. Mitchell would know that, it wouldn't be a betrayal of any kind . . . Guilt bubbled, but subsided as someone knocked at the door.

'Come in,' she called, her voice calm.

'Put her on the line,' McIntyre snapped.

The early-morning New Mexico sun glared from the terminal building windows of Albuquerque's airport and the scent of aviation fuel was heavy on the air coming through the open door of the aircraft. Four or five miles away, the towers of the city huddled on bottom-land that, at that distance, appeared as arid as the airport's immediate surroundings. From the window beside Fraser's seat on the other side of the aisle, he could see dark-treed mountains thrusting up into an already leached sky. As he waited, he could hear the rush of fuel into the tanks from the bowser parked beside the airplane.

As McIntyre gripped the receiver, his hand was clammy with tension rather than perspiration. His free hand clenched and unclenched in a fury of disappointment.

'Yes — who is this?' he heard. Fraser's smirk, as he listened on his own handset, infuriated. Gant's wife, trying to tough it out. She knew the flight plan — had to — but it didn't matter whether or not she told him. Kennedy was checking it out. He wanted to bruise her. He owed her some fear.

'Special Agent McIntyre, Mrs Gant,' he ground out.

'My name is Barbara Vance,' she replied, her

voice tiredly challenging.

'Vance — Gant, I'm not interested!' he growled. Chris' head and shoulders appeared in the doorway, blotting out the glare of concrete, but the young man ducked back as their eyes met. 'It's not you I want, lady — it's the guy you used to be married to. You've aided and abetted a fugitive from justice. I could — and I will — bring charges.' The threat was heavy in the morning. 'You're in enough trouble as it is, Barbara *Vance*.'

Her intaken breath was a source of immediate, sharp pleasure, as if he had aroused her.

'Why do you find it necessary to threaten me, Agent McIntyre?' she managed. 'Is threat what you get off on?' Fraser snickered in the seat opposite.

'Don't make me really angry, lady. I just want *him*. You don't count — but I can still make things bad for you. So *cooperate*. Tell me his flight plan.'

McIntyre glanced at his watch. It didn't have the right to be this hot before eight in the morning. Already, the hills seemed masked by a smog of heat and to have retreated to a greater distance. The terminal building was a single great mirror.

He listened to her silence which reminded him of a machine making noiseless but tangible and important calculations. Then he added: 'Listen to me, Ms Vance. I only have to instruct my agents who are with you, and I can have you arrested for harbouring a fugitive *right now*. But you realise that, I guess?'

The silence continued. Then, with a sigh of

admission, the woman answered him.

'OK, you can make trouble for me, Agent McIntyre. And I don't need any more problems right now. Mitchell is flying to Oregon, to the airfield at Redmond —'

He covered the mouthpiece of the receiver and gestured violently at the maps that lay unfolded on Chris' empty seat. Fraser moved, collected them and smoothed them out on his seat's folding table, which he jutted out into the aisle. McIntyre tugged on his half-glasses.

'Why Oregon?' he asked.

For a moment, Fraser appeared both disappointed and on the point of asking him a question of his own.

'I — I'm not sure,' Barbara replied. 'He didn't confide in me — just borrowed the executive jet.'

'How long will it take him to fly up there?'

'Most of the morning.'

McIntyre clicked his fingers impatiently at Fraser, who opened a map of the north-western states and awkwardly tried to adjoin it to the one already spread out. McIntyre studied the distances voraciously, as if discovering a quarry's spoor.

'Why did you agree to loan him your jet, Barbara? You knew the situation —'

'Like you said, McIntyre — I used to be married to the guy. He deserved a break.'

'The last one he's going to get, Barbara.' He grinned at Fraser. 'Put my man Kennedy back on the line. You showed good sense —' He realised that she had already gone, heard the murmur of her voice as she summoned Kennedy. 'Fraser — call Chris and the pilot in here.' Then: 'Kennedy, you hear that? What's the confirmation on the flight plan?'

'We're still checking —'

'Five minutes is all you've got. Move ass —' He looked up from the map as a shadow fell across it. The pilot's shirt was already damp beneath his arms from the morning heat. 'Can we fly all the way up to Oregon from here without another refuelling?'

'Where in Oregon, sir?'

'Redmond.'

'Sure.'

'So, he won't have to refuel, either.' His thick fingers made leaping, attacking movements on the map. 'How much longer before we can take off?'

'You want a change of flight plan — maybe thirty minutes.'

'Cut that time in half.'

'Is he headed for Oregon?' Chris asked with due deference.

'Kennedy will confirm that in a couple of minutes. If he is, then that's where we need to be.'

'Why Oregon?' Fraser asked.

'How should I know — the guy's running scared.'

'I don't think so, Mac. And neither do you.'

McIntyre shrugged. Looking up at the pilot, he said: 'Get that new flight plan logged. I'll confirm when I hear from Phoenix.' He grinned. 'The schmuck is running and we're right behind him. He's an hour ahead — can we make that up?'

'We won't drop behind him. Depends what he's flying,' the pilot answered from the doorway of the flight deck.

'Vance's personal jet.'
'A Vance Executive is slower than this baby. We can maybe cut thirty minutes off his lead —'
'OK, let's get out of here as fast as we can.'
As Chris moved away, Fraser whispered urgently:
'Think, Mac — for God's sake, *think*. Why is Gant so interested in Oregon? Is Strickland in Oregon?'
'I don't know, Fraser — but Gant's on his way there, and that's who *I* want!'

'Sure,' Gant murmured into the receiver. 'No, you did right to protect yourself. It's OK, I *understand.*' I counted on it, he added to himself.
Two hours into the flight, she had called via SELCAL. Like picking up the phone. Vance's personal jet had had that facility installed. Satellite phone links to the entire planet. He had wondered whether she would call and now felt a tinge of guilt that he had doubted her. She would have had to inform the FBI, and he had known they would check his flight plan — it couldn't have been kept secret.
'Thanks,' she murmured, as intimately as if she had been seated in the co-pilot's chair. 'What will you do?' There was an urgent, demanding interest in her voice.
'You don't need to know, Barbara.'
'I have to go — it's difficult.'
'OK.'
'Good luck.'
'Yes.'
He closed the channel, recognising as he did

so the strange intimacy of their conversation.

Thirty thousand feet below the aircraft, northern California was beginning to lurch mountainously upwards. The peaks of the Sierra Nevada were to starboard, the Pacific too distant to port to recognise other than as an emptiness as large as the sky.

What will you do?

The question had plagued him for more than an hour after the draining tension of the violent take-off from Vance Aircraft. For a long time he hadn't been able to concentrate, had been incapable of making any decisions. He had turned, whole minutes after he should, on to his northern heading, passing west of Phoenix . . . crossing the Grand Canyon, lifting over the Sierra Nevada before the solution had come to him.

He couldn't land at Redmond, unless he wanted the FBI to arrest him moments after touchdown. If he declared a fake Mayday and diverted, he would reveal his eventual destination as surely as if he phoned McIntyre to tell him. He needed somewhere to land and hide the airplane . . . somewhere secret. Somewhere within driving distance of Three Sisters and Strickland.

McIntyre was at Albuquerque — had probably taken off by now, and was maybe only an hour or so behind him. McIntyre could land at Redmond, just fifty road minutes from Squaw Camp and Strickland . . . The certainty that they would be there ahead of him narrowed the perspective of choice until it was a tunnel with no light at the end of it.

Los Angeles had been a sprawl to starboard,

then the Sierra Nevada and the Coastal Range had formed the high perimeters of his flight path. Somewhere amid the northern straggle of LA had been Burbank, masked in a morning haze. It had been ten minutes of flying time before the hazy recollection of the Skunk Works and the secret planes he had helped test for Lockheed reminded him. The flight path he was following he had flown before, tagging on behind commercial flights or flying above and below the commercial airways in ugly black Stealth airplanes, testing their radar invisibility. North from Los Angeles towards San Francisco and Oakland, then across northern California and southern Oregon to . . .

. . . *Warner Lakes AFB.* Long closed and *abandoned.* One of the airforce's secret facilities, linked to test flights of machines manufactured in the Skunk Works.

He hadn't needed the map. The topography and the distances had unrolled in his head like something on a Stealth fighter's navigational screens. It was tucked into the south-east corner of the state, amid salt lakes. It was *nowhere.* He had grinned, phrasing it like that. Some comic based there had once erected a crude road sign beside the one that declared the identity of the airforce base — *Fort Nowhere.*

It would take him hours by road from Warner Lakes — *after* he had found a vehicle to hire or steal. But the Exec would be hidden and he would be lost. It was the only option — even though it meant he wouldn't reach Strickland until late afternoon, and McIntyre would be waiting for him.

It was too late now. He had already initiated the deception. On leaving LA Centre's control boundary and before he contacted Oakland Centre, he had faked poor radio transmission. When he tried to contact Oakland, the problem appeared to have worsened.

All he was doing was switching rapidly between the two radios, Box One and Box Two. It reduced his transmissions to interrupted phrases, broken contact. For the ground centres, it would appear that he had a real problem . . . one serious enough to have him diverted off the airways, drop his altitude, head for wherever they suggested he land.

He had entered the Warner Lakes coordinates into the inertial navigation system of the Vance Exec. He opened the channel.

'Oakland Centre — Victor Bravo. Are you receiving me any clearer?' he enquired, flicking the transfer switch from one radio to the other.

He had to disappear —

The Learjet lifted into the New Mexico morning sky, swinging out over the suddenly small city below, then across the narrow blue strip of the Rio Grande. McIntyre's fingers, like those of a miser counting coins, pudged their measured way across the map, tracing their flight path. Fraser glanced at his watch. Five past nine. Flying time to Redmond, two hours fifty minutes.

Fraser was careful to conceal the smile that so insistently folded the corners of his mouth. The bribes had worked even more easily than he had promised Winterborne they would.

A golden hello, the title of vice-president in charge of company security, the health care and pension schemes, the promises of frequent bonuses . . . He had agreed to everything, and had managed a stubborn, almost pained submission on his face when he'd said: *OK, forty thousand down immediately* . . .

Fraser had realised, even as McIntyre had been speaking to Gant's ex-wife, that the man knew why Gant was heading for Oregon and who he expected to find there. He had asked for the alias, the location, and McIntyre had immediately held them to his chest like high cards. They had negotiated in whispers for ten minutes. The price was a great deal below what Fraser had been prepared to pay.

McIntyre had visited Strickland in Oregon once, years before, while he was still his CIA Case Officer. Strickland's hideout, not unlike the farmhouse in the Dordogne, was a lodge on a hillside. The place overlooked a lake — *Bonner Lake,* McIntyre had pretended to remember with great difficulty. He eventually recalled Strickland's alias was *Peter Ford.*

Firm up the offer, make it real, McIntyre had said. Fraser had done so. End of story. They'd get Gant and Strickland together, two birds with one stone. The price made it an excellent bargain.

McIntyre looked up at him and Fraser adopted a warm smile.

The Santa Fé National Forest was below them, the shining ribbon of the river gleaming amid the darkness of trees.

Strickland and Gant . . . His own bonus, from

a grateful Winterborne, would also be substantial. More than the forty thousand McIntyre wanted up front, a lot more . . .

From Warner Lakes AFB, where he had left the Exec abandoned in the shadow of a dilapidated hangar block, it had taken him two hours of walking in the morning heat to reach the few scattered dwellings of Plush, under Hart Mountain's western escarpment. There had been no vehicle for hire, but a young mother, with two bored and restless children in the rear of her people carrier, had offered him a ride into Lakeview. She had spoken of it as some kind of metropolis. Gant knew it slightly from his air force days when he had been flying in and out of Warner Lakes.

It was a government agency town of maybe two and a half thousand people, dusty and bleached despite the Federal money. The Forest Service, the Department of Fish and Wildlife, the Bureau of Land Management all had regional headquarters in Lakeview. The town had a movie-house and no cable TV. It was the place he was born — at least, the mirror-image of Clarkville, Iowa; but he no longer hated such places.

The young woman — her name was Betty and she had been unfailingly cheerful in the face of his own taciturnity — dropped him in the town and headed with an aura of delighted anticipation, towards the market. He had thanked her, and hefted Alan Vance's rifle in its hunting case on to his shoulder and pulled his rucksack from the rear of the vehicle. As he did so, one of the children, the boy, had stuck out his tongue at him.

Another hour had gotten him a four-wheel drive, a sheaf of maps, supplies and a rancher's soft hat against the day's glare and heat. He left Lakeview, diminishing in the driving mirror as if it was slowly drowning in the pale, oceanic air, and headed north on US 395, towards Riley and the junction with US 20, which would take him north-west to Bend and Three Sisters. As the town disappeared behind him, it was eleven in the morning. He had almost two hundred and fifty miles between himself and Strickland. McIntyre would be no more than an hour away from his quarry.

He accelerated, making the rear-view mirror blind with dust, even though there was no possibility he could reach Strickland before McIntyre.

It was difficult, almost as if he had regressed to early childhood, to make meaning from the hands of the big, white-faced clock high on the wall of the hospital corridor. Nine-fifteen . . . ? Yes, a quarter past nine on the evening following the night Campbell had been killed in a car accident at the junction of the Avenue de la Reine and the Rue Marie-Christine. The night Marian had *almost* been killed —

Aubrey paused in his futile meandering beside the immobile, carved figure of Giles Pyott. His liver-spotted hand ceased its movement towards his friend's slumped shoulder, then regained the comfort of its companion. His hands clasped each other behind his back, as if he were posed to inspect the hospital. Two passing nuns, one carrying a bedpan under a white cloth as carefully as a relic, moved away down the corridor as if mounted on castors, their habits rustling, the faint click of rosary beads excited by their movement.

That Marian was alive, even though sedated, seemed to mean little to either of them. Their mutual terrors for her had exhausted both old men, from the first telephone calls to the taxis, Heathrow, the Belgian taxis, the warmth of the hospital. They had passed most of the day there, without eating, drinking coffee only occasionally, without much conversation. The X-rays and the soothing, accented English of the doctor had fallen heavy as blows, but on numbed senses.

A policeman — a senior officer very evidently aware of their mutual, past authority — had described what his people understood of the *accident.* Of which there was no doubt, of course . . .

Marian had not been wearing her seatbelt as the truck had ploughed into the driver's side of the BMW — *into* Campbell, buckling him even more easily than the door pillar, shattering him more easily than the side windows. At the moment of impact, Marian had been attempting to open her door and get out of the car. A white van had torn aside the door like a flimsy curtain and flung Marian over its bonnet, bull-like, towards the pavement . . . And shift-workers on their way home had crowded round her still form in a panicked, shocked instant — and had saved her life, Aubrey had no doubt whatever.

Neither of the drivers involved had fled the scene. With supreme confidence and great innocence, their stunned recollections agreed with one another. Campbell had jumped the lights, making the collision unavoidable. The pedestrians had been unaware until the noise and the moment of impact, *they could not say, m'sieur . . . it is true the lights had only just changed, and people do not notice until their attention is attracted . . . you understand?*

Aubrey had given up at that point; quietened an enraged Giles and allowed the senior policeman to go his way. Four witnesses, the two drivers and two people in a car, had sworn it was nothing but a tragic accident, and they had not been contradicted. It would remain an accident. A young man from the British embassy had appeared some time in the early afternoon, but the enquiry he bore was unsolicitous and prompted by Central Office and the Party Chairman. *Would Marian have recovered sufficiently to vote in the House next week under a three-line Whip?* Giles' dismissal of the man would have abashed any of his old RSMs. After which outburst, his friend had sunk into a lethargy that would have suggested the numbness of bereavement to anyone passing him in the corridor.

Aubrey realised how much Marian was loved. Her accident, however traumatic for himself, had been as appalling as her death to Giles.

Aubrey cleared his throat softly. His mouth was dry. A small, pert Madonna observed him from a wall-niche. She might have aided Giles, had Marian died — Giles' faith was cloudy but persistent — but not himself. He heard a door open, but it was not Marian's room. His chest seemed to slump lethargically once more. Giles had not stirred.

Marian had sustained a broken arm, a broken pelvis and leg. A wound in her side had bled copiously, she had lost a great deal of blood before it was staunched in the ambulance. Three cracked ribs, bruising to most of her body, severe trauma. Scalp wounds, other serious abrasions. A brain scan had been carried out. Thankfully, there seemed nothing other than the concussion. Aubrey suppressed a shudder . . . a damned close-run thing. *Too* close —

The tired anger was dismissed by the door of Marian's room opening. Giles at once looked up as the diminutive nun who was the hospital's chief surgeon came towards them, her habit rustling like a drift of leaves. Giles stood up stiffly, towering over the doctor's slightness. His face remained ashen. The proud, bluff widower did not live his life through his child; she was, however as much his life as she was her own.

'You will try, as her father — and her friend — not to disturb my patient.' It was not a question. Giles still appeared as if he were about to be asked to accompany the sister to the hospital mortuary. 'You may stay with her for five' — something in his expression touched her — 'no more than ten minutes. I insist. She must not be agitated —'

Giles' voice broke through his numbness like a thaw. 'She — she will be alright, *now?* You have no reason to change your earlier assessment?'

The doctor shook her head. A small, serious face framed by her wimple. 'No. Her recovery will take a great deal of time. She must not be *pressured* into denying the seriousness of her accident.' The young man from the embassy had sought reassurance that Marian's was a very temporary indisposition. The surgeon had banished his insouciance as witheringly as if by excommunication.

'We understand, Doctor,' Aubrey murmured, smiling. 'May we — ?' She nodded.

He took Giles' elbow and steered him towards the door, as if through a tight crowd of people. The doctor accompanied them, then allowed them to falter across the threshold.

Her head was bandaged. Her face was the colour of putty in places, raw liver in others. Her arm was in plaster, a tent of raised bedclothes was over her lower body. Her eyes were preternaturally bright. Aubrey's smile faltered like an old bulb, then flickered on once more. He gently thrust Giles towards the bed, on her free hand's side. It was lightly bandaged, badly scuffed like a worn shoe.

'Daddy —' she muttered thickly, as if her tongue had swollen.

'Oh, *Tig — !*'

Aubrey moved to the slatted blinds across the single window of the small, bright, warm room. The noise of tears did not distress him. It was politeness that moved him, the priorities of intimacy between father and daughter.

In a few moments, sniffing loudly, she said:

'Hello, Kenneth. Brought any grapes?'

He turned, chuckling, his eyes pricking. He shook his head. 'The shops were closed.'

She winced as she blew out her cheeks in exaggerated, comic relief.

Giles blew his nose unselfconsciously loud. His eyes were damp and fierce, his mouth and jaw quivering with reaction. 'Are you alright, dear?' he asked.

'Hurts like hell — everywhere,' she replied. Her eyes glazed, perhaps remembering Campbell. *'God . . .'* she breathed.

Giles' old hand lay on hers, still twice its size, even though Marion's was padded with gauze. It was the light, careful grip of a boy who had caught a butterfly.

'He —' she began, then: 'Tape recorder . . . You'll need that, Kenneth —' She was tiring already, and he saw Giles resented his presence. He came between Giles' relief and a desired innocence. *Accident* without design. It would remove her from further danger.

Aubrey took from his pocket the list of Marian's personal effects that had been given him by the senior police officer. A second list described the contents of the car, Campbell's possessions. He scanned them, sensing his own lack of breathing, his utter stillness in the warm room. Eventually he nodded, then crossed towards the utilitarian cabinet in a corner of the room.

'Ben' — Marian swallowed painfully — 'confessed. The fraud — David's part in it.' Almost at once, she was half-asleep.

Aubrey rummaged in the black plastic bag in which Marian's possessions had been returned to her. Pulled out the tiny tape recorder and turned to Giles in triumph. Pyott's expression was one of foreboding; then he became angry with Aubrey.

'Your confounded *curiosity,* Kenneth,' he growled.

'Is this it, my dear?' Aubrey urged, moving close to the bed.

Her eyes fluttered open.

'Kenneth,' Giles warned.

'That's — it . . .' Marian managed. She smiled briefly, as if someone had told her she had passed an examination. Then, in another moment, she was asleep.

Aubrey, despite Giles Pyott's irascible expression, switched on the tiny recorder. A youngish male voice, Campbell for sure . . . speaking from the mortuary.

'. . . the decision was David's, the *planning* was his . . . He needed people like me, Laxton — he called us the European connection — to shuffle the cheques from one envelope to another . . .' The voice was heavy with fear.

Aubrey continued to listen until Campbell's voice died away and there was a long, hissing tape noise which masked the small, distant noises of traffic. Realising the calm before the storm, he stopped the tape running.

Giles' hand gripped his wrist, the fingers of his other hand snatching the recorder from Aubrey's grasp. Angrily, his eyes glowering, he switched on the recorder.

'Look out! Ben, for God's sake, *look out — !*'

Then the screaming of the car's metal as the undoubtedly arranged accident occurred. Only then was the tape silent.

Giles looked up at him after staring at Marian for a long moment. His face was ashen, his eyes like last hot coals.

'Did he — ?' he began, but his voice failed almost immediately, like a poor and distant radio signal.

'David?' Aubrey nodded gravely. 'Oh, yes, Giles — he *did.*'

Giles had returned his hand to his daughter's, and pressed it ever more protectively.

'She's safe now, old friend. I promise you. David thinks he has closed the last gate behind him. He must be feeling secure. Until I confront him with this . . .'

Aubrey turned away from the bed. There would be nothing on the tape concerning the sabotage. Campbell wouldn't have known about it. David may have trusted people like Fraser, but never Campbell with that kind of knowledge. But . . .

David had to pay the entire price.

It was as if he had written it on the wall of the room in huge black letters. For Marian's injuries, for Vance's ruin, for fifty and more deaths, David must pay in full. They had to prove the sabotage against him, not simply the fraud.

There had been no word from Gant. He was still out there, somewhere, like a perturbed spirit in pursuit of Strickland. He *had* to find him. For fraud, David might receive a token sentence — if he went to prison at all. Everyone, including most of the Cabinet and the European Commission, would want *no fuss,* would rather there was no evidence at all against David. Murder, however, they could neither excuse nor bury.

He turned to glance once more at Marian, pale as death, symbolising how close she had come to her demise. Mitchell, he thought, as if attempting some kind of telepathic contact . . . *find me the proof.*

Otherwise, David might yet slip through their hands. Marian would be safe, of course — but David would, in all probability, just be reprimanded for fraud; he would be *damned* only for murder . . .

Was Gant even alive — ? The thought chilled him.

'Strickland, this is beautiful,' McIntyre said. The man's hand was heavily, unreassuringly on his shoulder for a moment, then he retreated to the armchair that had been dragged out of the sightlines of the two windows of the room. The enthusiastic, ingratiating tone of his voice had been denied by the greedy stare of his eyes.

'A man has a right to protect himself, Mac. Even a duty,' he replied studiedly.

'You take your duty seriously, Strickland.' That was Fraser, who was more subtle and deliberate in his mockery. The ambient music that seeped from the speakers like an anaesthetic gas seemed to have no dulling effect on their anticipatory malevolence.

The electronic surveillance had been disarmed when the FBI arrived. He'd been in the bedroom, packing for Vancouver the next day. Their guns had been drawn as he opened the door of the lodge, while his was still concealed behind his back, not wanting to cause alarm to a neighbour. McIntyre and Fraser had arrived in the early afternoon, with the bustle of businessmen after a long flight. There were now a half-dozen of them in and surrounding the lodge.

The lights of the den made it full dark outside. Only he was visible from the windows — to Gant, who they promised with malicious humour was coming. He sat before the surveillance console and its bank of monitors and screens. They wanted Gant to see him alone. From scraps of their conversation, Gant must know they had beaten him here — his airplane had disappeared from radar. He'd been forewarned.

They promised him protection from Gant, assuring him that Gant wanted to kill him . . . as they did. Fraser was there as if deputised, but it must be he who was leading the parade. McIntyre's pension could go up in pieces — he, Strickland, held the grenade — because of the things they'd gotten away with in Latin America in the eighties. McIntyre had to let Fraser run the show.

Strickland swallowed carefully. His mouth and throat were dry as he watched the screens. The low-light TV cameras showed him the small clearing, the grey-washed trees, the flicker of a big owl between branches, the movements one of them made as he patrolled. But not Gant — not yet. The ground-level radar he had installed swept its arm across the screen. Most evenings, it revealed the presence of bears, the occasional dog or cat, the quicker blips of nightbirds.

He realised the very sophistication and thoroughness of the electronic surveillance would be his downfall. There was no way Gant could penetrate it undetected. They knew that. The two armed men outside were surplus. Gant would appear on the TV monitors, the radar, and wouldn't be able to get to him. Strickland knew Gant was his only chance. Maybe he didn't want him dead, at least not right away. Perhaps he wanted proof, a confession. A gap of time in which Strickland might turn the tables, kill Gant. Not like Fraser and McIntyre. He was absolutely certain of their desire to eliminate him.

The bear lumbered away on the TV, remaining a shadow on the radar. The clearing was empty, the trees, massing like an army around the lodge, were a grey fence. McIntyre scratched at his stubble. Fraser — he listened intently, to be certain — had begun checking his pistol. In anticipation.

CHAPTER FIFTEEN

Night Action

Now, he was certain. The night-vision glasses wearied his eyes, the single, cameralike lens heavy in his grip. But he was certain. Low-light TV cameras fenced the clearing around Strickland's lodge, moving slowly but ceaselessly, able to pick up anything that might come out of the surrounding forest.

He put down the binoculars and was shocked by the darkness. He could only make out a thin, last glow on the western horizon, with the closest of the mountains, South Sister, a ghostly snow-glow to the north.

The electronic surveillance was as he had anticipated. Strickland protected himself as naturally as an animal; his claws and teeth were TV cameras and radar. He returned the binoculars to his eyes. Maybe he didn't always use it, but it was operational now . . . Strickland —

— there. Framed like a painting in the window of the room on that side of the lodge, helpfully lit. Watching his screens, waiting. Gant had seen no one with him. Just one shadow moving in another darkened room, perhaps the kitchen. He could not know how many there were — other than the two outside and McIntyre, who just had to be there.

Gant was seated with his back against the bole of a withered, stormstruck pine, on an outcrop of rock only a few hundred yards from the lodge. He could look down like a raptor into the clearing, into the single lit room. The two patrolling men in the trees went about their business without imagination or variation.

A little after four, he had left the jeep two miles away around the shore of Bonner Lake, then skirted the tiny settlement of Squaw Camp. Those were the cabins and lodges that had formed the background of the snapshot that had betrayed Strickland's location. He had climbed up to Strickland's lodge in its small clearing by means of a hiking trail that wound up the side of the mountain. Knowing all the time that McIntyre would be ahead of him.

In the late afternoon, he'd caught the reflected light off what was, to all appearances, nothing more than a satellite TV dish. It hadn't been moving when he first saw it, then, just before dusk, it began swivelling on the low roof, back and forth. It was a radar dish used for military surveillance. Its one blindspot was the lodge's chimney . . .

. . . which problem the low-light TV system cancelled. The four cameras covered every foot of open ground. They could just sit and wait for him to step out into the clearing.

He ate a bar of chocolate and listened to the

rush of an owl's wings somewhere near, even heard the intensified rustling of its landing in undergrowth and its almost immediate takeoff. Heard beyond that the grumble of a bear, like the noise of a car that wouldn't start. Farther off, the dim noise of music from the little encampment of wooden buildings down by the shore. The lake seemed to hold the last light as if it was irradiated by a nuclear-spillage.

Carefully, he checked the equipment he had removed from the rucksack. Especially the stubby tube of the fifty-round helical feed magazine that belonged with the Smith & Wesson Calico 9mm pistol. Alan Vance had a collection of guns — like so many Americans who had never seen anything that wasn't feathered or furred blown apart. It came in useful now, though . . . the Ruger rifle would even take the short-range thermal sight, big as a videocamera, that he had found. Barbara had told him where to look. It was a patented design of Vance's early years in electronics.

He silently slid it home on the mount and raised its surprising lightness to his eye, rifle butt against his shoulder. The eyepiece showed him the night trees on a miniature screen. Two minutes later, it showed him one of the patrolling FBI agents, walking cautiously, just inside the trees. Clear shot —

Gant put down the Ruger Mini-14 carefully. The air was still soft, the evening breeze hardly evident. He smelt pine resin and the fainter scent of something frying. Soon, he would have to move again, try to discover how many of them there were. He pushed aside the thought that he was going up against the FBI. The body-count would be in Federal agents . . . Even if he could prove what Strickland had done to Vance Aircraft, and on whose behalf, there would still be charges that he had assaulted, wounded, even killed, FBI special agents.

The last of the light had gone and big stars had begun to appear in the moonless sky. It wouldn't be up until around midnight. South Sister was just an afterimage on the retinae; the other, more northerly volcanic peaks had vanished. The lit window in the clearing shone out more warmly. There were dotted lights down by the lake, the chug of a small motor as a boat slipped across Bonner Lake, its lights as much like specks as the stars.

He raised the binoculars to his eyes. There were two sedans and a four-wheel-drive vehicle parked close to the lodge. That could mean as many as ten people or more in total, plus Strickland. It hadn't seemed that many, from whatever vantage he had observed the lodge during the last hours of daylight. Two men outside, Strickland posed at the one window, the blinds down or the lights not on in other rooms. Could there be as many as another *eight* he hadn't seen? The stars gleamed like silver. He studied the lodge, after glancing at his watch dial. A little after seven. He had to wait, maybe for most of the night, just *wait* . . . And count.

The room he had decided was the kitchen registered a tiny spillage of light a little after eight. To the infrared binoculars, there was a shadowy shape in the room, a human heat source . . . By nine-thirty, he was certain there were two more men in an upstairs room, its window jutting like a wedge from the steep slope of the roof. Presumably, they were sleeping. In the trees, the two on patrol continued their routine. An occasional engine fired from the lakeside settlement, even laughter, raucous and abrupt, once. Then it was cut off as if a door had closed on it. The binoculars showed smoke in the starlit sky from a couple of tourist cabins. Faint noises from a small boat that had put out from the jetty on which Strickland had been photographed years before.

Ten-fifteen . . . There were six of them beside Strickland. Just before ten, an anonymous hand had passed him sandwiches and beer, the body to which it belonged kept carefully from view. McIntyre would be in the room with him . . . just *had* to be.

Strickland had become increasingly restless as the evening had progressed. The lit window, the proximity of whoever was in the room with him, eroded him, made him begin yawning. His head had turned occasionally, at other times he appeared to be responding to someone, even challenging the man Gant couldn't see but who had to be McIntyre. The two men upstairs were still resting heat sources. There was, from time to time, another figure in the dark of the kitchen.

His surveillance gave him power, control rather than weariness. *They* were the ones really waiting, growing uncertain and edgy with heightened nerves. He glanced at his watch. Ten-twenty. They would believe he was outside. They had waited long enough to begin to imagine he must have some strategy, that he was waiting out of confidence in the darkness of the trees . . .

They could wait some more. He had all night. He was ready. Time was on his side, not theirs —

Eleven-thirty. The three minutes since McIntyre had last looked at the big dial of his watch had dragged inordinately. The enforced silence of the lodge, the brightness of the lights in the room, the flicker of the monochrome TV screens, the wash of the arm of the radar screen — unnerved. Fraser and Strickland had begun to irritate, like a rash on his arms and chest, then slowly, deeply anger him, as if they were three prisoners unwillingly flung together and confined, he the only innocent man.

The thought of Gant, who *must* be out there in the darkness, able to see Strickland, spotlit as he was, was a goad, prodding him out of confidence with sapping electric jolts to his calm and assurance.

McIntyre chewed at the last uneaten sandwich on the plate that had been placed between himself and Fraser. The bottles of beer were empty. Their chairs were squeezed into the angle of one of the room's corners, out of sightline from both windows. It was, this late in the evening, as if he was tied into his, unable to break out of biting constraints. Eleven-thirty-one.

He heard soft footsteps from the bedroom above the den and shuffled restlessly in his chair. A few moments later, Chris opened the door. The young man hovered, bleary-eyed, in the doorway.

'We — Sam and me'll relieve the others now . . . sir.' The respectful politeness was added like a tag from a dead language, strange-sounding. Chris' tired blue eyes seemed troubled, uncertain. Scared of the dark, McIntyre thought dismissively, and of who's out there.

'OK, keep alert, Chris. Keep moving, keep quiet, keep alive!' Fraser snorted derisively. Chris' cheeks reddened.

The young man glanced once at Strickland, as empathetically as at a fellow-prisoner, then nodded.

'Sir.'

Chris closed the door behind him on Fraser's brief laughter, the sound of nails scraping down a blackboard. He shivered, then reluctantly opened the lodge's main door and stepped furtively on to the verandah. The stoop seemed betrayingly silvered with the first moonlight. Sam's breathing was laboured behind him. Chris fitted the earphone and checked his mike's throat-strap to greater comfort. He adjusted the harness of the transceiver that hugged his left side like a poultice. Then he murmured:

'OK, you guys, come on in. We'll cover you from the verandah —'

'Thank sweet Jesus,' he heard in response.

The night was chilly — or was it just the change of temperature from the warm tension of the lodge? Chris couldn't be sure, but his skin shivered at the touch of the cold. Sam remained to his left, an infrared monocular pocket-scope clenched in his hand. It was as if he were giving some freedom-fighter's salute. He scanned the clearing in front of the lodge methodically, nervously. Chris knew he should be doing the same. Gant — everyone said — was out there for certain, just waiting to get to Strickland. And he could only get to him through a half-dozen FBI agents.

So he was desperate. He wouldn't be stopped from even taking on the Federal authorities . . . The first of the two-man patrol emerged from the trees with exaggerated, comic caution, then began hurrying across the open ground, hunched as if against taunts rather than a bullet. But *why* was all this happening? It had no real shape. What was Strickland to Gant?

The second man came out of the trees. A night-bird shocked him into rigidity, then he hurried for the lodge. The two men passed them with laboured breathing, their fear palpable. The door closed behind them with a dull, carrying noise and Chris whirled on his heel to remonstrate —

'Well?' Sam asked.

'OK — here goes nothing . . .'

He walked off the stoop into the moonlight, senses alert, nerves stretched. They crossed the clearing with moonlight between them. On the bole of a tree, a low-light camera swivelled like the nose of a scenting dog. Chris felt observed rather than reassured. His feet hurried him into the trees. Sam disappeared fifty yards to his left. Moonlight filtered weakly, like some powder dusting his shoulders and hands. He gripped the Springfield carbine more tightly, pressing it across his stomach as he began his patrol.

Gant . . . The murmurings and asides of conversation between McIntyre and the Englishman, Fraser, flitted through his thoughts, as alarming as the rustle of investigating wings above his head. Fraser was relying on McIntyre — using him? There was a mutual, fierce determination to kill Gant rather than arrest him . . . and Strickland, too, was destined to be shown the end of the pier and invited to dive off . . . Gant?

He shook his head, making the infrared pocket-scope's image of the ghostly trees joggle like something in a child's toy. He almost expected snow. The trees massed again, white-grey, the darkness between them empty. He began circling the perimeter of the clearing, a hundred yards into the trees. A brief gap showed him the flanks of South Sister, gleaming with moonlit ice and snow. A glacier like an old man's beard. From a rise, another gap revealed the sheen of Bonner Lake below. Gant . . . was sitting out here somewhere, maybe even aware of him right now.

He flinched at an owl's delight in its ability to kill . . .

. . . In the silence of the lit room, the owl's cry intruded sufficiently to alarm them. Strickland's shoulders twitched as his eyes automatically swept the bank of monitors. The four cameras revealed nothing. His stomach was cramped with sitting, with the effort of calm. It was hours now since he had begun to *want* Gant to be out there, his imagination describing the manner, the exact distances, the precise route by which Gant could fox the radar. Strickland knew Fraser wanted him dead. He had orders to that effect and no other.

That much was obvious — he'd traded Gant for himself, and the FBI agent had gone for it.

'He's not coming,' he heard Fraser taunt McIntyre in a whisper.

'Yes he *is*,' McIntyre snapped back.

Strickland watched the screens. Nothing. Fraser's next words surprised him.

'You *would* tell us, wouldn't you, son, if and when the man comes walking out of the trees? You wouldn't keep it to yourself, just for long enough to give him the smallest chance?'

'No,' Strickland replied sullenly as a schoolboy. 'He wants to kill me, doesn't he?'

Fraser merely chuckled.

'Leave the guy alone,' McIntyre said. 'Christ, you'd give anyone the heebie-jeebies with that laugh of yours.'

'Sorry, Mac — I didn't realise you were so sensitive.'

Fraser lit a cigarette. Strickland's inside knotted with a puritanical, angry revulsion.

'Eleven-forty. Is he waiting for midnight, do you reckon? It's when most suicides happen.'

McIntyre's stomach rumbled. There were faint noises from the kitchen as the two men relieved of patrol duty made themselves something to eat. His impatience bubbled and grumbled like indigestion. Where in hell *was* Gant? Was he even coming?

'Anything?' he asked Strickland sharply.

'Nothing.'

'He isn't coming,' Fraser taunted, his features smug with assurance that Gant would come. 'You've screwed up, Mac.'

'I'm right,' McIntyre replied, as if rehearsing some old and boring script . . .

. . . and so it had gone on, hour after hour, Strickland's hunched, aching shoulders reminded him. The window he could watch without attracting their attention was a black square, looking on nothing. It failed to promise Gant, who had become Strickland's only image of rescue. Listening to their pathetic banter during the last eight or nine hours had worn him down. He'd been so *confined.* They could never, even with a psychological profiler on hand, have devised a better means of undoing him. Exposure at the lit windows was less wearing than the time-tunnel of their slow wrestling for dominance.

'Put money on it,' Fraser mocked.

'Shove it,' McIntyre sulked in reply.

Cat-and-mouse, cat-and-mouse, endlessly . . .

His temples tightened as the idea came to him . . . Expose them, make *them* move into the light. Gant had better be watching —

'There!' he announced quickly.

They lurched together out of their chairs, towards the console and himself.

'Where?'

'I thought there was something . . .' But he could not keep them within the frame of the window any longer.

'Arsehole,' Fraser concluded, but without suspicion. His breath was hot on Strickland's ear, his hand heavy on his shoulder. Strickland shivered with sudden, icy cold, at once regretting what he had done. Fraser's intention had somehow communicated itself through the man's touch. If anything went wrong, if Fraser felt threatened, then his first move would be to kill him. If Gant looked remotely like succeeding, he knew Fraser wouldn't hesitate.

McIntyre and Fraser sat down again, unaware that they had walked on to a stage.

Had Gant seen them? Strickland almost hoped not . . .

The thermal sight was at his eye, the rifle butt resting against his shoulder. Two others were obviously in the room with Strickland. He recognised McIntyre's blunt, thick-necked head and broad back. And the face that glanced sidelong at Strickland, with an evident sneer. It was Fraser . . . he remembered the picture Aubrey had shown him . . . Winterborne's man. *With* McIntyre *and* Strickland. They would see nothing on any of the screens, except their own two-man patrol moving in regular, undeviating progression.

The two men dropped quickly back out of sight. The screens had been blank. Could it have been a signal from Strickland . . . ? Gant was nervous of completing the idea. Strickland could just as well be working to their game plan. Even so, it had shown him not only who was in the room with Strickland but also that they couldn't see the screens for themselves if they remained concealed.

Eleven-fifty . . . The moon was reflected like a pale lantern in the smooth water of Bonner Lake. Time narrowed. The images through the thermal sight and binoculars, the sense of the Ruger and the Calico beside him, all fitted like the technology of a cockpit. The hours of waiting had drained him of Aubrey, Vance, Barbara, the general's daughter, the general — even his own circumstances. He stood upright, away from the bole of the stunted tree, holding the Ruger in one hand. The Calico was slung across his chest. There was a target and, like a missile, he locked on to it. He swung the rifle across the trees below him, picking up the first man then, after a few seconds, Chris.

The young man's features, white-on-grey, were distinct and recognisable. The map of the terrain in Gant's head began to unroll as clearly as on a screen he had just switched on. He began moving silently down the slope towards the first man, his awareness a receiver to be updated by his senses. An owl's cry, something rustling through the undergrowth, disturbed by his passage. Distances, time, location, all precise.

He stopped, using the binoculars now that he was closer to the first man. Waited —

— struck the man from behind with the butt of the Ruger, then squashed his limp form upright against a pine until he could safely let it slide soundlessly to the ground. He heard his own breathing, the FBI man's unconscious snores. The earpiece had flown from the man's ear as he'd struck him, his throat mike had risen above the collar of his shirt. Gant listened for Chris, for any noise. The light from the lodge was visible through the outlying trees.

Chris —

He slipped away from the unconscious man, towards the sound of dull, regimented footsteps.

Their clockwork patrol brought them together at —

— this point. Ten seconds. Chris' footsteps, the hoot of an owl, Chris' footsteps on the other side of the tree, his breathing. Gant raised the Ruger and —

— Chris' voice.

'Nothing, sir —'

Chris' features half-turned to him, his shoulder and head already flinching away from the rifle butt. Mouth open, throat moving, struggling to shout. Chris' weapon half-parried the Ruger's swinging butt, jarring Gant's grip. His hand left the rifle, grabbing at the short-barrelled, folding-stock Springfield, twisting the barrel up and away from them as they plunged together like awkward bullies. The Springfield flashed, deafened. Chris fell back with a groan, his only sound. Through the retinal flare of the gunshot, Gant could not locate the source of the noise. His boots touched something yielding and he bent down. Blood on his fingers.

'— can't *see,*' he heard. 'Can't see, Christ —'

There was the tinniness of an urgent voice coming from the loosened earpiece. Chris' curled, terrified body became an outline on the ground. The tiny voice squeaked like an injured mouse. They were alerted. *Move* —

He assessed his alignment with the lodge. Moved thirty yards farther. The cameras would pick him up, but he was in the radar's blindspot, where the main chimney jutted from the deep rake of the roof. Ten seconds since Chris went down — nearer fifteen — his eyesight would be coming back by now, the muzzle-flash clearing from his vision. No one on the verandah, Strickland still at his console.

He placed the rucksack on the ground after removing the flare pistol he had taken from the aircraft. One hundred and twenty thousand candela, burn time five seconds. He raised the pistol and fired it into the air. Tension gripped his stomach like a steel band.

Starshell burst. The clearing seemed to be blanched, made lifeless by the exploding flare cartridge. Anyone watching would be dazzled, he no more than a guessed-at moving shadow on their retinae, and the low-light TV cameras would be glare-blind. He ran, head down and in a straight line, across the narrow clearing —

— Strickland knew Gant was there, coming straight out of the trees. There was something moving on two of the screens, insubstantial as a bird's wing that had fluttered too close to the cameras. He felt himself tense, as if the flare-wash in the room was a fire.

'Is he *there?*' Fraser demanded, almost thrusting him off his swivel chair, his large hands seizing the console as if to shake some confession from it. Already, the light from the flare or whatever it was was lessening. 'What's that — ?' His finger jabbed at the betraying screen. On the radar there was nothing. Gant was in the blindspot.

'I — can't see, dazzled —'

Fraser didn't believe him. McIntyre was on his other side, the material of his coat sleeve rubbing against Strickland's cheek. There was a gun in his hand, at the corner of eyesight.

'I can't see *shit!*' McIntyre bellowed as if in pain. 'Is there anyone *there?*'

'Maybe there is,' Fraser grunted. 'Maybe —' He turned towards the windows, then glowered at Strickland. 'And *if* there is . . .'

'He can't be trying to get *in* — ?'

'There are two men *down!* He's stopped playing with us, you pillock!'

Do it now, Fraser told himself, as night returned beyond the windows. *Just in case.*

He moved towards Strickland, drawing his pistol as he did so. Winterborne's priority was the only one that mattered now, whatever deal he had with McIntyre. Strickland's eternal silence —

'What the hell are you — ?' McIntyre began, but Fraser motioned him away with a waggle of the gun.

He moved on Strickland quickly, as if pouncing at the man, thrusting the pistol towards his head —

— Gant saw Fraser advancing across the garishly lit window towards Strickland. It was like a bleached photograph taken at the moment of an explosion. He was close enough to recognise the fear on Strickland's features, see his hands trying to fend off Fraser, the purpose in Fraser's movement.

He raised the Ruger to his shoulder and squeezed off three shots. The window shattered. Fraser's head seemed to dissolve in a red, splashing haze in the instant before his body was flung aside and out of sight by the impact of the bullets. Strickland and McIntyre appeared frozen in the moment. Gant hurtled himself towards the verandah as he glimpsed McIntyre move from the window —

— McIntyre, struggling out of the shock of Fraser's death as if out of a clinging swamp, lumbered towards the door, switching off the lights before opening it, then yelling:

'Any of you *see* anything?'

— *see anything,* Gant heard as he crouched on the verandah beneath the suddenly darkened window.

Under the overhang of the roof, the verandah was dark, protecting. He could hear the fizzle of the flare in the clearing. If they'd seen him, they were afraid to come out. He listened above the thud of his heart.

'No, nothing —'

'— nearly blinded me!'

Both voices were calling from the direction of what he presumed was the kitchen. The lodge creaked now with their soft movements, echoing their tension. He felt rough wood against his cheek.

'Check every room, every window!' McIntyre.

Two down and Fraser dead. McIntyre, three others . . . Strickland. He was poised like a runner, then crabbed along the verandah, scuttling on his haunches, to the room next to Strickland. 'Are you assholes *checking — ?*'

Panic remained in the air, like the scent of the flare cartridge after its light had vanished. He stood up beside the window as he heard noises, saw the faintest glimmer of light as a door was opened —

— smashed the window, fired the flare pistol,

ducked back. The cartridge exploded against the far wall of the room or in the corridor beyond. The verandah was flooded with a sinister, nuclear light. Two seconds, three —

The window slid upwards and he heaved himself over the ledge into the room as it fell back into shadow. Listened. Moved quickly as someone stumbled unsurely through the door head shaking as if to rid himself of plaguing flies. He struck the body in the stomach with the rifle, then across the side of the head as it came within reach. Hauled the man aside. Corridor . . . McIntyre was in the room to his left, with Strickland. They hadn't moved out of it, even in their near-panic. The flare fizzled at his feet as he crouched back against the wall, the Ruger slung across his back, the Smith & Wesson Calico now in his hands.

Footsteps overhead, from a bedroom, someone coming down the stairs cautiously, one step at a time, long pauses between each movement on the open treads. He could see feet, legs coming into —

— the Calico ripped gashes in the banister, the panelling of the wall. The legs disappeared and he ducked down, the Ruger banging against the corridor wall. He heard shots go past his head, imagined he felt the heat. Two more wild shots from the stairs drove him back into the darkened room.

He heard his own stertorous breathing, that of the unconscious man on the floor. Moonlight reflected from the surface of a table. Faces of plates watched him from a dresser.

McIntyre was still in the room with Strickland — and Fraser's body. What remained of the face that had looked out at him from Aubrey's photograph, and which he had recognised in France, would be staring up at them in shattered surprise. Two men upstairs, unhurt.

Feet on the stairs, as his blood ceased to pound in his ears. Creaks faint as beetles in the wood. The slightest of clicking sounds —

He flattened himself against the wall, hunched into a position of abject surrender beside the sentrylike shape of a longcase clock, as the automatic weapon emptied its magazine into the floor, the room, what remained of the window. The rug moved under the impacts, the window frame shattered, the unconscious man was no longer breathing when the noise subsided into silence.

Another clicking noise, a new magazine engaged. The din began again. Plates on the dresser disintegrated, there were gouges in the walls, along the polished surface of the dining table, in the wall near his head, the inlaid wood of the clock. The body on the floor bucked with the impacts long after it was dead. Gant pressed his hands over his ears, over his head, curling into himself, hunched smaller, his body jumping involuntarily like that of the dead man.

Silence again, except for the slight, unnerved jangling of the clock's weights, its mechanism. His ears stopped ringing. He waited, watching the torn, pocked door that had swung half-open, pushed by bullets. Watched the window. Listened, waiting for the man on the stairs to empty another magazine into the dining room. He crouched back against the wall, swinging the Calico to cover the window, the door, the window, repeatedly.

'Bobby?' he heard hesitantly, a hoarse whisper. 'Agent McIntyre?' It was the man on the stairs. Bobby's dead . . . What was McIntyre doing? Nerves stirred his left foot. The tiny crunch of glass beneath his boot surprised an exclamation of breath from the staircase. Were both men on the stairs? There were no noises. Window, door, window —

The acrid scent of powder on the air, the roll of gunsmoke visible in the pale moonlight. Glass-littered floorboards, glass sparkling from the torn rug. The pale light reached the door. He could not move to the window without exposing himself to the automatic weapon aimed at the doorway.

He heard mouselike stirrings from the room that contained McIntyre and Strickland. The man on the stairs moved, but he wasn't making any approach to the door that stood half-open. Presumably, the second man was crouched near him. There were no sounds of anyone trying to climb on to the roof, get outside.

If he tried to close the door and escape through the window, the grumbling of glass under his feet would alert them —

— noise of something slithering, wood against wood?

'Who's left out there?' he heard. McIntyre's voice.

'Hyams — sir. And Billings,' from the stairs.

'Can you see him?'

'No, sir. I can see the door and the window. He can't move.'

'Good.'

'Gant — ?' An unfamiliar voice.

'Shut up, Strickland!'

Before long, Chris and the other guy outside would recover, begin to think, start to outflank him.

— that sliding noise again, the shuffling of bodies from the other room?

'McIntyre?' he called.

'What — ?' It was as if the man had been caught stealing, his hand in the cookie jar. 'You're finished, Gant. Give it up, asshole.'

'Not yet.' Beside him, the clock ticked comfortably, as if denying its circumstances. 'It's more like a Mexican standoff from in here . . .'

He listened. McIntyre wasn't swallowing the bait. He had only minutes now before —

— car engine starting. He looked wildly towards the window as headlights leapt out like another flare. Tyres screeched, beginning to retreat almost at once.

'Agent McIntyre!' he heard Hyams from the stairs. 'What's going on, sir?'

Another voice growled: 'Asshole's gotten *away — !*'

Then Hyams called out: 'Strickland? Hey, Strickland!' There was silence from the other room. Both of them were in the car. McIntyre and Strickland.

Gant stirred, then restrained all movement, listening to the car engine retreat down the narrow, twisting mountain track towards Bonner Lake and Squaw Camp. McIntyre would be driving very slowly. It wasn't much more than a hiking trail, following the contours of the mountainside for more than a mile before it reached the highway.

The deep, slow ticking of the longcase clock was mocking him now, as if to lull him into inertia. He raged inwardly against McIntyre's easy escape. The guy had just climbed out the window and gotten into his car — ! The clock was like someone guarding a prisoner, a matter of feet from him along the wall. He couldn't *move.* Its ticking was arrogantly assured, certain of his immobility. McIntyre was making for his airplane at Redmond, had to be . . . Strickland would disappear forever —

He pressed back into the angle of the wall. The Ruger was near his left hand, the Calico suspended on his chest from its short strap. He braced himself and raised his booted feet as if they were tied together, measuring distance, force. Glass pricked at his palms as they took his weight . . . he lunged —

— jangle of weights, heavy clockwork, the creaking of the case interrupting the clock's tall assurance. It toppled slowly, noisily, alarming the men on the stairs. The weights banged against the case like a heart against ribs. Then it fell across the doorway, shutting the door with a slam. Hyams' voice was cut off. Gant was on his feet, two steps taken, before all noise of the glass underfoot was drowned in the clock's bedlam as it struck the floor. Three more steps, into the moment of moonlight and the sense of nakedness, his hand on the window ledge —

— shots ripping through the door, the deafening noise of the clock's distress drowned by gunfire. Shards of glass and wood drifted down onto him like snow. Impact of his knees with the boards of the verandah, ricochets coming through the window. He rolled away then got to his feet, already running before he was upright. Orientated himself in the small clearing, running hunched, swerving and dodging like a footballer in a complex play. There was no shooting behind him before he reached the trees.

He plunged in out of the moonlight, stopping his flight against the rough bole of a tree. Thirty seconds since McIntyre's engine note had disappeared into silence. The scent of gasoline still pungent in his nostrils. That way —

— map in his head, clear as on a screen unrolling in a cockpit. The smudge of the lake, the little dot of Squaw Camp, the place he had left the 4WD, the hiking trail twisting its way down the mountainside.

He was running through the trees, his arm up against the whip of thin branches. He plunged uphill towards the vantage point he'd used to keep the lodge under surveillance. Forty-five seconds. McIntyre, headlights blazing, bucking down the hiking trail. He'd never cut him off, *never* —

For a moment, he could see the few scattered lights of Squaw Camp through the trees, and the silvered dish of Bonner Lake. Then the forest of lodgepole pines closed in around the car again, and the rear wheels slithered menacingly as he lost the hiking track, then jerked the sedan back on to it. The trail folded itself like a vast, lazy snake around the mountainside, its coils slipping lower and lower till it met the Cascade Lakes Highway at the settlement.

McIntyre cursed the wedges of the tree trunks that constantly seemed to spring to attention in the headlights. The hiking trail was determined to lose itself among them, hide away from him. Strickland was holding his seatbelt as he might have done a coat lapel. The indicator needle waggled around thirty, its erratic movements like the measurements of McIntyre's heartbeat. The driving mirror, the wing mirrors, remained black. Then, as if beckoning, the lake again for an instant through thinned trees, and the lights of the settlement. Three Sisters stretching away northwards, Mount Bachelor, snow-flanked still, to the south. Stars hard and big above the headlights . . . He realised he had slowed the car, as if to inhale the scene into choked lungs, and accelerated. At once, the car skidded on pine-mush, the rear nearside wheel spinning, the engine racing.

Strickland glared at him.

'For Christ's sake, Mac — !' It sounded as if they were still field operative and Case Officer.

'Don't throw up!' McIntyre snarled contemptuously, righting the car, the sweat cold beneath his arms.

The trail bent away from the prospect into dark trees again. Their crowded intent seemed malign, angering McIntyre. The sense of exhilaration he had felt in escape had dissipated in the effort required to negotiate the hiking trail. He'd paid no attention when they had ascended it in the afternoon light, it had been the driver's problem.

Gant couldn't get out of the trap he'd thrown himself into . . . He was pinned down, would remain so . . . McIntyre would have to alert a backup team when he got to the airfield at Redmond — have to call the pilot on the carphone and get the ship refuelled, a flight plan filed . . . to where?

He joggled the wheel in his hands, feeling his palms slip damply on the mock-leather. Where should he take Strickland? The guy knew the name of the man who'd hired him, the guy Fraser had promised would take care of *his* future . . . Now Fraser was dead, and his future was blown out of the water unless he could get Strickland to tell him the name. He was already more than half-persuaded that Gant wanted him dead. To stay alive, he *had* to trade the name for his survival. But it might need time to make him see things that way . . . so, where to take him?

He glanced across at Strickland. The man was quiescent, withdrawn; almost detached. He jerked the wheel again as the trail bent away and dropped, and the headlights bucked wildly, as if terrified. An animal glanced aside into the trees, a deer or something.

'I'll watch out for you!' he shouted as the engine note rose and fell like a protesting wail. 'You got to trust me, Strickland.'

'Why?'

'Because the guy back there — Gant — he

wants to kill you. You screwed up his family, his career —'

Strickland tossed his head, flicking his long blond hair away from his face.

'He wants to *know*, Mac — just like you,' Strickland jibed.

McIntyre braked gently. The rear offside wheel rose over a rock and settled. A momentary glimpse of the shining lake, the headlights staring out into empty air, then the trees again.

'Sure. But I'll keep you alive if you tell me. We can cut a deal — I want the name of the guy who hired you. Gant wants you doing hard time for what you did to him and Vance. Think about it —'

They were over halfway down the mountainside now, had to be. The headlights gleamed back from the tree trunks. Then there was maybe a forty-minute drive on good roads to Redmond. He had to decide what flight plan should be filed, call the pilot. Fear of pursuit fell away. The lake was closer, the lights of Squaw Camp brighter. Strickland had no other real choice. He'd come to see it that way, in a while. But as yet, the guy didn't seem about to fold up. The *Preacherman* would still take a lot of persuading to give McIntyre the name. He wasn't even grateful he was still alive, for Christ's sake!

McIntyre loosened his grip on the steering wheel. It would come out right. *He* had Strickland, the man belonged to him, not to Gant or the mysterious employer —

— wheelspin. He righted the sliding car confidently, almost relaxed. The headlights gleamed out through another brief gap in the trees. Bonner Lake was bigger, even closer, shining in the moonlight. It was coming out just right —

The car's headlights glared out through the trees far below him, then became muted again. He could not catch his breath, could not admit that it might be too late. From the outcrop where he had paused, he plunged into the trees again, catching foggy glimpses of the Three Sisters, other whitened mountains, the moon gleaming on Bonner Lake. All the time trying to ignore the weariness of his body, the strange, thudding fragility of his heartbeat.

They were much too near the lake already . . . The realisation, pounding in his ears like the noise of his blood, could not be admitted. Thin branches whipped at his face and hands and the ground seemed to snag and pull like mud at his boots and ankles. He swerved and dodged through the trees, the slope steepening ahead of him, dropping blindly downwards. There was no trail, just the sense of his descent to guide him.

He blundered out of the trees on to the scratch of the hiking trail. Vaguely saw tyre marks, the signs of a skid. The trail wound away down the mountainside, marking the way that McIntyre had gone. He'd crossed the first of the tracks — just the first — and the car was already nearing Squaw Camp. He plunged into the trees, his blood pounding more loudly than ever . . . then he heard something else. A wall of sound —

He cannoned away from a narrow tree bole, winded. He forced himself on, his hand touching a chain set in rock as the trees parted suddenly like a curtain being drawn. There was something ahead of him, blocking his path . . .

The waterfall arched out over the descending slope which led around the outcrop. It confronted him like a high, impenetrable wall, gleaming in the moonlight as if it was an enormous steel shutter. The chain was slippery to his touch, moss-covered. Ferns decorated the rock face. The din of water and the visual assault threatened to engulf him. The clock in his head ticked on, measuring the distance between himself and McIntyre as it increased, became hopeless. His breath came in exhausted, heaving gulps. *Too late* —

The main hiking trail avoided the outcrop and the waterfall, but the mountain had thrown it like a barrier across his line of descent. He edged forward, unnerved, the noise intensifying, his moonshadow creeping beside him, enlarged and more fearful. The chain clinked against the rock each time he shifted his grip. Spray dashed into his face, daunting him, like the sense of time slipping away. The cascade arched out over the trail — he had to be able to pass behind it, otherwise the chain wouldn't be there . . . His shirt and jacket were sodden, his ears deafened by the sound. The waterfall seemed no more than twenty or thirty feet across. The knife-scratch of the trail *had* to continue on the other side.

Trail — ? A ledge of rock along which he and his shadow moved with a helpless, unnerved caution. He was blinded by the spray. The sense of his feet and their shuffling movement forward seemed remote, not to be trusted.

The moon and his shadow disappeared . . . as did the chain. The water banged on his head and shoulders, trying to knock him to his knees in surrender. He was chilled to the bone. The water was silvered with moonlight. The cave behind the cascade seemed immense, featureless. He moved on fearfully, his foot slipping on a wet rock. He slid one foot carefully in front of the other, unseeing, deafened by the noise. His hands were stretched out in front of him to balance his body, to be ready to adjust —

— foot slipped again. He fell to his knees as if the noise and darkness had beaten him down. He wanted to scream. The noise that now enveloped him intimidated, appalled . . . He struggled to his feet and moved on. First step, second, third —

— behind him, suddenly. The world no longer entirely composed of water and noise. Moonlight. His shadow rejoined him on the ledge of rock as he grabbed at the reappearing chain.

He staggered away from the cascade, around the outcrop until the trees closed around him again and he could hear his heartbeat above the noise of the waterfall. The mountainside dropped away steeply once more. He hesitated. The lake was a faint sheen of light through the trees, but his bleary, clearing vision could not locate headlights.

Then he saw them.

The headlights of McIntyre's car were swivelling round, hundreds of yards below him, as they emerged from the trees. They were no longer bobbing with the undulations of the hiking trail but shone out clearly towards the lake. McIntyre had reached the highway, was turning on to it. Gant had been beaten. The Calico weighed heavily on his chest, the rifle hanging limply from his left arm. Yes . . . The headlights had steadied, like a poised runner, then they accelerated below him, confident, shining out along the strip of the blacktop as it threaded itself beside the shore.

Too late . . . He could not stop them now, McIntyre was clean away, Strickland with him. He had the *only* proof . . . Gant was shivering with rage, with the sense of being beaten. He wanted to raise his head and howl at the moon like an animal in his desperate frustration, raise his head —

— raised the Ruger, flipping up the waterproof lens cover of the thermal-imaging sight. Through the eyepiece, the headlights of McIntyre's car seemed like grey strips of rolled steel on the tiny video screen. The car, enlarged as it was, was at the extreme range of the rifle. But it was his only chance. The car was a rectangular box behind the headlights, its windscreen another tiny TV screen on which there were two shadows, escaping him, as he moved the rifle, tracking them —

— squeezed the trigger, again and again. The windscreen shattered. The headlights of the car wobbled like torches held in drunken hands . . . Gant felt a fierce elation fill him. He raised his arms in a salute as the car below him visibly slowed, lurching from side to side on the highway, the headlights glancing off trees, off the water's edge. Slowing all the time . . .

Then it left the road, the headlights nose-diving

towards the water, slipping into it, so that they gleamed out feebly as they began to drown. He could hear the protest of the car's engine, its revs far too high even though it hardly seemed to be moving. He watched it slip into the water eagerly, directionlessly. He'd stopped them . . . only to drown —

He was running, wildly. Heard himself growling through his teeth as he crossed the hiking trail. Then trees again, and darkness, after a brief glimpse of the headlights becoming more faint, bleary. The roof of the car was still above water. Black desperation prodded him on, taunting him with the sense that it was too late to save Strickland, that he was already dead in the car that was slipping beneath the lake. He cannoned off the bole of a lodgepole pine and blundered on, a deer startled out of his path, alarmed by his noise and flailing arms.

A brief glimpse of the lake from an outcrop of bare rock. He couldn't see the car, its headlights had vanished beneath the water —

'No!' he heard himself shouting. It was an elongated, unending noise that seemed to want to empty his lungs as he ran. His body was difficult to hold upright, propelled only by the arms he waved violently, futilely. He tripped, collapsing exhausted, rolling down the slope, the Calico bruising him, the rifle lost . . . *Too late* —

The surface of the blacktop was hard, jolting him into stillness, numbing one arm, knocking the breath from his body. The highway, he realised he had reached the highway, and forced himself to his knees. He looked round him desperately. The surface of the lake shimmered with moonlight, undistressed, peaceful. There was no sign of the car, or of where it had entered the water . . . He lurched to his feet and staggered to the shore. Treadmarks in the moonlight, on the narrow grass verge, indentations across the brief, pebbly shore . . . Calm water had closed over the roof of the car, drowning it.

Nothing disturbed the tranquillity —

— until he plunged into the water, wading out into the chill of the lake. The water passed his thighs, stomach, chest. He shivered as it robbed him of the heat of his exertions. Swallowing air, he ducked beneath the surface into sudden, icy darkness. Swam blindly, praying . . . The moonlight was a faint, ghostly light above him. His chest began to tighten, his throat bulge with the effort of holding his breath. A yard to right or left and he would never see the car . . . The headlights would have shorted by now, the engine would have stopped. It was *here,* somewhere, just feet away, somewhere . . . His chest ached, his arms flailed wildly as if he was still running rather than trying to swim —

— touched something. Right hand. Something hard . . . He gripped it, straining to make it out. Driver's mirror . . . he ducked into the ragged gap where the windscreen had been. The driver — McIntyre — was dead.

Passenger? He thrust his head further into the car, his lungs bursting. A white, bloated face moved feebly. Gant reached in and unbuckled the seatbelt that was trapping Strickland. The man was still now, as if he had finally blacked out. Gant pulled — his breath expelled itself involuntarily with the effort and he began swallowing water — and Strickland came free like some octopoid creature that had been anchored to the car. Gant had hold of his shirt as he felt the bonnet of the car beneath his feet. He thrust away from it with his remaining strength, pulling Strickland after him up towards the ghostly shimmer of the moonlight.

His head broke the surface of the water like that of an otter and he gasped down air, coughed water. Fought the air into his aching lungs, even as he clutched Strickland against him. Gulped air again and again, as if it would be snatched from him.

He swam awkwardly, pulling the lifeless body with him, the dozen or twenty yards until he could stand upright and haul himself and the inert Strickland across the pebbled floor of the lake. Then he flung the body down on the shore, pouncing on it as if he wished it further harm. The shirt, pants, flesh seemed unstained with blood. He pumped the man's arms grotesquely, angrily. Strickland had cheated him . . . He had blown it, trying to stop the car. McIntyre was dead, Strickland was drowned —

— turned him over. The night air was cold, Gant felt his own body shivering and the lifelessness of the body beneath his own as he straddled it, pummelling at the man's back, squeezing his lungs, pumping in the silence . . .

Strickland coughed. Water dribbled from his gaping mouth. An eyelid fluttered, then Strickland's lungs began pumping of their own volition as he choked air into his body. Retched, choked again, continued breathing, lying on his stomach, face twisted to one side.

Gant rolled away from him, exhausted. Satisfied. Heard his own heartbeat become calmer, quieter. As his night vision improved, he saw — or believed he saw — the black pinpoint of an otter's head breaking the calm stillness of the lake's silvered surface.

He sat watching the unmoving otter. Perhaps it was similarly watching him. The sound of Strickland's raucous, regular breathing and his quiet groaning were the noises of success. They seeped into his weariness, strong as liquor, warming him.

POSTLUDE

1st June, 199–

Directors, dealers through holding companies,
Deacons in churches, owning slum properties,
Alias usurers in excelsis, the quintessential essence of usurers,
The purveyors of employment, whining over the 20 p.c. and the hard times . . .

And the general uncertainty of all investment . . .

Ezra Pound, *Canto* XII

The Special Branch officers were downstairs, being served cups of tea by David's housekeeper. There were two anonymous saloon cars parked outside in the morning sunshine of Eaton Square. He and David Winterborne confronted one another, Aubrey taking a certain, tangible pleasure from David's discomfiture. The Home Office official, Baird, remained in his selected corner of the large drawing room, just beyond a stream of sunlight from one of the tall windows, as if he possessed no interest in either of them.

'This is, as I said, all very unofficial, David. For the moment, at least.'

Winterborne, unwarned of their early arrival, was already dressed and breakfasted. The scent of coffee lingered in the room, even though the housekeeper had removed the tray. Aubrey's own breakfast had been meagre, a failure of appetite. The cramp of agitation that had kept him awake for most of the night remained knotted in his stomach.

'Why? Why *you*? As you say, you are *un*official, almost a non-person as far as these matters go.' He glanced across at the man from the Home Office, perched on a narrow Louis Quinze chair, studiously analysing the intricate pattern of the Persian carpet near his feet. 'You have absolutely no authority, Kenneth. Why should anyone in their right mind have let *you* come?'

'A favour — of a kind.'

Aubrey had remained standing throughout their brief encounter, leaning heavily but firmly on his walking stick.

'A chance to gloat, then?'

The Home Office type had informed David of the reasons why he must accompany them, what allegations had been made. Customs & Excise were raiding his offices, those of Complete Security, other companies under the Winterborne Holdings umbrella. David was being taken into custody pending consideration of a State Department request for his extradition to face *serious criminal charges.* Aubrey had hovered at the man's tall shoulder like an ancient Nemesis. He had persuaded old acquaintances in the Branch, the DS and Customs to seize the opportunity to begin the surgical dissection of David's finances.

'Not to gloat — to ask,' he snapped, his temper suddenly heating him. Winterborne faced him, his back to the window, making Aubrey squint into the sunlight. 'To ask *why?* And to ask, how did you *dare?*'

His anger was difficult to restrain; his reserves of hauteur seemed to have boiled away like steam. Marian was safely ensconced and comfortably recuperating in a Sussex nursing home. Giles and he were constant visitors. As was David's father, Clive. Giles' anger had died away, as if it was measured in a U-shaped thermometer; as Marian's health rose, his rage subsided. But not his own. Especially not now, confronting David.

'You mean dear Marian, of course,' Winterborne replied arrogantly.

'Of *course*, Marian! How could you try to have her killed?' Aubrey hissed. 'The rest of it I can see. The deaths of strangers for a clear advantage — nothing more than items on the television news. But Marian . . . ?'

'Marian placed herself in the path of the train,' he replied evenly. It seemed a remark often rehearsed, something he had coached himself to believe. 'She was the last, the only obstacle . . .' His dark eyes blazed and his nostrils flared. 'She was so *persistent — !*'

'The final barrier, then. To success? Or to being what you really are, David?'

Winterborne moved closer to Aubrey, his back turned to Baird. He was tangibly pleased at the slight flinch of Aubrey's old frame. 'I was fighting for my very existence. For the survival of everything I had built up over a decade and more.' His voice was an intimate, hard whisper. 'I did not intend to lose *any* of it.' His eyes registered Aubrey's contempt and he turned away sharply towards the window. 'I'm tired of this, Kenneth. It serves no purpose.'

'No,' Aubrey sighed. 'Perhaps I did come to gloat. To watch you fall.'

'You wish.'

'Strickland has been very cooperative — in great detail. The FBI are determined. Links will be forged, connections made. It *is* over, David.'

Winterborne was silent for a long moment, then he said, without turning from the window and its view of the square:

'Shall we go? As soon as I have called my solicitor?'

'Yes, I think so. I — I'm lunching with your father . . .'

Winterborne's shoulders twitched, then in a calm voice he said:

'Then you will have a very uncomfortable task to perform. An entirely *indigestible* one. I wish you good luck. Now, excuse me while I make my call —'

As he stood beside the ornate French desk, the morning sun glared in at the window. He was haloed by the light, his shoulders unbowed, his tone easy as he spoke to his solicitor. Aubrey felt an overwhelming desire to break his walking stick across David's back.

Instead, he reminded himself of the Special Branch officers downstairs and Baird's silent presence in the room. The cars parked outside in the morning sunlight. It *was* over. At least to the extent that Gant had been cleared of all charges, all suspicion, When the story broke, very soon now, in the US media, his Medal of Honor would be mentioned, his service record. He would be entirely rehabilitated . . . presumably to return to his chosen career.

And David would know that he had been beaten by Marian, Gant, Giles, himself. He would probably, if only for a short time, go to prison. He would become *untouchable* by people of influence, by financial institutions, by governments . . . It did, after all, seem sufficient punishment, a proper justice.

The thought stimulated him as he waited for Winterborne to finish his conversation.